Magical Academy for Delinquents

Ann Denton

Copyright © 2020 Ann Denton

1st Edition

All rights reserved. No part of this publication may be reproduced, distributed, or transmitted in any form or by any means, including photocopying, recording, or other electronic or mechanical methods, without the prior written permission of the publisher, except in the case of brief quotations embodied in critical reviews and certain other noncommercial uses permitted by copyright law. For permission requests, write to the publisher, addressed "Attention: Permissions Coordinator," at the address below.

Le Rue Publishing
320 South Boston Avenue, Suite 1030
Tulsa, OK 74103
www.LeRuePublishing.com

Cover by JV Arts

ISBN: 978-1-951714-42-0

To all the book besties who like to share their favorite worlds with others, play book bingo, and fight over book boyfriends. May this book cause epic arguments and let you share swoony sighs.

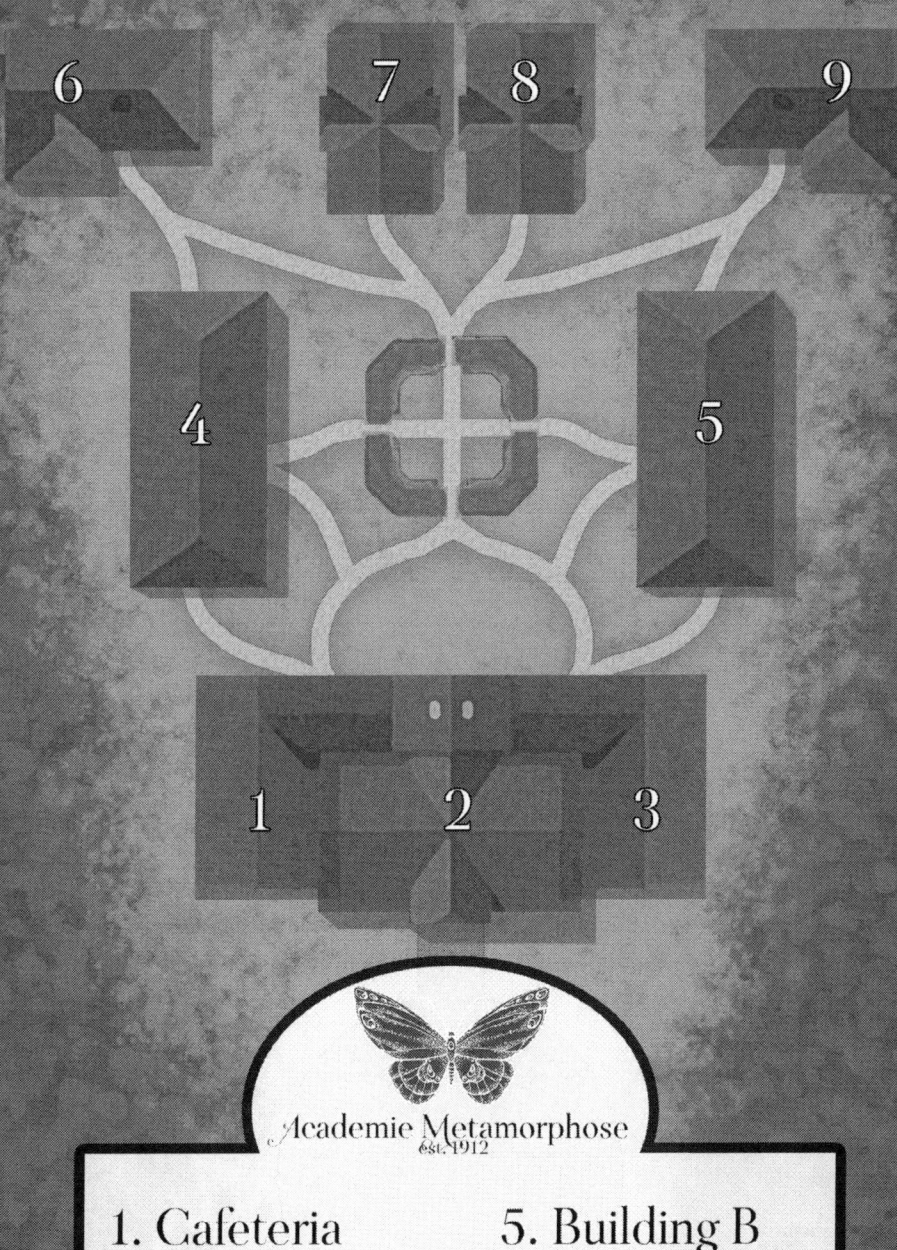

Académie Métamorphose
est. 1912

1. Cafeteria
2. Admissions
3. Library
4. Building A
5. Building B
6. Girls' Dorm
7. Gym A
8. Gym B
9. Boys' Dorm

1

WE HAD a substitute professor in Journeyman Spell Writing—easy pickings. She was more timid looking than most, a pale, young woman in a bright yellow suit, which clashed horribly with her skin tone and the flushed patches on her cheeks. Any other day, she would have been prey. I would have snapped her fragile ego in half and sent her running and sobbing down the hall. My reputation would have required it. But I glanced at the clock. Today, I didn't have the time. I had twenty-three minutes before life as I knew it exploded.

My eyes traveled back to the substitute. She didn't look like she'd ever run a single classroom before; her posture was hunched, she chewed her lower lip, and she was hiding halfway behind the desk. She set her small brown suitcase on the desk and a shaft of afternoon sunlight hit it. I spotted a scratch that marked the bag as faux leather. I nearly clicked my tongue. She should know better than to show signs of poverty here. The shallow idiots would want to rip her apart.

"Newb," Terra Lysour called out as she took a seat, eyeing the sub as she flicked her crappy pink extensions over her shoulder.

"Did you just say boob?" I asked, as loud as I could, mostly because I hated Terra's guts. A big-boned girl who'd had boobs magicked to match; she was a total bitch. Unfortunately, she was also top of the class. She'd apparently passed last year by writing her own spell for her boob job and executing it perfectly in front of several professors. She'd caused quite an uproar, but since she was a fourth year, and over eighteen, there hadn't been anything anyone could do about it. I loved reminding her about her whorish claim to fame though.

Chuckles erupted as Terra turned back to me and glared.

"Rude, Terra," I scolded. "Not all of us are obsessed with your sweater puppets."

A cluster of students walked in just then, passing between us and deflecting whatever brilliant comeback Terra had. It was usually "fuck you."

Around the room, students grinned when they saw the sub. As they took their seats, every eye in the room turned to look at me expectantly. I raised my eyebrows at them and shifted in my seat. *Dammit. Time to put on the show. Arrogant rich girl ... and go.* I hardened my expression. Then I dismissed them all, looking down to brush lint off my navy blue, pleated skirt, feigning boredom. I traced a pleat that the dry cleaners hadn't gotten quite perfect.

Inside, I buzzed with nervous energy. But not for the same reasons as the rest of the class. No, I wasn't excited about a sub or the beautiful possibilities of torture. I was excited for something a bit grander. Half an hour ago the faculty had all received a very important message.

I had to bite down on a smirk and control my emotions for what was about to happen. Patience was key. It was the key to pulling off big stunts. It was the key to my real goal. For me, every day for the past three years had been a practice in patience. I smoothed my expression back to disinterest as I grabbed my wand case out of my leather book bag.

A silent sigh seemed to go through the room, as expectant excitement turned to disappointment; the entitled peanut gallery didn't think I was going to give them a show. I nearly smiled at that. If only they knew. They were waiting for me to cause chaos, but they'd have to wait a few more minutes. I had bigger prey than professors in mind today. Because I was an illusionist. They all thought I was one of them. But they were wrong, and they'd never know it. They only ever knew what I showed them.

A guy with awful, Ken-doll, plastic-looking, gel-heavy hair sat next to me. I thought his name was Dan, but I wasn't sure. He scooted over in his seat so he could elbow me, an iridescent scar from spell writing gone wrong zagging up his arm. "Whatcha' gonna do?" he asked.

"If you wanna screw with the sub, you'll have to use your brain for once and think of something," I told him as I shoved his elbow away.

The trembling substitute clutched her skinny latte like it was a shield, like that caffeine would protect her from the abrasive scorn of the teenagers that sat in front of her. I unzipped my wand case and pulled out the slim, pure gold stick. Medeis Academy—an academy with a tree branch so far up its ass it didn't even realize nobody knew how to pronounce its crap Latin name—might have been one of the most exclusive academies on the east coast, but wealth didn't prevent people from being assholes. Myself notably included.

Under the hawk-like eyes of my classmates, I grabbed an inkwell and set it next to my wand. I set out a thin roll of parchment, half as wide as a store receipt, on my desk next to it. I then reached down into my backpack, pulled out a compact mirror, and clicked it open. I studied my straight brown hair and the orange streaks I'd given myself just last night; I frowned at the couple of freckles sprinkled on my nose. They were my least favorite feature, but unless I caked on the foundation, they always showed. At least I had pretty blue eyes. I fingered one of my orange stripes, debating whether it made my freckles stand out more or not. I deliberately ignored the sub and my classmates.

My indifference toward the magic professor caused her to sigh audibly in relief, and the other students to grouse as they turned back to face forward. I smiled to myself as I shut my compact and shoved it back into my bag. They'd get their entertainment. But they had to wait for it. For twenty-one more minutes.

The bell rang and the sub tottered forward on heels that were clearly too high for her. "Good morning, everyone. My name is Miss Tameka —"

"Nobody cares." An anonymous male voice called out from the back of the class. Titters erupted around the room. Miss Tameka whatever-her-last-name-was swallowed hard and turned to the professor's desk. She opened her cheap suitcase and pulled out a stack of papers. As I stared at them and recognized the light blue cover sheet used by the magical government, my stomach dropped.

Dammit, even after all this time, part of me wanted to prove I could do it. But I wouldn't. I clenched my hands into fists and turned to stare outside across the marble campus buildings toward the dormitories as if I didn't care about those papers in her hands. I pretended the dead tree line was more appealing as the winter wind picked up and made the branches dance.

Ms. Tameka turned back around to face us. And then her voice lashed out with a bit more attitude than I would have expected from her wilted-flower persona. "Well, perhaps you might care what my name is when you hear I'm here to administer a surprise examination. The Pinnacle has an internship opening this summer—"

Immediately, several of the goody-two-shoes straightened up, all alert, when seconds ago, they'd been as willing to dismiss this woman as the rest of us. But dangling the carrot of working at the magical government center was too much. Their inner nerd popped out like a zit. I shoved mine deep inside and let it fester. Because screw that. I focused on thinking about my room, about the suitcase I'd packed and shoved under my bed.

Miss Tameka's eyes settled on me. Even as I stared out the window, I could feel her gaze and see students turn to look at me again, this time with questioning expressions instead of expectant ones. I knew exactly what that meant. Dammit. Mom had pulled some strings. This internship quiz showing up in my advanced spell writing class was one of them. Internally, I shook my head. The woman's faith in me was unshakable. A little piece of me cringed at the thought of disappointing my mother yet again. I knew she wanted this for me—a solid future. But I'd already committed myself to something else long ago. My future, or lack thereof, was set.

I took a deep, bracing breath and turned away from the window. I stared defiantly into Miss Tameka's beady eyes as she told us to put away our wands and get out pens. "This will be a test of your spell writing speed and accuracy," she stated, "but we don't want any accidents as this is a level six spell."

"Level six? I thought only level eight through ten were used at the Pinnacle," some nerd with five spell writing scars dotting his cheek asked.

I'd put money on the fact that he'd tried to magically get rid of his acne and failed—multiple times.

Ms. Tameka replied, "Level ten is only for professionals. No intern will be expected to do a level ten spell. Six is quite hard enough. So, this will be a theoretical, not practical test. No wand-writing, pens only."

Wands were the only way we could do magic that we weren't born with; we could write spells and create all kinds of fantastic things. But wands were dangerous. One wrong wave of the wand, one wrong symbol, and everything could go *poof*. I rolled my eyes, doubting that the test was dangerous in any form whatsoever, but put my wand away. I didn't pull out a pen like everyone else. Instead, I folded my hands calmly on my desk and faced forward. I started playing *Rage Against the Machine* songs in my head. They'd been my brother's favorite and they were a good distraction from the temptation of that little blue packet.

I tried to watch impassively as the sub, aka government test administrator, started to hand out examination papers. "Everyone who takes this examination must be a minimum of seventeen years old in order to qualify for the internship." Seventeen was younger than the Pinnacle normally allowed—typically their internships started at age eighteen. Mother definitely had a hand in this, since I didn't turn eighteen for another couple months.

A super-nerd second year at the back of the room groaned and pulled out a book to read, since he didn't qualify; he was only sixteen. "Fucking bullshit," he muttered, but not loud enough to get in trouble.

Miss Tameka slid the booklet underneath my folded hands, the crisp paper rustling as it rubbed against my skin. She stood right next to me as she said, "Inside this test, you will read a scenario. It's not a real-life scenario but theoretical. You will have to use an illusion spell to disguise a person as an object. You will have exactly thirty minutes to create an original spell to counter the issue presented here. Those who succeed will get to move forward to an interview. Those who complete the interview will be subjected to a magical probe—"

A few grumbles arose at that, because a lot of my classmates were into taking illegal potions. Bubblehead was incredibly popular in the girls' locker room. I usually had to shove aside pedicured feet to get to my gym locker, because those idiots would be floating with their heads bouncing along the ceiling. When magicals got high on Bubble, they did it literally.

I openly grinned at the mention of the magical probe and shot a look at Terra Lysour. Terra had big Pinnacle ambitions. But she was a total Bubblehead. In every way.

I wondered briefly if she'd ever written a spell to flush out her system and erase traces of illegal Bubble magic. If she hadn't already, I was pretty certain she'd try if she made it to the magical probe round—legality be damned. Because this opportunity was a rarity, the Pinnacle typically only took magicals who'd become Unnaturals.

My mother's voice popped into my head, cutting off the music. "Only the most advanced magic workers of their generation get to be there, Hayley. I know you're one of them. Your natural gifts plus your spell writing…"

I cut off the memory of her lecture by searching my bag for gum. I shoved a stick in my mouth and leaned back in my seat, letting the taste of mint distract me as I glanced at the clock. Nineteen minutes.

Leave it to my mother to think that I'd earn an internship as only a third year when most of this class was filled with fourth and fifth years. I looked down briefly at the Pinnacle symbol on top of the test packet, a tower much like a chess rook, with a diamond above it, radiating light. I kept my hands off it, though Miss Tameka had set it down crooked on my desk and I kind of wanted to straighten it. But if I opened the test, I'd be too tempted to solve the problem. Years of racing my brother had ingrained me with a competitiveness that was hard to let go. Not to mention that tiny, niggling feeling in the back of my mind that wasn't so certain about what I was doing.

I let the test sit crooked and turned to look at the clock on the wall. I didn't want to be part of the magical machine anyway. I had better things to do. Like disrupt the fuck out of it.

But then Miss Tameka dealt me a death blow. "This internship will be in the science and research division."

Quick as a flash, I bent over and grabbed a pen. I flipped open the pages. The scenario was deceptively simple. I read it over twice before everything clicked. My pen raced across the paper. I might not get the fucking internship. But I wanted the damn interview. I had to rush because I was already on a countdown clock here. Fuck. I glanced at the clock. Only seventeen minutes until everything would blow up. I willed my hand to go faster, pretending Matthew was sitting next to me, racing me. As I wrote, I didn't have grand ideas about internships leading to cubicles and cubicles to offices and offices to jet-setting airplanes and tropical meetings. I thought about maps and codes. I thought about verifying locks and guard patterns. I thought about learning employee habits. I had criminal thoughts.

Fifteen minutes later, I finished the final spell symbol with a bit of flourish and set my pen down. My eyes met Ms. Tameka's and her brows rose as she approached. I shut my test packet and handed it over to her, unable to prevent the arrogant smirk on my face.

She walked back to the desk; nose buried in my test as she scanned my spell writing. When she met my eyes, I knew exactly what she was thinking.

'It's perfect,' her expression said.

I know, I thought as I folded my fingers on my desk like a good little girl.

A loud shoe squeak sounded in the hall and then the classroom door was yanked open.

Every eye in the room turned to look as my worst nightmare walked through the door.

Tall, stacked, with a jaw that could cut glass, my nightmare brushed his black bangs up and yanked off his leather jacket, revealing chiseled arms under a short sleeve uniform shirt better suited for spring than mid-winter. When he slung his jacket over his shoulder like a douche, his untucked white shirt pulled tight against his abs, which were perfectly formed. Behind me, a girl audibly gasped at the sight of him.

"Sorry. New transfer." His deep blue gaze traveled around the room until he saw me. He knew better than to smile, but his lips curled up just a little, like he couldn't help it. And damn him for having the world's hottest fucking smirk. That asshole.

Another girl sighed. Stupid Terra Lysour pushed out her fake tits. Fools. He might have been built like a quarterback, but it was all a facade. Before he'd become an Unnatural, he'd been a skinny, dweeby nerd who liked to read comics and fuck around with cameras like a norm. My lips naturally curled into a snarl at the sight of him. Fucking Evan Weston was a stalker.

This was the third school he'd suddenly transferred to shortly after me. It must have been harder for him to transfer this time around. He was a few months behind.

Evan winked at me before I turned away, clenching my fists. He was an asshole. And—as far as I was concerned—a murderer. Rage heated my spine and crawled up my neck like a little red devil. It whispered in my ear. "Fuck him." I was not going to sit through class with Evan Weston. I could not—*would not*—do it. I stood up as he made his way to a free seat in the back of the advanced class.

"Miss Dunemark, please sit—" the sub requested.

I grabbed my bag, ignoring her. I'd win an interview no matter how pissed she was. She wouldn't be able to help it. Not with how fast I'd finished.

And, perfect timing. My countdown had ended. *Let the nuclear meltdown commence.* I heard a buzz flit around the room, like a swarm of bees had flown inside. Students pulled out their phones.

"Phones away, this is an exam—" the sub protested.

Everyone pretended not to hear as they unlocked their devices and pressed play on a video that had just been sent to the entire school email list.

I started walking toward the door, smirking at Evan as I passed him. "Enjoy Medeis Academy. They're just your kind of people."

His initial confusion turned to anger when he realized the implication of my words. His mouth opened, but the loudspeaker interrupted him.

"Miss Dunemark, report to the headmaster's office immediately."

I smirked again and gave a little wave. Evan's stalking was fucked. For now, at least. I savored the look of disbelief and fury on his face all the way down the hall. It looked like two things might work out in my favor today. Time to face the firing squad.

2

The headmaster's office was meant to be imposing, with its oil paintings of previous headmasters cozying up to world leaders, signifying how much the norms depended on magicals to keep the world afloat. The red carpet and red velvet chairs were Baroque monstrosities that were so busy, you couldn't focus on one thing. Trophies that had been important to someone at some point littered every surface.

I sat down across from Headmaster Grogney, taking my time to compose my face as I put my book bag on the floor. I tried not to smirk, but it was difficult. I mean, a video of your headmaster masturbating at his desk as he rubbed a gerbil all over his bare chest—that was grade A material, right there. Especially when you knew said video had just gone viral throughout the school.

All over campus, magicals were snickering, and Headmaster Grogney's self-proclaimed love for animals had taken on an entirely new meaning.

I sat in his office, watching the vein pop in his forehead as he fast-forwarded through a genuine work of Photoshop and Adobe

Premiere art. Instead of homework, I'd spent the last week in my dorm room creating that masterpiece, uploading it from a computer I knew his ridiculously incompetent IT professor could trace. And I'd done it all by hand too, so it would be identifiable even by a norm—which our IT professor was. I hadn't magicked a single part of it.

I settled back in the plush red velvet of Grogney's visitor seat and stroked the arm, letting the material change from lighter to darker and back again with each pass I made. I was kind of annoyed that Grogney wasn't watching my hard work—he was missing out on the terrified little animal squeaks I'd painstakingly put in. Those finishing touches made all the difference. He wasn't watching it, but he wasn't yelling yet either. *Seriously? Wasn't this enough?*

He was pissed, yeah, but he hadn't said the words. The portly man was nearly purple with rage as he set down his wand on the desk (he'd nearly snapped it because he was squeezing it so hard); but really, Grogney had only himself to blame. Did he need another little push?

"You know this is all your fault, right?" I asked.

"Excuse me?"

"I've spent plenty of time in this chair." I'd given him plenty of opportunities to kick me out before this. There was the obvious plagiarism that I'd done, buying crap spells off some fifth-year students and turning in word for word replicas. There was the fight I started in the bathroom with that bitch, Terra, who'd said vamps were worthless shits that needed to be put down. I'd pulled out a chunk of her fake pink weave. None of it—nothing—had gotten me kicked out. I shook my head at Grogney. "You're too soft. You went with in-school suspension."

"Young lady—"

"Shit, I even tried to get the combat teacher to make out with me." That had been a sacrifice on my part, because while the man was ripped like a god, he had a nose the size of the Mississippi. "But a big donation from mommy made you shut up about that one." The combat professor had been forced to quit, which I did feel bad about, but what asshole made out with seventeen-year-old students, anyway? Gross. I was doing some poor girl somewhere a favor, getting him out of the academy. What it all boiled down to was that it was Grogney's fault that we were sitting here today. If he weren't so blinded by deep pockets, or if he had any damn moral compass, he wouldn't have subjected the students and professors to my bullshit antics.

Still, he delayed.

What the hell was it gonna take? I took out a pen and a notebook, squeaked my chair closer to the desk, and posed my pen in my hand. "So, Headmaster. What's it gonna be? Lines this time? Time out? Or do you prefer spankings?"

I leaned forward and smiled as I watched him visibly shake with the effort of holding back. He didn't even notice my hands sliding along the desk. Of course, I exuded a tiny bit of power to make the desk blur a bit in his vision, but I don't think he noticed in his ire.

"Hayley Dunemark, you're expelled," he growled, jowls trembling. He was too worked up to get anything else out.

Finally. Shit, that was the most work I've had to do to get kicked out of an academy, I thought as I sat back, replacing my notebook and items in my bag. Then I stood and extended my hand to shake his. "It's been a pleasure knowing you, Headmaster."

He did not take my hand. I shook my head. Even after you lost a duel, you were supposed to shake hands with your competitor. Poor breeding. So, I simply reached up to my hair and pulled down my oversized rhinestone sunglasses, gave him a finger gun salute and tongue click, and walked out the door. I waved at his prim little secretary as I left. I was sure she and her other turtle-neck-wearing, wand-waving windbags would enjoy gossiping about me tonight. She was probably sending out a group text already.

I walked down the halls to a mixed reception—there were as many hushed whispers as there were high-fives and catcalls from magic prep kids who wished they had half the guts I did, but not really. They were all just teenage posers, trying to get through the five stupid years of academy training before being unleashed on the world as full-scale magicals at age twenty. I did my best to ignore the uniform bunnies—as I'd started to call the timid, rule followers—beyond an extra little sway in my hips. A girl had to have a little sway to go with a badass performance like the one I'd just pulled. But not too much. Getting kicked out of yet another exclusive, magical academy was the easy part of my plan.

I pushed up my sunglasses as I unlocked my locker and started stuffing books into my backpack. I thought, *I gotta stay on my toes.* Acting like a badass was easy. Acting like a victim was harder. And I still had Act Two of this charade to pull off.

"Hales, you're a fucking idiot!" Tia slammed her hand into the locker next to mine and I stiffened.

I stood and turned to see her worrying the black spikes in her hair. With her apple cheeks, short stature, and slightly rounded body, Tia did all she could to fight the label 'cute.' Her dark makeup and spiked hair were accented by chunky silver necklaces and leather bracelets that rode the line between emo and BDSM. As soon as Tia saw my eyes flicker toward her nervous habit, she lowered her hand from her hair. She leaned in close and whispered, "I know you want out of here. But don't go fucking up your chances for any kind of career. That was too much."

What she said pulled at my heartstrings. She was sweet. And she cared, which was more than I could say about most people, other than my mother. But she didn't know what I was up against. And what I'd done so far was nothing compared to what I was going to do next. I snorted. "Like I'd ever want to work for the Pinnacle anyway." That wasn't a lie, not completely anyway.

"What—you want to work for the norms?" Tia shook her head and narrowed her brown eyes. Her eyeliner was so thick that when she did that, her eyes looked like black streaks, you almost couldn't see the whites. Creepy.

"Yeah. Have my heart set on being an accountant," I winked. I felt like ruffling her spikes but resisted.

She laughed. "Yeah, I always pegged you as a number cruncher," she quipped, flipping off some nitwit first year dude who'd turned to gape at us. When he turned away, she looked back at me and asked, "Are you sure you want to go … there? Metamorphose?" She whispered the last word.

I leaned toward her and nodded. "Still think you can get your aunt to get me in?"

She inhaled and pressed her lips together. "I've been working on her. But this bullshit you keep pulling—"

"Makes me a perfect fit. I'm a tortured little rich girl who's acting out and in need of rehabilitation; and mom can more than afford the tuition—"

Tia shook her head. "I don't think you know what you're getting yourself into. Those kids have problems. Serious problems. Some of them are dangerous."

I narrowed my eyes at her. We had been best friends since we were twelve. I'd originally been separated from her at fifteen, because I'd been sent to the most exclusive magical academy of them all—Niveus. I'd gradually made my way to Medeis. At first, it had been awesome, reconnecting with Tia. And I had to admit, she made for a great ally. Tia was one of those people who knew people. Car broke down? She had a second cousin. Diamond fell out of mom's earring? She had an uncle. Her family was like this massive networking association almost by design—like her great-grandmother had been picking careers out

ANN DENTON

for everyone for the past ninety-four years so that none of them had the same job and all of them could keep their cash in the family.

Tia had been more than excited to help me with part of my plan. I hadn't told her all of it. Couldn't tell her all of it. I wouldn't tell anyone the entire plan, because it was crazy, because it was highly illegal, and because I didn't need anyone trying to talk me out of it. That plan was my only hope.

"You aren't backing out, are you?" I tried to keep the panic out of my voice, but a little of it leaked through. My chest grew tight at the thought that I might get kicked out of here and not make it to my goal. I needed Tia, desperately, to get to the next stage. Her aunt worked at Academie Metamorphose, which was the prissy name for the school that everyone actually called the Magical Academy for Delinquents or MAD—the magical equivalent of a rehabilitative school for teens with attitude problems, legal problems, natural-born power problems. They called it rehab, but the people I'd spoken to who'd gone there called it a prison. And it was exactly where I needed to be.

Tia worried her lip-ring, and that set off all kinds of alarm bells inside my stomach.

Time to give her the lie again. "Grayson Mars is my destiny, T. I just know it."

She rolled her eyes. "I never woulda' pegged you for the lovesick kind."

"Dude. Trust me. I know. But there was this party..." This completely fictional party, where I met him and we talked, and all our parental issues came spilling out like beautiful little fluttering fairies. And it was magical. Bullshit, bullshit. Bullshit bullshit bullshit. The lie spilled easily from my tongue. I'd practiced it enough that it was almost real in my head, like a false memory.

Tia's eyes softened and I knew I had to press my point home.

I grabbed her hand and squeezed. "Tia, I need to get in there. Now." Matthew had been gone three years. And after I'd come up with my plan, it had taken me two and a half to get to this point. Who knew how long it would take to get through the rest of it? I needed into MAD. I needed in, like, yesterday, because every night my brain buzzed with anxiety. I was nearly eighteen and I hadn't gotten halfway through my plan yet. I pulled her hand up and held it between us as nervous sweat started rolling down my back. "Please..."

"I'm not backing out." She flicked me with her fingers in annoyance until I dropped her hand. She hated when I held her hands or exhibited any kind of PDA like side hugs. "But you and I both know that place is for crazies. You're better than that. You could do better than anyone else in this entire fucking academy."

I shoved the last of my books into my bag. There were no kitschy items in my locker as I'd never planned on staying at this prick school anyway. I slammed the locker closed. "Maybe I can't."

"That's a lie! You're a fucking Darklight," Tia seethed. "Like one fucking percent of the population—"

"My power has nothing to do with what I choose—" I started.

Tia cut me off. "Don't give me that crap. Your magic tested off the charts. And you've got the fucking rarest strand. You know you get special treatment because of it. Your entire life has to do with your powers. Every natural-born magical's life does. It's how it is."

Her words were a slap to the face. "It doesn't have to be."

She rolled her eyes. "Don't be naive. And don't throw away your chance. I know you've been in a weird place since Matthew—"

"Don't." The single word warning was all she was gonna get. Tia was sweet underneath her tough-rocker girl persona, but she wouldn't understand the things going through my fucked-up head. I couldn't trust her with this. I couldn't trust anyone—because anyone else would think I was insane. I could only rely on myself. Because there was no one else in the world who could save Matthew. Even *I* didn't know if I could. But I'd fucking die trying.

3

BEFORE I HEADED to my dorm to grab my suitcase, I stopped off at the girls' restroom. I yanked open the door and strode toward the obnoxiously pink stalls. I was pulling open a stall when I heard the telltale signs of two people making out. *Gross. Seriously?* That happened enough during school hours. But school was out. *Find a car, go to the forest, shit—go do it on your parent's bed for all I care, people,* I thought. Just not the nasty-ass, germ-filled bathroom. You'd think rich bitches would have standards. But nope. Half of them were desperate to secure their posh lifestyle with rings during fifth year. Gag.

I bent down and looked along the tiled floor. The third stall was the one with two feet under it. I momentarily wished I had written a spell to stink people out without having to smell anything myself. Why hadn't I done this? I made a mental note—that would probably be a good spell to have at Metamorphose when I needed to work on plans. I didn't need everyone seeing my diagrams of the top-secret levels of the Pinnacle.

I was about to yell and tell this couple that they had an audience when the guy's voice whined.

"Come on, baby, I just need a little extra juice for practice."

Wow, a romantic. Let me fuck you for a power boost. Asswipe, I rolled my eyes. And a cheater, since that was technically illegal for all sports. Norm and magical schools played against each other and magicals weren't supposed to use power for sports.

"I have to go see my parents after this. They're gonna want to know about that internship thing. I don't want to be flaring. They'll notice if my magic's out of control." The girl's voice whispered but I recognized Terra's nasal pitch.

I almost backed out of the bathroom right then, doubly disgusted because someone was making out with her—the vamp-hating snob. But the guy's next words pissed me the fuck off.

"You want me to go find some of your friends instead? Fine." The guy's hands slammed against the bathroom stall wall in anger.

For a second, I saw white. Then black. My own power flooded me and then tingled at my fingertips. That asshole did not just threaten to sleep with Terra's friends. And to physically intimidate her? I might hate that bitch, but what the hell? That was pathetic. It was low. I waited to hear Terra rip him a new one. But she didn't.

"Johnny don't—" Terra whined, and I realized who the guy was.

Our quarterback. Fan-fucking-tastic. *Way to fit the athlete asshole stereotype,* I thought. And Terra was so caught up in this petty bull she didn't even stand up for herself. I shook my head.

"Strip, then." Johnny ordered, in a jerkwad tone.

I heard Terra whimper.

And I'd had enough. Rage lit my neck on fire. Terra might be a bitch. But no one should be coerced like that. From both their tones, it sounded like this was a regular occurrence. I debated leaving, wondering if what I could do would make a difference anyway. Terra might just run back to him tomorrow. Girls often did when they were in shit relationships—my mother included. Somehow, they thought anything was better than loneliness.

They were wrong.

I heard Johnny start to groan and I snapped. It might do no fucking good. But I did it anyway. I lifted a hand and sent a narrow blast of power in the direction of their bathroom stall. Purple light streamed from me, bounced off the stall door, refracted toward the ceiling and then bounced down again. The stall they occupied started to glow like a giant light bulb. Brighter. Brighter. Blindingly bright as I fed my rage with more power.

"The fuck?" Johnny Castlebrook stumbled out of the stall and fell to the floor, clutching his eyes. I lifted my hand and let the light recede.

The stereotypical quarterback in a letterman jacket with the symbol of Medeis—a wand—on it, he had wavy hair and a decent, though boring, face. But his head was set like an ape on his shoulders. The boy had no neck. Blech. Terra had terrible taste—for so many reasons.

Terra followed after Johnny, still buttoning her uniform skirt back up. Her collared shirt looked rumpled, one of the buttons might even have been torn off. I wasn't sure.

"Professor—" she started to come up with some lame excuse. Until she realized it was me standing there. Her dumb, doe eyes widened. She was shocked at first, but it didn't take long for that shock to turn to fury. "What the hell?" she bellowed at me. "Get out of here, you stupid freak!"

And that was just one of the many reasons, I loathed her. "You're gonna scream at me for stopping him from forcing you into sex for a power boost? Which, by regulations, he's not allowed to have, anyway?"

Terra's face grew pinched and I knew then that I shouldn't have bothered. I was gonna come out the bad guy in this situation. Luckily, I was used to that role by now.

"It wasn't forcing," Johnny stood and lumbered over to me. "She's lucky I'd touch her."

I laughed. "We both know she's got more power in her pinkie toe than you do in that dick of yours—though they're roughly the same size."

Johnny's hand shot out and grabbed my shoulder. His other hand rose, as if he were about to use his power on me. But then his eyes looked past me.

A roar filled the room. A deep, inhuman, animalistic roar.

Fucking no! This is not happening! Instead of the sound filling me with fear, I was filled with irritation, like someone had put tape across my forearm and yanked.

Johnny let me go and I turned around, eyes narrowed, heart pumping hard.

A giant, brown grizzly bear stood in the doorway of the girls' restroom. It reared up on its hind legs, kicking aside shredded bits of white and blue uniform (a casualty of shifting from human to animal form), before trudging over to stand next to me like a protective, overbearing furry dick.

Goosebumps rose on my spine, even though I tried to force them away. I dug my nails into my palms and ground my teeth. "I was handling it."

The bear beside me growled in disagreement. Johnny thought it was growling at him and scrambled backward, knocking Terra to the floor. He wasn't even gentleman enough to help her up. And he was definitely ungentlemanly enough to move behind her and use her as a human shield. Fucking coward.

At least Terra called him on it. "Hey, asshole!" she cursed him.

I rolled my eyes at all of them and turned and strode toward the door. I'd find another bathroom. Thank fuck I was done with idiots at Medeis Academy. Criminals would be better than this. At least criminals had the skills I needed. Terra and her boob jobs were as magically self-absorbed and useless as the rest of the losers here.

The bear tried to lumber along behind me, but I shook my head. "Don't you dare, Evan." *Motherfucking interfering stalker. Follows me from school to school and tries to fight my battles? Who does he think he is?*

I slammed the door shut on his big, hairy snout.

I CHECKED MY PHONE TO MAKE SURE MY DRIVER WAS ON THE WAY, THEN unlocked my dorm room, struggling with the stupid door and banging my hip on it three times before it opened. Once I was in, I tossed the key on the table; I wouldn't need that sorry fucking thing anymore, thank goodness. For all that this "prestigious institution" bragged about the finest amenities, this building was built in the early 1900s and I doubted that the locks had ever been changed.

My roommate, Zaira, sat on her bed and gaped at me, playing with the ends of her braids. She hadn't bothered to get up and let me in. She was *that* kind of rich and lazy.

I ignored her and went straight for my bed, bent over, reaching underneath to pull the overstuffed wheeled suitcase out, eager to leave this upright, uptight place. My heart tap-danced with excitement, listing off my next steps. Home. Then hopefully MAD to recruit some badass motherfuckers. Then I'd head to the Pinnacle. Just not the way Mother wanted. I'd go in the dark of night. And I'd take from them what they'd kept from my family, from so many families. A cure for the madness that hit magicals who wanted to be like Evan, magicals who tried to write the spell that was powerful enough to give them the permanent power to shift; magicals who were good, great even, but had made one little mistake with their wands ...

Zaira interrupted my thoughts. "I can't decide if I should be all 'Yas Kween,' that was an epic vid, or if you're totally just thirsty. Mommy too busy fucking Wall Street dudes to pay attention to you?"

I wanted to punch her out, but assault charges would fuck up my plans. I wanted to get into MAD, not to have to go to the clink first. "Yup. You got me pegged. You're *so* smart. Damn." I flipped Zaira off as I wheeled my suitcase out the door.

"You one damn cray cray bitch, that's for sure. I'm glad you're gone, Hayley."

I should have let it go. I really should have, but my grip tightened on the suitcase and I stopped. I pulled open my backpack.

Zaira stiffened on the bed, then rolled and grabbed for her own wand, which was sitting on her dresser. "You'd better not—" she warned, pointing her wand at me. But Zaira was an Icefire, the most common of the magicals. And she skated by. We'd only made it this long as roommates because I didn't ever come home and see her stupid face.

I arched a brow at her when she aimed her wand at my throat. "What a threat! Are you sure you're pointing the right end of that thing at me?"

She wasn't. I rolled my eyes before I pulled a slightly tarnished silver wand out of my bag and tossed it on the bed. Then I winked at her. "Have fun explaining to Headmaster Grogney how you got his wand."

Zaira gawked.

God, I loved seeing people stare in wonder. It was the best feeling in the world—watching disbelief, panic, and admiration declare war on their features. It was an all-out micro expression explosion, which often made for hilarious combinations—flared nostrils, a raised brow, and a smile. If I hadn't had plans, or been so excited about my goal, I might have taken out my phone and taken a few snapshots of Zaira. But I had places to go and criminals to meet.

I shut the door on her stunned face and went whistling down the hall. I ignored the glances that came my way while I walked through the quad toward the entrance. I was so over Medeis. But just as I got close enough to see the driveway that would lead me to freedom, a hand gripped my arm and swung me around.

A furious Evan glared down at me, chest heaving. He'd clearly run all the way across campus to the guy's dorms to grab clothes before booking it back to me. He hadn't thrown on a jacket. His light blue t-shirt molded to his abs even better than the uniform shirt, and the points of his nipples were visible in the February chill. His hair was mussed. In short, he looked like every sexy fantasy I'd ever had about him when we were growing up. My mouth dried out. Fucking shit. I tightened my grip on my suitcase, reminding my body that we hated him, that we had goals. My nipples didn't seem to care.

Evan's face crumpled, like he was sad or disappointed by what he saw when he looked at me. Inside, that made part of me wither. But it made another part of me want to smack him across the face. *How dare he judge me after what he'd done?* I yanked my arm out of his grip. Fuck him. Fuck Evan Weston. At least he couldn't follow me where I was going. He was too prissy for that. Because I was done with his constant attempts to distract me.

"Hailstorm. Please. Please stop doing this to yourself," Evan's words were a whisper so low that I could hardly hear them. It took me a minute to piece together what he'd said.

I swallowed hard; my stupid mouth was touched by this murderer's concern. *Fuck him. He can jump off a cliff*—my heart wouldn't let me think that. *Fine, he can wallow in mediocrity behind a desk his whole life, discontent, and bored and getting daily paper cuts,* I amended my thought. My heart seemed okay with a lifetime of menial torture, because it let me get away with that.

"I'm not doing anything to myself," I seethed through my teeth, turning to walk away from him as quickly as possible.

Of course, the stalker wouldn't just let me walk away. He didn't have it in him. Evan's long strides easily overtook mine.

"Hayley, you're punishing yourself. For what happened to Matthew and then your dad. You're spiraling."

I gave a bitter laugh that materialized as a white cloud in the afternoon chill. "I'm not punishing myself."

"What the fuck do you call this?"

I shook my head as I spotted my driver and the sleek, black town car. And maybe it was my excitement over the car, and the promise of warmth that it held; or maybe it was my excitement about being on the brink of the next stage of my plan, but I accidentally said more than I intended. "I call this Operation Matthew."

Evan stopped short; his six-foot, four-inch frame stunned into statue-like stillness. That name alone was like slamming a baseball bat into his gut. I knew, because whenever anyone used that name and I wasn't expecting it, I felt the exact same way. That name was sacred. To me, at least. It should be to him, too, considering Matthew used to be his best friend.

"Hayley, I don't know what you're thinking, but whatever it is, you're wrong. He's *gone*." He cringed as he said it. But still, he fucking said it.

I glared at him, fury rising like a tide. How dare he fucking give up on my brother. "That's what the Pinnacle wants you to think."

"What's that supposed to mean?"

Shit. I'd said too much. But there was no taking the words back now. There was no way to scoop them up out of the air and put them back into my mouth. I'd have to count on Evan's guilt to keep his mouth shut. And maybe write a spell for it once I was out of sight, so that he couldn't go running to his mommy or mine and give it all away.

Dammit. I was a bit furious with myself. I needed to control my rage around him, or I was going to make a mistake worse than a slip of the tongue. I gave Evan a haughty look before turning and walking away. I didn't feel bad about leaving that fucker emotionally bruised and battered on the sidewalk as I walked to my car. He could drown in a blood-red puddle of his own guilt for all I was concerned. Because even though he'd apologized and cried and said he didn't mean for it to happen, he couldn't erase the past. And the events of the past stood like a chasm between us. He was who he was. He'd made his mistakes. I was making mine. And we were on separate paths. He was the youngest Unnatural in fifty years—he'd been the first seventeen-year-old in decades to perfectly write the spell to give himself shifter powers. A spell my dumbass brother had tried to do with him. Now, Evan was the Pinnacle's golden poster boy. I planned to be their worst nightmare.

I gave him an arrogant little wave of my fingers before I handed my backpack and suitcase to the driver and slid into the car.

I pulled out my wand and parchment and wrote a quick spell to make Evan unable to remember our conversation. The spell turned into magic, sparkling gold dust as I wrote, the parchment burning as each symbol I drew magically came to life. I opened the window and let the magic trail out of the car as the driver pulled away from Medeis. Then I pushed Evan out of my mind. I had two hours to review my plans to break into the Pinnacle. And I wasn't going to waste a minute of them.

4

"Hey kiddo."

I jumped in my seat. I glanced over and realized my dad was sitting at the far end of the town car bench. My eyes flew to the driver, a norm guy who stared straight ahead, oblivious. I immediately put up the privacy partition so my driver couldn't hear me sounding like a mad woman—talking to myself ... because my father was a ghost.

Once the partition was up, I took a second to calm my racing heart. I hadn't expected Dad to show up during daylight hours. We usually met once a week. We had scheduled to meet up tomorrow. But sometimes he lost track of time. Over the past few years, he'd lost track of more and more things ... he'd forgotten the color of my mom's eyes. What we were doing. Sometimes he even forgot my name.

It was a blessing and a curse. I still got to see him, hear him. He wasn't completely gone. But he was a shadow of himself. That thought almost made me laugh bitterly. We were all just shadows of ourselves anymore. My chest ached to be whole, like it had been four years prior. But wishing for the past was an exercise in futility.

I carefully put away my wand and the rest of my roll of parchment before I turned to face my father, wondering what version of him I was going to get today. Was he going to be lost and befuddled? Or would he be on the ball, full of information? My chest buzzed in anticipation, balanced on the razor's edge between hope and despair.

I studied him, trying to read his gaze. Dad wore brown slacks, an Argyle sweater, and a brown fedora trimmed with a plaid ribbon.

"I told you I hate those hats," I muttered. Fedoras were so douchey looking.

"Why do you think I wore it?" He grinned, patting the brim.

I rolled my eyes, but inside my heart gave a little happy jump and kick. If he'd worn something to bug me, that meant this was a good day. After three years, I would have thought I'd have gotten used to the bad days, but I hadn't. Each bad day he had was like a punch to the gut— even though it was his memory loss that had let me institute my plan in the first place. When my dad had first appeared to me—he'd been hit by a train, driving distracted only a week after Matthew's accident —he'd shot down every idea I'd had to save my brother. But, as his memory grew weaker, so had his will. He'd let information slip about his lab and the studies there. The lab that had been bought up by the Pinnacle, because assholes like my stepfather—

"So, why are we in this car?" Dad's question interrupted my train of thought as he glanced around at the black leather interior.

"Got kicked out again," I told him.

"Congrats. I hope you did my name proud."

I bit down on a smile and gave a little shrug. "Harry? You want me to make the name Harry proud? I think I'd have to stop shaving and join a commune for that."

Dad laughed, and it accentuated the wrinkles around his dark brown eyes. But not in a bad way, in a way that said he'd been laughing for years—at the world and life and everything. When he was alive, he'd always been ready with a smirk or smile. My heart tugged at me hard. I wanted nothing more than to curl up under his arm and give him a hug.

Though being a Darklight allowed me to see ghosts, I couldn't touch them. They were only specters of light too far outside normal vision range for anyone else to see. And they were rare, even more rare than my power. Darklights were one in a hundred. Ghosts were maybe one in ten thousand. My dad was only the second ghost I'd met in my life.

We'd debated telling Mom about him at first ... but then she'd tried to kill herself the first time, and it just felt like the revelation would make things worse. I shoved down the hurt of that memory, the fact that she'd tried to leave me alone in the world. But I still felt the tears sloshing inside my stomach. There was an ocean of grief under my skin. I was just floating on top of it, on a rickety raft that was this damned plan.

Dad's laughter trailed off, and he swiped at the corners of his eyes— out of habit more than anything, because he couldn't cry anymore— he propped his foot up on his knee and linked his fingers together over that leg. "Alright. I've got updates. First off, Claudia is a douche."

I chuckled at dad's name for mom's new husband. "Agreed. But is that relevant?"

"He's cheating on her."

Zap. It was like I'd been stuck with a cattle prod. I stared at him, shocked, as the car went under a long bridge and cast us into shadow. Dad's form flickered in the dark. We sat in silence until we emerged from under the bridge. A million images and awful words filled my mind. I pictured myself choking the life out of Claude. The fantasy was satisfying as hell. But when I pictured my mother's face after ...

The asshole was going to get to live. God, I hated that. I smoothed out my face and grabbed my laptop out of my bag. "Who?"

"Secretary. Of course. Doesn't have a creative bone—"

"Let's talk work," I snapped. Dad might be pissed about this, but I had to face the fucker in a few hours. He didn't. I had to restrain myself. He didn't. I was already two seconds from boiling over any time I saw 'the Clod'— which was my nickname for the thickheaded, brutal bastard. I didn't need to be all worked up when I saw him today. Not when I had fucking goals to achieve. Dammit. I blew out a breath.

Calm down. Focus on other shit, I told myself.

I started up my laptop. Then I pulled a flash drive out of a hidden compartment in my necklace and inserted it. It was old school, the flash drive, but it worked to keep the info I wanted away from prying eyes. I opened the encrypted file where I'd saved folders and articles about my targets. To anyone else, a secret "Crush" file might look like guys I jilled off to, but the file was so much more than that. It was my list of potential recruits. Because I wasn't arrogant enough to think I could break into the Pinnacle with just Dad to help me. Not quite.

I'd need manpower if I was gonna get the serum that Dad said was down in their vaults. And professional established criminals weren't likely to listen to a two-bit chick like me. I'd tried that route already. Been shot down for a year before I gave up on that track.

I needed bad boys. Didn't just want them. Needed them desperately.

Assholes like my mother's shit of a husband, Claude—who sat around on the Pinnacle board getting served coffee and blowjobs by secretaries all day—had decided that since testing had blown up a magical, and a building or two, that the continued search for a serum to cure Matthew and others like him wasn't safe or in the public's best interest.

What those dickheads didn't say was that they were goddamned liars. My dad's lab had been testing a cure without any explosions. And it had worked—once, at Dad's lab—before Matthew tried to go Unnatural. Before the government vultures had swept in and "bought" the lab and all its research.

My dad leaned over to look at the screen, and by the crease in his brow I could tell that the lost ghost was gone, and my father was back.

He said, "The serum is in box 94, but the only way to access it is through the vault. But even getting down to the vault is gonna be hard, Hales. You have to get to the vault first, which is no easy matter —let me just tell you—and unravel a level 10 spell that locks the vault door. Then, only one person can enter the vault wearing an Honesty Amulet. Even if you get the serum out of the box, you can't leave the vault without declaring your intentions. And the vault won't let you leave if you honestly mean to steal the serum." Dad was my scout for this whole operation. He'd been shadowing people at the Pinnacle so that I could pull this off when I was ready.

I waved off that last bit. I'd worry about the Honesty Amulet when I got there. That seemed light years away anyway.

"Were you able to watch the guy unravel the spell?" I asked.

He lifted his fedora and scratched his head. "Not enough to see what he wrote. I forgot to add, as far as I can tell, there's still the timer."

"Fuck." I ran a hand through my hair.

"We're gonna need a Tock to give you enough time to write the spell."

"I know," I growled. Only about four percent of the population had the power to manipulate time. It didn't give me a ton of options. My damn pick for Tock had gotten himself arrested for felony breaking and entering. Stupid ass Andros Traylor. I pulled out my laptop and hacked into the Hidden City police reporting system. "He's on hold. Meaning another state wants him." I pursed my lips and shook my head. If I could go break into the Hidden City prison and fucking smack him across the face, I would. Of course, if I could break into the prison and get to him, I'd probably drag him right to the Pinnacle to help me. But the chances of pulling off that kind of break in and going unnoticed … I needed the Pinnacle to be my only job. I didn't need people looking for me before I even got to it.

"What state? Are they gonna transfer him?" Dad asked.

I shook my head. "Doesn't say. Lazy ass admin probably hasn't gotten around to figuring it out and typing it up." As pissed as I was at the cops for finding him, I was twice as pissed at him for getting caught. Stupid fucking criminal. As far as I could tell, the bank break in was a drunken dare or something. I rolled my eyes. "Now, I don't even know if I want him, if he can get caught so easily."

Dad sighed. "Well, you better start looking for another."

I rolled my eyes. "I know."

"You could try a girl."

I shook my head. All the recruits I had in mind were dudes, because, frankly, they were less drama than women. Plus, I had zero time for romantic theatrics and shit going down in my group, so I didn't want a mix. We needed to get in, out, and move the fuck on with our lives. Like a one-night stand with no fake phone number exchange afterward and no regrets. Mutual benefits followed by mutual disinterest.

I was not gonna hash out the old girl versus guy topic with my dad again. So, I pulled open some other profiles. "My two other top picks are solid."

To even get inside the Pinnacle's main building, I'd need someone to cause chaos and distraction. Malcolm Bier fit the bill there. I swiped to open the file that held all his personal details, from favorite breakfast cereal to anarchist magazine cover with him on it. He was blond-haired, blue-eyed, and shirtless, because All-American hot abs were clearly the best way to recruit new anarchists, at least that seemed to be Resist Magazine's strategy. Malcolm was an Icefire, like seventy percent of the natural born magical population. But … he was also a nineteen-year-old prodigy with a penchant for using his fire power to blow things up. His anarchist tendencies were what made him appealing. Not the six pack abs or that 1950's flip to his blond hair. Definitely not the chin dimple. I went back to the magazine cover and pinched, zooming in to see if they'd photoshopped that in. But nope. Looked like Malcolm scored a 10/10 for brains and brawn. I studied his eyes and hoped that his hatred of the Pinnacle would help tip him over the edge and get him to help me.

"Anything new on Malcom Bier?" I asked.

"No, he's been low key since the bombing. Staying at that school. Probably trying to keep the heat off him so he doesn't end up caught like that Traylor fellow."

I sighed and nodded. "Well. He's still a go then. He and Grayson are both at MAD."

I closed out Malcolm's file and pulled up the picture of Grayson Mars. Again, this guy was on a magazine cover where he (eyeroll) posed in his underwear, showing off his rich-boy-has-a-personal-trainer body. His chocolate eyes bored holes into me while I reread the gossip. He was the son of the billionaire who'd gotten us commuter rockets to the planet Mars. Now there was an entire colony being built there. All because Grayson's daddy could work wonders with air. His hardworking father was an African American with incredible natural born Force power, power he'd passed onto his son. I looked back up at Dad.

"Grayson Mars?" I asked. Whenever Dad could slip away from the Pinnacle, he was shadowing these guys for me. When he remembered, that was.

"Cops still can't prove he started Crush," he reported. Grayson was rumored to have spearheaded the first magical motorcycle gang. "But seems like he skipped out of MAD at least one night last week and met up with a couple guys on bikes. I saw him make one of the bikes hover."

"Nice." My heart beat faster. Hovering a motorcycle took a shit ton of control. I licked my lips as I pictured it. The gossip magazines called him the orgasm king, because he could use his force to create the best suction. But air pressure, lifting objects—I was far more interested in that.

"Not proof of concept," Dad warned. "We don't know if he can hover a person. A machine is a lot less fragile."

I waved away his concern. "It's totally proof of concept." Grayson had bad boy streak and an ability to cover his tracks. Perfect qualities in a man. And he hated his daddy with a passion—hatred that was good for me, since his Dad was running for a Pinnacle seat. I hoped his hatred of Daddy would translate into hatred of the Pinnacle.

The billionaire's son part was the worst of it, because Grayson had proven multiple times that he had an ego and sense of entitlement a mile long. It meant the way I'd have to go about recruiting him would be … unique. I glanced at my father. I was definitely gonna have to keep Dad busy while I brought these guys around. Because I'd do whatever it took to get them on board. No need for my old man to get all ragey.

"You could always just climb the building to the seventh floor," Dad protested. The seventh floor had the least protection, because the Pinnacle security team didn't think people would penetrate mid-building. The bottom six floors and the top three were where most of the security was focused. Where a helicopter might try to land, or where most magicals would try a first or second floor entry. But most magicals weren't Grayson Mars. Lucky number seven was going to be our entry point.

"If I'm climbing, I can't be covering all of us in shadow. If we fly, I can basically make us invisible," I countered. "I can suck all the light out of that patch of sky. We need Grayson."

"His dad has a press conference coming up for the election."

"Is that relevant?" I asked.

Dad shrugged. "I dunno." He blinked and his expression dulled as he looked around the car. "Wait. What are we doing in the car? Where are we going?"

And there it was—his memory had gone out again. I pressed my lips together. I had difficulty swallowing for a minute as I watched his animated expression fade. But I didn't quite give up. Not yet.

"Dad?" I tried. Once in a while, prompting his memory helped. "Do you remember that time we went to the grocery store and I announced I was a fruitarian?"

Dad's eyebrows furrowed and he didn't respond.

I pursed my lips and blew out a breath, trying to stay focused on him even though a sheen had started to form over my eyes. "Do you remember how you went out and hired this chef to make meat fruit?" He'd hired some guy to make a minced meat dish dipped in custard and painted to look like apples. "I almost puked to death." I laughed at the memory, triggering the tears that had built up in my eyes. They splashed down my cheeks. But as Dad's face remained impassive; the tears of laughter turned into tears for another reason.

My pain bloomed like an African daisy, a flower that opened and closed each day; but instead of the regularity of the sunrise and sunset, my wound tracked Dad's unpredictable memory. Each time he faded into a stranger, it felt like I lost him all over again.

I swiped at my cheeks. I shook my head and tried to shut the tears down, but it was a minute before I could get myself under control. When I could, I stared right at him and clasped my hands in front of my chest, hoping that he'd take my directions right now, even when he wasn't quite certain who I was.

"Dad, I need you to go back to the Pinnacle."

He blinked several times and took off his hat, staring at it. I couldn't tell if he was listening to me or not. But I had to try.

"Dad, I need you to shadow Edward Newsome. I want you to see if you can find that spell he uses to open that vault that holds the serum." I tried to speak slowly and clearly, but my throat was still a bit clogged.

Dad gave a faint nod and disappeared. I stared at the spot where he'd sat for a minute, wistfully, my heart a brick inside my chest, cracking my ribs.

I set down my laptop and leaned back in my seat, breathing deep, trying to reset my emotions. I reminded myself that I was another step closer—closer than I'd ever been. And this time I had Tia's help. I focused on that for twenty minutes, visualizing my next steps until my stomach fluttered like I was sitting on top of the roller coaster. *It's finally happening.* I pictured Malcolm, Grayson, a mystery man, and myself all standing at the base of the Pinnacle, staring up at it. Then I looked down into my hand, where I held the glowing green vial of serum.

I texted Tia one last time to make sure she'd pull through with Academy Metamorphose.

-*Did you talk to your aunt?*-

-*Frothing much? Yeah. She sent your mom a packet.*-

I fucking fist-pumped and then gave a thumbs up like a nerd, though there was no one to see it.

-*When?*-

-*Last week.*-

-*Yes!*-

This was more thrilling than that time when I was twelve and idiot Evan had lent me his signed comic book and brushed his fingers against mine. It was twice as intense as the last two mediocre orgasms I'd had with random hookups at Medeis.

I looked out at the scenery rushing by, and a name for this venture popped into my head. Because I was going to MAD and I was going to convince three guys who didn't know me from Adam to join me, 'Madness' seemed like the perfect fit.

5

I TOOK A COUPLE DEEP BREATHS, squared my shoulders, and slid out of the town car. I brushed off my skirt, straightened my tights, and slid my defiant teenager mask into place.

Round ten was about to go down. And I was in it to win it.

I slammed the front door behind me, letting the echo boom across the polished marble floor. I kicked off my Mary Janes, but kept a wide, confrontational stance. I hoped someone besides our maid, Maria, was here, or else I'd look like a jerk for slamming doors.

I didn't even have a chance to move before my "stepfather" pulled open the door to his study. Just the sight of him made spiders crawl up my spine. Claude leaned against the door jamb, his ice blue eyes making me freeze. He was near fifty, but wrote spells to slow his aging, so he appeared closer to forty. He had a gut, even though he was tall. And he had turned out to be just as sweet as the home-brewed moonshine he made as a hobby. Everything about him made my throat burn. Particularly now that I knew he was also a cheater.

"Hayley," he uttered that one word and it felt like ropes had coiled around my wrists. The room grew cold with mutual loathing, and goosebumps formed along my arms.

"Claude," I mocked his reprimanding tone as I crossed my arms. I scanned his over-starched shirt and two-day, grey beard. There'd been a time that I'd thought of him like an uncle, back when I was young and ignorant. He and Dad had been so close before he'd broken off to start his own company and focus on magical weapon manufacturing. But now, I didn't know how my mother could stand him. "Where's Trudy?" I asked. He hated when I called my mother by her first name, thought it was the height of disrespect. Which was why I always used it in front of him.

Claude took a step toward me, letting his power fill the air and send the room plummeting to below-freezing levels. His natural-born gift was Icefire. He could control heat and cold, though with me, he always seemed to choose ice. Maybe he thought it was the more painful option. Or maybe he just didn't want to burn down the precious mansion he'd bought with money he'd essentially stolen from my father.

"How's your secretary?" I sneered. "Or should I say sex-cretary?"

Claude's power lit the room with a pale blue stream of light as coldness slammed into me. My skin prickled painfully.

But I was used to it. Unknown to my mother, the Clod often liked to vent his ire with me using cold burns, or tiny fire burns that could be explained away by things like curling irons. My skin was dotted with gifts from him, scars he'd given me over the past two years whenever I didn't bow down to his magnificence. My neck was his favorite target.

I saw him lift his hand, his eyes dropping to my throat.

I unleashed my own power. A pale purple stream of light, ten times stronger than Claude's pathetic power, filled the room. At the edges, my power flickered with the shades of the rainbow, while the main beam grew so bright that Claude had to shield his eyes with one hand, meaning he could only use the other to cast. His blue beam dimmed to half its previous power.

"Fuck!" Claude grunted as my light rays seared his skin.

I pushed harder, letting my light beams flip over from visual light to the UV spectrum and grow brighter; I tried to ignore when Claude's grunts turned into yelps of pain.

I recalled the first day I'd met Claude. The first time he'd seen my Darklight power, he'd just laughed and called me rainbow girl. Until I'd used my darkness to take away his sight. I spread my hands apart and decided he'd had enough light. My beam disappeared and blackness filled the room. I could see perfectly, but I knew the change from light to dark would blind my stepfather.

His grunt proved me right.

And right then I wanted to crow at him, to lord it over him that I knew about him. His stupid affair was only the tip of the iceberg. I knew about the Alchemiken studies he oversaw. I wanted to tell that fucker that I could see every fucking encrypted Pinnacle email about shields and amulets he was sending. The fucking asshole had only gotten a council seat by riding my father's coattails and then taking—

"You worthless piece of shit, Hayley," Claude moaned. "What a waste of potential, that could be put to better—"

"Worthless? Which of us can't see well enough not to piss on their own shoes right now, *Claudia*?" I taunted.

"Your mother's right. You're fucked in the head." The words hit me like a nine-iron to the gut. I didn't even notice when he lifted his hand and a tiny jet of flame, as narrow as a laser, shot out at me. He burnt a line onto my stomach, through my shirt.

Damn! The fire cut right into my skin and it felt like I was getting stabbed. I twisted away and the flame sputtered out. But the scent of burnt flesh remained. My fury rose like an inferno. "You want to see fucked in the head?" I screamed. "Dad!"

My father appeared. Thank God, Dad's face appeared clear and not blank this time. Or I might have lost it. I pointed a shaking finger at Claude—the man we both despised. Without another word, Dad rushed at the man and forced his way into Claude's body. Claude couldn't see Dad—Claude still couldn't see anything with my darkness clouding his eyes, but he would be able to feel the cold, haunted, vulnerable feeling that went along with being possessed by a ghost.

I walked forward and latched onto Claude's hair. I yanked his head back. "Did you want to repeat yourself, *Claudia?*"

A sudden gust of orange-tinted wind pushed me over with the strength of a hurricane and flattened me against the marble floor. "Hayley! What the hell are you doing?" My mother's voice echoed throughout the foyer as I lost my grip on the darkness and the gaudy chandeliers restored themselves. Dad leapt out of Claude's body and bolted for the sky, like he always did whenever Mom came into a room. Even after all these years, he couldn't bear to see her with someone else.

Mom strode forward, her hand still outstretched to pin me down as she checked on Claude, clucking over his sunburns.

My teeth clenched when I saw that. Not once did she ask who started it. She wouldn't believe me if I told her anyway, so what did it matter? I'd spent the last two years convincing her I was a rebellious shithead. And she might love me, want a better future for me, but when it came to me or the Clod? There was no competition. Only one of us funded her habit. Staring at me only reminded her of what she'd lost.

I ground my teeth together and stayed put as she yelled for Maria to grab some Aloe vera.

Only after she'd safely closed Claude back in his study, with a bottle of Aloe and a promise to check on him, did Mom turn to me. My mother stared down her straight nose, her brown eyes flashing, but only with a quarter of the fire she used to have. She saw the burn hole in my shirt and came forward. She checked it over. "You're lucky he has good control. This is minor. Doesn't even break through all the layers of skin. Hayley, why must you attack him? That's the third time I've seen you physically go after him."

I didn't bother to argue. I wouldn't win.

Mother shook her head, patted her perfect French braid, and turned to stride out of the room, her beige heels clicking against the marble floor. She didn't even ask me to follow her. She just expected me to do so. I rose slowly, taking a long and careful inhale to refill my lungs with air. My mother was a Force—like Grayson Mars. After any face off with her power, I was always left a bit breathless. I walked slowly, giving myself time to counteract the light-headedness.

Mom sat down in a chair in the living room, smoothing out her dark brown dress, a dress chosen to match the exact shade of her hair, before turning to me. The bags under her eyes looked deeper than the last time I'd seen her. I wondered if the track marks in her elbow were worse. I guessed they were. She'd been taking Calm spells for years now, and it was showing, despite the spells she wrote to slow her aging and enhance her appearance.

"Well?" she demanded an explanation, folding her fingers. But I saw them tremble, despite how she tried to hold still.

My heart drooped a little, thinking she might be worse than I knew. Calm was a mellowing spell, but typically, the side effects. didn't emerge unless you were doing it more than twice a day.

She was bad—she'd just gotten home, and withdrawal tremors were taking over. I pretended not to notice. Noticing would start a fight. Discussion would start a fight. Mom hated fights. Only one thing would work on her. I responded with stony silence, just like she expected me to.

Mother's nostrils twitched and she wrung her hands just as I tended to do. She closed her eyes for a moment and chose her words carefully. "I can't do this anymore, Hayley."

This? What—parenting? The bitter part of my mind wanted to lash out at her and tell her she hadn't done it for years, but I didn't. I stayed silent. Mom hated uncomfortable, drawn-out silence. She'd fill the void, talk, think I was agreeing, and then finish with a hug.

She gave a harsh laugh. "God, I wish this wasn't happening. I wish you had gotten knocked up or something—"

"Mom!" I scolded. She'd actually shocked me.

She smiled ruefully at me. "Teen pregnancy is an issue I know how to deal with." She shook her head, referring to the fact that she and Dad had gotten pregnant with Matthew way too young.

She never talked about the past. She must have been feeling down. I couldn't help but want to make her smile, even if it was just for a second. "Well, I'll get right on that then," I told her. "If you're so desperate to help me raise a baby—"

"Shut up!" She gave a broken cackle that turned into a half sob.

Hearing her cry hurt. I knew that Mom was just as full of jagged glass inside as I was. I wasn't trying to make the pain worse. But she didn't understand. She'd been part of the problem, turning away from life after Matthew's accident, after Dad died. She'd abandoned Dad's business, encouraging the Clod to sell off the research division to the Pinnacle. She'd sent me off to the first of many boarding schools. She'd tried to escape.

I went over and sat next to her. I gave her a side hug, pulling her against me and realizing how rail-thin she actually had become.

Mom took a deep breath to calm herself before she spoke again. When she did, her words were heavy and measured. "There isn't another magical academy that will accept you. You've stormed out of every counseling session I've ever sent you to. Evan's tried to watch over you; you've rebuffed him. I talked to Tia. Even she thinks you're out of control."

I bristled slightly. Tia had spoken to my mom about me. I'd known she hated my plan, but the betrayal sliced at my ribs. Good thing I hadn't trusted her with the full truth. My arms crossed and I braced myself for whatever came next. *You know this is the hard part,* I told myself. *Mom is always the hard part. Just get through it.*

Mom shook her head. "I know that after what happened with Matthew, and your father—you were shocked. Hurt. Angry. And I don't blame you. You lost half your family in a week. It would have wrecked anyone. I've tried, Lord knows, I've tried to be patient and supportive, darling. But we can't go on like this. I can't do it anymore."

My throat grew tight. Those words were like physical blows coming from her. I'd expected them, or something similar, but still each one was a punch to the heart that left me bruised and broken. Even more broken than I'd been before.

"I think you need to see a counselor again."

"I don't want—"

Mother stood, interrupting me. "I don't care what you *want* anymore, Hayley! You've pushed me to my limit. I'm done! See a counselor. And I'll figure out a damned tutor or something since you can't—"

My eyes widened. *A tutor? Fuck no! That would screw everything up!* If I was locked up here at Claude's twenty-four/seven, I'd never find the people I needed. My plan started to unravel before my eyes, like a sand painting, a piece of art so carefully constructed, only to be wiped away with one careless gesture. My breath came short and quick as I fought a rising tide of panic. I couldn't let this happen. She couldn't do this to me. "Mom, you can't—"

"Hayley, this is your last chance. I hate to say this. But, if you back out of counseling again ... if you don't take this seriously, you're going to be disowned."

If she'd stabbed me through the heart, it might have hurt less. Those words curdled like poison in my ear. They soaked into my bloodstream and tainted my bones. She'd let go of me? Could she really do that? I was all she had left. She was all I had left.

I stared up at her hard face. Her lip trembled a bit, but her jaw was tight and set. Of course, she could let go of me. She'd already tried to leave the world and me behind twice. Cutting me off was just another way of doing it.

My stomach churned and I felt ill. I stared off at the wall, at some stupid vase full of flowers. I closed my eyes and tried to resist curling up, knees under my chin, arms wrapping around myself.

What was I doing? Was I doing the wrong thing? Ever since Matthew had tried to become an Unnatural, tried and failed, my only thought had been to save him. I'd risked everything for this plan that was finally, finally fucking coming together. Everything I'd done, everything I'd become ... the light was there at the end of the tunnel, gleaming down on me. Yeah, I had a few details to work out but still. Right fucking there. A future for Matthew. Could I give it up?

I watched my mother walk out of the room and I wondered if it would be possible to save my brother and keep any kind of relationship with her. Or would I have to choose?

6

I DROVE to the counselor's office with a sense of trepidation. Counselors always gave off an air of superiority and judgment. Typically, they were norms who couldn't contain their glee at the fact that a magical couldn't handle life.

I didn't want to go, not at all, but after mother's ultimatum two days ago, I didn't think I had much of a choice. I needed to give her something. I needed to give her hope, so that I could ask for the thing I wanted most. To get into the worst magical school in the country. The school that claimed to rehabilitate juvenile offenders; and the only place I'd be able to find people both heartless and talented enough to do what I needed done.

Come on Tia, I mentally pleaded. I hoped she was working her magic right now. The letter clearly hadn't been enough. She was supposed to meet with her aunt this weekend.

I'd sent her an endless stream of annoying texts this morning, checking on her progress.

Her responses had been less than thrilled.

-Chill okay? We're still driving. She lives two hours away when she's not on campus. Which is across the country BTW. I can't believe you're gonna leave me again!-

-I know.- I'd texted back. -I'll miss you. But, truth? Can't wait until I'm a whole plane ride away from the Clod.-

-He's so creepy. Those eyes are totes serial killer.-

-I know. Think your aunt will let me in?-

-Did I or did I not fail Psychic Predictions?-

She'd failed horribly. Hadn't been able to write a spell to predict a storm on a cloudy day.

-I'm just nervous.- I'd told her as I'd texted from the breakfast table in an empty house. The Clod and Mom had both left for work before I'd gotten up.

-Yeah. Obvi. Drink some of Clod's shit.- Tia's response about busting out Claude's God-awful homemade moonshine made me giggle.

-And pass out for three hours? I've got to meet my new 'therapist.'-

-Make sure you tell them how awesome I am.-

-Will do. Make sure you tell Auntie the same.-

-Not sure awesome will get you in.-

-Awful, awesome. You know. Whatevs. XX-

-XX-

I parked my pretty red Porsche, double and then triple checking the address. But it was correct.

I stepped out of the car and stared for a second. This office was a bit *different* from the others, to put it mildly. It was in a strip mall, for one thing. It was right next door to a Chinese buffet that smelled as delicious and unhealthy as it was possible to smell. Unlike the uptown offices that I had been to before, this counselor's office had blinds on the windows and when I stepped inside, instead of a bimbo with blindingly white teeth smiling at me, the reception desk was empty except for a sign in book, which was old school paper and pen—not even electronic. I signed in on today's page and chuckled to myself as I walked over to the seats and tapped the blinds. I watched them sway in the window. Blinds. I couldn't remember the last time I'd been to a place with blinds. Maybe when I was a kid, before my dad's energy company had done an IPO and the stock had skyrocketed. Nothing was more of a sure bet than a natural's magic power.

I looked around the office, wondering if the plants were fake, too. How long had it been since I'd seen a plastic plant?

I couldn't resist. I leaned over to touch one. To my shock, it was real.

I tried to sit but found I had too much nervous energy. When I stood, I looked down at the carpet tiles, and realized that a trail had been worn thin, where other patients had obviously tracked back and forth as they awaited their own appointments. I wondered about this therapist. If his patients couldn't even sit to wait, what kind of success rate did this douche have?

Just because, I let my feet wander the path that others had made.

"Hayley?" A soft feminine voice called.

I turned and was nearly startled out of my skin. In front of me wasn't some prim receptionist in a suit, but a short, red-haired woman with a jagged scar that ran down the length of her face and was clearly the cause of the empty black socket on her left side. She smiled and the scars stretched around the crater, which she hadn't bothered to cover with an eyepatch or anything. Her face was so gruesome that it was hard to look at, and so my eyes swept the floor. "Yes, ma'am," I sputtered.

The red-headed woman walked to the front door and turned the lock with a click.

"Oh, don't pull that meek bullshit with me. I hear you've got quite the attitude." The red-headed woman chuckled. "No need to get all formal because I've lost an eye." She turned back to me and I just couldn't maintain eye contact. It was too unnerving. She strode closer in her flowing, flowery dress. "Unless you think I might take yours as a replacement."

I looked up in shock. Was she joking? That had to be a joke. Only, she grabbed onto my chin. Hard.

Her face took on an evil, evaluative tone as she studied my eyes. "Yours are quite beautiful. Lovely shade of blue. I bet there's a spell writer out there who'd be happy to steal them for me."

I jerked my chin away from her and took a few steps back. *What the fuck?*

She watched me and laughed. "You can dish it out, but you sure can't seem to take it. I've heard you pranked a ton of your headmasters recently." The woman pulled out her wand and a piece of parchment. She opened up an inkwell on the reception desk and dipped her wand into it. Then, quicker than a blink, she scribbled onto the piece of parchment. It lit up with a golden glimmer as she wrote, and the paper burst into flames. As the paper burnt itself up, the gaping hole in her eye socket suddenly disappeared. Her left eye restored itself, but the eyelid drooped a little, and the jagged scar on her face remained.

Holy fuck. This woman had to be a Delusionist-level spell writer! That was fucking perfection. A level 10 spell. And fast, too. She hadn't hesitated once to ensure she was writing the right thing. Every professor I'd ever had urged caution. Whenever they demonstrated spells, it was always slow and steady. Because if you messed up writing a spell ... you had to suffer the consequences. A slip of the hand, an extra line, could change your life forever. If she'd messed up, she could have lost an eye, or both.

I rubbed a hand across my face, more shaken by her performance than I wanted to let on. Impressive, yeah. Fucking nuts? Also, a big hell yeah. "Okay. That was a pretty good one." I could admit when I'd been had. I could even admire it a little. "You wouldn't mind giving me that spell, would you?"

The counselor laughed. "From what I hear, you write pretty good spells for yourself. You were in fourth- and fifth-year classes as a third year at Medeis. But if you need a little incentive, maybe want to freak out your mom one night, I might be able to be persuaded to give it to you, after you actually show up for five appointments, of course."

Bribery in return for my participation. That wasn't a new technique, but no one had ever bartered something I'd wanted before. The bribes had all been money or threats from my mother. This pitch almost had me intrigued.

I tilted my head as I stared at her. Her hippie flowery dress and random office did not seem like something my mother would have chosen for me.

"Did Claude pick you?"

The redhead avoided answering me and extended her hand. "I'm Dr. Meg Potts. I specialize in hopeless cases."

"Hopeless cases? You're very tactful."

She waved her hand dismissing me. "Your family thought you might like to talk to somebody else who was also a bit traumatized," she gestured at her face, "when a spell writing attempt to become Unnatural went wrong."

The skeptical part of me wondered whether or not the scars she'd left on her face were also just a spell she'd written, but the curious part of me won out. If she'd been hurt during an attempt to go Unnatural, those weren't just scars on her face. They were claw marks. "What kind of shifters did they end up becoming?" I asked.

"The ones that shifted all ended up becoming wolves, surprisingly enough. It was unusual, since Unnaturals don't get to choose their shifter form. I theorized maybe that the massive amount of magic in the air somehow influenced the animal ultimately. But no one else has ever replicated the conditions because it's too dangerous." Her voice grew thin. "There were seven of them."

I took a step back in shock. That was a lot. Most magicals that tried to go Unnatural attempted the spell in groups of two, three at most. The spell writing was so dangerous that a lot of people were dissuaded from even trying, though shifter status was considered the highest level of magic. Only those that became shifters earned the official title of Delusionist-level spell writer. Chances were less than one percent that a person would get everything exactly right—it was like the chance of a norm becoming an astronaut—but every year, nearly a thousand magicals tried.

I stared again at Dr. Potts face, surprised she had survived that night at all. "They. You didn't try? Why were you there?"

Her eyes were solemn and didn't look at me as she recited just the facts, her voice thin as she recalled that night. "I was attempting a PhD in Spell Writing. My dissertation was on writing under pressure."

"Oh."

"Why were there seven magicals? Did they—"

"Three of them made the transition. They completed the circle and their spell writing was perfect. Their bodies were able to absorb the magical blast. It's black, did you know that? Kind of looks like a black light. A big, dark black mass with purple edges. Scary." She shook her head. "Three became full-fledged wolf shifters. But four of them didn't. They went rabid. And turned into ..."

She trailed off. But she didn't need to say it. I knew exactly what they turned into. The same thing that my brother had turned into. Anyone who attempted a spell to become a shifter and failed turned into a bloodlust-filled monster. A vampire.

7

My session with Doctor Potts was ... odd to say the least. She didn't ask me to sit in her office and talk or anything. Instead, she made me stand out in the lobby the entire time. And she seemed to talk about herself more than anything else. I learned she was in a bowling league with a bunch of norms, and a lot of other trivial stuff.

At one point I asked, "Aren't you supposed to ask shit about me?"

She shrugged. "Kinda. But my strategy is to bore you enough that eventually you'll want to talk just so I'll shut up."

I laughed. "We're not there yet."

"Don't worry. I have two cats. And an iPhone. We've got about a thousand pictures to go through."

I thought she was joking. She wasn't. I only made it through one-hundred-eighty-seven photos before I caved. "OMG. Ask me something. No more Buggles. Please."

Potts smirked up at me. "You're pretty easy to break, know that?"

I narrowed my eyes at her. "You challenging me to keep silent?"

"Maybe."

"I don't think you're a counselor at all. I think you're a crazy old lady who wants to talk about her cats—"

Her laugh was a raspy, throaty sound, like a smoker's laugh. "You got me pegged. You know, most of us only become therapists because we're so messed up, we want to study ourselves. It's all very narcissistic."

"Is this reverse psychology or something?" Was she seriously telling me she was nuts?

She grinned at me. "I dunno. Is it convincing you to trust me?"

"Nope."

"Then it wouldn't be very good reverse psychology, would it?"

I squinted at her, trying to determine her true purpose.

"Let's take a drive." She jerked her head toward the door and started walking that way without waiting for me. She switched off the lights, leaving me standing in the dark in the middle of her office lobby. I could still see using my infrared vision, but it was weird, and rude as fuck.

"Hey!" I scolded, following after her.

She just waved me out of the way so she could lock the door. And then she marched right over to my car. "This fancy one's yours, right?" she asked, trying the handle.

I almost felt like my car had been insulted. Fancy? Ugh. Cool would have been an understatement. Fancy was just awkward. Then again, Dr. Potts was anything but normal. I couldn't even come up with a response more than, "Um..."

"You lock your car?" She looked at me, shocked.

"Yeah."

Potts raised her eyebrows. "I thought you'd have written an electric shock spell or something by now to keep people back."

"The voltage for that can be hard to manage with temperature changes," I lied. Voltage was a bitch, but I really didn't change the car for nostalgic reasons. I wanted it to stay exactly as it had always been.

Potts eyed me up and down. "Did you fake your transcripts?"

My mouth dropped. First she kind of insulted my car. Then she'd definitely insulted me. "No."

"You're a Darklight. I know you're school-hopping, soul-searching or whatever. But you should have a handle on temp changes by now. Damn. You're gonna be a lotta work for me."

I shook my head as I neared the car and my fob automatically unlocked the Porsche. "Should have charged my mother more."

She agreed as we slipped into our seats. "Yeah. Seeing this thing, I probably could have charged double." She stroked the leather seats. "You're spoiled."

I shook my head. "This was dad's old car, and I'd been begging him for it since I was eight. So, technically it's a hand-me-down."

"Still," she snorted before pulling out her phone and pulling up a saved address. "Alrighty, I'm in charge of music. You just follow the turns the map shouts out."

I raised an eyebrow at her. "You aren't touching my music."

She just smiled, ignored me, and hooked her phone to my dash. Then she turned on the most godawful polka music I've ever heard in my life.

I slammed the volume button to mute it, but her hand went right back to turn it up as soon as I started driving. She turned the volume up bit by bit, slowly, smiling as I clenched my jaw.

I made it through two songs and about six minutes of driving. But when the third song started, I said, "I can't listen to another one."

Potts pretended she couldn't hear me, until I reached over and turned the music off. "Oh." She smiled at me like a lion smiles at a gazelle. "Don't like the music? I guess you can talk instead. Tell me about your childhood."

Clever bitch! I shook my head. I couldn't help but be amused and annoyed. "I'm gonna find your house and pay someone to toilet paper it."

"You aren't allowed to pay someone. If you do the legwork yourself, you're more than welcome. Childhood?"

I rolled my eyes and turned left as the instructions dictated. "Good. Normal I guess."

"Favorite game to play with your brother?"

Memories drifted up at that question. "Matthew liked everything, pretty much. He really liked to make up scenarios. We were cowboys and space aliens at the park. We'd be underwater undercover agents at the local pool…" I trailed off as I remembered Matthew chasing me under the water, freaking out the norm lifeguards when he used his Icefire magic to lift all the pool water and transform it into a frozen arch high in the air above him so he could run away, but melted it right behind him with his fire powers, leaving everyone around him in the water, forced to swim after him. Marco Polo with him had been a nightmare. It was only when Evan and I teamed up that we even had a chance. My lips curled into a nostalgic little grin as I got onto the highway, picturing Matthew's freckled face laughing at me from the pool ledge. I hated my freckles, but I'd gotten lucky. Matthew had gotten a face full of them. He even had one on the bottom edge of his lip that stretched when he smiled.

For whatever reason, Potts gave me a few minutes to reminisce before asking another question.

"You two ever fight?"

The question tripped me up. Nobody asked that. Not about a vampire. That was about as bad as asking if a dead person had been an asshole. I glanced over at Dr. Potts, but she gestured back at the road. "Watch that bus, please, I'd prefer to get there in one piece."

I drove for a few minutes in silence, trying to dissect her question. "He didn't tell me that he was going to try to become an Unnatural, if that's what you're asking."

"Not what I asked. What did you guys fight about?"

I shrugged. "Regular stuff. TV. He hated that I could change the channel to whatever I wanted with my magic. I used to make him watch Barbie movies non-stop."

Dr. Potts chuckled. "You're a true sadist. More so than me."

I laughed. "I was just a sweet six-year-old."

She shook her head. "Nope. Not buying it. What else did you fight about?"

I took a deep breath as my mind flickered through my memories. It had been three years since I'd tried to bring up a bad memory. I'd only ever brought up the ones that pushed me forward. "We fought about him joining dad's company. I thought he should go back to his old dream of helping sea magicals."

Potts grunted as she absorbed that information. She leaned an elbow on the car door. "What did he say?"

I had to dig deep to remember specifics. "Something about wanting to do something bigger. Matthew wanted to do what had the most impact."

"And what did he think that was?"

That part of the memory was right on the surface for me. And it wasn't a pleasant one. It was one that haunted me. It blew like a cold wind through my body and chilled my insides. I went cold and my face grew stiff. My fingers tightened on the steering wheel. It was a minute before I felt capable of answering. "He thought it was curing vampirism."

"Why?"

"Because he said we lost some of the best magical minds to madness when they attempted the Unnatural Spell."

"Why'd he think joining your dad's company was such a great idea?"

I avoided answering. The lab experiments Dad's company had run weren't exactly Pinnacle sanctioned. I made another turn, and I started to get a sneaking suspicion about where we were going. "Where are you taking me?"

"I asked first."

"Dad's company had a contract with the Pinnacle. They were investigating potential causes of the extreme reaction." Officially anyway. Unofficially, they'd also been experimenting with cures.

"Why would an energy company do that?"

I pursed my lips. "Because my father was eccentric and couldn't imagine spending all his money on yachts. So, he set up a non-profit lab and hired some scie—" I took a final turn and I knew exactly where Dr. Potts wanted to take me. I turned to her. "My mother doesn't want me going ..."

"Your mother doesn't realize you've already been sending blood once a month, like clockwork? Nice magical regeneration spell, to do that by the way."

My body grew hot and my face paled. It took a few seconds, but I fought to answer nonchalantly. "What?"

Dr. Potts rolled her eyes and turned back to face forward, toward the wrought iron gates of the Institute for the Vampirically Insane.

The building loomed in front of us cold and imposing. It was at least four stories and made of grey stone. Unlike a normal building, it had no windows. The parking lot was nearly empty, which wasn't a surprise, magicals who became vamps weren't discussed, they were discarded like an embarrassment. Some families straight up shot their vamps—out in the country, that was still legal. In the cities, institutes like this had sprung up.

Melancholy started to seep into my bones at the thought that my brother was trapped inside this awful tomb-like building, but Dr. Potts didn't let me wallow.

"Chop chop! Get a move on. Your session only lasts another hour."

I rolled my eyes and unbuckled. When we made it inside, the check in process was more pathetic than any of the academies I'd ever been to—so long as Dr. Potts and I signed our lives away with their waiver, we were let in. No ID check or anything to ensure we were relatives. WTF? Where were the vamp rights activists on that one?

I hissed at Dr. Potts as we walked down the hall toward the room my brother was supposedly assigned. "Anyone can get in here. It costs a shit-ton of money to keep Matthew safe here. They're not even keeping track to keep him safe from jerk offs?"

"Oh, way worse than jerk offs come here, sugar," she said as she shook her head. "That stupid dare, to see if you can live long enough to cum in front of a vamp—those kids aren't a threat, even though I think one in ten of them ends up eaten."

"What?"

She shook her head. "You think they invest in ballistic level glass for this place? Bullshit. Get those vamps worked up enough and they'll bust through. But … what was I saying? Yeah. The real threat are the purists."

I glared at Potts. "That does not make me feel better!" The thought of those crazies always ripped me open like I'd been stabbed.

"It wasn't supposed to." Dr. Potts lifted her finger and pointed. "102, right?"

We opened the door, which wasn't even fucking locked, and stepped inside. I'd never actually been able to visit my brother before, and the room wasn't at all what I expected.

It looked like one of those observation rooms in a cop show. There was one-way glass dividing our little segment of the room from his. Looking through it, we could see Matthew pacing like a tiger inside his cage. And that's all his room was, a 12x12 cage of solid walls.

His red eyes gleamed in the darkness, and when he scented us, he let out a roar that sent a shiver down my spine. He rushed to the glass and banged against it, slamming his hands on it again and again. His claws raked down the glass, scratching it.

The brother I had once loved and admired had been reduced ... to this. His dark brown hair and freckled face were the same, but everything else about him—his hunched posture, the massive white claws extending from his fingers, the two huge saber-tooth like fangs that overlapped his bottom lip, and his mind—had been overtaken by the darkness.

The sight made my chest raw. It was like standing on a bridge railing, peering down at the water, seeing the end writhe and snarl and spit at me. I knew if that glass window broke, I would die. My brother would kill me—I knew it without a doubt. My nerves lit up with that knowledge and terror made me want to back away. At the same time, my heart keened. In that moment, I knew exactly why my mother had never wanted me to visit in person. She hadn't been trying to stifle me. She'd been trying to protect me. Because seeing Matthew rabid was the most awful thing that I could imagine.

I shrank back, both in terror and in sadness.

"Least he made himself a bit of a nest," Dr. Potts observed, pointing to a back corner of my brother's dark chamber. His bed had been torn apart, but he'd used bits of fluff from the mattress to create a pile in the corner. "That's more than most vamps can think to do," she continued.

She took a step toward Matthew, unafraid that he was now scratching white streaks into the mirrored window with his jagged claws. She sat down in one of the folding chairs I hadn't noticed.

"What cushy visitor accommodations they've got," I snarked, focusing on the chairs instead of my brother. I kept my eyes trained on Potts and tried to ignore the fact that Matthew was trying to break into the room to kill us. But the snarky attitude I normally kept up cracked like ice. I swallowed hard.

"You gonna sit or you gonna donate?" Dr. Potts asked.

She had a real knack for interrupting my moments, it appeared. But I was grateful for the distraction. "Donate?"

She pointed to a ghetto IV set up in the corner. A tube and needle dangled from a small hole in the wall. The needle glinted like an evil nurse's wet dream. I walked over and looked at the setup. It was a very primitive, very awful-looking contraption. Whenever I donated and mailed in blood to Matthew, I always used a HemoLink, a little device shaped like a ping-pong ball that had four needles to puncture the upper arm in a spot without nerve endings. I'd never used a needle to draw directly from a vein. "That needle doesn't even look clean. And what am I supposed to do—just stab myself and hope I hit the right spot?" This place didn't even have people to help you if you came to feed your kin? Fuck this place.

Potts rolled her eyes, then she came forward. She pulled out her wand and a tiny slip of parchment. She flipped the end of her wand and the tip turned dark with ink. Apparently, she'd splurged on a self-inking wand. As Potts muttered her spell, the parchment crinkled and dissolved into a gold mist. The mist enveloped the needle. The second she stopped spell-writing, the needle went from grimy to shiny and then the little barb plunged itself into the crook of my elbow.

The needle stung when it bit me, but I didn't focus on that. I'd just seen Potts write a two-part spell. I had to work to keep how impressed I was off my face. Her spell writing skills were superb. Apparently, there was more to the chatty doctor than there seemed. I wondered for a second why she'd never tried to go Unnatural herself. But I thought I knew the answer, so I kept my mouth shut and focused on my arm.

Dark liquid filled the tube and traveled through the wall. Matthew's rabid scratching stopped and instead I heard him snort and scuttle over to the corner. He picked up the other end of the tube, which looked more like a heavy-duty garden hose than a delicate medical tube. I realized why when he started chewing on it, slobbering on himself and grunting as he slowly drank my blood.

Tears filled my eyes and I turned so Potts couldn't see. More memories of Matthew surfaced, of the time he bandaged my knee when I fell off my bike—after he'd pushed it too hard, of course. There was the time he'd switched the tags on our Christmas presents and pretended to be so excited over his new hair-color-changing doll. Of course, he'd relented when I'd opened my 'really smokes when it shoots' army tank; he'd offered to swap if I gave him a dollar and the toy. He was such a shit.

My hand reached out and touched the glass. He didn't stop slurping and didn't move to match his claws with my fingers, but he did eye me. And everything inside my chest ached to have my asshole brother back. Anything. I'd give anything for him to steal my stuff one more time.

"Hayley, that's probably enough. You can't give too much," Potts said.

I blinked, like I'd come out of a trance.

Somehow, Potts was right next to me. And she yanked the needle out of my arm before I could protest.

She pulled me from the room as my brother realized his blood source was gone. A wild yowl went up. But as she shut the door behind us, I swore I heard a word between all the slavering cries. I swore Matthew said my name—"Hayley."

It sounded like a plea.

8

Four days later, I clicked the online order button with a little bit of glee. I'd just scheduled Tia a male stripper in thanks. She'd motherfucking done it. She'd gotten her mom and her aunt drunk on mimosas over the weekend and then brought up my sad little story, prodding her aunt's ego until the woman was bound and determined to save me. They'd called my mother and gone to brunch—the rich female socialite's version of 'golf'—it was where things got done.

My mother wasn't able to resist Tia's mother and aunt, especially not when they'd combined their heartfelt pleas with a little visit from one of Metamorphose's 'reformed' students. A hot dude in his mid-twenties, covered in tattoos, sat with my mother and drank tea, talking all about how Metamorphose 'saved his life.' Now he's got some awesome Pinnacle job and is all straightened out, the picture-perfect walking advertisement for the reform school.

This morning, Mom had informed me that I'd just been accepted, which was bullshit because I'd hacked her email and seen the interest letters going back and forth weeks ago while I was still 'struggling' at Medeis. What she really meant was this morning she transferred over the cash and made it official.

Fucking yes—MAD here I come, I thought.

Then I texted Tia.

-Expect a "big package" after school.-

-?-

I just smiled but didn't text her back as I grabbed my purse. It would be better if it was a surprise. And she really deserved it.

My packing had been half done, since I never fully unpacked from all the prior academy returns anyway.

I really only had to pick up all the magical magazines I'd bought in a search for a better motivation for my team. I'd scoured all the scientific and magical breakthrough articles, looking for something brilliant to tempt them into helping me. I didn't have an answer for that yet; I didn't know quite how I'd get them on my side. But intuition was telling me I'd find it.

I shoved the magazines in my backpack with my air gap laptop, regular school laptop, and tossed in my gold wand and two spares. Other than the backpack and a coat, I didn't have too much to pack, since MAD was cross-country in Washington state, where weather was brisk, but nowhere near the godawful extreme cold of New York.

I was looking forward to the weather as well as meeting my new soon-to-be partners in crime. I did a little shimmy as I added some lip gloss, blew a kiss at an old family photo of the four of us—Mom, Dad, Matthew, and me all smiling as we stood in front of a waterfall. I'd manipulated the light and Matthew had manipulated the water so that a rainbow curved over us. It was the perfect happy family picture. Of course, Matthew had let the water fall just after we'd taken the shot— drenching all of us. But even that was part of the perfect memory for me. At the last minute, I decided to add the pic to my bag and bring it with me.

I had to remind myself not to grin as I tossed on my go-to black sweater. I wasn't supposed to be thrilled about this school. It was supposed to 'teach me a lesson.' I tried to control my face as I went down the stairs.

I embraced my mother in a crushing hug. "I'm sorry, Mom," I apologized to her for all I'd done and all I was about to do. "I love you."

"I hope they can help you there, I really do," she murmured into my hair. "You're only a plane ride away. I'll be there if you need anything. Just call me. And Doctor Potts still has a Facetime appointment with you every Sunday. Do not miss one."

I sighed and pulled back. "I won't. I promise."

Mom's hands came up to gently grip my cheeks. "I love you, Hayley Dunemark. Please make me proud."

All I could do was smile weakly, because there was no chance in hell of that.

I turned to leave, but Claude stopped me. His back was to my mother as he turned to face me, so she couldn't see the expression of pure evil on his face. "Don't you want to give your dad a hug goodbye?"

If my mother hadn't been there, I might have hit him with a bolt of UV light and tried to undo all that fucking youth magic he'd used on himself. And then I'd fucking burn his face until it was a roasted lobster. Maybe do the same to his dick if my beams could penetrate. But I couldn't do any of that. Because then I wouldn't get to walk out the front door, which was already open, beckoning me. So, I just glared at him and turned without a word.

Then, all too quickly, I was outside and in the private car, watching as the driver pulled away from Mom. The separation hit me hard when I couldn't see her anymore. Next time I saw my mother, I might have my brother back, I might be a criminal, or I might be dead. I put up the divider. The thoughts running through my head were too much, the emotions too big and bulky to hide with sleight of face. I couldn't do it.

I hunched over and breathed through my nose, shoving everything else from my mind. I tried to focus on inhaling and exhaling and nothing else.

It worked—kind of. I held off on the tears during the car ride, but after I'd strapped myself in on the jet, I let loose. It felt like I'd just taken an irreversible step. And that scared me more than I thought it would. But by the time the plane touched back down, my mask was back. I was one hundred percent sass.

I changed in the airport restroom. When I came outside and found a town car waiting with a hot guy holding my name on a white board, I signaled. As he grabbed my bag, my driver wolf whistled.

I grinned and winked at him. He was kinda cute, if you were into the whole bulked up and bald thing.

"Jailbait," I responded. "For three more months. Wait. Shit. Two." I laughed and said, "I forgot it's February first."

"Well, sugar, you can hold onto my number 'til you're legal. And then I'll give you anything you want." He winked, but in a good-natured (aka not creeper) way that let me know he was half-joking.

I laughed. "Good to know." He couldn't have hit thirty yet, so I wasn't totally grossed out. In fact, I might have briefly even considered his offer if I'd been some other girl. But by the time I was eighteen, I fully expected to either be in prison or in the Bahamas, depending on how shit went down.

He shut me in the backseat, and I adjusted the black leather halter top that I'd put on instead of the normal, collared uniform shirt that MAD required. The halter had a silver zipper down the middle, and I unzipped it halfway as the driver climbed into his seat and watched in the rearview mirror. His eyes glittered as he caught a glimpse of my black bra. I rolled the plaid skirt once to make it a little shorter. The driver's fingers tightened on the steering wheel.

"Damn, girl. You better not do anymore or you're gonna make me have a wreck," he said as he started the car.

I said, "It's important to make a good first impression." I tossed on a leather bracelet. Then I re-tied one of my chunky high-heeled boots.

My driver groaned. "You're breaking my heart, girl. This get-up is all for some guy, isn't it?"

"Yup."

"He's not worth it if you gotta change up everything for him."

I laughed. "Thanks for the life advice." And then I stared out the window. Because my driver had no idea what he was talking about. The guys I was heading toward were worth whatever it took. Because all my hopes hinged on them.

When we pulled up to Academie Metamorphose an hour later, it felt like pulling up to a magical mafia compound. The walls were made of brick stacked high above. The wrought iron gates were flanked by two guard towers with armed men inside them. It gave me the warm and fuzzies, staring up at them.

I swallowed down any nerves, though. This is what I'd wanted. What I needed. My leg jangled up and down despite my efforts to keep still.

The driver stopped at the gate as a guard inspected both our IDs and the trunk of the car before we were buzzed in. The car rolled slowly forward as a furious wind whipped past, just inside the gate, hurling dead leaf fragments north. But as soon as the gate was open wide, the wind died down to nothing. I unbuckled and turned in my seat, glancing up at a guard tower. One of the guards had his hand extended.

Interesting. They protected the gate with Force powers.

That wasn't in the brochure, I snarked internally as my driver navigated down the curved road. I rolled down my window and stuck my hand outside to feel the band of thick air pressure that hovered just beyond the edges of the car, waiting to be released so it could bat at the leaves again. As soon as we were twenty feet from the gate, the wind whistled and rushed back across the road, an invisible wall of cold, whipping fury that blocked the gate. I watched it carefully. It extended about five feet on either side of the wrought iron, and then died off at the towers so that the guards had a clear line of sight in every direction.

I might need to split my time between recruiting and ensuring I can slip in and out of here at will, I thought, settling back into my seat as we drove for ten minutes through a forest. In the distance, I saw a group of students running. Their shirts were slick with sweat, even in the cold weather. I stuck out my tongue. *Gross.* I didn't approve of that part of this damned school at all. But physical education seemed to be a big part of MAD's 'keep the fuckers in line' strategy.

We rounded another curve and the forest opened to a sprawling lawn. I blinked when I first saw the stone lion. Of course, I'd swiped the letters from mother's desk and hacked the emails on her computer, so I knew the school had two enchanted stone lions prowling the grounds for students' "safety," which was a shit cover for their real purpose—keeping us inside the walls. But I hadn't been expecting the lions to be so massive. One tromped toward the trees, its feet making divots in the dirt. The fucker had to be ten feet tall, at least. And its eyes glowed an eerie red.

Damn.

I nodded my head in respect. This place was gonna be a bit more of a challenge than I'd thought. Going off campus would be good practice for the Pinnacle.

The car pulled into a circle drive made of grey pavers with a marble fountain in the middle of the turnaround. The fountain wasn't running because it was February, but it was still an impressive piece of classical sculpture: a nymph turning into a butterfly. *They take their bullshit transformation logo far too seriously,* I thought, rolling my eyes. Thank the Lord we did not have to wear little butterfly patches on our uniform shirts. I might have puked.

The administration building was at the very front. I studied it after I exited the car. It was a flat-faced stone building with a pitched roof that made me think of the school for girls in one of my favorite childhood books, *The Little Princess;* the building looked proper and grim at the same time.

A woman with a tight white bun and a crisp black suit came down the steps to greet me, reinforcing that *Little Princess* governess theme. Her heels clopped along the stones like a horse and her smile was wide and toothy as she said, "Hayley, welcome. I'm Josephine Nazer, Director of Admissions." She didn't shake my hand, though her smile widened a bit at my outfit, in a way that made me cringe and want to zip my shirt back up to cover my bra. I couldn't tell if she was planning evil things or checking me out, but I didn't like either option.

Nazer gestured toward the front door. "Go ahead and leave your suitcases here. We're just waiting for one more student to arrive and then you can start your first class."

"No orientation?" I asked, as we started to climb the stairs together.

"Not here," she clapped her hands. "We believe in just tossing you right into the fire." Her laugh was a little too manic for my liking. That, combined with the weird smile, changed my opinion of her governess vibe. As did her next words. "I hear you like to pull shit on faculty, Ms. Dunemark. Just be aware, here, the faculty has the authority to pull shit back. So, don't go stirring the pot. This is your only warning." I glanced over to see her eyes drilling into me.

I nodded, keeping my face neutral. For once, I didn't give a crap about the faculty. This place was just another means to an end.

9

Ms. Nazer pulled open the heavy wooden front door. The hinges screeched so badly that I clenched my teeth. *Note to self, don't sneak into or out of the admin building through the door.* I eyed the windows. The second floor wasn't too high. If I did ever need to sneak into the building, after I made it past the lions, those windows looked like they'd be acceptable entry points.

The massive entryway was par for the course at every academy I've attended. There was a lot of marble, some giant paintings of magicals in history—guiding Joan of Arc, melting the glaciers and helping people across the Bering Strait, some pompous dead fat dude in a feathered hat that I should have known but didn't. Overhead hung a chandelier that never got used as the practical wall sconces were all that anyone really needed anyway. But rich people never could get over wasting money on sparkly shit—my mom's overstuffed jewelry safe was evidence of that.

Nazer gestured to a stairwell at the right and we made our way up a set of carpeted stairs to a hallway full of nondescript offices. Her office had the standard bowl of candy that people who feel insecure put on the desk to bribe you into liking them. She had Werther's Original in the bowl, so I snagged one.

I sat down in the guest chair the director pointed to while I sucked on the grandma-licious candy. The chair was plain wood, much less opulent than those at posh schools I'd previously attended. And it was set kinda high so that my toes barely touched the ground. I briefly wondered if that was on purpose, to make me feel like a kid, or if the fact that guys outnumbered girls at this reform school eight to one had influenced the furniture choices. I decided the latter must be the reason for the chair.

Nazer grabbed my schedule off a spartan desk and went to hand it to me. As she did, a strange, humming awareness took over my body. Goosebumps rose on my neck and my skin flushed. What the fuck? I turned, and my nose slammed into a guy's torso.

Eyes watering, I grabbed my nose, trying not to curse as I looked up at whatever freak had just invaded my personal space.

I froze when my eyes crawled up the torso of the hottest guy I'd ever seen in my entire life.

My smarting nose receded to a dull throb in the background as my eyes drank him in. Holy fucknado. I felt like I was back at the entrance gate and caught up in that windstorm. Only, instead of wind blowing through me, it was lust. And instead of feeling cold, it felt like fire. Shit. My mind crumbled to pieces as I tried desperately not to visibly lick my lips.

This guy had bad boy written all over him.

He wore black basketball shorts and a plain white tank top—idiotic choices for February but fucking delicious choices for me. His muscular arms were sleeved in tattoos. Lickable outlines curled across his veined forearms and up his biceps. More tattoos were visible through his shirt and covered his defined pecs. Part of me wanted to ask him to lift up the shirt just so I could see all the designs. Another part of me wanted him to lift up his shirt so I could see if he had the full six pack that I imagined he had. And all that smacked me right in the lady bits before I even looked at his face. His face was a punch to the heart.

He had dark brown hair that was buzzed on the sides and a little longer on top. It was styled to the side with gel but was a little sloppy and spiky instead of nice and neat. It was just-fucked hair. My fingers clenched as I brought my hands down from my nose. I loved guys with just-fucked hair. His straight brows shadowed deep brown eyes and a good jawline. His lips were puckered in a hot-as-sin smirk. Something about him reminded me of a lion. He was predatory.

He eyed me appreciatively, his eyes roaming down my body and lingering on my legs. But he didn't introduce himself. Instead, he shoved a hand in his pocket—not so subtly adjusted his package—and then turned to the admissions director. "Nazer, good to see you."

Ms. Nazer's voice was curt. "This is your last shot Kieltyka."

He leaned forward and gave her a wink as he snagged a hard candy. "Yes, Drill Sergeant."

Nazer shook her head and shoved his schedule at him. He stuffed it into his pocket and unwrapped the candy, turning to look at me again as he popped it into his mouth. He rolled it on his tongue suggestively until I shifted my eyes away from him. He was obviously an attention whore. I knew how to deal with them. I stared out the window, ignoring him.

Out of the corner of my eye, I saw him tilt his head toward Nazer. "How long do you think she'll last?" he asked her, clearly indicating me.

I stiffened slightly before forcing myself to relax and ignore him. *Yup. Can't stand not having attention.*

Nazer just shook her head and pointed at her desk. "Leg up, Zavier." She unlocked a metal cabinet in the back corner.

"Ms. Nazer," Zavier's hand flew to his chest in an exaggeration of innocence. "You know I'm shy! If you wanna see the goods, you gotta ask me when we're alone." He batted his eyes at her when she turned around holding an ankle monitor.

The older woman's face was as flat and rigid as the hair pulled back in her bun as she retorted, "I'd have thought you got enough of showing your goods off in jail."

Zavier shook his head. "Nobody pretty enough there for me. Nobody as pretty as you." He smiled up at Ms. Nazer as he swiped a couple more candies from her bowl and put them in his pocket.

I bit down on a chuckle. Dickhead was actually kind of funny.

Ms. Nazer just rolled her eyes and said, "If you don't want to put your leg out for me, I can ask Coach Lundy to put this on you."

Zavier tossed his foot up onto her desk immediately. "Way to ruin the mood."

Nazer deadpanned. "What mood? Annoyed?"

I snorted. I couldn't help it. Maybe Nazer wasn't as bad as I'd first thought. I liked how she'd swung back at him.

Zavier turned to look at me and grin as Nazer snapped the ankle monitor on him. "Like the sight of me getting restrained? I'm down to explore that later."

"I'd like the sight of you holding a *restraining order*," I retorted.

Zavier jutted out his lip. "Only if you make it for five hundred miles so then I can sing The Proclaimers' song." Zavier cleared his throat and launched into the lyrics.

"You fall down at my door, you'd better be dead," I told him.

Zavier just grinned as he started an air-drumming solo. I couldn't help but crack a smile as he skipped around the room air-drumming on the cabinets and Nazer's desk while he sang, "Dah-dah-dah-dah."

God, this guy was giddy on another level. Something about him was so jovial, so teasing, and so fucking cute at the same time—gah! The feelings rumbling through my chest were the same as that time I'd babysat my four-year-old cousin and asked her if she wanted a snack. She'd said, "Yes, I want a chocolate poo-poo!" And then she'd collapsed in giggles and run from me because she knew she was being naughty. Zavier had the exact same smirk in his eyes, and it made me want to burst into laughter.

I resisted—barely—and asked Nazer, "Is he always this bad?"

Nazer snapped her fingers and Zavier stuck his foot back up on her desk, bowing to us as we ignored him.

"And the crowd goes wild!" He waved his hands in the air like a grateful rock star at the end of a set while Nazer pressed a button on his new anklet so that a blue light started blinking.

Nazer gave me a dry look. "Actually, *this* is good for him." The director tucked a flyaway hair back into her bun, then she gestured toward the door, before going to her seat. "Mr. Kieltyka, I trust you can show Ms. Dunemark the way."

Dickwad smiled at me and held the door open. "I always let ladies come first." His eyes glittered with mirth. "Oops, did I say come? I meant go."

Oh my God. He was ridiculous. At the same time, delicious images flitted through my head because he was fucking hot. Yeah, he was an attention whore. But he had this weird, twisted pervy charm. I kept my look hard because I knew he was searching for a blush. "No, you didn't. You meant come. Problem is, you've probably never seen the real thing. I bet all your girls fake it." I stood up and brushed past him. He followed too close, close enough to rub against me as we went back down the hall.

"Nobody fakes it with me," he argued.

"Guys can never tell."

"Yes, we can!"

"How?"

"Truth spell," he said.

I scoffed. "Liar! What guy takes the time to write a Truth Spell before sex?"

"Well, let's have sex and I'll write one before. Then we'll both know I know," he winked.

"You are about two seconds away from a punch to the dick," I told him.

"Still a hand on my dick …" He gave a wink.

He was funny, not that I laughed and let him know it. I kept my face passive as I raised a brow. "That desperate, huh? Might want to try a different strategy."

"Well, give me your expert advice."

"Be a gentleman instead of a walking horn dog."

Zavier protested my dismissal. "What? I'm the ultimate gentlemen. That back there was a slip of the tongue. My tongue likes to slip a lot." He hurried in front of me so he could walk backwards, and waggle said tongue suggestively at me. "In fact, maybe you could help me with that. I really need to get my tongue in shape. We could meet up later, work on tongue curls." He demonstrated his tongue curls for me, crossing his eyes at the same time.

"If you didn't look like a drunk duck that might be tempting. But hard pass, perv."

I was getting sucked into conversation with him when I should be doing more productive things with my time. I pushed past him and started down the stairs, scanning the few students roaming the first floor to see if my targets were there. No dice.

"What? No! I meant we could be like gym buddies. Workout our tongues. Other body parts." Zavier hurried after me.

"Yeah," I snorted, glancing through the open doors on the first floor.

Zavier wouldn't be ignored. He grabbed my hand and pulled it to his chest, forcing my attention back to him. "You're taking this all wrong." He pasted on the fakest innocent face I've ever seen, one that I knew had fucking worked a zillion times because it was so goddamned cute, I wanted to laugh and strangle him at the same time. He wrapped his fingers around my hand and pressed it down against his hard, firm pec. "I'm just trying to be nice here. You're twisting what I say, making it *dirty*." His face fell on the last word as if he was disappointed in me.

I couldn't help but bark out a laugh. "What the *hell* do you want?"

A grin split his face open. He knew he'd fucking won. And he was not a gracious winner. "I wanna know if you wanna be dirty or flirty friends."

"What?"

"You wanna be my nutty buddy? My frenefit? My peener pal?" He started to slide my hand down his chest toward those abs.

Part of me really wanted to feel them. And that was bad. I yanked my hand away. "I'm gonna have to go with no." Because my body really wanted to say yes. But I had other things to do. And Zavier looked like he was a high-maintenance kind of distraction.

"Okay, cool. We'll have a flirtship then." He slung an arm across my shoulders and the feel of his hand trailing down precariously close to my chest had me catching my breath.

"A what?"

"We'll be flirty friends until you give in and want to be dirty friends."

A shiver traced its way slowly down my spine as Zavier traced a finger over my forearm. My core lit up like a fucking nuclear reactor

—but letting this happen would be a damned disaster. Zavier's proposal sounded dangerous. I shrugged out from under his hold. "I don't think so."

"So, you wanna skip right to dirty friends? Perfect. There's a janitor's closet—"

I held up a hand. "No. I mean I don't want to be friends."

Zavier froze, his dark brown eyes going hooded as he stared down at me. "You don't mean that," he said huskily.

And damn my body. I fucking blushed like some innocent fucking schoolgirl. Where the hell was my composure? Fucking shit.

He grinned when he saw it. He leaned forward. "That's okay. You're allowed three mistakes. That was one. The outfit is two."

I glanced down. "What the fuck is wrong with my outfit?" I'd picked it specifically for Grayson's tastes.

Zavier leaned forward and whispered in my ear, "Because your nipples are about to get so chafed and raw in that leather top ... and I'm gonna spend our entire run imagining I'm the one making them that sore."

His proximity and naughty words had my panties soaked. It took me a second to process *all* the implications of his words. "Run?" I asked.

Just then, a short man who was far too tan for his light brown hair and blue eyes, walked up to us. Just like Zavier, he had on running shorts, shoes, and a t-shirt. "I'm Coach Lundy. Welcome to Metamorphose. Let's start with the run. Shall we?" The coach jogged off without another word.

I looked down at my leather boots and fucking cursed. I could ditch the run. But on the first day? When I didn't want to get kicked out of this place?

The coach looked back at me. "Dunemark, move it!" he barked as he held the door open for us.

Zavier jogged ahead of me, turning to grin back at me as we entered a spacious courtyard full of sidewalks and grass and the occasional bench. The February afternoon was bright and sunny, but cold.

Grumbling, I picked up my feet and jogged. I caught up with Zavier, already feeling the weight of my boots making me clumsy. "You could at least be a gentleman and offer to let me have your shirt," I groused.

"Sorry, I only give out clothing to dirty friends." Zavier winked at me. Then he held up my bracelet—the fucker had swiped it! —and jogged ahead to ask something of Coach Lundy.

Asshole! I zipped up my leather shirt—no reason to let the zipper rub my stomach raw—and fucking cursed the fact that I'd chosen heels. I tried to jog on the balls of my feet. I was left behind as we made our way out of the courtyard and onto a dirt path with some trees. I could see Zavier's glutes flexing through his basketball shorts. I could see the definition in his calf muscles.

Fuck.

Here I was at Metamorphose in the final stage of my plan. And I didn't have time for interruptions. But Zavier Kieltyka was too hot and annoyingly irresistible to easily ignore.

He was gonna be a problem.

AFTER MY FEET FELT READY TO FALL THE FUCK OFF, COACH LUNDY ended our run. He stopped outside a gym. He pointed at it. "Shower off. Ten minutes 'til your next class. Kieltyka, you have Norm Technology with Dryden. Dunemark, you'll be in Building B with Ho for the Intersection of Magic and Science."

"Um, clothes, sir?" I asked as I brushed my disgusting sweaty hair off my face, trying to ignore how Zavier grinned wickedly at me. My feet throbbed and my nipples were sore, though not quite as sore as my stomach, where the damned zipper had rubbed despite my best efforts. I'd almost unzipped the shirt and thrown it into the fucking trees, but that would have given Zavier a free show or revealed my powers if I used shadows to cover myself. I wasn't quite ready for the students here to know I was a Darklight.

Lundy just pushed open the double doors of the gym with his back and gestured for us to walk inside. I did. The atrium of the gym was a long, tiled hallway filled with glass cases of trophies and a couple random red doors.

Lundy cleared his throat and pointed right. "Girls locker room is that way. We have spare uniforms for students to wear after the first day run," he said. "We find that most students here don't follow dress code when they arrive."

My inner frown was so intense that it was hard to keep from glaring at Lundy. Spare uniforms? Like the kind my cousin Sara's preschool kept on hand for when some kid pissed their pants? Spare uniforms? Patched, misshapen, oversized grey monstrosities filled my head like monsters. There'd be no fading into my seat with that shit on. There'd be no impressing Grayson or Malcolm.

I sighed and made my way to the girls' locker room. Nothing I could do about it. I crossed my fingers and hoped my hacking into Metamorphose's class schedule had stuck. If it had, then I'd have P.E. with Grayson and I'd have Malcom as a tutor. I needed those ins.

I turned the shower on and let the water warm up. Then I sat on a wooden bench backed by red and grey lockers and stripped off my leather shirt. I carefully lifted one of my sore feet up so I could untie my boot.

A sound had me turning around, palm out, ready to let my power flare.

But then I saw it was just fucking Zavier. "Get outta here, perv!" I was actually annoyed at him this time. My feet were fucking throbbing.

Zavier held up a bundle of clothes in his hand. He was still wearing his running gear. "Our spare clothes 'accidentally'" —he used air quotes—"got switched. Normally, I don't mind parading around naked, but since Ms. Nazer's serious and this is my last shot here, I thought maybe you'd be cool with swapping out. Unless you want to wear guy's clothes."

I sighed. "Have at it." I gestured over at the basket on the wall labeled "spare uniforms."

Zavier walked by me and dumped a plaid skirt and black button up top on the bench beside me. "Thanks." He rifled through my basket and pulled out some guy's clothes, MAD issue dark red pants and black collared shirt. I noticed his ankle monitor was missing. Hmm ... I eyed him suspiciously. Suddenly, I had a whole new appreciation for his drum solo.

"Know who switched em?" I asked as I eased the first chunky shoe off with a hiss. Dammit, that hurt. I carefully peeled off my sock to see my foot was swollen and raw on the bottom.

"Nah, could be anyone around here. You're gonna wanna watch out," Zavier warned as he walked back toward me. "In here, not everyone is as nice and innocent as you."

I didn't roll my eyes, but only because I was busy untying my second boot. "Yeah, that's me. Perfectly innocent."

"I figured you were. Otherwise, you'd have known better than to turn me down." He winked.

I laughed, and the sound echoed off the lockers and the tiles as steam started to fill the room. "Get outta here."

"You sure? I'm an expert at rub downs." He looked at me in my bra and then rubbed his own nipples through his shirt, making the world's most ridiculous face.

"Zavier, don't make me use my powers on you."

"Aw, sweetheart, don't freeze me out," he said, assuming I was an Icefire.

I let him keep his assumptions. As soon as people found out I was a Darklight, there was always a little cluster of annoying groupies who wanted me to perform on demand. I glared into his deep brown eyes. "Don't call me sweetheart."

"Don't be so tempting."

"Don't be so impossible." I chucked a boot at him, which he ducked, laughing. Dammit. There he went again, flipping my annoyance around to amusement. Fucker!

"Alright. Alright. Do you want help with those feet real quick or not?" He pulled a silver wand out of his basketball shorts and tossed the guy's uniform on the bench next to me.

I grimaced, wondering how he'd kept his wand in there, how he'd kept it clean—maybe he hadn't—how he hadn't stabbed himself with it while running. My confusion must have shown on my face because he laughed as he pulled out a tiny, finger-thick roll of parchment out of his pocket. "I have a shrinking spell on it and a hidden pocket. Or … if you like … I'm a grower not a shower."

I shook my head. "You're a walking, talking headache." But internally, I was taking notes. When I broke into the Pinnacle, a shrinking spell like that could be useful. I'd have to practice on my gear.

Zavier sat on the bench next to me and took my foot into his hand. I winced as he touched it, and another hiss escaped through my teeth.

"Damn, sweetheart, those don't look good," he commented as he examined my foot. His hands were big and rough and warm, and in other circumstances, I might have caught my breath for other reasons. As it was, I just clenched my teeth together and tried not to scream.

"I can write a healing spell real quick, if you just let me use your wand," I offered. Healing spells took time to work, because they had to penetrate through the skin to the bloodstream to take effect, but still, if I limped through my shower, I'd hopefully walk normally by the time I was opening my classroom door.

"Nah, I got this," Zavier set my foot on his lap and then clicked a button on the side of his wand. Blue ink appeared on the tip. Then he unrolled a bit of parchment, laid it on my calf, and scribbled onto it, the magic swirling around the parchment and burning it up nearly as fast as he wrote. The magic heated my leg, but only slightly. Magic didn't really burn unless someone intended it to. When Zavier finished, he ripped the parchment, leaving the rest of the blank roll for another spell, as the piece with writing burnt to a crisp from the strength of the magic, leaving a floating orange ball of light. He put his hand on my ankle and held it steady as a soft orange light from the spell he'd created penetrated my skin.

Seconds later, both my feet felt like they'd been encased in water. I writhed as they stung from the astringent created by the healing spell, but then, just as suddenly as the wet sensation had appeared, it evaporated. What? Shock and disbelief filled me as I stared down at my feet. They looked fine. Perfectly fine. The red, sore, raw patches were gone. But ... that couldn't be. That happened fast. Way too fast. Even faster than the time I'd fallen off my bike as a kid and had gotten stitches at the local magical hospital.

"What kind of spell was that?" I asked, careful to keep my tone soft and the awe out of it. If I'd learned anything from running with the rougher crowds at my old academies it was never be too impressed. But as I glanced at Zavier's face, I didn't just see a hot guy with an overconfidence issue anymore. I saw potential.

But Zavier just smiled at me and said, "Trade secret." Then he stood, letting my foot fall to the floor. He gathered up his clothes and left me alone in the girls' locker room, wondering what the hell had just happened. I puzzled it over as I stripped down and walked into the stream of hot water. *What Zavier did was unheard of. Even master spell writers can't—*

Banging on the locker door interrupted my thoughts.

"Dunemark, class is about to start!" Coach Lundy boomed. "You're gonna be late!"

Fuck.

10

When I walked into the Intersection of Magic and Science, it looked like a young Jackie Chan had hijacked a classroom. Professor Martin Ho was short and skinny but wore all black—at first glance, at another school, he might have been a target for student ridicule. But when I glanced around the room and saw no one was slouching or hiding a phone under their desk, not even the guy with the teardrop tattoos under his eye, I knew Ho was a hardass.

The professor had a vicious gleam in his eyes when I stepped inside late with wet hair. His eyebrows rose slightly, and I wondered if he'd expected me to show up in a guy's uniform. My eyes narrowed as I thought back to the admissions director. She was the first administrator ever to ignore my skanky, first-day, bad-impression uniform. Suspicious.

I'd have to ask Zavier if the uniform swapping had happened before. He hadn't seemed too shocked. I wondered if the faculty didn't have a low-key hazing system set up for shithead students. If they did, they'd just gained an ounce of my respect and resentment simultaneously.

Ho didn't appreciate the moment I took to have this revelation in the doorway of his classroom. "Ms. Dunemark, we're so *privileged* you decided to grace us with your presence. Please, since you've interrupted my lecture, come to the front and tell the class all you know about Alchemiken." He gestured wide, stepping to the side of his desk and leaving a gaping space in front of his whiteboard for me.

Great. Unlike other academies, where teachers were intimidated or bribable, Metamorphose seemed to staff jaded sadists: coaches who liked to let girls run in boots and leather and now professors who wanted to make an example of me in my first three seconds. The snickers started up from my classmates and my stomach started to churn. I shoved the discomfort away. I let the energy buzzing under my skin build just a bit so I could ride the adrenaline. *Fuck that Ho,* I thought, internally high fiving my own punniness.

Ho didn't know it, but any attempt to put me on the spot was just practice for later. What if I got caught in a restricted area in the Pinnacle? There was nothing else for me to do but pull this the fuck off with an arrogant, bored smirk on my face.

I walked down the aisle, stepping over a guy's foot when he stuck it out and attempted to trip me at the last second.

I kept my eyes off the students, and on the projects that were clearly displayed on a table behind Ho's desk. The first magically-assisted construction project in history—a bank or something in Hong Kong—had been recreated in foam board. It was shaped like a snowflake, or a lace doily set on its side. The windows were all black to create the illusion of holes. My father had taken me and Matthew to see that building when we were younger. Matthew had been in awe of it. I'd been sad that they didn't have falling snow effects as you walked through the front door. My nine-year-old self had found it lacking. The foam board replica was decent, but someone had gotten lazy with the knife. On foam board, you had to replace your razor every few cuts. Otherwise it got jagged. My Pinnacle replica at Medeis had had the same issue. I stopped myself from clicking my tongue.

A couple mediocre, saggy cardboard messes were next. Finally, there was a very precise rendering of the Pinnacle building in black, which was interesting, because the Pinnacle building, in all its hubris and glory, was pure white marble and ridiculous fake gold paneling reminiscent of the ancient Greek Colosseum stacked thirty stories tall. The metaphor of god-like superiority was a little overstated in my opinion. Way too overstated, per the person who'd turned the gods and goddesses carved on the friezes above the arches into snakes and salamanders. Interesting. I'd have to be nosy one day and find out whose project that was.

I turned once I reached the teacher's desk and hopped up on an empty corner. I crossed my legs, letting the loaner uniform skirt (that was two sizes too big and rolled at my hips so it wouldn't slide down) flare out. I tossed some wet chunks of hair back over my shoulder and grinned out at the class. Twenty faces, in various shades of smirking or bored disinterest, stared back. I scanned them quickly. Eighteen guys. Two girls. Fucking shit, that was a lotta guys. I'd seen the numbers before coming here. But the real-life vision made me momentarily question how many of these idiots broke out of here to get laid. I was betting a lot of them did.

My eyes stopped when they reached a guy in the back corner, partially hidden by shadow. I let my vision brighten a bit so I could see him better. It was Malcolm—the blond hair with the fifties side part, the blue eyes made grey by the burnt-out lightbulbs above him. The sense of confidence that radiated from him was palpable across the room. Even though he wore the same black collared shirt and red pants as the rest of the guys in the room, he was different. His vibe wasn't tough guy or machismo. It was sexy, 1950s Rat-Pack, smooth operator confidence. Immediately, I felt like I knew who had made the Pinnacle replica. Malcolm stared back at me with bored disinterest. Of course, he didn't have a file on me.

I, on the other hand, knew that he ate mac and cheese nearly every day, read philosophy but often cursed the writers as he read, and loved nothing better than a good debate. He'd been on MAD's debate team before it was disbanded for devolving into a brawl during a tournament. I deliberately licked my lips, drawing his eyes to them. Then I turned away, to face the class.

"Alchemiken," I said, adopting a nasal professory voice and steepling my fingers in front of my lips, "is a highly controversial topic." The nasal thing got annoying, so I switched to my normal voice. "Named after alchemy, the age-old proposition of turning lead into gold, this *delightful* term is what magical and norm scientists around the world are searching for: a magical gene. In other words, a genetic key that would turn a norm into a magical." I waggled my fingers like I was sprinkling fairy dust, exaggerating my tone and earning a snort from one of the guys in the front row, a dude with a fro.

"What have studies found so far?" Ho demanded.

"You mean our published studies or the ones in third world countries where they inject rats and chimps and babies in China with supposed *magical genes?*"

I saw Malcolm's eyes widen a bit and it was a struggle not to look directly at him. I'd gained his attention. Now I had to keep his interest. I knew I'd come across as a suck up and a nerd. But I didn't care what Ho thought of me one way or another. I cared what Malcolm thought.

"Why don't you tell me about any study you know?" the professor said.

"Well, the test tube babies were a bust," I stated. "China's tried at least three times to 'breed' magical children like livestock. One of the doctors initially claimed success but then it was discovered he was falsifying his records."

"Animal studies?"

"There was a claim that some rats got Icefire. But here's the thing. Your subject has to be intelligent enough to use the magic in order to prove it to me."

"You're citing the Vandillon studies. You don't believe them?"

"I need more than a few frozen rats to believe they had power and weren't chucked soaking wet into a freezer."

"What about any local studies?" Ho asked.

A spitball hit me in the face.

I flushed. My nostrils flared and my toes curled as I gripped the desk. It was a little early to build a rep for myself by lashing out.

Ho sped up the aisle and yanked a student out of his seat so fast that I didn't even have time to wipe the spitball off my cheek. The professor pulled the guy backwards by the hair down the aisle as I stared in shock. I had to remind myself not to let my jaw drop when Ho eye gouged the dude with the teardrop tattoo.

The other students looked on with interest. But they didn't pull out phones like would have happened at any of my prior academies. They didn't document the incident and plan to get their five minutes of fame on social media from it. They probably knew if they did that they'd be in for the same treatment.

Ho opened the classroom door and said, "Out."

The dude nearly ran into the door jamb on the way out, his eyes red and streaming with real tears to match the ones he'd had inked onto his cheeks.

Ho turned back to glance around the room imperiously. His gaze dared anyone to challenge or disrespect him. Utter silence met that gaze. When Ho's dark eyes turned back to me, even I had to force myself not to cringe away. His hand rose to his cheek and his index finger stroked it oddly.

That's when I realized I hadn't wiped away the spitball. I did so, trying to feign nonchalance. Maybe at MAD, this sort of thing was normal. Maybe professors bodily dragged students around every day. But it took me a second to recover. I was a little taken aback. Nazer had warned me professors didn't take things lightly, but damn.

My eyes scanned my classmates, many of them marking me as prey. Great. I looked like I didn't know what the fuck to do in a fight.

Shit. I debated showing off my power, but that was just as likely to draw in the crazies who wanted to suction it out of me like vacuums.

"Ms. Dunemark, please continue," the professor said calmly, as if nothing had happened.

I glanced back at Malcolm, scolding myself, reminding myself that I needed to be impressing this dude, not anyone else. To my surprise, Malcolm gave me a small, encouraging head nod.

Shit. That almost made this harder. Fangirling started up in my chest, like a whole live stream of jumping, screaming little thirteen-year-old girls going "he looked at me." I was doing this. I was actually doing this. Malcolm fucking Bier was looking at me. Focused on me. I closed my eyes. *Don't fuck up,* I told myself.

Then I opened my eyes and stared back at Professor Ho. I couldn't look at Malcolm or I knew I'd lose my cool. My cheeks were already threatening to go red as it was. "The studies here in the U.S. have been minimal because of human and animal rights concerns."

From the back of the room, Malcolm called out, "The published studies have been minimal, you mean."

"Right," I cleared my throat. My palms were sweaty. My palms were never sweaty. Dammit. I tried again. "The Pinnacle and the government of the United States haven't been able to come to an agreement about citizenship if a human became a magical."

Ho's eyes twinkled with mirth as he said, "I thought, with your stepfather overseeing the research for the Pinnacle, that you might know a bit more about the unpublished studies."

Any admiration for him dried out and burnt to a crisp as fury rolled through me. The fuckwad had gone and cut off my legs with a single sentence. The atmosphere in the room went from bored to hostile in two seconds flat. Dammit to hell. The Pinnacle was the enemy to most of these damn students. And now they knew my mother's shit husband worked there. Way to put a target on my back. As if I didn't have enough with the nerd thing. Day one was not going well. I ran my tongue over my teeth, wondering if I could salvage this. How I could salvage this.

One girl at the back of the class said, "So you're a stupid chess piece?" That's what the underbelly, the criminal underground, called people who played by the rules.

I narrowed my eyes at the girl. She stared straight back, her dark curls and the leather collar she wore screaming defiance in a way that was all for show. I ran down my mental attendance sheet. She had to be Laura Whitehall, recent plaything of Grayson's, if my PI was correct. Not officially a girlfriend, though she wanted to be. Interesting that she'd hate chess pieces since Grayson's daddy was angling to join the Clod at the Pinnacle. The question became, did I make her a friend or an enemy? Which one would get me closer to Grayson?

"If I was a chess piece, would I be here?" I asked her.

"Maybe you're a nark," Laura stretched her legs out under her desk and crossed them at her ankles, displaying an ankle monitor just like Zavier's.

Ohh, that monitor is so badass, girl. You show it off, that's right, I thought sarcastically snapping my fingers in the air for her. I wondered if she'd paid extra for the ankle monitor just to look more hardcore.

From all my research about the people here, she'd only ever gone down for repeated shoplifting. High dollar stuff? Yeah. But nothing dangerous or crazy. I smiled at Laura as I studied her brown eyes and bright red lipstick. I saw a chance to redeem myself in front of the jerks in the front row, who were leering at me, eager to find me in the hall after class and give the new little nerd a taste of the dark side.

I put a finger to my lips and tapped. "If I *was* a nark, I'd probably know all about the fact that you blew that cop who arrested you in order to get him to change your felony to a misdemeanor, wouldn't I?" I nodded to myself, pretending to be thinking about it as suddenly the room buzzed with energy, on high alert. Gazes ping-ponged back and forth between me and Laura. The guys in the front row leaned back in their seats, no longer leering.

Fuck. Sometimes I loved being me.

Laura's eyes narrowed and she glared at me.

"I didn't do that."

I pulled Zavier's innocent bullshit face. "July 17th last year? You sure? Looked like you in the photo. Pretty sure the court minutes still have you on parole for shoplifting, you scary thing, you."

Snickers kicked off as Laura's fingers clenched on the edges of her desk. Yup. One enemy made. Hopefully she'd run to Grayson. And either he'd cast her off or come to defend her. Either way, I'd be on his radar. With a billionaire's son, that was always the first step. Yes-men and coattail riders were a dime a dozen. But opponents? Bitches? Those were few and far between in the land of the wealthy.

My grandmother used to say you'd catch more flies with honey than vinegar. She obviously didn't know that fruit flies were obsessed with vinegar. Grandma just repeated what she'd been told. She was a bit of a chess piece. But fruit flies were drawn to vinegar like moths to flame. They were so attracted that the fuckers would drown themselves in it.

I was gonna compel Grayson Mars to come to me until he begged me to drown him.

Professor Ho stepped in front of me. "And you're done. Thank you, Ms. Dunemark. You've gotten detention on your first day. Take your seat."

I strode to the back of the room, head held high, adrenaline and success buzzing in my veins. I considered sitting down in the empty seat next to Malcolm, but that might be too aggressive. He was a bit of a loner, possibly shy. I'd see him at tutoring anyway. Plus, I had a point to prove.

I sat down right next to Laura. That earned me another round of stares from the other students as Laura's hands fisted on her thighs underneath the desk. I could have taken the third empty seat all the way across the room. But that wasn't how the game was played. The alpha, bullshit dominance game meant that I needed to be up in her face all the time until she submitted.

I leaned back in my seat and focused on Ho, who was trying to regain control of his classroom. But the energy had changed. He knew it. I knew it. Glances kept floating back my way.

A wide, shit-eating grin spread across my face before I could stop it. Next to me, Laura Whitehall thought I was mocking her.

"You'll get yours, bitch." Her tone was low and dark.

And I couldn't help turning to let her see my full-toothed smile. This was the best lesson ever. Because I'd impressed Malcolm and made my first enemy. But as I glanced over, Malcolm's face was one of disappointment.

Aw, fuck. He didn't really expect me to let her bitch me out, did he? Was I supposed to stand there and take it?

"Ms. Dunemark!" Ho barked. "Back up here!"

I slowly slid out of my seat and strutted forward. They took this hazing thing seriously.

"Since you seem so eager to have the class watch you, you can just stay standing up here, so they have a better view." He placed me just in front of the corner, like timeout, his eyes glaring at mine, ordering me to stand down. But once I'd slid on my bitch persona, it was sometimes hard to slip off. I glared defiantly back at him.

"Alchemiken rights debate. Where do you stand?" Ho challenged me.

I glanced at Malcolm for half a second. I wasn't sure if the Laura thing had lost him completely. I didn't know if I could get back on track. I took a chance on the professor's question. "I think they're putting the cart before the horse. Alchemiken hasn't even been proven. There is no such thing as a dual citizen yet. Meanwhile, we have a vamp population—one that neither side wants to take responsibility for—locked away in institutions. They don't have magical representation in any legal system, they don't get—"

A black-haired guy in the front row stood up, acne pitted face furious as his chair smacked to the floor behind him. "A fucking vamp killed my grandpa," he said.

Ho held out a hand. "Take your seat, Mr. Therrian."

"I'm sorry. But was that vamp nearly starved to death before that happened?" I asked, leaning around Ho. "They've been known to get more aggressive when they haven't eaten regularly."

"Fang-loving whore!"

Ho marched over to Therrian and stared the kid down. Then he turned back to me. "Get out of my classroom."

I went to grab my bag, but Ho stepped in front of me. "Go directly to the Admin building. Room 208. Your detention starts now."

11

DETENTION SUCKED. I had to spend three hours butchering half a cow, hacking at it and trying not to puke from the smell. And then I had to feed four of the professors, who transformed into their Unnatural wolves for supper. My heart raced as their claws had clicked across the tile floor and headed for me, growling. The way they ripped apart the meat, raw tendons hanging from their huge fangs like red ribbons … it had been so sick I'd nearly puked. It was so creepy and disgusting that even after I went back to my dorm room, that nightmare of a detention invaded my dreams. Wolves stalked me through the fog.

I was ripped from sleep by something sliding across my throat. My brain immediately screamed, "Fangs!" My eyes flew open and a dark face leaned close to mine. A hand pressed down further on my neck.

I gasped in surprise and from the need for air. Fear raised goosebumps on my arms, but I refused to let my stomach churn.

You knew something like this was coming, I told myself. *Buck the fuck up. It's better than a wolf.* Matthew used to tell me to take it like a champ when he tickled me until I couldn't breathe. This wasn't that different. Hardly breathing. I focused on taking slow breaths.

Grayson Mars pressed a hand down on my neck as he sat on the side of my bed. His fingers curled into my neck threateningly. His features were highlighted by the moonlight in a way that made him appear quite menacing. Menacing and handsome. His thick lips snarled, and his brows were drawn down. But even with the anger in his expression, he was undeniably good looking. That was a completely irrelevant, half-asphyxiated thought and I scolded myself for it as soon as I had it. Goals. He was here. He was angry. My plan had worked. I flexed my fingers, trying to decide if I should burn his eyes or blind him with darkness.

I quickly decided against darkness. He'd still be able to squeeze. And he was strong. The biceps near my face were huge. They felt massive compared to what I'd seen of him across the room at the stupid socialite functions mother dragged me to attend. My heart tapped nervously at my ribs, reminding me to stop fucking analyzing every little detail and get some damn oxygen into my body. I pulled at his fingers and he relented the tiniest bit. Good. He wasn't actually out to kill me. Yet. I was sure that if he wanted to, he could probably curl his hand completely around my neck. If he wanted to, he could snap it.

I gulped in air.

The shuffle of footsteps made my eyes fly across the room. Beyond the foot of my bed were two guys and a girl. They wore black sweats and jackets but didn't bother to hide their faces in the moonlight. One of the guys smiled at me. He was the guy with the teardrop tattoos under his eye. That made me reevaluate Grayson's intentions. Gangster tattoos for murder were a little farther than I wanted to go.

I let my body go limp and I didn't move. I'd let them make the first move. Because I needed Grayson ticked but not murderous. I needed to push him, but not too far. I needed him to see me as a challenge, as an equal, but not as someone worth eliminating.

Movement jerked my eyes to the corner. The girl opened my closet door, making a shadow crawl across my wall. Based on the curly haired silhouette, I assumed the girl was Laura, though I couldn't see her face. I hadn't given anyone else reason to hate me this afternoon.

The girl bent down and rustled through my freshly unpacked things. I relaxed a bit more in Grayson's hold. They wanted to screw with my stuff? *Real fucking original.*

Grayson leaned down toward me and his breath was hot against my ear as he whispered, "Heard you think you're hot shit."

His voice sent a shiver down my spine. But not the scared kind. I stared up at him. I tried to force a couple tears into my eyes, let him think he was getting to me.

Laura giggled as she started pulling my shoes out of the closet. She lined them up on the far wall of my room, where I could see each and every pair. My Louboutins and Saint Laurents were placed in the center of my boots and other shoes.

Grayson yanked the back of my hair roughly and pulled my head up just a fraction, so it was resting against his hard, hickory-scented chest. Damn—the guy had good cologne.

He made sure I had the perfect view of the far wall and his companions. He kept the tight grip on my hair and an unimportant question flickered through my head. *I wonder if he likes it rough?* I shoved that idiotic thought aside and Grayson jerked my head forward to make sure I was focused on the wall.

After all my shoes had been laid out, like firing squad victims, Laura skipped forward and pulled the lid off a huge, covered, metal pot.

Rank steam filled my room.

I had to tamp down on my gag reflex. Laura covered her nose and giggled as the two guys walked toward the wall and slowly poured steaming hot noodle soup over my shoes. I was pretty certain they'd added some kind of rotten meat to it, because the smell coming from it was horrifying. The soup splattered against my walls and sank into the cheap utilitarian carpet. The carpet was actually the worst of my worries. Even a spell to remove it wouldn't be fast enough. That nasty smell would linger. I'd have to pay to get that shit replaced ASAP.

I took deep breaths through my mouth, as deep as I was able with one of Grayson's hands still on my throat.

Laura turned to watch me, obviously expecting some kind of reaction. So, I let out a moan. "Oh!" I felt like saying, "Oh, my poor fucking shoes, how will I ever live without you? Tragedy, agony! And thus, with a heel, I die!" Did they think I was that fucking shallow? Or that fucking stupid? Apparently.

Laura's eyes flared with anger at my reaction. I guess it hadn't been big enough for her. Dammit. Maybe I should have gone with the Shakespearean death scene shit. Fuck me.

Her eyes glanced around the room and I knew she wasn't satisfied. I tensed in Grayson's arms and he chuckled.

His chuckle was a low, smoky sound, like some jazz singer had turned laughter into music. I worried my lip with my teeth as I watched Laura head over to my dresser.

When all of my shoes had been ruined, the guys set the pot in the middle of the room.

Laura opened the top drawer and dumped out my socks, so that they rolled across the floor.

My heart crashed into my ribs like giant ocean waves smacking against the rocks. Fear foamed inside my chest. For the first time since these fuckers had come into my room, I felt scared. Sweat beaded on my brow. My flash drive was hidden in the middle of one of my sock rolls. I'd taken the necklace off and stuffed it in there to hide it. That flash drive held all the fucking Pinnacle floor plans and student profiles and every damn thing I needed for this heist.

My fingers clenched and I tried not to physically give myself away. But I felt like puking. I felt like blinding then burning the fuck out of all of them. *Shit.*

I forced myself to stare back at the dresser and not at the socks that littered the floor.

It felt like minutes passed, though it was probably only seconds, before Laura opened a second drawer and found my underwear.

Yes, bitch, yes! I screamed inside. Outside, I writhed and moaned, like I was humiliated.

Laura smiled, feeling triumphant. She pulled the drawer out and walked with it over to the still-steaming vat of sludge. She dumped it over, sending the entire drawer of lacy thongs and bikini briefs to their permanent end. Even if I could write a spell to get rid of all this soup shit—and I would—the smell would have soaked in and ruined everything. I didn't have a hard on for car upholstery or crime scene clean up magic. I didn't have spells laying around for how to get shit stains out.

Behind me, Grayson's laugh rumbled through his chest and vibrated against my back. I focused on that sound. Then I made my muscles go limp. I tried to curl myself into a ball, like I'd been defeated.

"Little girl, don't mess with the big dogs," Grayson's voice wrapped seductively around me before he shoved me roughly forward onto the bed. My face hit my comforter and I turned sideways, watching as he stood. He zipped his coat and nodded at his lackeys as they climbed out my window. Grayson turned before he climbed out himself. "This is your only warning."

"Understood," I rasped, my throat still sore from where he'd grabbed me.

Grayson tossed a leg up onto my ledge and then gave me a wicked grin before he hopped out my window. My third-floor window.

I pulled myself up out of the bed and hurried to the window nearby. His little crew members were climbing carefully down the walls, using what appeared to be niches carved into the stone. Good to know those were there. I assumed some enterprising students had magically added them to the architecture for nighttime visits like this.

But Grayson didn't use the niches. His Force power let him levitate through the air. His hands were pointed at the grass like Iron Man's rocket-blasting mechanical gloves. I could see the wind he emitted whipping the dead winter grass below his palms and flattening it like some balding man's crap comb over. Grayson slowly lowered the amount of Force he used so that he sank little by little until he stepped easily onto the grass.

Holy shit! I was right! He can lift people! I licked my lips. That level of control was rare. Most people with Force power could send a blast of wind, but couldn't funnel it, direct it, turn up or down the volume like a song on the radio. Grayson's power sang.

He waited for his minions to finish their descent and glanced up to see me staring down at him.

His grin was absolutely wolfish. He honestly believed he'd threatened and scared me.

I had to hide my grin back. Because Grayson was so cute. He thought he was the predator.

He wasn't.

He was the prey.

I couldn't wait to catch him.

12

THE NEXT MORNING, I woke up early. I'd had to cut away the nasty soup-stained section of my carpet and toss it in the dumpster. A jagged circle of old wooden floor peeked up through that hole now.

I'd saved a pair or two of shoes and tossed the rest. But the only panties I had left were the ones I'd been wearing and the ones in my go-bag, a pack I kept underneath my bed in case anyone ever found my flash drive and I had to bolt. Those panties were not flattering. Granny panties meant for comfort in case I had a long bus ride ahead of me, they were patterned with daisies. They kind of looked like an elementary schoolgirl's panties. Not something I wanted to be seen in. And I expected them to be seen. Laura and Grayson wouldn't go to all that work for nothing. It didn't matter that I'd let them leave on top. Entitled bullies liked to feed their egos a consistent diet. I harbored no illusion that I'd be off the hook.

That's why I was up before dawn, ordering replacements and then sitting at my desk, tapping my wand against my lip, trying to come up with some kind of retaliation that was significant enough to tell Grayson I wasn't a pushover, but not significant enough to make him my enemy forever. I watched dawn crawl across the sky, as tired and groggy as I was. The sun rose slowly. But finally, I had an idea. I dipped my wand into my inkwell and started to write.

As I'd expected, Grayson's crew didn't make me wait long. They hadn't developed the same sort of patience that I had. Their goals were short term, they had no long game.

I had hardly stepped outside the girls' dorm room to head to breakfast before a blast of wind hit me and sent my skirt flying up, displaying my panties for everyone.

I made eye contact with Grayson; his dark face unreadable in the grey cloud cover of morning. His hand was extended, keeping my plaid skirt aloft, dancing in the wind almost like a Marilyn Monroe snapshot.

A smile stretched across my face when Laura's hyena-shrill laughs stuttered. Because nobody saw my granny panties. I'd spelled them to glow neon—flashing from green to red.

"I figured if you were gonna make me show the goods, I might as well make the goods a light show," I winked, letting them eye my color-changing panties. "Anyone want to play red light green light?"

Grayson's lip quirked up. He didn't speak, but his expression said, "touché."

I gave them all a little finger wave before strutting toward the cafeteria, not bothering to push down my skirt or hide my panties.

I ignored a couple catcalls and the cell phones that came out to photograph my ass. I did take note of those students, because I'd hack their phones later to delete the footage. But there was no reason for me to start shit with them. I already had Mr. Mars to contend with. And I was pretty happy with the way things were going. But derailing their prank this morning wasn't enough.

Grayson still had to know he couldn't get away with shit like last night. The billionaire's son wasn't untouchable. He was about to learn that.

I entered the cafeteria. The doors closed behind me and my skirt finally fell normally over my thighs. I walked inside, wondering what Grayson and company were thinking, hoping they hadn't eaten yet.

The cafeteria was a big beige room full of round wooden tables and chairs. Skylights were scattered around the ceiling as were potted plants across the floor. Other than that, there was no decoration to speak of—other than their grand entryway—MAD liked things spartan for the students.

I headed toward the metallic serving area and grabbed a tray, thankful that a lot of students seemed to have eaten and the place was only about a quarter full. I tried not to wrinkle my nose at the choices. No need to piss off the staff who cooked, though I kind of wondered what the qualifications for the job were. Hatred of teenagers? Appearance on that norm show, *Worst Cooks of All Time*? I prayed that my mom would soon relent on my credit card restrictions—she'd been pissed about the stripper for Tia and only made an exception for shoes and undies when I took a picture of my damaged goods and told her that a box of my stuff had gotten dropped in the mud—and I could order some premade meals and a microwave and avoid this nonsense all together. I regretted my generosity when I smelled the tuna surprise that was today's main dish. I shook my head at the middle-aged dude serving it and put together a wilted salad with a lot of shaved almonds, tomatoes, and some ranch. I grabbed an apple and a banana, and some toast with apple butter, then found a seat away from everyone. I set myself up in a dark corner, partially hidden behind a plant.

Grayson and his entourage entered. *Score.* Laura and her wild mane of black hair clung to him like a fuzzball on a sweater. If I'd had someone to bet against, I would have put up all my millions to wager she'd never once contradicted him. Ever. I rolled my eyes. But that part didn't matter—yet. I still owed Grayson for last night.

As they got their food, I unrolled a piece of parchment. Then I wrote the spell that I'd brainstormed this morning. It was a long spell, one of the longest I'd written, but I wanted to be sure it wouldn't be easy to unravel.

I watched the paper burn, leaving a little snake trail of ash on the table as the golden cloud of magic arose. It glittered in front of me for a minute before it disappeared. I put my things away carefully. There was a time delay on the spell, and I wanted to be out of the way before it activated. But I did plant a small camera—I zip tied it to the leaves of the plant in front of me. I checked the video feed to my phone and tilted the camera so that it was square on Grayson's table. I hoped the sound was good enough. Then I rose, very careful not to skip or smile or betray my glee. I was careful not to react when Grayson and his friends saw me.

Of course, he blew my skirt up again, letting the entire cafeteria get a good laugh. But I gritted my teeth, kept my eyes on the door, and didn't acknowledge any of the bullshit. I knew that sycophantic laugh track would soon go wild with unbridled mirth at his expense.

As I stepped outside the cafeteria, I was right.

I ran to the gym number two and hid in the broom closet before I allowed myself to open my phone. But once I did, I collapsed in laughter. I was fucking brilliant. After I'd walked out of the cafeteria, my spell had activated. And not thirty seconds later, Grayson had reached for his water bottle. As soon as the plastic touched his lips, it turned into a giant sparkling pink dildo. To the rest of the people in the cafeteria, it looked like Grayson was sucking a giant dick.

Stupid Laura did what any class-whore clinger does. Her eyes widened in horror and she pulled the bottle away from Grayson. Of course, as soon as it wasn't touching his lips, it turned normal again. Presto change-o.

"Hey!" he growled, "You've got your own. I wasn't finished—"

"Your bottle just turned into a dildo."

"What?" he scoffed.

But another of his cronies shook his head. "Dude, it's true."

Grayson picked up his water bottle. "Looks normal to me. Does it look normal to you?"

"Right now, it does," Laura said, uncertain.

Grayson put it to his full lips again. And a big pink dildo re-emerged as he stared cross-eyed down his nose. "That bitch!" he said, but there was half a smile on his face.

That's right, fucker. Not everyone's too intimidated to mess with a rich boy.

Grayson turned to Laura. "You try it."

She swallowed hard and her eyes darted around the room.

"Come on, chicken," I goaded her through the screen.

Of course, she couldn't say no to Grayson. Girls like her and Terra Lysour thought that saying no would get them kicked to the curb. I winced when she took the bottle even though tears had formed in her eyes. She was going to do it, though she really didn't want to, though she was anticipating humiliation, just because he told her to. I wanted to shake girls like her and just tell them to grow a spine. But there was nothing I could do.

Laura lifted the water bottle to her lips with shaking hands. But it stayed a water bottle.

"What the hell?" Grayson said. He took it back. As soon as it touched his lips it turned into a dick. And the triple activation part of the spell started up. Since this was the third time he'd touched the dick to his mouth, it started to vibrate, splattering water across his chin.

The roar of laughter that went through the cafeteria was brilliant. It must have vibrated the floors. Part of me wished I could be there in person to witness it, but I was pretty sure that if I was there in person, my person wouldn't exist much longer. Grayson would kill me.

He set down the water bottle and shook his head, his prior amusement gone as he grabbed a napkin and dabbed at his face.

"That tricky little thing," he said.

"Don't worry, baby, we'll get her." Laura put her hand on his broad shoulder, trying to comfort him, though the expression on her face still hadn't changed from the relief she'd felt when the water bottle hadn't turned into a dildo on her.

Grayson absently patted her hand as his eyes scanned the room, looking for me. As he glanced around, his dark expression made the laughter sputter and falter, dying off.

Nope, buddy, not dumb enough to sit there and wait for you to kill me.

"We'll make sure she knows—" Laura started.

But Grayson stared down at her. "No. I will. She's clearly calling me out, baby."

"But—"

He stood, ignoring her and leaving his innocuous-looking water bottle on the table. "I'll take care of it."

Then he grabbed his bag and walked out, leaving her behind.

I grinned to myself. He was going to spend all day thinking about me instead of her. Yeah, he'd be hating me the entire time. But love and hate were just milliseconds apart. They were both energy that boiled over to the point of irrationality. Both impulsive needs driven by the mind, intense feelings that burned like fire. I was gonna scorch Grayson until he couldn't tell the difference between the two.

And then, I was gonna proposition him.

13

TIA TEXTED me Saturday morning before Cross Country.

-Lady, that hot guy you sent was epic, up until his tiny briefs. Too many steroids. Not enough going on downtown.-

-LOL. Sorry.-

-It's cool. I still ogled him. So, gimme an update! Have you snagged the hot guy?-

-It's a work in progress.-

-He better be worth it.-

-He is. I can already tell.-

Of course, I didn't mention that Grayson was probably planning my murder. Some things Tia didn't need to know.

When I left the gym after Cross Country on Saturday morning, Zavier ran across the grass toward me. I hadn't seen him all day Friday as I'd hidden out in bathrooms and closets between class to avoid Grayson's steaming temper.

"Holy shit, you have lady balls!" Zavier crowed, referring to my dick spell.

"Those are called ovaries," I said, tucking my still semi-damp hair into a black beanie. I'd minimized my shower time because a couple of the girls in the locker room had decided to help Grayson out by punishing me with hail instead of water from the shower head.

Apparently, everyone at this school tested positive on the asshole scale. I was used to being one of the few. Being just one asshole of many would take some getting used to. But on the other side of things was Zavier. He didn't seem to fit in here.

Looks-absolutely. His sleeved tats were drool-worthy and to-die-for. He was showing them off a little today despite the cold weather, cuffs rolled to his elbows. But Zavier's happy smile and the chin nod he gave everyone we passed didn't fit. Even the way he slung an arm around my shoulders was way too innocent.

"Do you not know that half the student body wants to kill me right now?" I asked, trying to shrug out of his hold. "You don't want to be seen with me."

"Oh, I *do* know you have a death wish. Question is—why?"

Death wish. That's one of those phrases Claude used on me, when he came to my room late at night and stood in the doorway, to tell me that I was a disappointment who was slowly killing my mother. He'd tell me it was my fault she had to take Calm, that she couldn't eat, that she'd fallen down the stairs.

I shoved the memories and Zavier off at the same time, trying not to let the darkness take control. "I don't. I'm just a bitch."

He evaluated me for a second before he took two long strides to catch up with me. And his damn arm went back around my shoulders. "A hot bitch. A bitch in heat."

"Dude, if either one of us is a dog, it's you."

"If I'm a dog, can I sniff your ass?" He started to snort and scooped me up, dumping me over his shoulder.

Shocked, appalled, embarrassed, and a tiny bit amused, I clamped my hands over my butt. "Put me down, you moron."

"Not until you come up with a more clever way to ask."

"Please?"

"Nope."

Ugh. I thought about burning his butt with gamma rays; I had a great view of it, but we were in the middle of the two buildings. And even though it was Saturday, that was just another school day here. Teachers and students swarmed all around.

He wanted something more clever. I replayed our conversation. The pun we'd been working off had been dogs. "Sit."

Zavier sat, still holding me, my ass still pointed in the air. But now, it was at hand level for most people strolling past.

"Zavier, anyone walking by could spank me," I hissed.

"You're no fun," he grumbled, finally relenting and pulling me down onto his lap.

I glared at him. "You're crazy."

"Nope. I'm rubber. You're glue."

"I'm gonna kill you and turn your bones into glue," I said, as I struggled off his lap without his help.

"Good one." Two seconds later, he was up again, grabbing my hand. "Come on, or we'll be late for class. Tell me more about your glowing panties."

I smacked his chest. My new undergarments hadn't arrived in the mail yet. I'd had to hand wash and enchant today's pair, which alternated between electric blue and pink light. "That's the real reason you scooped me up, you perv."

He gave a shrug. "I had to see the truth for myself."

"You're ridiculous."

He squeezed my fingers and asked, "Are those regular LED panties or are they spelled? I want that spell. Oh man. Can you imagine Professor Huchmala with glowing panties?" Zavier chuckled as he held open the door to Building A. His enthusiasm was as high as a preschool boy's in the sandbox.

He led the way to Magical and Norm Intersections, my only class with him, painting bright mental pictures of Huchmala in disco-ball style undies. I had to admit, his idea had appeal. Professor Huchmala was the art therapy professor. I'd met her Friday, and she had an awkward vibe that she spread around like peanut butter. It stuck to the roof of your mouth after you left her class. She was an older woman with shoulder-length silver hair, crow's feet, and blue eyes that never made eye contact. She always looked slightly to your right. She wore a lot of sweater dresses which meant the light from luminescent panties would penetrate, drawing attention all day long. Joy for every student —until she noticed.

I bit my lip and debated helping Zavier out. But I'd used my natural magic for the panties. I didn't really want anyone to know I was a Darklight yet, and so far, the faculty were keeping it under wraps. And while he came across as harmless, the guy was on his last shot here. That meant he'd done something big.

"Sorry, they're just norm panties," I shrugged, lying as we sat off in a corner of the lecture hall by ourselves.

Zavier sighed. "That's okay. Now I'm totally gonna fuck off in class and try to think of how to write a spell to do that."

I laughed and shook my head. "Instead of that, can you tell me what the fuck is up with my tutor? He was a no-show." That pissed me off to high heaven because I'd worked damn hard to ensure that I got Malcolm assigned to me. I'd had to hack the system twice, because some dumb admin troll had changed it back.

I worried that I'd ticked Malcolm off in class the other day. I ran a hand across the back of my neck.

A girl with cherry-red pigtails and gauged piercings in her ears sat down in the chair next to me. I glanced over at her, because no one had bothered to sit near me yet at this school. Grayson's scorn apparently carried some weight. But this girl smiled at me before she sat. I realized she had gold earrings looped through the steel tunnels in her earlobes. She dug her book out of her bag and ignored us, flipping open to the current chapter—The Great Fog. It was all about the 1960s war between technology and magic, each trying to muddle the other's power. I could see the page was highlighted in several marker colors. I briefly wondered what a nerd of this caliber was doing at MAD, but then Zavier spoke to me.

"Who's your tutor?" he asked.

"Malcolm Bier," I said.

The girl looked over at me, her earrings jangling as she turned and blinked cat eye makeup at me. That's when I realized she had a nose-ring, lip piercing, and a piercing through her dimple. The first words out of her mouth were a warning, "Shit. Even I've heard of him. He goes here? If that guy ghosts you, it's a good thing. Trust me. You don't want to be mixed up with all that. He's on like eight countries' watch lists."

"Sorry, who are you?" I asked. This girl wasn't on my list of students. My eyes roamed her suspiciously.

"Emelia."

"New transfer?" Zavier asked, stretching and sliding an arm not-so-subtly behind my back.

"Potential. My mom's trying to scare me into compliance by sending me here for a week," Emelia laughed nervously. "I think it might work."

"Know the feeling," I responded, easing back against Zavier's arm because I liked the feel of his bicep against the back of my neck. I probably shouldn't have done it, considering it would probably only encourage him, but the way his fingers curled possessively around my shoulder and pulled me closer felt good. Even if it was only a momentary distraction.

Emilia eyed us for a second before the professor—a white haired man with a ponytail—called us all to attention. When Emilia turned to face forward, Zavier leaned in. His breath was hot against my ear as he whispered, "Giving in already, dirty friend?"

I fought against the tingle that ran down my spine at his words. "No, you're just a good headrest," I replied.

"You'd be a good headrest too. But not for my face ... for my—"

"Mr. Kieltyka," Professor Wolfe called out, saving Zavier from a good punch to the nads. "Please step on down here for a demonstration." Wolfe smiled, which made his wrinkled face double the number of ripples in his skin. He shoved his hands into his tweed pant pockets and waited patiently as Zavier uncurled from around me and made his way down the steps toward the wooden podium. There were quite a few steps on the way down, because at least a hundred students fit into this room, which was set up as a semicircular auditorium with a small raised stage at the front. I imagined that quite a few faculty members were huddled in their lounge, drinking coffee and complaining about us while Wolfe took a good chunk of the student population off their hands.

"Now, we've already discussed how norms and magicals have had quite a terrible history of violence," Wolfe stated. "I know we live in a somewhat segregated society as a result. It's proven easiest. Most of you have only gone to school with magicals. Most norms stick to their side of any given town. But, it's very important we cultivate positive relations with one another. Today, we're going to go over some of the proper protocol for when you meet a norm."

Wolfe turned to Zavier, who dwarfed him by at least half a foot. But the professor didn't seem intimidated in the slightest. In fact, from what I could tell (this was only my second class with Professor Derby Wolfe) our professor was just one of those genuinely happy guys. He constantly strove to crack jokes in class. Some fell horribly flat. But he was the only professor I'd ever known to make that kind of effort. And I appreciated it.

Wolfe said, "Mr. Kieltyka, you're going to be my assistant today. But, instead of dressing you in sparkles and sawing you in half—"

"Boo!" one student called out.

"Do that instead," another guy shouted.

I just laughed as Zavier struck a feminine pose that showcased the blinking ankle cuff he wore as he said, "Don't worry everyone, I'll still be eye candy no matter what."

A couple erasers were thrown at Zavier. One hit Professor Wolfe, but he didn't seem to mind. "Today, I'm going to play a norm. Once in a while, you might encounter them at the bank or grocery store. They often hold administrative positions, even within our own government or prisons. While we no longer have to wear patches on our sleeves to identify ourselves as magicals, it's considered polite to identify yourself as such if you engage a norm in conversation."

"Why, though?" one of the guys I recognized as Grayson's lackey, a dude with a buzzed head and a septum piercing, asked. "I mean, what's it to them if we've got magic?"

Wolfe sighed. "Norms are very particular about their confidence levels. Ever since the invention of the Unnatural Spell, one hundred seventy-two years ago, there's been additional friction between our kind and theirs."

"Why though?" A lazy-looking guy with white-blond hair called out from the back of the room, waving his wand in the air. "We were their little bitches for centuries. Only fair that they take their turn."

"Well, now, that is an interesting philosophy." Wolfe didn't just shoot the asshole down like he should have. He acted like the statement had some kind of twisted merit. Which is why the students here loved him. Wolfe cleared his throat before he continued, "Before the Institutes were created, the Unnatural Spell used to cause more than just heartache when it went wrong. One moment." He left Zavier standing by the podium and went behind it. He grabbed his wand. He dipped it in the inkwell and tapped it against the podium in a quick staccato rhythm as he unrolled a parchment and wrote a quick spell. His hands weren't what they used to be. Age was catching up with him. His left fingers got singed as the parchment burnt beneath him, the magic racing his writing ability. Wolfe finished just before the fire reached the tip of his wand. "There we are," he said, before sucking on one of his burnt fingertips.

Above his head rose a circle, that shimmered like a mirror. Derby glanced up and then out at the class. "Those of you who know me, know that I've been one of the lucky ones able to slow my aging process down. And while it's generally not polite to ask a Norm their age—particularly the women—I'll let you in on a little secret. I am one-hundred-seventy-six this year."

I knew that already from researching the school. But clearly, based on the silence that sliced through the room, not everyone did. Gasps went around the room. Magicals had normal lifespans. Unnaturals had normal lifespans with the added hazard of getting eaten or run over or whatever while they were in animal form. Some magicals used spells to slow their aging. But the longest I'd ever heard of anyone lasting, before Professor Wolfe, was a hundred and thirty. His spell writing must have been incredibly badass.

I glanced over at Emelia. She was leaning forward in her seat, fascinated. While the other kids were impressed for a second, they'd already relaxed back into their arrogant, 'don't give a fuck' poses. *Yeah, this girl is not gonna fit in here,* I thought as I turned back to Professor Wolfe.

Derby gave a small smile before gesturing up at the floating mirror. "I've had the luck, or misfortune, depending on your position, to witness the creation and change the Unnatural Spell has wrought." The mirror above him flickered and came to life like a movie screen. A small town, in late evening, lit by twinkling lanterns, came into view. The shops were mostly closed and deserted as the view from the mirror gazed down a raised wooden sidewalk. A woman's hand clutched a small one in front of us. Our view tilted up to look at her. The woman wore a long-sleeved white blouse and a full mauve skirt half-covered by an apron. She held a lantern aloft. Her resemblance to Derby made it clear that we were seeing his memories, and this was his mother.

"Just a bit further." Her British accent was musical and warm, though her eyes darted around. "Next time don't wander so far when you're catching frogs! You know that tonight your father and uncle wanted to try that new spell just in from Paris." Her voice scolded but her arms pulled Derby closer into a hug, and for a moment all we got to see were her skirts. "Come on then," she muttered, pulling away and setting a quick pace.

Derby and his mother passed a gentleman in a waistcoat and evening jacket, who stopped and tipped his hat.

Derby turned backward to stare at the man when his mother didn't stop. "I want a hat like that when I grow up."

His childish voice made me guess he was maybe four years old.

"Come on, we need to get home." His mother's voice was stern. The view jerked and then whirled as Derby was tugged along by his mother and swung back the other way.

A house came into focus. Though it looked just like all the other buildings on the street, Derby's eyes focused on the little clapboard three-story stuffed between two taller row houses. Clearly, this was home. A metal gate and a small garden separated the house from the sidewalk. Derby's mother dropped his hand to open the gate.

Derby dropped to a crouch to stare at a beetle crawling along the ground.

A girl's scream lanced the darkness. The sound was so piercing that even some of the guys in my class jerked in surprise. I met Zavier's wide eyes across the room. I glanced over to see Emelia still leaning forward, but now her fingers clenched around the desktop.

What kind of memory was Derby showing us? Dread filled my stomach.

On the mirrored screen, Derby's young voice called out, "Maggie!" He stood, eyes on the door of the house.

His mother yanked the gate open and started to run toward the house. Derby scrambled to follow his mother, our view bobbing up and down as he ran as fast as his little legs could take him.

His mother ran up the steps to the home, which was cast into shadow by a big tree in the front garden. She called out, "Alvin?"

A boom sounded inside the house, like heavy furniture toppling over. She tried the latch, but the door was locked. She pounded on the wood. "Alvin!"

Another crash sounded. And another scream.

Bile rose in my throat.

"Bugger," the woman cursed and dug into her skirts. "Maggie?" she yelled as her fingers tried her pockets, then her apron. "Maggie are you alright? Alvin, come get the door!"

No one answered her calls.

But a strange slurping noise started.

And the screams stopped…

Derby backed slowly away from his mother, into the bushes on the side of the house as she frantically rechecked her pockets and called out, "I forgot my key!"

We watched as Derby's small hands latched onto the white siding and wooden planks were all we could see. Each rough splinter came into focus as Derby climbed the wall of his house and grabbed precariously onto a window ledge.

My heart thrummed in my chest. My hand clenched onto the chair arm just as Derby's little hands clutched at the wall.

The sound of young Derby's struggle to pull himself up onto the ledge filled the auditorium, all of us held our breath as he peered between the curtains into the parlor.

At first, all we could see was a dull grey room, embers glowing in the fireplace from a fire that clearly needed tending.

His mother banged on the door again, making me cringe.

"Don't do it!" someone in class whispered.

But she had no choice. Her husband and child were inside. She continued to bang.

Young Derby watched the drapes flutter as a shadow entered from an open door near the fireplace. A shadow with long arms ending in claws.

"A monster," Derby breathed.

Cold sweat trickled down my neck. I wanted to look away, but I couldn't blink.

A bang and a creak sounded as Derby's mother was finally able to open the front door.

"No!" Derby cried, his head turning toward the stoop, hand extended toward his mother. He fell backward, into the bushes, as his mother was dragged into the house.

The mirror went black and then dissolved into golden specks that evaporated, the spell used up.

Silence reigned.

Professor Wolfe faced us solemnly. "My father and uncle were not successful with the Unnatural Spell. And it was so new at that time, news traveled so slowly … there were no restraints in place for those who attempted it."

No one asked what happened. It was obvious. An awkward, pity-filled silence weighed down the room for a moment before Wolfe added, "They killed sixty-seven people before they were caught."

"Caught how?" a guy asked.

Wolfe shook his head. "I don't know. They didn't keep records back then. As far as I know, they didn't even know how to kill vampires back then. That development came after the spell had become more commonplace."

"I've never seen one. How do you kill them?" one insensitive asshole asked.

The always-good-natured professor didn't seem to mind. Or maybe, after over a century, the memory had lost the sting for him. His answer was curt and factual. "Beheading. Only true method. And it must be with a silver blade. But we've gotten a bit off topic. Today, we're supposed to discuss norm and magical interactions on a much more mundane scale. This," he gestured through the air at the spot where the mirror had displayed his most horrific memory, "is simply an example to give you an understanding of the deep-rooted fear and powerlessness that a norm has when faced with a magical. It's quite similar to what a magical lower on the power scale, say a thirty or so, feels when facing an Unnatural. Or a vampire. Norms like to know who they're dealing with. It's also been known to prevent a fight or two."

"Cause we can wipe the floor with them." Grayson's lackey called out as my brain pulled up his name from the school records. Jerome.

"Exactly," Derby Wolfe's finger shot into the air. "It's an unfair fight. And it's been statistically proven that if you announce your status immediately, there's a sixty percent decrease in aggressive behavior from norm men."

"There's also a ninety percent decrease in sexy times from norm women," Zavier grumbled from next to the professor. His comment immediately lightened the mood as the class dissolved into titters.

Derby bit his lip. "Well, now that might be true for *some* of you."

A wolf-whistle went through the class. Even I participated.

"Show me your ways!" Zavier dropped to his knees and bowed, hands and forehead to the floor, earning a laugh.

"That," grinned the Professor, "is exactly what I'm going to do."

14

I LEFT the class with sore ribs. Professor Wolfe had really put on a show to drag us all away from the horror of vamps and into the absurdity of norm and magical interactions. Of course, Zavier had been the perfect pick to help him with it. The boy ate up attention like it was candy.

"Excuse me, can I get past you to grab some pickles?" Wolfe had pantomimed pushing a shopping cart.

"I prefer pickle tickles myself, but sure. Oh, by the by, I'm a magical." Zavier had winked as the class had guffawed. Wolfe didn't even bat an eye.

"Pickle tickle, is that a magical kind of pickle?" he'd asked, his British accent lending a posh feel to the naughty joke.

"Oh, it's magical for sure," Zavier had responded.

"I cannot believe they're talking like this." Emelia's face had gone white as a sheet and she'd put a hand to her mouth as the professor allowed all kinds of dirty innuendo throughout the rest of class, feigning innocence.

I'd just clutched Emelia's shoulder and laughed until tears streamed down my eyes.

Zavier and Wolfe needed to go on the road. Start a comedy show.

Zavier had to run off to Cross Country after that, because every fucking student had to participate in that class once a day, seven days a week.

"Enjoy the misery!" I yelled after him.

"It'll only be miserable because I won't be able to stare at your ass the whole run!" he called back.

I rolled my eyes as Emelia stepped up next to me.

"I've got Amulet Creation with Barron next," she said, holding up a schedule and looking confused. "Can you point me in the right direction?"

I was only three days into MAD myself, but luckily, the Academy layout was pretty simple. There were two massive gyms that sat between the girls' dorm and the guys' dorm on the north side of the campus. Above and around these buildings were trees. Lots of trees. In the middle of campus were two long, white stone buildings lined with windows and more goddamned blinds on all those windows than I'd ever seen in my life. Dr. Potts would love them. And the fact that they looked covered in dust.

Each of the classroom buildings sat on either side of a grassy quad, which was currently as dead and out of season as the damned blinds. The buildings were labeled—Building A and Building B—clearly the faculty believed in the Keep It Simple Stupid naming system. The cafeteria, library, and administration offices were all part of the same long building at the front of the school grounds. And all of it was nestled cozily in the woods where we students were made to run over pinecone strewn paths full of ankle-twisting potholes. Metamorphose was super charming like that. It was especially fun on yesterday's run when one of those damned stone lions jumped out at us, startling us as we ran. *Fucking Cross Country.*

I shook off my thoughts and glanced over at Emelia—her cheeks were nearly as red as her hair as her eyes gazed around at the blatant Bubble sales going on in the hallway in front of us. MAD students didn't give two fucks about drugs. Or detention. Most had seen the inside of the pen. Professors seemed to turn a blind eye to Bubble; it was better than Rapture, which made the jerks who took it temporarily invisible, or Elation, which made people laugh until they puked. Those sales went down in the dorms, amulets with little spells tucked inside exchanged for massive amounts of cash. Or blowies. The lack of girls at this school made BJs a hot commodity.

In addition to Zavier, whose antics were mostly harmless, I'd been propositioned about ten times a day. My threats to turn their dicks into literal popsicles made most guys back off. The fact that I couldn't actually do that since I wasn't an Icefire was completely irrelevant.

A fifth-year dude walked by, and seeing Emelia's open mouth, he winked and said, "Need something to fill that hole?"

Fucking academy guys. Even though I'd just laughed through a class full of innuendo, there was something about the way Zavier delivered his bullshit that made it silly instead of slimy. This dude did not have that gift.

"Sorry, Slim Jim, she's more of a bratwurst kind of girl," I retorted.

"Fuck off, Chess Piece," he glared at me.

Thanks, Professor Ho, thanks a fucking lot, I thought as I flipped him off and grabbed Emelia's hand. The only upside to everyone here thinking I was a Pinnacle-darling was that they wouldn't suspect me of stealing from it. "Come on. I happen to be in that class too."

"So, is it always like this?" she whispered, as we walked outside onto the dead grass and headed for the other building.

"As far as I can tell," I said, narrowing my eyes as Grayson strutted past, his arm around that curly haired bitch's shoulders. Laura, of course, mad dogged me, because women are vengeful like that. But Grayson's handsome, sculpted face had evaluated me coldly before turning away, like he was unaffected and had better things to do.

I knew better, of course. He'd been hitting up spell casters online. I'd been paying them off not to create spells for him. My eyes followed the handsome boy as he disappeared around the corner. I wasn't going to let him buy his way into beating me. He was going to have to do it himself.

When I looked back at Emelia, her green eyes studied me.

"Why are you here?" she asked.

"Cause I'm a bitch," I responded, linking our arms and leading her to Barron's class.

"Well, that's obvious. You've been nothing but mean to me."

We both giggled and for a second I felt like a normal teenage girl. But I wasn't. I turned the question back on her. "What about you? Why's your mom threatening to send you here?"

Emelia bit her lip and leaned over to whisper, "She caught me having sex."

I unlinked our arms and stepped back, hands in the air. "No! What? A teenager having sex!" I put my hand to my chest. "What's the world coming to?" I laughed.

She gave me a half-grin, but then she pressed her lips together. There was more to this story.

I tilted my head and studied her. "Okay, but still. This place is extreme."

She gave a single-shoulder shrug. I doubted she'd tell me, but maybe I could guess what kind of sex had been so outrageous a mother would threaten her daughter with reform school.

"Televised sex with someone in a furry costume?" I guessed.

She cringed and giggled, "Ew."

"You were suspended by your nipple rings from the ceiling?"

"I do have nipple rings. Now you're giving me ideas."

I busted out laughing and pulled open the door to Barron's class, which was not a big lecture hall like Wolfe's. Amulet Creation was set up like a science lab. Only sixteen students could fit at the eight stainless steel tables. Beakers and tubes crowded a countertop on the left wall. The right wall looked more like an apothecary's shop, with candles and dried herbs and flowers hanging from the ceiling. Stone mortars and pestles were stacked on the floor.

It was a weird amalgamation of science and old-world sorcery. I led Emelia over to the table in the back right-hand corner of the room and we took our seats just as the professor entered.

Though Zavier and I made fun of Huchmala, that was nothing compared to the comments that flew around school about Barron.

Leena Barron was a MILF. Even I thought she was hot. She was a blonde in her early forties who'd been a model when she was young, but then had a couple friends OD. Apparently, that "inspired her" to work with troubled youth—or so the interview she'd given in *Candid* a few years back had said. Professor Barron wore low cut shirts and had a tattoo of a dragon that curled around her breast.

Today, her white shirt revealed his head, while the flames disappeared under the rounded collar. I suspected the professor was less savory and 'savior-y' than she led people to believe; if her eyes were any indication, she had a taste for the older male students.

The guys leaned back in their seats, shirts rolled up, untucked and unbuttoned, flexing and trying to hold it like stupid ass primates. The jerkwads got away with anything in her class if they were somewhat ripped. But I shut my mouth. Because if my dad taught me one thing, it was that you don't fuck with an amulet maker. Amulets could be good, could be healing, or they could be goddamned horrific.

My eyes flickered across the posters of ancient Egypt behind the professor's desk; the place where the first magicals had surfaced. Back then, they'd made all kinds of amulets for the pharaohs. Some of those had lasted thousands of years—cursing anyone who broke into a pharaoh's tomb. Even though spell writing was more commonplace nowadays, and more revered in our fast-paced society while amulets were considered stodgy and time-consuming—inefficient—a proficient amulet maker could fuck you up. And your progeny after you.

Leena Barron started her lecture right after the bell finished ringing. She hopped up onto her desk, crossed her legs in a way that made her dark blue skirt pull tight against her thighs. Her voice was low and syrupy-sweet when she said, "This week, we're going to work on Recollection Amulets, or amulets that help enhance your memory. While these amulets aren't allowed in school and will be held in our repository until your graduation, many industries like their employees to learn more quickly and easily. A Recollection Amulet can be a valuable tool when you enter the workplace."

A guy or two nodded.

Emelia was the only one in the class who took notes as Professor Barron went through the steps to create the amulet. It would require simmering lilac and gladiolus petals in a bath sprinkled with a scorned woman's tears—because scorned women never forget. Once that solution had sat through the full moon (due to rise in four days), you had to dip your parchment strip into it, then dry it over an eternal flame that had been burning for at least a hundred years.

"How are we supposed to get access to a flame like that? The Pinnacle has all those," Emelia scoffed.

I slid my torso across the table away from Emelia as Professor Barron stared coldly at the new girl. "Excuse me, aren't you simply here for the week? Emelia Berringer?"

"Yeah," Emelia replied, fidgeting with her earring.

"Then you won't be here for that portion of the amulet creation," Professor Barron slid off the desk, smooth as silk, and flowed down the aisles to swipe Emelia's notebook. "It's so unfortunate you won't get to see it. My dear friend will be lending us his eternal flame for this project. He's a big supporter of Metamorphose graduates."

Emelia's face flamed but she kept her mouth shut as Professor Barron took her notebook. The professor sashayed back to her desk and dropped the notebook onto her desk.

"Bet that friend got his flame illegally," Emelia muttered.

I'd never looked into eternal flame, but I bet it went for a pretty penny if it was black market. Hard to hide and transport though, since you couldn't let it go out.

Professor Barron gave a wide, fake smile to the class. "Now, why don't you all go ahead and get started?" She gestured toward the dried herbs on the wall. "First one to identify gladiolus gets ten extra points on this project."

Well fuck. I was out. But it was funny as hell to watch the clueless guys in class try to fake their way through examining the flowers, each of them trying to be all secretive about searching their phones.

"Hayley, why don't you stand up and give it a shot?"

Every part of my body stiffened on being called out like that in front of the class. My eyes met Professor Barron's and her blue orbs were cold and aggressive. Her easy demeanor was gone. Dammit all to hell. She wanted to have a pissing contest? Here? Why the fuck was a professor like her challenging me? I turned to see the guys in the room also staring at me, arms crossed. Oh. It was because she had backup. Lots of it, by the look of those muscles. But why put me in my place right now? She had to know I'd just met Emelia too. Other than the naughty uniform when I'd shown up here, I'd kept my head down for the past couple days. I hadn't fucked with her or the other profs at all. She'd have no reason to hate me. Unless she was another Grayson lackey. I eyed her, trying to decide if she was working on behalf of the faculty or the Mars' billions. The urge to blind her with darkness and break her pretty nose came on fast and hard. I had to clench my fists to hold my power in.

Deep breath, I told myself. It was hard not to retaliate when I'd been screwing with faculty for years.

I glanced over at Emelia, expecting to share a sympathetic look with her. But she had an odd expression on her face. Her eyes flickered from me to a spot on the wall and back again. I glanced over at the wall, where a long-stemmed floral arrangement with a rainbow array of flowers shaped like soft stars, their points blunted, sat in an earthen vase. I quirked an eyebrow. *Who the hell knows what a gladiolus looks like? Other than a grandma who gardens?*

But, since my go-to method of humiliating professors was out, I gave it a shot. I stood and pointed to a bright orange spear of flowers.

The professor's face lit up with surprised delight.

"Brilliant, Hayley. Bring them on up."

I stood and grabbed the vase. My eyes were on Barron's, trying to decide if she was genuinely happy or just planning to extend my humiliation. That's why I didn't notice when the door opened, and someone walked in. I didn't even turn around until I felt a presence at my back. A presence that was dark and looming.

Then a voice. The voice of my nightmares.

Evan Fucking Weston reached around me and handed a slip to Professor Barron. "New transfer."

I dropped the vase.

Dammit.

15

I DIDN'T KNOW what the hell Evan had done to get transferred here so quickly. I didn't try to find out, even though he stood next to me at the table I'd been sharing with Emelia in a tension-filled standoff for the rest of class, smelling like fucking Guess cologne—a scent he'd worn for years that drove me insane. I used to steal Matthew's pillowcases after Evan slept over so I could sniff them like a freak. That memory created a knot the size of a walnut in my throat.

I almost screwed up and let my gladiolus petals boil over because of him. His presence was like a hornet sting or a chainsaw hovering over my head. It exacerbated my need to get a move on with my recruitment so I could get the hell out of this school and away from him. I avoided looking at him, didn't even let my mind ask how he'd already gotten a Metamorphose letterman jacket on his first damn day.

I ditched Emelia when the bell rang and fled the room. I was not talking to that fucker and I didn't care if it made me a bitch to my newest ally or not. Part of me felt bad about it, but the boiling hot furious part of me wanted to blame him for that, for losing me what seemed to be a new friendship. He made me so angry I got fucking illogical. And that was bad.

I had work to do. I needed to avoid him and find out where the hell Malcolm was hiding. There was no way I was letting him out of tutoring me. I ditched P.E. to find the Detonator. But he wasn't in the Spell Writing class he was registered for, wasn't in the nurse's office where I had to fake a blush and ask for a tampon and a note for gym class in order to excuse my search. I broke into his dorm room. He wasn't there either.

I took a minute to snoop, fingering his jackets where they hung on pegs on his wall and carefully checking his drawers for illegal substances. But Malcolm's room was as empty and lifeless as they come. Other than the stacked boxes of microwavable mac and cheese in the corner by his fridge and microwave, the only thing that indicated he even lived here was a framed picture of him and his mother on the desk. I picked it up, noting how pretty she was. He got his blond hair from her. But that was not fucking useful.

Dammit all!

I opened his closet, slid the doors apart, and found an entirely different side of Malcolm. Stacked inside the closet doors were at least thirty board games. I picked one up. Azul. I read the back. It was a tile game with a little bit of strategy to it. I put the box back.

"So … he likes games." That was something Dad hadn't seen, or at least hadn't remembered to report when he'd visited Malcolm's house over Christmas.

Malcolm was here, on fucking campus, according to other students I randomly stopped in the halls, like a crazy stalker. For a second, I wished he wore an ankle monitor like Zavier. It would make him easier to track down. But then it would make him a hell of a lot harder to get off campus. My mood disintegrated as I checked several guys' bathrooms and had to temporarily blind some fuckers and burn one who grabbed me in order to get them to back off the BJ talk. I let them all think I had an amulet in my pocket when I did so, because if they realized I was a Darklight then the talk would only get worse. The guys at MAD were ten times as aggressive as my prior academies.

My phone dinged with a text from my mom at lunch.

-Honey, I'm so proud!!! Why didn't you tell me? We just got the letter from the Pinnacle for your interview!!!-

She used a lot of exclamations and then three smileys. Mom never used emojis. Ever. Seeing them made me give a tiny smile, even though her excitement over my interview was the exact opposite of my excitement. She wanted me to scope out a job, but I was going to go scope out the security.

I texted her back as I ate.

-Awesome! I didn't want to tell you because it wasn't a sure thing.-

Technically, it hadn't been, though I'd known my spell writing was kickass.

-Use the card if you need to get anything for it. Suit. Shoes. Will they let you off campus to get your hair done?-

I laughed as I imagined asking Josephine Nazer to let me leave campus to get a blowout. That was gonna be a big hell no. Immediately, though, I pulled out my phone and hit buy on a couple of random items I had in my cart. A little jar of UV activated paint. Either I could use it somehow against Grayson or use it during the interview and mark a path through the Pinnacle with it. I also ordered some granola bars, dried fruit, a new set of thigh high lace socks because they looked cute ... then I went back to texting Mom.

-Doubtful I'll be able to get out of here to do my hair. I'm gonna need a flight too. What date?-

I put the date she mentioned in my planner. Eight weeks away. Over spring break. How convenient. I'd already be home in New York. I crossed my fingers and made a wish that I'd have the guys on board by then. Recon would be easier if I knew what I was looking for on their behalf.

-Gotta go to class. Love you.-

-Love you too, sweet pea.-

She called me by my childhood nickname. She never did that anymore. I had to clear my throat as I slid my phone back into my purse and navigated the crowded hallway. A fight broke out in the knot of students in front of me. Fireballs started flying. I ducked and ran to the nearest stairwell, climbing and using the second-floor hallway, taking another staircase on the far side of the building back down. Luckily, by the time I got back to the first floor, Professors Ho and Lundy seemed to have frozen the arms of the perps in blocks of ice and were dragging them off.

Never a dull day at the Madhouse, I thought as I pulled open the door and walked into Study Hall. That class was my fifth period on Saturday, and boring as all get out because no talking or eye contact were allowed. Professor Torrez, a chubby guy with a goatee, looked up from his magazine and beef jerky when I came up to his desk.

"Yes?" The gap between his teeth was full of jerky and the teriyaki smell of it made me swallow hard.

I made some dumb excuse about research to him so I could escape the scorn of Grayson-influenced classmates and go to the library.

That was where I found my quarry.

What the mother fuck? What damned delinquent student hangs out in a library? For fuck's sake.

The asshole was in a private study room, alone, surrounded by twenty ancient-looking, leather-bound books.

I yanked open the door to his study room and tromped in, thankful that the window into this room faced away from and not toward the librarian's desk—in case I needed to smack him. I studied his golden hair, his heavy-lidded blue eyes. He wore his uniform shirt tighter than most of the guys, with a narrow black tie that added a fifties vibe to his look. But, despite his wholesome appearance, Malcolm gave off a vibe that was incredibly dangerous. When those lazy blue eyes rose to meet mine, I felt like someone held a knife to my throat. My breath dried up. Just from his look. And yet, despite my brain knowing I should be scared, I wasn't. I felt high.

That heady sensation gave me the confidence to say, "You ditched me."

Malcolm didn't even offer an expression before he turned back to his books. "I don't like attention whores."

His dismissal burned. Fire lit inside my belly and spewed out in my tone. "Excuse me?"

"Challenging Laura Whitehall is a power bid. You care about the ridiculous illusion of social status here."

"I can't care about that *and* school?"

"I won't waste my time finding out."

Anger lit me up like a forest fire. He had no idea why I did what I did. And it was all for far more important reasons than attention. I slid into the seat next to him and leaned over until my chest brushed his elbow, invading his personal space. "You know, blowing things up to get yourself a magazine cover is about as attention-whorish as it gets. Guess your anarchist tendencies didn't extend to rejecting the media that props up all that power."

His brows lowered and he finally turned away from his book. His blue eyes punched me in the throat as he said, "Get another tutor."

"No."

I saw him swallow hard against some impulse when I defied him. But the swallow was all I got. No fist curl, no jaw clench. Malcolm was hard to rile. I studied his face. He was so fucking handsome that it almost hurt to look at him in real life. He was one of those beautiful people that had the potential to make you hate yourself. But instead of his beauty, it was his energy that was all-consuming. He had this dark, cold presence that made goosebumps rise on my arms and my nipples pebble under my shirt. None of the magazine articles had talked about how enchanting his presence was.

I ran my hand down my arm to stifle the cold and cover my nipples as Malcolm and I engaged in a staring contest.

I saw the stripes of blue in his eyes, the tiny freckle on his left cheek. I saw a minuscule scar under his eyebrow, one no one would normally notice.

I let out a breath, and my breath curled into a mist in front of my face. Glee filled me up like dancing champagne bubbles when I realized Malcolm was even more magnificent than I'd ever thought. An Icefire, the most common natural magic. Normally so mundane. But Malcolm's deft precision was amazing. He was using his magic to chill the air around us, to physically intimidate me and make me want to leave. *That* was his fucking presence. He was turning the condensation in the air colder, almost (but not quite) freezing it. It was a delicate balance of ice and fire at the same time. Beautiful. It was a manipulative masterpiece.

God, it made me want him. In more ways than one.

I leaned forward even further, parting my hands and letting my breasts press against his arm on the armrest. I let a bright smile cross my face when my lips were only inches from his. "I chose you. I don't want anyone else."

That got a response from him at last. Malcolm leaned back in his chair and his eyes traveled down my torso and then back up. *"You don't get to choose."*

Heat flared across my panties. Heat I knew he'd just put there with fire magic. But heat flared inside me too, caused more by his words than his magic. Because, suddenly, I knew exactly how to get Malcolm on my side. "Okay then," I relented, leaning back and then stretching, extending my hands far behind me and closing my eyes so that Malcolm could look his fill. "I'll just have to make *you* choose me."

He laughed. And it was a dark, bitter sound, like black coffee. But it was just as steamy and hot. "That's not gonna happen."

I gave a little shrug as I leaned back in my seat. "We'll see." I snatched a paper from his stack and then grabbed his pencil. I started putting dots onto the paper.

"What are you doing?"

"We'll play for it."

Malcolm paused. The aura surrounding him lightened, until I could feel the crisp dry air from the wheezing, centurion heating system again. He didn't grab the pencil away, which I took as a good sign. I'd intrigued him again.

I tried not to glance up at his face as I created our game board, twenty rows across and twenty rows of dots down. "You know how to play?" I asked.

He shook his head, smirking. "Nope."

"We take turns drawing lines to connect the dots. You can only go vertical or horizontal, not diagonal. When you get to make the last line in a box, put your first initial inside. That's your point. Whichever one of us has the most points by the end wins. Note: If you can finish one box with one line and that helps you finish an adjacent box, your turn keeps going. You can keep completing boxes one line at time until you can't complete them with a single line."

I held the pencil out toward Malcolm. He slid it out of my hand, careful not to touch me.

Hmm. Interesting.

The first few minutes passed in silence as we filled in random lines around our makeshift game board. His eyes darted to my face consistently, measuring me up in between turns. I pretended not to see him. I also pretended not to see the first box, letting Malcolm build his confidence.

Then I got a triple score. I leaned in and slid my hand over his as I gave him the pencil. "Want to concede?"

Malcolm scooted back, eyeing me. "Why do you care if I'm your tutor?"

"You're the smartest guy here."

"You aren't behind."

"I have to have a tutor. It's required."

"It's a stupid requirement. Why follow stupid requirements?" Malcolm tilted his head and focused on me, his gaze as bright and sharp as a laser.

I tried to gauge what he wanted. Tried to think of what he wanted to hear. But my stupid eyes glanced right. Even I caught it. Malcolm's eyes hardened and he anticipated a lie.

"Get out."

Fuck.

I closed my eyes and took a deep breath. And instead of trying to outwit him, I told him the truth. Part of it, anyway. "If I get kicked out of here my mother will cut me off and I'll lose the one thing I've always wanted."

"Which is?"

But I kept my eyes closed and shook my head. "I just met you."

"Fair enough."

I let out a sigh of relief, opened my eyes, and grabbed onto the seat of my chair. I squeezed it, trying to expel some of the relief flooding me. He wasn't going to kick me out. The truth had been the right choice.

Malcolm gave me a sidelong glance of amusement and tapped his pencil against the table. "You still don't need a tutor. Everyone has different degrees of control over their natural magic." He studied the sheet intensively, like a doctor about to perform an operation.

"I agree it's stupid. But I don't want to be stuck three nights a week with some dude who only knows how to make ice shanks." I rolled my eyes.

"Ice shanks can be useful."

"I'm hoping I can stay out of prison." I crossed my fingers and held them up for him. "Besides, your subtlety is so much better," I told him. "The way you make me get goosebumps..." I swallowed hard as another tingle of heat flashed between my thighs. "And *that*. I've never known an Icefire who can do that."

Malcolm's face remained impassive. He acted like he hadn't heard me. He stared at the sheet for another minute before he leaned back in his chair. He studied me. I felt like a piece of art. Like a sculpture set out in a museum. His eyes traced over me from head to toe. But not the way a horny teenager did. Not the way the other guys at school did. His eyes traced me like he was a sketch artist and he was searching out all my shadows.

It made me nervous on a level I'd never been before.

I clasped the seat to avoid shaking. My normal facade of confident bitch faded as I watched Malcolm. An awkward laugh burst out of me for absolutely no reason and my hands flew up to cover my reddening cheeks.

That's when he leaned forward with a smile, this time invading my space, forcing me to lean backward. He made a line on the page. And then another line. And another. He filled in boxes one by one, and though my eyes flitted to the page occasionally, I couldn't help but stare at him. His profile, his features, they were beyond handsome. But when I stared at him, I didn't see those things. I saw control. And concentration. I saw the rigid, upright need for honesty.

All of it made me feel vulnerable. Another flash of heat hit me, and I gasped.

I'd proposed to play a game with Malcolm.

But whatever game he was playing wasn't just on the paper.

It was something else. It was a game I was sure I'd lose.

16

Malcolm annihilated me during the dot game. And then I sat next to him in Ho's class, like a fucking starstruck nerd.

He didn't say anything, but he bit down on the tiniest grin when I stood at the seat next to his, waiting to see if he'd tell me to get lost. I didn't want to overstep and piss him off again, like I'd obviously done last class. I also wanted him to reject me and get it over with if he was gonna go that route, because we were the first into the classroom, even Professor Ho hadn't gotten here yet.

Malcolm nodded once and I slid into the seat beside him with relief, glad he wasn't sick of me yet. As I reached down to the floor to dig into my bag, I wanted to kick myself over being relieved. *What the hell is wrong with you Hales?* I asked myself.

I didn't get to answer that question, because someone kicked my arm.

Fucking hell!

I sat up and yanked my throbbing arm to my chest. I looked behind me to see Laura standing in the aisle. She sniggered down at me, her plum lipstick pursed in the universal, snotty kiss-face that bitches seemed to agree upon as their calling card. Her skirt was rolled so that it just covered her crotch.

"Grayson needs you to take on his fights for him, huh?" I asked.

Behind me, Malcolm cleared his throat. I clenched my fingers into fists and turned around to face him, frustrated. Did he seriously expect me to back down from that?

Laura's hand yanked on my hair and wrenched me backward. *Oh shit!* My hands flew to my head and a sour taste filled my mouth. I didn't recognize it until I swallowed. I'd bitten my tongue and it was bleeding. I thought she'd try to rip out my hair and let go, but I saw ice flash in her hands.

The bitch was gonna try to cut me.

I didn't have a choice. Light started to brighten my palms. Hopefully, she'd feel the burn and back off and everyone else would just think it was close range fire.

Laura growled and gasped. But she didn't back off. Dammit. I'd have to do more. The professor still hadn't come in, so I couldn't count on his help. Suspicious. Either I'd have to out myself as a Darklight or … "Dad," I whispered, trying to be subtle.

Dad materialized by Ho's desk, glancing around the classroom. As soon as he saw me, I knew today was a bad day. My heart cracked when he tilted his head and squinted, hand raising to his lips, tapping as he tried to work out that feeling of déjà vu when he looked at me.

Shit.

The ice blade reached my neck. Adrenaline spiked. I had to take low, deep breaths to counteract my racing pulse and ensure I didn't pass out. Laura left me with no choice. I had to use my power more. With one hand, I blasted Laura's hand holding the knife with burning hot white light. With my other hand, I shot darkness at her eyes.

"Argggghh," she screamed as the skin on her hand turned red, then bubbled with a second-degree burn. My light melted her blade and it soaked my chest as she pulled away and stumbled to the back of the room.

I stopped the light as soon as she moved but kept the shadows over her eyes as I swiveled in my seat.

She tripped into a low cabinet by the back wall and fell to her knees on the off-white tile floor. She started to sob as she cradled her burnt hand.

I stood and walked over to her. I held out a hand to help her up. And only then did I stop blinding her. I stared at her. "You are not my enemy. Don't become one."

Her eye makeup was smudged, and her lip twitched. I could just see her aching to lash back at me.

Luckily, Professor Ho walked in just then.

"Good evening all, sorry, I got caught up in the hall with a student question—"

I raised a brow at Laura. She'd planned her attack then. She got points for that. But she needed to save her wrath for someone else.

Ho was immediately at our sides when he saw us standing at the back. "What happened?" he asked sharply.

"Laura was trying to show me how to hold a fireball and it got a little bigger than we expected," I said, tossing on my 'sincerely regretful' face.

Ho turned to Laura for confirmation.

Her eyes flashed and then she stuttered, "Yeah. Um. Yeah, can I go to the nurse?"

Ho nodded before turning to me. "Ms. Dunemark, you've earned yourself another detention. A Sunday detention."

I swallowed the snarl in my throat and nodded. I glanced at Dad, who was wandering aimlessly around the room, trying to pick up books he couldn't touch. I wanted to tell him to disappear, but I couldn't. The room filled around us and my view of him became only the occasional glance between students as Ho started the class. I stayed trapped in the room with the memory of my father, hidden in the crowd, feeling forsaken. He hadn't meant to leave. But still, here I was, alone.

It was a sobering hour.

The only saving grace was that Dad disappeared before the final bell of his own accord. It gave me a second to collect myself before Malcolm grabbed my hand and stared into my eyes.

His hand was warm and soft and twice the size of mine.

"What you did … don't do it again. We'll talk Monday." With that vague order, he let go of me and disappeared.

I didn't know what to think. What didn't he want me to do? Fight? Defend myself? Or use my powers? I scuffed my Mary Jane against the floor as I walked to my final class of the day, annoyed at him, pissed at Laura, heartbroken about Dad. I was in a funk. And I was ready to take that out on someone.

Fencing should have been the perfect outlet.

It wasn't.

Huchmala fucking sucked as a hippie-dippie Art Therapy professor. But the old lady kicked my ass in fencing because I could never tell where she was actually looking with her weird eyes staring off to the side. I charged and screamed and thrust and all that crap and got the shit beat out of me.

It was cathartic, in a way. I didn't normally wear myself out physically. Not the way Metamorphose did. But fencing was better than running. Getting to pretend to hurt someone was better.

I didn't even want to analyze myself when I thought that as I showered and changed for dinner. I sighed and rolled my neck as I walked through the quad. With the number of showers I was taking, after daily Cross Country, P.E., and then fencing every other day … I was gonna need to order new shampoo next week. Or shave my head.

I laughed hollowly, wrung out as I headed to the cafeteria to eat dinner. My calves burned with every step. I also needed to order supplements or some kinda something or I was gonna be limping through the Pinnacle's secret passageways. I put that on my list of things to Google as I planned for my break in.

I gulped down the first half of my meal as rapidly as those wolf-shifter professors had the other day. I didn't even taste the crap they called cheese and broccoli casserole.

Once I didn't feel like I was about to fall face first into my plate, I decided to test out what I'd learned from Malcolm as I ate. I'd never thought of giving myself an aura with my powers before. But it was so fucking cool and I was pissed this was the first I'd heard of it. I put a hand out under the table as I ate, letting the shadows grow a little bit darker near me. But keeping it subtle was hard. I accidentally made a light go out near me. A couple students looked over and then I had to keep up the damned facade and make it look like the light had just burned out. That was annoying. I kept up a stream of power to zap the light as I ate a salad, wondering how long it had taken Malcolm to master the aura thing.

As I thought about him, I rubbed my thighs together. Everything about him was just damn hot. His eyes, that control. I had to force my legs apart and close my eyes. I knew I needed him and Grayson on board before I came here. But now, I didn't just need him.

No damned romantic complications, Dunemark, I scolded myself, biting into my apple. I tried to shake off thoughts of Malcolm. I pulled up my phone and messaged a hacker I knew while I ate. By the time I'd finished my apple, the guy was sending me the deets on Evan's transfer here. I shook my head as I read through them. The big furry idiot had gotten into a fight with that Medeis quarterback, the one harassing Terra. Evan was such a fool. And such a fucking stalker. I was going to have to figure out a way to take him and his hulking grizzly ass out of the picture. I sighed. As if I didn't have enough to do.

17

Sunday bitch-slapped me. I mean, who started their Sunday with a four-hour run? Idiotic movie stars who didn't have a mind, so they had to sell their body. And Professor Lundy. He forced all first year or transfer Metamorphose students to wake up at the ass crack of dawn to run.

His diabolic plan to break me almost did the job because not only did I have to run, I realized Laura Whitehall was a transfer this year too—so I got to spend the morning with her. Grayson's curly-haired hoe glared at me. She looked like shit in the morning, her normally slick curls were like a frizzy creature clinging to her head, her burnt hand was wrapped in bandages. I hoped it had bugged the crap out of her while she slept. Maybe that would make her think twice before she attacked me again. I smiled and blew her a kiss, just to help make her day a little worse. Because I'm petty like that. And if she wasn't gonna take my warnings, I was gonna push her buttons.

But fate zapped me for being a dick. I turned away from Laura only to see Evan stalking toward me. He wore rip away black pants and a black hoodie that did nothing to hide the bulk of his shoulders.

Why couldn't he just look like a grizzly bear all the time? "Why doesn't he at least keep the hair?" I grumbled under my breath. If he had nasty hairy arms, despising him would be so much easier. When Evan got within five feet, I zig-zagged through the other students like an idiotic rat in a maze. Dammit all! Was every Sunday morning gonna be torture surrounded by people I couldn't stand? I took a deep breath and decided I'd just have to use the time for planning. Lord knew I needed it because the schedule here was intense.

That's when Emelia walked up, gym shorts looking awkward on her punk rocker body. Her long-sleeved black t-shirt showcased some band I'd never heard of, who were apparently really big on broken skulls. I walked over to her with a little wave, but she turned away from me. Damn it. I deserved that for ditching her yesterday. I went over and apologized anyway.

"Look. I'm sorry. I was an ass. Evan makes me do irrational things."

"The hot guy?"

I nodded as Emelia glanced over at him. She gave him a once over and said, "Yeah, I'd be doing the opposite kind of irrational things if I was you. Why are you avoiding him?"

"Long story. Point is, he's a jerk. And I'm a jerk."

"Sounds like you're perfect for each other." She grinned.

I pointed a finger at her. "I'm about two seconds from retracting my apology."

"Fine. Accepted." She held out a hand to shake on it. I did, even though that made me feel like I was thirty.

"I'll try not to do it again, but if he comes near—"

Lundy's whistle startled me. I turned toward him, where he stood in a green beanie, looking like a Keebler elf. But the short, buff dude had lungs. "Shut your traps and give me twenty! Now!" he barked.

For a second I wondered if MAD was actually a military academy disguised as a reform school. But that second of wondering earned me five more damned pushups. Lundy was an ass. I didn't know if it was because he had Napoleon syndrome, being so short, or he was just naturally inclined to evil.

I finished, arms shaking, only to sit up on my knees and find Evan right in front of me. *What the hell?*

Lundy barked, "Stretch out. Grab the person in front of you and I want to see leg and back stretches. Go!" The whistle chirped.

Evan grabbed my wrists and pulled me toward him. We were so close his sweatshirt rubbed against my shirt. I swallowed hard, looking to the side, anywhere but at him. Someone else had already grabbed Emelia as a partner. Dammit. The only person without a partner was Laura Whitehall. Fuck it. Even she was better.

"When are you gonna forgive me?" Evan growled in a whisper when I tried to twist my wrists out of his grasp.

"Never. Thought that was obvious." When Evan wouldn't let go, I let my wrists go limp. I couldn't give into the urge to claw his face, so I shoved my anger down and recited multiplication tables, though I really thought he'd look better with a few scars. Maybe of the Potts variety.

"That's bullshit. You can't hate me forever."

"Well, it's bullshit then. But there's nothing you can do that can make me forgive you."

"I think there is." Evan's blue eyes struck mine like a lightning bolt. He pulled me forward so that I leaned over, back arched like a cat, as he sat down on the ground, still holding my wrists. He stuck his legs out on either side of mine and locked my ankles in place. Then he leaned forward and said, "Pull on my hands. We have to stretch."

My nostrils flared. But Lundy walked up behind him just then. The coach eyed me like he was just waiting for me to give him an excuse for extra punishment. I slowly turned my hands over and wrapped my hands around Evan's wrists. I hadn't touched him since my dad's funeral. Not since the hug that had made me melt like chocolate, before I knew everything. Before dad's ghost told me that Matthew's accident had happened because Evan had drunkenly dared him that night, overconfident and stupid and reckless. I stared over at Evan, his dark hair and his perfect features, and saw the future I'd once wanted. I used to picture how our babies would look so often when I was a girl that I was shocked my ovaries hadn't exploded. They'd felt like ticking time bombs. Every time I'd seen Evan, it had felt like I'd gotten one click closer to detonation.

Our eyes locked. And damn my body for betraying me, but I felt another click. That stupid chemical pull, that hormonal reaction, was still there. I'd programmed my stupid self to be attracted to Evan Weston. And apparently a decade of programming didn't just disappear. Even in the light of terrible facts. Even if I wanted it to. Feelings I thought I'd let go of swirled in my chest like tie dye, mixing with the sadness and turning it into this twisted, messy vortex. I swallowed hard.

So did Evan.

His eyes shouted things at me. But he was smart enough to keep his damn mouth shut. Because if he'd opened it, I don't know what I would have done. Something that got me kicked out of MAD, that was certain. I lowered my eyes to the dead grass and pulled up Grayson's face in my mind. *Goals. Focus on those,* I told myself, ignoring the fast pulse beneath my fingertips.

Anticipation hit me hard. Grayson hadn't retaliated yet. I'd intercepted two more of his emails to spell writers on the dark web last night. I'd even pretended to respond as one of them. I couldn't wait to see how that played out.

"What's that look?" Evan whispered, as Lundy wandered over to another group of students.

"What look?" I still avoided eye contact.

"That's your 'I've been naughty' look."

"There's no such thing as a look for that," I scoffed.

"I've known you your whole life, Hales. I know your looks."

I rolled my eyes and scoffed, dropping his wrists and sitting on the ground. "My turn." Anything to turn the tables and get on to a new topic. Evan jumped up. But instead of grabbing my outstretched hands, he stepped behind me and pushed forward on my shoulders, kneading them. Dickwad. Trying to soften me up into forgiving him. It wasn't gonna work. Still, I had to bite down on a moan. Huchmala was a bitch with her foil and she'd made me go through all kinds of 'assaults'—as she so accurately called them—last night. I'd been overeager, emotional. And now my shoulders moaned in delight. Evan's fingers trailed up my neck.

Dammit. I shoved my body down, bending in half over my legs, stretching to touch my toes, trying to get away from his fingers. I pictured Matthew's face, that horrid vampire institution. I had work to do.

"Hayley—" Evan started to say.

Luckily, Lundy blew his whistle and it was time to run. I scooted forward in the dirt and stood, brushing off my ass and making my way toward Emelia. I jogged beside her, trying to shake off whatever had just happened with Evan.

I needed to check in with Dad. I'd have to call out for him later today or tomorrow and hope he could come for a visit. I hoped his memory would be better than yesterday. Then we needed to discuss who he might know in the industry that could broker a deal for me. I could steal that serum and cure Matthew. But if I could find a lab or a scientist … find a buyer … then I'd be able to sell the serum to people who wanted to try the spell. I'd be able to use it to cure other vamps. I fell behind the pack as my thoughts grew focused and a slight mist started to fall. My skin grew soggy and I slowed further. We neared a bend in the path, and the people in front of me went around it. That's when I realized I'd become dead last.

I slowed to a walk.

I heard voices through the trees, which made me slow further. Some instinct made me crouch. Even though it was mid-morning, and not dark at all, I felt the need to stay hidden. I backed up against a tree and opened my right hand, letting shadows drift across my body.

Two figures walked past, off the path, talking in low voices. They were careful not to step on any twigs or make a lot of noise, which made me wonder what they were doing. Once I thought that they wouldn't notice, I followed along behind them and quickly realized they were some of the guards from the gate. They wore black uniforms with the idiotic Metamorphose butterfly stitched above their breast pockets.

"Fucking think they could just magic this shit up themselves," one muttered.

"Could you fucking magic up a stone deer all by yourself?" the second scoffed, halting their progress. "This is good enough. We need to get back."

"Headmaster don't want it close to the path," the first man protested. He turned, and in the dim light under the trees, I could see he was missing a tooth. "Don't want the students to see."

Didn't want us to see what? I squinted at the stone deer for a second, before I realized what the fuck a stone deer might be used for. Why students might not want to see it. I swallowed hard and tried not to make a sound as I backed away through the trees. I heard a growl in the distance.

Dammit.

Instead of trying to run, I looked around at the trees, weighing my options. Fucking all bullshit pine trees! I sprinted up a rise as the two guards ran in the opposite direction, cursing.

"They weren't supposed to let the damned things out yet! Amulet isn't set to go off for five more minutes," I heard one yell, before his voice faded away.

I spotted an oak and ran for it, heart stumbling. Damn motherfucking curiosity! I scrambled onto the lowest branch, scraping my hands so badly they bled. I hoped like hell that stone lions didn't give a shit about blood. I glanced back at the stone deer, whose body still looked like stone, but whose eyes had started to glow red. I had no idea what its insides were like. I pulled myself up a second level of branches just as the earth started to tremble.

The stone deer blinked and then suddenly ran—right toward me.

"No, you fucker!" I cursed under my breath and latched onto the tree like a toddler latches onto his mom's legs. *Fucking fuck!*

The sound of brush snapping filled my ears and felt as loud as a war drum. I fought to control my breath, my brain trying to tell my body who was in charge. My body wasn't having any of that shit. I started to close my eyes so I could meditate.

Something whacked against my tree, making my teeth clang together and send painful vibrations up my jaw. I saw a stone lion's ass charging away from me—it must have clipped the tree—and it leapt through the air, tail whacking one of the tree branches ahead and breaking it—that tail was like a damned spear.

The stone predator was too fast. The lion leapt, its stone teeth latching on to the doe. A horrible scraping sound met my ears as the lion ripped the stone animal apart, flinging boulders ripped from the deer's body in different directions. I cringed as I watched the massive stone cat chomp the deer's head, breaking the poor thing's face into bits of gravel. Tiny stones dribbled from the lion's mouth as it chewed. After eating about half of the stone deer, the lion gave a satisfied grumble, and laid down to sleep right next to its kill.

Well. At least I knew what I could do to get past the fuckers. That was something. But damn. I didn't want to be anywhere near them when they ate. Ever again.

I retreated slowly, eyes always on the lion, grateful I happened to be downwind. I took a deep breath as I returned to the path, clutching my heart. I hadn't been on the path for five steps before Lundy appeared around a bend, arms on his hips, frustration in his eyes.

"Where have you been?" he thundered.

After seeing the lions, his threats registered at about a two out of ten on the fear scale—possibly equivalent to a screaming toddler who might bite me. I simply stared at him dully for a second before I realized he expected an answer. "I couldn't breathe," I finally rasped.

His eyes narrowed but he didn't dispute anything. "Get over to the nurse then."

I nodded weakly and Lundy jogged off. Clearly, my medical issues were a top priority. Dickweed.

I stumbled back to my dorm and showered. I let the suds seep out of my hair and wondered if I was taking on too much. I was recruiting two dudes, one of whom was an asshole and the other one ... I swallowed hard. The other one knew I was a Darklight. I had to get them to agree to this crazy plan. Then we had to get past guards and lions to get out of here, break into the Pinnacle, steal the serum, and sneak back in time for Lundy to think I was just a brain-dead idiot and not a criminal.

I took a deep breath. Nope. None of that shit. No pity party. Life was hard. I just had to work harder. One step at a time. I was working on the guys. I had to be patient with that. I had time. I stepped out of the shower and realized I didn't have that much time.

I had two hours to hit up the dark web and research Tocks before my Sunday detention with Ho.

I sighed. School was getting in the way of my life. The only upside to the day was that my new panties had arrived. So I got to slide into a lacey new pair before I lounged across my bed and scrolled through my phone, answering texts from Tia, who wanted Grayson updates, and trying to find the perfect, "just released from prison and desperate for money" Tock to add to my operation—just normal, everyday teen criminal stuff.

18

I'D FORGOTTEN about my appointment with Potts. My phone rang when I was grabbing banana nut muffins from the cafeteria. As soon as I saw the video call request I cringed. Despite the morning terror in the woods, I headed back that way. It was still the most private place on campus.

I made my way to a spot where I could watch the guards at the gate. Might as well do some recon while I appeased mommy by talking to Potts. If I was gonna sneak out of here sometime next fall, which was the earliest I thought I might be able to bring these guys around, I'd need a plan to get past the gate.

Dr. Potts answered on the third ring when I called her back, looking a little unkempt, which I found surprising since she'd been the first to call. Her hair was mussed, and she was still drinking coffee. Since she wasn't taking this that seriously, I set down my iPad and took a bite of my muffin.

"Hey failure," she greeted me.

"Hey Scar," I said in response. "Planning to kill your brother today?"

She looked confused.

"Lion King reference," I rolled my eyes at her.

"Oh. Huh. I woulda' thought you were too cool for Disney references."

"Only in public."

She gave a gruff laugh. "Alright. How's the first week been?"

"Productive," I said, through a mouthful of muffin. And it had been. I was pretty certain I could convince Malcolm. Grayson wouldn't forgive me for a while. But Evan. I shook my head. He was a problem.

"What's that?" Potts wouldn't let me get away with anything. "What's that head shake mean? What are you thinking about?"

"Nothing."

"I've got cat videos this week. Not just pictures."

I sighed. "Fine. This guy I hate just transferred here."

"Ohh, I sense gossip. Let me refill my coffee so I can pay good attention." The video wobbled and showed bits of sky and ceiling and a furry patch that I sincerely fucking hoped was one of her cats and not—

"Okay! Ready!" Potts set the iPad on her end down on a table or something. My view of her was still slightly askew, but it was steady at least. She held up a coffee mug shaped like a toilet bowl and took a sip.

I cringed. "Seriously? How can you drink from that thing?"

She chuckled. "It was my Christmas present to myself. Nobody steals your coffee mug when it looks like a toilet full of liquid—" She tilted her cup so I could get a full view of the interior.

I set down my muffin. "Now I'm not hungry."

"Good," she countered. "That's less I have to wait for you to talk."

How could she be so annoying and endearing at the same time? She reminded me of Zavier. "There's a guy here who's just like you," I told her.

"Not today. Today I want to hear about the guy you hate. Deets. Gimme."

I sighed and picked a berry out of my muffin. "Fine. He's ... he was Matthew's best friend."

"Ah." Potts leaned on her hand and stared sympathetically at me on the screen. "He made the change, didn't he?"

I nodded, turning away from the pitying look on her face to stare out at the trees. "And it was all his fault."

"His fault?"

"His idea."

Potts took a deep breath and let it out. "You know, the guys that made it through that night I was there?" She didn't specify, but I knew she meant the night she observed the Unnatural spell. "Two of the three of them committed suicide."

I sucked in a breath and stared back at the screen. "What?"

"Survivor's guilt. It's a real thing. When you know you didn't deserve to make it through any more than the next guy." She shook her head. "Especially with all that new talk about vamp security."

"What about the other guy? The third one." I asked, searching for anything to think about but *that*. I didn't want to picture *that*. Didn't want to picture Evan doing *that*. I just wanted him to go away. I didn't want him to die.

"The other guy ... well, I fuck his brains out every now and again, so I think he's doing okay." Potts winked at me with her good eye.

"Are you trying to give me an eating disorder? Because seriously, between that mental image and your coffee cup, I don't think I ever want to eat again."

"Your loss."

"My loss is your loss. Because if I starve then mommy's not gonna pay you."

One of Potts' cats jumped onto her lap and she ignored me for a solid minute before turning back to our conversation. "All I'm saying is, hate him with a little bit of discretion. No matter what he did, he's hurting inside. Just like you. And unlike you, you nasty little spitfire, he's got a whole lotta self-loathing mixed in."

My face closed down. I did not need this woman to tell me to be nice to Evan Weston. That was never gonna happen. "Is the hour up?"

"Not yet. I get to torture you a bit longer," she retorted. "I'm thinking about getting a new cat. There's a guy down the road who found some feral kittens. Was thinking about naming one Marlowe. After Christopher Marlowe."

"Who?"

"Don't you read the classics at the rich-kid school?" Potts took another sip of coffee. "He wrote Doctor Faustus. That play about selling your soul to the devil."

"Hmm." I stared down at my nails, which were starting to chip. I doubted MAD would give me a pass to leave campus for a manicure.

"You know, the moral of that play is that a guy thinks he's getting what he wants … but he's not. He doesn't realize the cost …" Potts kept talking, but my thoughts drifted away, and my responses started to go auto-pilot. One lecture a day was my limit and I wasn't ready to deal with another. If Potts was going for a one-two punch, she was swinging at the air because I'd already lain down and gone to sleep.

Mentally at least. My answers became a random mix of the following: "Yes." "Mm-hm." "Sure."

"Great!" Potts yelled into the phone. "I'll tell your mother you asked for me to come down there and meet you in person! Next weekend's meeting will be so much better!" Then she broke into song, this ridiculous seventies number that my dad used to sing to us: *So Happy Together*.

I just stared at her dancing around for a minute before what she'd just said sunk into my brain. "No. Wait."

"Too bad kid. You're my ticket to a free vacation. I have it all on video. You said yes. I'm not letting you ruin it for me."

I rolled my eyes. "If you come down here and lecture me ..."

"Then I'm doing what Mommy paid me for. Getting you off this crap track you're on ..."

I hung up on Potts, closing the tablet. I wasn't on a crap track. I was on the right track. I wasn't making a deal with a single devil. I was recruiting a whole team of them. And if they wanted my soul, so fucking be it. I didn't need my soul. I needed my brother back.

I ate breakfast.

Then I served the world's most awful detention. I had to plant twenty-five new trees with the groundskeeper because the stupid stone lions kept knocking entire trees down when they clawed them like kittens.

My arms were shaking by the time I reached Sunday's midday P.E. class. I almost cried when Coach Blafield, a woman with a man's haircut, told us we were playing croquet. My hands couldn't do it. They were raw because the groundskeeper wouldn't let me wear gloves to dig and they shook from holding the same position for an hour and a half. When I tried to clutch the mallet, I couldn't. I ended up kicking my ball whenever the Coach wasn't looking.

It earned me dirty looks at first, but soon the other girls in my group were doing it too. Because seriously, croquet was for old people who like spiked lemonade and gingersnaps. As soon as that torture was over, I stumbled to the cafeteria. I hadn't eaten enough in the morning. I had two sandwiches and a couple glasses of orange juice, sitting at a table all by myself.

And willing or not, Potts' words started to roll around in my head. Ugh. I didn't need that. I tried to shove them away, but melancholy followed me, dogging my footsteps just like Evan did.

I grabbed an armful of fruit to take with me, since my feet ached, and I didn't want to have to come back across campus for a snack. Then I headed back to my room, ready to wallow in self-pity and make a list of every reason I was justified to hate Evan. I waved weakly at Zavier when he tried to flag me down from where he stood in line.

"Project," I called out to him. It was a lame excuse and it earned me some weird stares. Two jerkwads at a table near the door tossed food at me.

"Kiss ass," one of them said.

I shrugged, staring down at him and his eyeliner. "I'm working on the next spell I need to put Grayson in his place."

The guy's hand froze, spoonful of yogurt ready to launch. "Well, alright then." He shoved the spoon in his mouth instead, proving not everyone cared for Richie Rich.

Zavier bounded over to me, finally abandoning his place in line. "Can I help?" he asked, an eager glint in his eyes.

I shrugged. "Grab your own food though. I don't have anything in my room."

Of course, the kitchen staff loved Zavier in a way they'd never love another student. He held up a finger to tell me to wait, then ran over to whisper to the lunch lady. He came back with a Tupperware container filled with lasagna.

"I didn't see lasagna in the line," I said, as he grabbed two napkin rolls filled with utensils from a crate by the door.

"They made it for the staff." He winked at me and I couldn't help but laugh.

I stared up at him in grudging admiration and he preened. I'd never seen a person do it before, but Zavier literally puffed up when I said, "Damn Midas. You've got the golden touch."

His eyebrows lifted. "Oh, I do. Girls say so all the time. And I'd love to prove it to you."

"I'd love to prove you're mentally defective. Your horny brain has taken over all your other senses." I pushed open the door and we walked outside into the brisk pre-dusk winter air. It wasn't raining yet, but the clouds looked droopy.

"I wish *you'd* take over all my other senses," Zavier grumbled as we headed past building A to the girls' dorm.

I quipped, "I'm trying to talk *sense* into you. Doesn't that count?"

"Well, why are you so *sensitive* about sex?" he asked. "Why can't we play hide the baloney?"

I burst into trumpet-like, snort-filled, highly unattractive laughter.

"You're full of baloney," I wheezed.

"You could be too," he grumbled, sticking one rolled utensil set in his pocket and unwrapping the other to unleash the fork. He put the rest of the packet into his pants pocket and then opened the lid. He began to eat steaming hot mouthfuls of lasagna as we walked. He ate so quickly I wasn't sure he could even taste anything. It looked more like a gulp and swallow technique.

"You eat like a dog."

He howled at the sky. Then he paused to lick sauce off his lips. He pointed his tongue and licked slowly, lapping at a bit of sauce that had dripped just off his lip onto his chin. His tongue couldn't quite get the right angle.

"Hold still," I said. I rolled my eyes and leaned up on my tiptoes, swiping the mess with my finger. For some stupid reason, I made eye contact with him. And Zavier's normal smirk disappeared, his eyes traveling the length of my face. Something strange happened to his expression. Or so I thought. But at that moment, the sun broke through between two clouds and light shone right into my eyes, blinding me.

"Ahh!" I reached my other hand up to shield my eyes.

Naughty Zavier took advantage and swooped down to suck the sauce off my finger. His tongue played against my fingertip, swirling and flicking.

"Zavier," I warned.

He didn't stop. And though I should have pulled my finger away from him, I couldn't. For some reason, I was stuck there, captive, until he released me when he blinked.

I glanced over at Zavier a few seconds later. I felt weird after the look we'd shared, like it had somehow messed up our light-hearted vibe. I verbally tried to stumble back to normalcy. Or the version of normalcy that Z and I had developed over the last week. "So, what's with the tattoos? Any of them mean something?"

"Bedpost notches." He grinned. He yanked down on his shirt, to reveal a bare spot on his swollen, muscular left pec. A pec he clearly waxed in order to showcase that hot body art. "But look, I left a spot just for you. Right over my heart."

I suppressed the urge to step forward and lick my spot like a five-year-old so no one else could have it. Instead, I rolled my eyes. "You are seriously so thoughtful. Now, would I get to choose the mark that you put there in my honor?" I touched my fingers together in the stereotypical 'scheming villain' pose.

He released his shirt and tossed his head back to laugh. "I can only imagine what you'd choose."

"How about ... a squished banana? A small, bruised—"

His hand flew to his junk. "My banana is thick and ripe. And delicious."

"You like banana? You taste banana regularly?"

He poked his fork at me. "You're bananas if you think I eat bananas."

Dammit, I was hoping I'd stump him. I chewed on my lip and scanned over his sleeves once more. He had a couple faces, some trees and a moon, a pocket watch, a wolf.

"Or maybe some text? Some text that's scrolly and fun and says, 'I'm a yellow turtle in a green canoe.'"

"What the hell does that even mean?"

"You'd have your entire life to figure it out. You'd get to stare at it day after day ..."

"Vicious! I'm gonna Google it later."

"You do that." I'd just pulled the saying out of my ass, but it was fun watching Zavier's face search mine and then stare off into the distance, pondering what the nonsense sentence meant. When he bit his lip, I had to turn away, because I had a sudden urge to do the same thing.

Z took another bite of his lasagna as he said, "I think an elephant raising his *long, thick trunk* to the sky would be a better image, don't you?"

"Nope," I deadpanned, though my eyes glittered with mirth. "You're definitely not an elephant. Though ... are you telling me your dick is grey and wrinkled?"

"Maybe," he closed his lasagna container and bounced around me, reminding me of a living breathing Tigger. "You'll have to see to find out."

I shoved his shoulder and Z nearly tripped into a guy playing a guitar on the grass. The hippie vibe from the dreadlocked guy on the grass was ruined when he pulled out a pocketknife and took a swipe at Zavier.

My guy had reflexes like a cat, though, and jumped out of the way in the nick of time. Zavier reached back and grabbed my hand, yanking me forward and away from the violent hippie.

"Don't mess with Stanley," Zavier warned once we were thirty feet away.

I glanced back at the guy, who'd gone back to tuning his guitar, his open knife on his knee for all the faculty to see.

"Why not?"

Zavier shook his head. "He got beat in the head a few too many times in the pen. He won't hesitate."

"You got away."

Zavier shrugged, a red stain crawling up his neck. He toed the ground. "Let's just say I'm glad he took a swing at me and not you."

"Why? Cause I would have kicked his ass?" I raised a brow.

"No, because I would have been forced to step in to—"

"I can handle myself," I interjected, a bit offended that he'd try to play knight.

"But dirty friends always defend one another to the death." Zavier made a 'duh' face at me.

"I thought dirty friends were only hit it and quit it friends."

"Well, *yeah*, until one's facing death. Then it's until death do you part. That's dirty friend code. You break it, you'll never find a dirty friend again. Word will spread and your dirty rep will be ruined forever. You'll have to have—*ew*—real relationships."

His face was the most serious I've ever seen it. His jaw was tight, his eyes focused. He was trying so hard to repress the laugh bubbling inside of him.

"I'm gonna need to see the dirty code. I didn't realize the rules were so extensive." I tried to imitate his face, but I couldn't hold it. I started to giggle.

"Your laugh makes me want to tickle you until you scream," he said.

"Your face makes me want to scream."

"As long as you're screaming my name, I'm happy."

"I don't think your dick's been less than 'happy' a day in your life."

"He was unhappy the day you denied his claim."

"His what?"

"Dick claim. When your dick points at something, it's claiming it."

"What if your dick points at a machete?"

"My dick would *never* do that." Then he crouched forward like a little old man with a fork for a cane. "Didn't anyone teach you about dicks young lady? They have a sense of self-preservation."

God, this guy was so preposterous. His mind was like a unicycle, entertaining to watch and at the same time, it just left me asking 'why?' I had to cover my eyes for a moment because even though I was mentally recording this moment for future playback, I just couldn't believe what I'd heard.

"Okay, new topic," I announced, searching for something to ask about. Zavier's ankle monitor blinked blue and I stared at it. "How'd you get that?" I asked.

Zavier straightened and sighed. "It's a long story that involves my ass of a cousin."

We reached the door of my dorm building and I swiped my wand over the scanner to unlock it. Zavier held it open for me.

As I ducked under his arm and we entered the girls' lounge on the first floor, I said, "Well, we'll be in my room, alone, on my bed ... what better to do than have pillow talk?"

He gritted his teeth together and stared up at the foam tile ceiling in the front hallway. "Why must you torture me?"

"You started it," I pointed out. "If you hadn't hit on me so hard—"

"I was trying to hit you hard enough to turn your head—"

"You mean to *get head*."

Zavier stepped inside and let the front door slam shut behind him. "You're the best flirty friend I've ever had," he said softly.

I couldn't see his face at all, my eyes were adjusting to the dim interior. But I felt sure he was joking. Zavier was always joking. I tossed my hair and said, "I'm wonderful, it's true. But I'm sure you say that to every flirty friend." I started up the staircase toward my room.

"Okay, fine," he hurried after me. "I might say it, but I don't mean it."

"Are you ever serious?"

"Yes."

"When?"

"I'm serious about getting you into bed."

I shook my head and walked in silence until I made it to the third floor and my room, which was at the very start of the hall. "I'm probably gonna end up pulling your hair out or spelling you to have a giant rash someday."

"As long as you spare my dick."

"Why would I do that?"

"Remember, he chose you. That's special."

"That's about as special as the special sauce at McDonalds, which they hand out to everybody."

"My dick's insulted. He's shaking his head at you." Zavier swung his hips side to side.

I reached my door and banged my head into it several times. "Why am I such a glutton for punishment?" Why was I hanging around Zavier at all? Why wasn't I avoiding him, focused on my pity party and my goal? Why did I let him tag along like the Pokey Little Puppy?

Zavier's hand reached out before I could smack my head into the door one more time. "Hey, now, enough of that. You're a glutton because you can't get enough of me." He slid my key out of my hand and unlocked my door, letting himself into my room.

I stood in the hall and watched him go inside, glancing around at my bare walls before heading to my dresser. He set down his food on the bare dresser top and pulled open a drawer. Then he rifled through my things. He had absolutely no respect for my privacy. But I didn't stop him. I just watched as he pulled open my underwear drawer and slid his finger through a bra strap, lifting it to check the size on the tag. When he realized I hadn't come into my own room, he dropped the bra back in the drawer and walked back to get me.

I shook my head as I stared up at him. "But why?" I was still stuck on our earlier topic. Why did I let him annoy me and razz me and touch my underthings?

Zavier grabbed my hand and gently pulled me inside, shutting the door softly behind me. He snicked the lock into place. And then he hugged me to him, softly stroking my back before he answered. But when he did, molehills became mountains, splinters turned into trees, drops became oceans. "I like you because you're quick-witted and hot as fuck but not obsessed with your looks. I like you because my chest does a happy dance when I see you."

My heart felt like it was sparkling. Like it was a diamond and it had just been pummeled with light and rainbows were streaming out of it. Then Zavier leaned down and whispered into my ear in his dirty, flirty voice, "You like me, because you're the saddest girl I've ever known. And I make you laugh."

I sucked in a breath. How did he know? How did he see that? No one ever saw the real me. The masks, the bitch face I wore, the clever little quips—everyone only ever recognized the surface level, things I chose to show them. How had Zavier, Mr. Fluff and Tease, Mr. Playful—how did he know?

For once, Zavier didn't laugh or bounce or giggle. He didn't make crazy eyes at me. He stroked my hair with his hands and folded me into an even deeper hug, like he was trying to crush me.

I felt like a piece of laundry that had been drying outside, cold and wet and caught in a time warp from a different era, flapping in the wind—completely exposed to the elements. But when he put his arms around me, he pulled me off that tight, thin rope I'd been clinging to and instead, I clung to him.

The silence stretched out, an admission in and of itself on my part. But I let it stretch too long. Because I didn't know what to say. Yes, I liked him. More than liked him. But … I was me. I wasn't this girl who fell for guys. I was someone on a mission. And I didn't know what to say without hurting both of us.

Then, like always, Zavier's silly side returned and ruined the moment. "Grab the phone and call Emelia. We'll make it a threesome."

I smacked him.

He curled away, lifting his hands and one knee in the air defensively. "Hey! Hey! I meant for movie night! Let's ditch the tournament and hang out here!"

"Can we ditch the Sunday tournament?" I asked. It appeared like a course on my class schedule.

"Well ... depends on how naughty you feel like being."

I narrowed my eyes. I didn't have time to mess around and get on the shit list of all the professors here.

Zavier sighed. "Fine. We'll go to the tournament. But I expect a naughty pillow fight after."

I grabbed my phone out of my purse. "You keep dreaming about that."

Zavier walked over and plopped down on my bed. He snuggled my pillow. "Oh, I will."

19

WHEN WE WALKED into the big gym for the tournament, I hardly recognized it. Blue lights lit the walls and gave everything a strange spacey-looking vibe. The bleachers were pulled out and full, and professors roamed the wooden basketball floor. The goals were gone. Instead, what looked like a giant glass sphere, fifteen feet in diameter, was suspended twenty feet in the air. My eyes flickered over it, and the two silver ladders on opposing sides that rose to a platform just beneath it.

I'd heard the tournament was a brawl—Zavier had explained that much on our walk over. Everyone was required to fight twice a semester. But most of the fights were done by volunteers—guys who wanted to get out their aggression. The tournament had similar rules to cage fighting—no eye or nut shots, permanent injuries, all that. I saw two mean-looking guys at the base of the ladders. Each wore a black outfit similar to a karate kartegi and one golden, magical-repression glove on their right hand.

"They're only supposed to use their left hand to create magical shields," Zavier explained, when Emelia asked about the gloves. "But everybody cheats."

I looked up again at the glass bubble.

"Seems like they'd crack that thing."

Zavier chuckled. "Nah, it's reinforced. And the sphere has gravity all around, so that competitors can walk up the sides, or even fight upside down. First couple times you see it, it's pretty cool. But after you fight in there …" he shook his head. "I don't like to watch it as much."

I glanced over, wondering why that might be. But Zavier's eyes were on the competitors climbing the ladders. When his face turned back toward me, he was in silly mode again.

"There's more," Zavier waggled his eyebrows. "But I won't ruin the surprise."

Emelia started to climb the stairs to find a seat, but Zavier grabbed her by the back of her collar. "Nope. We can't sit there."

She reversed and came back down, her tongue ring clacking against her teeth as she asked, "Um, why?"

Zavier steered us farther into the gym before he answered. "That's where the Zoo sits."

Emelia's eyes immediately widened. I leaned around Zavier so I could look at them. I'd researched all the individuals here, but their files didn't necessarily give their gang affiliation.

The Zoo was a gang made of Unnaturals who did major weapons and drug runs through the Midwest. I eyed the five students who sat huddled together. They all looked like fifth years, but other than that, they were different as could be: a blonde girl, a skinny Asian dude, two black guys and a Hispanic guy. All of them wore navy colored shirts. And the way that they sprawled out in their section showed they had utter confidence.

"The Zoo always sits on the northeast side. Fangs sit on the southwest." Zavier said as he put his hand on my back and helped me up the bleachers to a spot at the top. We sat and I looked around. We had a good view above the floating net here, but not the best view of the opposite side of the gym. I had to twist and crane my neck to try to see the Fangs. Other than vague forms, I couldn't really make out faces.

"They're the all-wolf gang, right?" Emelia said. "I read an article that said they have a commune and a huge wooded area not too far from here." Emelia's face scrunched as she tried to remember.

"I dunno. I just know to stay out of their shit here. Zoo, Fang, or Crush—stay away." He'd named off Grayson's gang in that mix. The motorcycle gang rumors were true, then. Zavier grabbed a lock of my hair and started to twirl it. He leaned into me and changed the subject. "If you get scared, feel free to clutch onto my massive biceps."

I laughed. Hard. Until tears came to my eyes. When I repeated what he'd said, Emelia laughed too, until Zavier got pouty.

"I think I'm gonna go sit where my biceps are more appreciated." He huffed and moved down a couple rows but glanced back with a fake pout that let me know he wasn't really hurting. Of course, he ended up sitting right next to Evan—that was just my luck.

They laughed together—of course, they did. Zavier could make friends with anyone, the big jerk. The guys glanced back at me and then bowed their heads and started talking earnestly. If it was just Zavier and some rando, I'd have sworn he'd done it on purpose to make me paranoid. But with Evan … there was a lot of shit Evan could tell him about me, like the time I puked all over the back seat after we went to Haunted Flags, the magical theme park. My inner gossip peaked around the corner wielding binoculars, tugging on my shoulder and making me wish I had time to write an Eavesdropping Spell.

Emelia sighed, rubbing her stomach after all the laughter. "He's something else," she said, gesturing at Zavier.

"Right?" I shook my head. "I've never met anyone more ridiculous."

She sighed. "I've met a few crazies, but none quite so amusing. It's too bad he's got a record."

I glanced down at him. That wasn't something I could judge him for, because pretty soon I'd have my own. But I glanced over at Emelia. "So, you like the good boys then?"

She shrugged, and opened her mouth to answer, but just then, the *Space Jam* theme song started to play—because I don't think any school has updated its 'pep rally' music since CDs were a thing.

The competitors reached the platform just below the sphere. They stood facing each other until the cheesy music faded. And then a trapdoor on the bottom of the sphere opened and they both used their arms to lift themselves inside. The trapdoor closed and sealed itself just as two red-tinted spotlights came on and outlined the students.

The guys bowed to each other. And then, somewhere on the floor, a professor blew a whistle.

The first punch echoed through the loudspeakers and made me cringe. *Shit!* They must have had that sphere magically hooked to the sound system. Around me, my classmates roared.

"Go Julian! Fuck him up!"

"Come on Chris! Get him!"

The blows went back and forth. Punches, kicks, sideswipes. My heart raced a mile a minute and my stomach twisted. I was not a fan of this level of brutality. I kept expecting the professors to call it off. But, other than Emelia, who stayed quiet and pale beside me, the other students were standing, screaming, roaring encouragement.

And then something strange happened. The side of the sphere closest to me flickered orange in the middle. Immediately, both the fighters froze, pitch black outlines highlighted by red spotlights. The guys stared at the orange light on the sphere. Then they sprinted for the opposite side. They ran up the wall just as the orange color burst into magical flames.

"Shit!" Emelia jumped in her seat and clutched my arm.

I was just as surprised, but I'd had more practice hiding my emotions. My eyes widened, but that was my only tell.

"Why do they have something like that at a school!" Emelia said, retracting her hand and pawing nervously at her bright red hair. "That should be illegal. What if they got burned?"

I shook my head. So far, Metamorphose didn't follow any of the rules that my previous academies had. As far as I could tell, these professors couldn't be bought, and they seemed to get a twisted sort of pleasure out of punishment.

I glanced down at the gym floor. Huchmala was smiling up at the circle, where the competitors were now punching each other even though they were sideways. Professor Barron looked like she was hot and bothered by the two males pummeling each other. Only Professor Ho looked bored, probably because he was mentally critiquing every move they made.

The flames dimmed and students around us yelled, "Boo!" but only seconds later, a blue light flashed directly under the competitors' feet. One guy—Chris—saw it. Julian didn't. The first guy sprinted up the side of the bubble until he was hanging upside down like a bat. His feet were firmly planted on the top of the bubble, but his long hair floated up around him.

Next to me Emelia gave a little squeak. "The gravity must be inverted. Instead of pulling in, it pulls out to each of the edges."

I started to ask what that meant but the blue light flashed and suddenly half the dome was covered in ice. Julian slid, arms pinwheeling. That's when Chris leapt down, jumping onto Julian's back. I expected him to pummel the other guy into submission, but Julian flipped their bodies so that he was on the bottom, sliding on his back along the ice. And then he tossed Chris into the air—as if the two-hundred-pound dude weighed nothing.

I hunched my shoulders and squinted, waiting for the moment that Julian would roll to the side and Chris would fall back down, landing smack on his back. But Chris didn't fall. He just floated, suspended, unable to move in the center of the sphere.

The whistle sounded again. And the screaming cheers started. "Fuck yeah! Julian!!!"

Zavier goaded the group near him into pounding their feet and chanting "Juli-an! Juli-an!"

The ice disappeared from the sphere, and I watched Professor Ho wave his hands. Chris was slowly lowered to the bottom of the sphere. When Chris stood up, the trapdoor opened, and the contestants descended.

Emelia turned to me. "Well, that was terrifying. So, what did you do today?"

"Stupid counselor appointment."

"Yeah? Is it because of your dad?" she asked.

My sense of indignation flared. I turned to stare at her. "Excuse me?"

"I mean, his death was kind of a big deal in the news. I don't know." Emelia played with her lip ring. "Never mind. Sorry."

I sighed and leaned back against the empty bleacher seats behind me, propping my elbows up on them. "Yeah. I guess it kinda is because of him." I didn't mention Matthew.

"Your mom remarried, right?"

"Stalk me much?"

If Emelia's cheeks had gotten any redder, I could have stuck her in an apple orchard and called her a tree. "Sorry. I looked you up this afternoon."

"Don't do that," I scolded. The idea of someone prying into my life gave me the creeps. I did it myself all the damn time. But that was different. That wasn't for stalker reasons. Then again, Emelia was only here for a week. It's not like she had to take the threats about going camping out in the wilderness of campus (Metamorphose's version of in-school suspension) seriously. What the hell else was she supposed to do with a relatively free Sunday afternoon?

I looked over and realized she was studying my face. So, I shot her an answer. "Yeah, my mom remarried. And I hate the guy."

"My parents are divorced. Dad remarried," Emelia admitted. "But I kind of like her. She's less crazy than my Puritanical mother."

"You're lucky. Claudia's the worst." Even the thought of him made me suppress a shudder. I almost moved to touch the wound that was still healing on my stomach. But I resisted. No one needed to know about that.

"Your mom married a girl?" Emelia looked very confused.

"Nah. I call him that to piss him off," I explained as two new competitors started to climb the silver ladders.

"I like Laurie so much I call her Mom most of the time. I try and stay over there as much as possible."

I cringed. "I'll never call the Clod that. I keep waiting for the day my mom sees sense and divorces him." I said that out loud, but I didn't really believe it. Mom was too broken to love herself anymore. Too broken to love me. I doubted she'd ever leave Claude. I stared glumly up at the two new competitors as they were sealed into the fighting bubble.

"What if she doesn't?"

I didn't want to think about Claude the asswipe-cheater any longer. I didn't want to deal with it. So, I asked, "What exactly got you sent here?"

Emelia blinked hard for a second before she lowered her voice and said, "My mom found out I had two boyfriends."

"You were dating around? So?"

"Not exactly. She caught me with them both, at the same time."

I turned to face forward, keeping my face neutral. But inside I burned with curiosity. What was it like? Was it good? Was it hot? My eyes traveled over the crowd, which was filled mostly with guys. If Emelia's mom wanted to scare her off having threesomes, this was not the place to send her daughter. MAD's guy to girl ratio made it the perfect breeding ground for female fucking harems. I'd never considered the idea before… but it had merit. After all, guys thrived on competition. And if they were competing for orgasms, how hard would they work? It was definitely something to consider. Not that I had time to consider it right now. I was way too busy.

"So, like, why are you here?" Emelia asked. "And what's your plan after you graduate?"

I opened my mouth to spout off a bullshit answer, but just then my right arm lifted and flipped my hair. *What the hell?* I stared at my hand. I hadn't meant to do that. My left arm lifted and did the same thing, flipping my hair. Then my right gave a giant flip. My left arm smacked Emelia as it rose again. My eyes went wide. Snickers floated over and I looked to see Grayson and his posse about twenty feet away, all their eyes focused on me. My arms started to pinwheel and I had to stand so they wouldn't hit the bleacher seats. I almost pitched forward. Only Emelia grabbing my back saved me.

More eyes turned to watch me as the staff continued to reset the floating orb and get it ready for the next round.

"Dammit. Grayson did this," I told her. *How am I gonna write a spell to unravel this if my arms won't stop?* My eyes must have shown my panic to Emelia.

She dug into her backpack and pulled out a notebook. "I'll try and write something to unravel it. But it might take a minute."

"Hold up," Zavier's voice cut across her. His arm came forward and held me by the waist. He ignored the fact that his new position made me smack him as my arms rotated.

Evan took the notebook out of Emelia's hands and glanced up at me. His blue eyes were analytical as he looked me over. "I got this. But I didn't bring my wand. Hales—"

I nodded frantically, nearly pitching forward again. Only Zavier's arms wrapped around me kept me in place.

Laughter started to echo across the gym as more students noticed. I didn't care, my attention was focused solely on Evan as he scribbled quickly on a roll of parchment, faster than I would have thought possible. The parchment smoked and burned and then a glittering blue magic swam through the air and encased my arms.

They stopped pinwheeling and I sank into Zavier's chest, breathing a sigh of release. My shoulders ached. "That fucker," I growled into Z's shirt. His arms rose and gently started to massage my sore shoulders without being asked.

I turned my head to look at Evan, whose face was strained, even though he should have been relieved. His jaw was tight.

"Thanks," I told him, a bit grudgingly. Damn Grayson for making me turn to my worst enemy.

Evan gave me a sharp nod, then started to put away my things. He immediately headed down the bleachers toward the floor. I watched him go, my brow furrowed.

"Hayley, you could be a little nicer, don't you think?" Zavier whispered into my hair so that Emelia couldn't hear.

I shook my head as I sat back down, rotating my sore shoulders, trying to shake them out. "He's part of the reason my brother's a vamp."

Zavier picked me up and sat me on his lap. "You don't mean that." He petted my hair. "Nobody can force anyone else to write the Unnatural spell."

I burrowed my face into Zavier's neck. "Can we discuss something else please?"

"You know he's in love with you, right?"

I pulled back and punched Z in the chest. "Don't say that."

Z rubbed his chest and mock pouted. "You hurt me!"

"I didn't hit you that hard, you baby."

"Kiss it and make it better, or I'm leaving," Z lifted his shirt. Holy abs! His entire torso was a work of art. And not just with the tattoos. His chest was like a magnet.

"Didn't you just tell me some other guy was in love with me? And now you want me kissing on you?"

Zavier shrugged. "You can love more than one person at once."

I leaned back. "I do *not* love you."

"Yes, you do." He leaned in and rubbed his nose against mine in one of those obnoxiously cute, coupley ways. "You wuv me wots and wots. Now kiss it, Dunemark. Make it bettuh."

Why did he have to be so damn cute? Why did his chest have to look like the sex equivalent of an ice-cream cone? Irresistible. I leaned forward and pressed my lips to the bare spot over his heart.

"Yeah baby, that's it!" Zavier moaned.

I leaned back and smacked him with a laugh. "Put your shirt down."

The sight of Evan coming out of the guys' locker room, dressed for combat made me freeze and I lost whatever humor Zavier's playfulness had ignited. Zavier settled me onto his lap, and I didn't even notice when his hands settled on my thighs.

My eyes followed Evan as he walked toward the ladders. Unlike the other competitors, who'd worn black, Evan wore some ridiculous gold-colored wrestling suit that was skintight. Everywhere.

Around me, people started laughing. Emelia and I looked at each other, confused. She asked Zavier, "Why's he dressed like that?"

"Newbs who fight have to wear that shit," Zavier answered.

Emelia stared over at me, disbelief etched on her face. "This school! I can't believe the stuff they do. This should be illegal."

More than the crap that the Metamorphose staff got away with, I couldn't believe that Evan actually pulled that suit off. He didn't look like an idiot. He looked like some goddamned fucking Greek statue dipped in gold. Fucking asshole. His eyes met mine. Of course, they did. Because after Potts' had planted bullshit thoughts in my brain, and after Zavier had said what he'd said ... I was obviously gonna be tortured, not just by Evan's presence, but by stupid niggling doubt.

"Why's he fighting?"

Z just looked at me and shook his head, pity stretching across his features.

I turned away from the tournament, away from Evan's bright blue eyes, with Potts' words about survivor's guilt and dark paths ringing in my ears.

"You know he's in love with you right?" Zavier's question scratched at the hole in my chest.

I couldn't think, couldn't deal with it.

I climbed off Zavier's lap and grabbed my backpack.

"Hey, we were cuddling," Zavier protested.

But I shook my head. I grabbed my earbuds from my pocket and slid them in. Then I took my phone and turned on this Norm heavy metal band, Mol. I pushed play on "Bruma" and let the screaming lyrics take over.

Once again, I turned away from Emelia and Z. *Maybe I'm just not meant to have friends,* I thought as I slid up a couple bleacher levels so that I could sit alone surrounded by lies and plans. That was who I'd become. That was the real me. Not the girl flirting with Zavier. Not the girl who wondered whether her brother's best friend might actually care for her or if he was just acting out of old guilt.

I kept my eyes deliberately off the fight and pulled up an app. I searched the dark web for a fucker who might know a Tock, and how I could get in touch with one.

20

Monday passed in a blur until I walked into tutoring. Malcolm sat calmly in our assigned study room, number 62, as though what was about to happen was no big deal. Maybe for him that was true. But I'd already pissed him off a few times. And though I'd come here expecting Grayson to be the bigger challenge, something about Malcolm was just... overwhelming.

The study room looked like any other. Just a couple beige walls, with a big window on one side so that the librarian could ensure 'propriety.' Inside was a wooden table and four chairs with a metal rolling library cart against one wall for unused books. But when I stepped inside, this study room was immediately twenty degrees colder than any other. My breath misted in the air and my nipples pebbled under my shirt. I was only wearing a sports bra, so they were incredibly obvious. I crossed my arms, backpack still on my shoulders and asked, "Sorry, but this is overkill, don't you think?"

Malcolm glanced up from his laptop. He closed it and put it into his bag. "Take a seat." He gestured at the chair across from himself and then bent to get something else.

I sat with my back to the window, facing him. But even after I'd shed my bag, I couldn't bear the cold. "My teeth are gonna start chattering in like two minutes," I warned.

Malcolm huffed but tossed me his jacket. "Idiots from Grayson's posse have come in here nonstop to tell me to fuck with you. I don't want them hanging around."

I slid my arms into his dark blue fleece, which was soft, and immediately cut down the chill. It had one of those freshly laundered scents to it that I noticed as I folded the extra length on the sleeves back so that it fit me. "Sorry about that."

"Told you not to get involved with that shit. Especially as a Darklight. You're lucky no one else here knows you have all that power. You wouldn't be able to fight them all off. You should leave Grayson and his gang alone."

"I've got a plan."

Malcolm set a deck of cards on the table and leaned onto his elbows. "Do tell." His bright blue eyes sparkled with mirth. Today he had on a big watch with a leather strap and a second hand that ticked loudly, filling the room with little clicks. It looked old and fit his fifties look perfectly.

I ignored his request and changed the subject. He didn't need to know all my plans for Grayson. Not until he trusted me. "What's with the watch?"

"We're gonna play a game," Malcolm said. He stared at me until I met his eyes. When I did, my breath caught, because there was a fiery intensity in his gaze. There was something dark and direct about Malcolm that drew me in.

The room grew colder, but a flash of heat crept up my thighs and settled there. The band of heat stroked up and down my legs until I swallowed hard. "Is this the game?" Was he trying to make me come by heat magic alone?

More cold crept down my chest and settled on my nipples, but nowhere else, making me agonizingly aware of them. The heat flicked again, this time over my slit and my stomach tightened. I tried to regain control, lacing my fingers on the table in front of me, clenching my teeth for a second until I could calmly say, "What are the rules of your game?"

Instantly, the heat and cold retreated, leaving me wanting and disappointed. It had been too long since I'd had an orgasm.

Malcolm didn't answer me right away. His blue eyes grew dark as he studied mine, and I didn't see any of his earlier humor. There was something eerie and fierce about him. But instead of repelling me, it just intrigued me. How could he make me nearly come, then be completely unaffected by it? Most guys would smirk, be self-satisfied, be telling me to beg. Zavier would have made himself a paper crown and tossed confetti in the air if he'd had that kind of control over my body.

Malcolm simply stared at me. He kept our gazes locked as he undid his watch strap. The way he unfastened it felt like a strip tease, agonizingly slow and full of longing as he painstakingly unbuckled and bared his wrist. He laid one side of the strap and then the other on the table.

He flipped over the watch. "We're going to play a game called Bullshit." He dragged over a paper and pencil, setting it beside him. Then he grabbed the cards and started to shuffle. The silence was long and intense as we traded breaths across the tabletop. When he started dealing, I rubbed my legs together in anticipation.

"You know the rules?" he asked.

I nodded. "We lay out cards face down in order, Ace through King. If we don't have a card in order, we lie."

"If you lie, I call Bullshit ... and..."

"If I'm lying, then I'll have to take the pile." I bit my lip in a false show of nerves. My nerves were actually singing from Malcolm's presence, but I was pretty fucking sure I could pull this off. I'd faked out all the dickwads at my former academies.

Malcolm set his elbow on the table and pointed at my face. "Bullshit. That face." He put a mark on the paper and checked the time on his watch. "Couldn't go twenty seconds without trying to lie to me."

I scrunched up my face. "Isn't that the point of this game?"

He just gave me a smirk, quirking up one corner of his lips in a delectable way that made me want to lean across the table. "I'm leaving twelve cards off to the side, so we don't know exactly what one another have." He stacked a little pile neatly face down. "You start, Hayley."

I pulled a single Ace from my hand and slid it facedown to the middle of table. "One ace."

Malcolm watched me for a second, then slid two cards to cover my ace. "Two twos."

I checked my pile, eyeing his expressions over them. I had two twos in my hand. Did he have the other pair or was one of them in the offset pile? His face was set like a stone. Impossible to read. I flipped my vision over to infrared to try to see if his body heat was rising.

"Are you using your power on me, little Darklight?" he asked.

"No."

"Bullshit." He made another mark on the page. Then he clicked his tongue. "It's going to be a very long night if you keep trying to lie to me."

"If you knew I was using it, why did you ask?" I returned my vision to normal and studied him again.

"I wanted to see if you'd lie."

I laughed. "Oh, okay. So, you just expect me to admit to cheating?"

"Yes."

"Why?" I shook my head. He made no sense.

He paused and waited until he had my full attention before he answered, "Because I want you to."

A shiver coursed down my spine and a flutter passed through my chest. I was scared and turned on at the same time. My heart thudded and it was a moment before I got up the courage to ask, "Why?"

"I think you know why." He gestured toward my cards. "Your turn."

I swallowed. I stared at my cards for just a second, then pulled two threes and a four from my hand. "Three threes," I said, sliding them over.

"Bullshit." He shook his head. Then he pushed the pile toward me.

I glared at him. "How can you tell?"

Malcolm didn't answer, just plucked some cards from his hand and laid them down. "Two fours."

"Bullshit."

He flipped them over. They were fours. *Motherfucking dammit!* How was he so good at telling when I was lying? He was totally getting under my skin. And that was making me screw up. I didn't do that. I was the one who fucked with everyone else, not the other way around. *Get a grip, Hales,* I lectured myself. I tried a few deep breaths before I grabbed the fives in my hand and tossed them down on the table. But I threw them too hard and one of the cards flipped face up.

Malcolm simply flipped it back over and asked, "Did the Pinnacle send you here?"

"What?" My jaw dropped in shock.

He evaluated me for a minute, his eyes drifting over my lips and back up. "I'll take that as an honest no."

"Why would the Pinnacle send me here?"

He shrugged. "They've done it before. They like to keep tabs on me."

Hmm. Not in his file. But I supposed, if the Pinnacle had covert operators spying here, it wouldn't be marked down anywhere easy to find.

"That sucks," I finally said. Then I felt like an idiot, because it was such an obvious, dumb thing to say. No wonder Malcolm was playing Bullshit with me. No wonder he wanted the truth. My cheeks heated as I realized the reasons that I'd thought he wanted me to tell him the truth were clearly very different from the reasons he wanted the truth.

A flash of heat across my thighs made me raise my eyes to his.

"Tell me what you're thinking right now," he demanded.

"That I'm an idiot," I said.

He studied me before giving a small nod. "Truth. That's progress. Two in a row."

"Tell me why you thought I was here for the Pinnacle." I glared at him.

He leaned his chair back so that it balanced on the rear legs and closed his fanned-out cards. "You have no real criminal history, yet you were sent here—"

"Half the kids here don't have rap sheets."

"I wasn't done."

I shut up. Malcolm's solemn face told me that was the only way I was gonna hear the remainder of his list of reasons.

"Your stepfather is on the Pinnacle board—"

"Don't call him that."

Malcolm raised an eyebrow but didn't ask. For that I was grateful. I didn't want to have to explain the Clod or our messed-up relationship.

Instead, Malcolm said, "Finally, I went into MAD's system once I was pinged as a tutor. I removed you as my student. Yet, somehow you managed to get reassigned."

My eyes fell to the table.

Malcolm dropped his chair and leaned forward. "That part you do know something about."

I gave a single shoulder shrug. "I hack a little here and there." I glanced up at him.

"So, you chose me before you came here."

Nervous energy gnawed at my bones. *Do I use the crush explanation? He seems to know when I lie.* Instead of saying anything, I just nodded. My cheeks flared red from the nerves, which shot off like fireworks in my stomach.

Malcolm's face lit up with surprise, and possibly a little bit of delight. "Oh. Well then." He fanned his cards back out.

"Well then, what?" I asked.

Heat flared across my panties, this time lingering longer, burning hotter, moving faster. My breath leapt like a ballerina and a tiny gasp escaped. The heat slowly receded. It took me a second, but when my eyes were able to refocus, I looked at Malcolm.

That self-satisfied smirk I'd expected to see earlier was present in full force as he leaned forward and said, "Well then, that changes the nature of our little game."

21

Tuesday, I woke up with soaked panties after tossing and turning and dreaming of Malcolm sending hot flames over my panties while Grayson played with my breasts and Zavier kissed me. After such a good dream, I should have been in a decent mood. But I wasn't. And I didn't quite know why. The weather wasn't overcast or windy for once. The sunshine should have perked me up. But I felt down and melancholy. I felt like a snake pit had formed in my stomach and the slithering, twisting reptiles were hissing at me.

Even Emelia noticed at lunch. "Lady, what's eating you?" She bumped my shoulder in a friendly way.

Normally, I ate alone, but she happened to enter the cafeteria at the same time. So there was no escaping her to go brood in miserable silence. I just got into line behind her and silently filled my tray.

After we sat down, she repeated her question.

I shrugged.

Emelia dug into her sloppy joe and then tried to give me life advice with her mouth full. "You know, whenever I get depressed about my mom or worried about my guys—"

"About that, how do you manage two guys?" I asked.

She shrugged. "I just told them up front."

"Don't they get jealous?"

She laughed and wiped away the Joker mouth she'd gotten from her last bite. "They got over that real quick—"

"How?"

She shrugged. "Dunno. But they're cool now. Like BFF."

Unease twisted through my stomach. And I realized that was what I was nervous about. I'd come here to recruit Grayson and Malcolm. But I still didn't know if they'd agree. I didn't know how they'd work together. I'd never seen them interact once on campus … other than in my dirty dream. I blew out a breath. I needed to think about something else.

But then Emelia made a statement that made turning my black mood around impossible. She said, "If my brother ever finds out, he'll kill them both." She laughed. "Overprotective big brother syndrome, you know?" Her eyes met mine.

The snakes inside bit me. My stomach turned sour. I stood, shoving back my chair. "I gotta go."

I left the cafeteria without really looking where I was going. I just kind of wandered. I ended up at the administration building and meandered through the halls until I saw a room I hadn't been to before. It was tall, with all kinds of brass safe deposit boxes lining the walls. But the door was unlocked. It was odd enough to distract me for a second. And I was desperate for any kind of distraction. I stepped inside and walked toward the nearest wall.

Each box had a little label on it. I bent to read one and realized it was a name. A last name. After scanning a few boxes, I realized they were in alphabetical order. I traced my fingers over the cold boxes with the little pull tabs. I yanked on one and it opened easily. I saw three envelopes inside. It was a mail room. I shut the drawer and continued on. And then I saw a box with my last name on it. Dunemark.

I pulled open the mailbox, wondering why the hell Professor Nazer hadn't told me about this when I'd been in her office. Inside the box was a letter from Tia and a pink slip that told me to go to room 107 to pick up a package.

I ripped open the letter from Tia first, which was full of gossip from Medeis. It was sweet that she'd written. And while I didn't care that Terra Lysour had broken up with football jerkoff—which was a long time coming—when Tia lamented the fact that her cousin Britney had gotten asked to the Unnatural Ball, the biggest celebration of the year back east for magicals, the one that all the Pinnacle big-wigs went to, I felt a bit nostalgic. I was sad I couldn't be there to comfort her with hugs and hot chocolate filled with Laughter-infused marshmallows.

I texted Tia. -*I can't believe you sent me a letter and didn't tell me already about the ball!!! Britney is a vapid idiot. Whoever she's going with is gonna have the worst time.*-

Her text back pinged right away. -*I thought you might like the snail mail. But it's totally been killing me.*-

-*The dumb admin never told me I had a mailbox. I got a package too. Is that from you?*-

- *:) They wouldn't allow the kind of packages I'd send you.*-

I smiled, the black cloud in my head momentarily lifting as I walked down the hall to room 107. I handed over the slip to a gruff looking guy with a chipped front tooth. He handed me back a box that had one corner crushed. I looked at the label. It was my blood draw kit. Medeis Academy had forwarded it here.

The sight of the box sent my mood tumbling right back down. I walked slowly down the hallway as Matthew's laughing face flitted through my head. He and Evan had completely embarrassed me on my fourteenth birthday. They'd bribed the janitor at my middle school and arrived at like the butt crack of dawn. They'd hung a huge sign outside the building that said, 'Happy Birthday Hayley!' It had flashed rainbow colors and had a unicorn on it—like I was six.

When I'd gotten to school, I'd been mortified to see that sign. But the prank had only gotten worse. When I'd walked into the hall, I'd found balloons floating all around at different heights. They weren't tied, or filled with helium, they'd been enchanted to hover just so—and fucking Matthew had written an Unpoppable spell on them so I couldn't destroy them before all the other students got to see.

My locker had been the worst. It had been wrapped in gold foil paper that had a note attached. "Happy Birthday! From the Birthday Bandits." Those shitheads had become legendary for their prank. I'd just tried to sink my head into my sweater like a turtle all day long. What fourteen-year-old girl wants people staring at her? I definitely hadn't.

My eighteenth birthday was coming up. Just about a month away. There would be no pranks for it.

Staring down at the box, at the contrast between what my life had been and what it was now, I had to swallow against the lump in my throat. My feet started to move, and my eyes roamed the admin building, searching for an open door so I could get out of the public eye before I melted down.

I spotted a meeting room and basically dove inside, moving to the corner farthest from the door and just sinking to the floor so that I could let the tears overflow. It hurt. It hurt so bad. More than all the burns that Claude had given me combined.

I could feel my face heat and my thoughts turn fuzzy as the tears turned to sobs and I replayed every prank I'd planned to hit Matthew with since his accident. Because sometimes, when things were rough, I'd pretend that nothing had ever happened. I'd pretend that life was normal, and I could do things to get revenge on my ass of a brother, like cover his car with maxi pads in the school parking lot or make an announcement over the PA system. "Matthew Dunemark, please report to the office. Your mother is here with your clean underwear." I started to laugh despite my tears, which just made me choke so I stopped that game and just sat against the wall, waiting out the tears. I cried until my eyes were red and I was pretty sure that lunch was over. But I only had Study Hall next so I didn't give a shit.

I hugged the box to my chest and stared at it a moment. Then I grabbed a pen out of my bag and stabbed the tape until it opened. I pulled out my blood donation kit and stuck the little half dome on my upper arm. I took out the collection bag and tube and attached them to the dome. Then I pressed down. Immediately, a pressure like a vacuum started on my arm and the donation device began to work.

I leaned my head back against the wall and closed my eyes. At first, I only saw patterns through the red of my eyelids, but gradually memories surfaced again, and the tears started back up. They were slower, since I'd cried so hard before. But they were steady, like I was a leaking faucet, broken and waiting for a repairman to come wrap me up in tape and glue and chemical crap or whatever the hell they did.

"Hey," a soft male voice, almost a whisper, said.

I opened my eyes and looked to my left. Evan stood in the doorway.

I didn't have the energy to scoff or to run. I didn't have the energy to fight or even turn my head away. I was wrung out. I just stared dully at him and watched as he glanced back into the hall, then closed the door behind him and walked over to me. Evan slid down the wall next to me and bent his knees.

"What are you doing here?"

"All shifters have to have a private shifting lesson over here. We work on controlling our animal instincts. Mine just finished."

I stared at his knees next to mine. He was so massive since the Unnatural spell. "Your legs are twice as wide as mine," I said, without thinking. My voice sounded like a rusty nail.

"Yeah, takes some getting used to. I have to eat like entire chickens now."

I turned to look at him, my cheek pressed against the wall. Before this shit went down, we'd been friends. Good friends. I'd thought of myself as his second-best friend. He'd probably thought of me as an annoying clinger. God how much had changed. My chest ached dully, lonely—nostalgic even for Evan after a day like today.

I could have stopped talking, could have just sat there in silence and let my donation bag fill up, but I didn't. For some reason, I didn't. I stared at Evan's pale cheek, the chin that had been strong and thick even before his change. I stared at his black eyelashes as he stared out the window across the room. And I said, "I send him blood every month."

Evan blinked, his lashes brushing his cheeks. Then his face turned and his eyes, damp with their own emotion, met mine. "I used to go and donate in person when we were back east."

"Why in person?" I shuddered at the memory of that institute.

"I wanted to make sure he got fed," Evan replied. "You see how they treat them?"

"There was no fucking security," I growled.

"Not just that." Evan reached over and gently untwisted a partial kink in my tube, so that the blood could flow easier. "I've seen the orderlies drag vamps down the hall. I tried to follow, but I couldn't see where they took them, they went into a locked hallway."

My forehead crinkled. "Why?" Vamps were hard enough to catch as it was in the first place. Why would anyone move them once they'd been contained? It didn't make sense.

Evan chewed his lip. "When Matthew first changed, that institute was full. He was on a waiting list until someone pulled a few strings—"

"Probably Dad," I commented. Mom had been way too messed up to think straight in the aftermath.

"Either way," Evan continued, "vamps don't die unless they're decapitated. So, where'd that opening come from?"

I shrugged. "I got forced into a couple vamp family support groups. One guy said the family eventually decided ... to ... you know ..." I shook my head.

"Well, I don't think that many families have decided on the ax. Last time I went to see him, that place was only half full."

My head swirled and I felt dizzy. "What? Where are they moving vamps?"

Evan shook his head. "I dunno. But I doubt their families are taking them back home."

A sad, angry laugh burst out of me. That's what I'd wanted to do. Originally, when everything had happened, I'd wanted us to keep Matthew at home. My parents had both been adamantly against it. It was too dangerous. I'd read a newspaper article about a family who'd tried it. They'd all been drained in their sleep.

"But they can't be exposed to windows or daylight," I murmured, thinking aloud.

"Yeah, I know. And at first, I thought ... maybe ... this is gonna sound awful ... but I thought there might be some serial killer at Matthew's facility. Like someone who'd found the perfect place to live out their twisted--"

I held up a shaky hand. "Don't. I can't handle that right now." The thought of some sick fuck with an ax in hand, strolling down the corridors of that awful place, whistling, opening the door and nodding cheerfully at a nurse who just averted her eyes and kept walking—I couldn't handle it. A shiver went up my spine. My stomach started to pulse.

Evan covered my hand with his own, which pulled my gaze to his long fingers. They wrapped up mine so perfectly. And the warmth offset some of the chill my mental images had created.

He confided, "I went to two other institutes. One near Manhattan. Another in Jersey." His eyes went navy-colored and his voice thrummed with anger when he added, "Both of them were half-full too."

Dread hacked at the warmth I'd stolen from Evan's fingers. "What does that mean?"

But, just then, the device on my arm gave a little beep. I glanced down and realized my donation bag was full. My reeling mind had to wait a few seconds for practicalities. I pulled the HemoLink device off my arm and tossed it and the tube into the trash can. I went to put the pint-bag into the refrigerated foam box that the donation company sent with their kits. But Evan took the bag out of my hands and did it for me.

I glanced up at him once it was all packed away and he'd cleaned up the rest of my trash. Evan reached into his bag and pulled out a sports drink. "Here."

I gulped the red liquid until half the bottle was gone. But when I wiped my lips, I was back to Nancy Drew mode. "Evan, why are all these institutes empty?"

Evan hefted my donation box and my bag for me, like they weighed nothing. "The only thing I can think of … is that someone powerful is using vamps for something."

"What though? They're wild, not tameable—"

"Immortal," Evan's words cut through mine.

I stared up at him.

Professor Ho's head popped into the room. "Excuse me, what are you doing here? Ms. Dunemark, you should be on your way to my classroom!" The short man glared up at Evan.

"Blood donation sir," Evan explained.

To my surprise, Ho's face softened a bit. "Alright. Get that in the mail ASAP so it doesn't spoil. Dunemark, walk with me."

Evan put my backpack on, gently sliding it over my shoulders, in a move that would have previously made me recoil. But maybe it was the fact that I was emotionally exhausted, or blood deprived, or he had stoked my fear and curiosity because I found it comforting. He looked over his shoulder at me and gave a little half wave, before pointing firmly at the drink in my hand. "All of it," he said, like he was pre-scolding me for something that hadn't happened yet.

I stuck my tongue out at him.

He grinned back.

As I turned away from him, I realized some little part of me had just started to forgive Evan Weston.

22

Grayson might have gotten me with pinwheel arms at the tournament, but it took him seven days to reverse my dick cup spell. He didn't figure it out until Wednesday. He'd thought leaving his water bottle behind last Friday morning would end it all. But I'd enchanted him, not the water bottle. So, anything he drank out of had turned into a sparkly vibrating cock until he figured out how to reverse it over the weekend.

It had earned him a couple of delightful nicknames from some of the prison-tatted students who didn't give a fuck about him and his money.

"Duck Sick."

"Cockle spaniel."

"Snurg gurgler."

I enjoyed watching his dark brown eyes search me out anywhere around the campus and burn holes through me. He'd hardly glanced at Laura over the past week as he'd tried to hire an Unraveler up to the challenge of undoing my spell work.

I'd hacked his computer and he'd reached out to at least three pros to try and get it done. That did add a bit of swagger to my step. Particularly when one old douche bag professional I'd tried to hire for my Pinnacle break in two years ago (a fat, living in his parents' basement jerkoff who'd turned me down) couldn't do it.

Mama's got skills, I'd patted myself on the back when I read that email exchange.

But all good things come to an end. And that beautiful spell did too.

Once Grayson got that spell removed, I was on high alert. I wrote all sorts of spells to protect my person from physical attacks. Most of my nights were spent checking Grayson's computer and trying to write spells based on what he wanted to do to me. I turned down another movie night with Zavier and Emelia because of it. And at first, I did well. But Spell writing can always be exploited by a loophole. Nothing's ever watertight. A good Unraveler could look at a spell and just see the chinks in the armor. A great one could untangle a spell quickly and efficiently by coming up with a counter spell on the fly. That's what I'd been practicing for the past few years, so that I could break into the computer and safe at the Pinnacle. Unraveling was going to be the key. And ultimately, Unraveling was how Grayson got to me.

Starting Monday morning, the bastard showed up randomly at the door to whatever classroom I was in (he was learning my schedule) and stared at me until I moved and waved at him. Then his face would grow dark and angry and he'd stomp off.

Twice, he found me in the hall. He even knocked on my dorm door once, staring after I'd opened it. He never spoke. But I always gave him my cocky grin and just-for-assholes finger wave.

Emelia told me it looked like he was hunting 'puss.' I laughed at her. She'd gotten the hunting part right. But he was hunting for my humiliation. To even the score. And I welcomed the day he would. Sort of. In a roundabout way. Because it meant he was focused on me. It meant I was a challenge.

But I wasn't gonna let him pay his way to superiority. I didn't need someone on my team who bought his way to the top. I need him to think his way there.

He did.

On Thursday, I woke up after another hot group sex dream and stretched, refreshed and ready for another shit morning of Cross Country with Lundy. Because every day started with a run after breakfast. My ass loved it—my skirts had never looked so good on me—but the rest of me could do without all the practice fleeing through a forest. The cynical part of me wasn't a fan.

As I tossed off the covers and climbed out of bed, my legs felt tingly and strangely energized. I glanced down at them but couldn't tell what was wrong until I tried to take a step. And that step turned into a skip. And another skip. And another.

Laughter and glee bubbled up through me. I felt like clapping. Grayson had been testing my boundaries, I was certain. But he'd broken through. I hadn't protected myself against skipping. Because who the fuck would think of that other than a five-year-old girl?

My giggle was interrupted by a knock at the door.

I knew exactly who it was.

I skipped over and threw the door open wide, not caring that I was in my pajamas—a light pink silk tank top and shorts.

Grayson Mars stood in my doorway wearing sweatpants, a white t-shirt, and a hungry, curious look.

I gave Grayson a wide smile and said, "You did it. You got me."

His eyes traveled down to my legs and his expression darkened.

My breath hitched. *Maybe he doesn't believe me?* But then my thoughts took it a step further. *Shit. Or maybe the spell he cast has some kind of delayed activation like the dick thing ... better to get it over with,* I thought, and I skipped in a circle around my room, hands flying to my chest to stop my breasts from bouncing too much without a bra.

Grayson leaned against the door jamb to watch the show. I couldn't tell if he enjoyed it. I could have checked—used my infrared vision to see if his body temperature rose—but I was too worried about waiting for the other shoe to drop. And drop it did. Right on my ass.

After a minute of skipping, I found the delayed effect.

My feet froze in place and my knees bent. My back bent forward of its own accord until my eyes were on my ugly gray carpet. I couldn't control my own body! Panic rushed through me like river rapids, because I didn't know where this was going. I felt like I was in a canoe, white water all around me, rocks looming.

I'd kept my retaliation on Grayson light-hearted with the dick thing, but had he done the same? Some of the shit he'd originally asked for when he tried to buy spells online was downright fucking evil. Was he going to make me poop myself? Pants myself? Stick a finger in my own ass in public? —He'd asked for that one twice.

Anxiety filled me like a swarm of gnats as my hands slowly went up my legs toward my thighs. Oh fuck. Oh fuck. *You're in your room idiot*, I told myself. *At least you're discovering this now and not in the middle of class. You have time. Not much time. But time to start figuring out a counter spell to unravel whatever he wrote.*

My body held still for a moment, as my anticipation built. And then, suddenly, my spine dropped and lifted. My back and knees bent, and my butt went up and down, faster and faster. My ass sped up until it felt like Jell-O attached to the end of my spine. And I couldn't stop. Not on my own. *Dammit!* The jerkwad made me skip and twerk!

It was embarrassing as fuck, since my short sleep shorts rode up to give me the world's most uncomfortable wedgie, freeing the lower halves of my ass to Grayson's stare. The wedgie burned like no wedgie had before, because the friction was awful. I couldn't stop twerking until some unknown timer that Grayson must have written into the spell went off. At that point, I was out of breath and my face was red as a tomato.

I turned to look at Grayson, emotions torn. Admiration and hatred. Fury and utter humiliation. That fucking ass! "How am I supposed to make it through a run with Lundy like this?" *Or a walk to class*, I thought. Shit ... this was way worse than what I'd done to him. It would take forever to unravel. And I had a damned test in Wolfe's class so I couldn't ditch the entire day. If I did ditch ... each of my detentions had been worse than the last. I didn't have time to waste on that.

I briefly considered finding another recruit—dropping Grayson and taking Dad's suggestion to scale the Pinnacle's headquarters more seriously. But then I glanced back at Grayson.

For the first time in days, a smile crossed his face. It wasn't a happy smile, or a mean one. For once, it was a proud smile. A 'hell-yeah, I did that' smile. It lit his face up. It softened his jaw. And for a second, I saw the guy underneath the Grayson Mars persona, underneath the bored little rich boy attitude he wore. I saw someone like me.

That only lasted for a second, because Grayson's proud smile turned dirty as his eyes roamed down my figure, taking in my silk sleep shirt sans bra. "Not my problem," he said in a gravelly tone before he pushed off my door jamb and walked down the hall.

I skipped toward the door and leaned out. "You know this means war!"

Grayson turned around and put both hands in the air, curling his fingers in a come-hither gesture several times. "Bring it."

I DID DITCH CROSS COUNTRY. THEN I ENDED UP CALLING ZAVIER FOR A favor. He'd arrived at the door of my dorm with an excited smile on his face.

"You need it *bad*, don't you!"

"If by it, you mean your help, then unfortunately yes," I grumbled as I tossed my hair up into a ponytail. Then I turned from where I was perched on top of my bed and held out my arms.

"Oh baby!" Zavier raced to my bed and leaped on top of me leaving the hall door wide open in his excitement.

"No, you weirdo!" I batted him off, though the feeling of his muscles encasing my torso made my vagina tell my brain that it was an idiot. "We have a test. I need you to carry me to class!"

Immediately, Zavier sat up and started examining me with his eyes and (of course, because he was him) his hands. "Did you get hurt again?"

I pushed him away, but he tweaked a nipple before I could get him all the way off me and by the glint in his eyes, he'd done it on purpose. It didn't help matters that I'd dreamed about him playing with my breasts last night. I had to shove down dream images as I said, "I'm fine. I just can't walk."

He raised one eyebrow, finally leaning back on one of his elbows and looking up at me. "How can you be fine if you can't walk? That's the definition of not fine!"

"I've been spelled. And I don't have time to unravel it before class."

Zavier's brown eyes studied me. "I think you could do it."

I shook my head vehemently. "I've already started making notes. It's crazy complex."

He checked his phone. "Still, we've got a whole five minutes—"

"Zavier, just please, I'm begging you. Carry me. You're my only friend here." Saying that out loud made me emotional for some stupid reason. I knew it was true. But still. I swallowed before I continued, "It's Emelia's last day. I'd like to be able to say goodbye."

That seemed to get his butt moving. Finally. He hopped off the bed and grabbed my backpack. He slung it over his shoulder and then came and picked me up so that I faced him. I felt odd. Was he going to carry me facing backward all the way to class? "Wouldn't you rather give me a piggyback ride?"

Zavier leaned in and nipped my ear before he answered. And the strangest part of it was that, for some reason, I let him. "A piggyback ride won't make you think about you and me, and how well we'd fit together as dirty friends—so no, I wouldn't rather give you one of those."

"We do not fit together," I growled, even as I wrapped my arms around the tattoos that floated up his neck. I traced a bird colored in greens and blues that flew toward his dark hair.

Zavier walked to my dorm room door. But instead of heading into the hall, he shoved me up against the frame. He pressed his pelvis into mine. "Yeah we do." His hands tightened under the backs of my thighs as he gently rotated his pelvis side to side. "Do you feel that?" he whispered as he started to get hard.

The friction felt good. So good. If Zavier was a whiskey, I would have been halfway drunk. His touch. His smile. And then he leaned forward and kissed my neck, right at the base so that my nerves sang. He leaned up and said, "Look. I could fuck you and kiss you perfectly at the same time."

And then he leaned in. His mouth edged closer to mine.

My heart raced and my stomach flipped. I shoved Zavier away and went skipping down the hall. "Run, run, run, as fast as you can. You can't catch me—"

That's when the twerking caught up with me the second time. "Dammit!"

After Zavier filmed it and laughed so hard that he gave himself a coughing fit, he turned into a gentleman, picked me up, and carried me to class.

"I'm saving you from public humiliation. You owe me two BJs for this."

"I'm not paying for you to get a Bachelor's in Journalism. Definitely not paying for two. What do you want to be when you grow up anyway?" I asked, realizing I'd never asked him anything like that before.

"An accountant," Zavier quipped as he carried me down the stairs.

I punched him in the shoulder. "No! That's my go-to sarcastic answer. You can't steal it."

He shrugged. "Didn't you know that I'm a thief?"

I scrunched up my face in disbelief. "Yeah, okay."

Zavier paused in his walk across the quad, shifted me to a hip so that he could hold me one-handed (which was hot) and pointed down at his ankle monitor. "What do you think I got that for?"

"Cause you're annoying and your parents want to make sure you don't run home?" I teased. But then I worried I'd gone too far. I leaned back in Zavier's grip to check his facials.

He didn't look hurt. He looked smarmy, greasy, too smooth and proud of it.

"Reach into my shirt pocket," he said.

I squinted at him, not sure how to read his change of topic. Slowly, I reached into his pocket. I felt some string, silk, lace.

I pulled out a brand-new pair of my underwear. "Zavier!" I seethed, squishing the thong into a ball and hiding it in the palm of my hand.

He laughed, and bounced me, returning me to straddle position.

"How did you even get in my drawers! I didn't even see you!"

Zavier's only response was, "A good thief never tells."

23

EMELIA'S last day was bittersweet. As much as I'd liked having her around to talk to or eat with once in awhile, I hoped she didn't come back. I needed to focus. I needed to game plan just how I was going to break the news to Malcolm and Grayson and get them to agree. Just the thought of telling them made my palms sweat and my throat grow tight. So much was riding on their 'yes.' And up to now, I'd really just learned to make myself a hated entity. A bitch.

I should have been able to shove emotion aside and just focus on next steps—that was what I'd done for the past few years. But I wasn't finding it as easy as before. Maybe because I was emotionally invested in these guys. *A little. Just a bit. Fuck.*

My attempts at sculpting deer in Huchmala's Art Therapy class reflected my lack of attention. I accidentally squashed two of the legs together and had to rip the entire back half of my clay sculpture off and start over. My annoyed huff drew the prancy teacher over.

"Ms. Dunemark, are you feeling okay today?" Her eyes stared at the guy behind me in class even though she stood right in front of me.

"Yup. Yeah. I'm fine."

"Oh dear, you know, denial isn't a healthy thing. Don't judge your emotions. Just let them be. They are what they are," she chanted, using the phrase she forced us all to recite like the fucking Pledge of Allegiance at the start of each class.

"They are what they are, and I just need to acknowledge them and let them go," I said her stupid line in the hope that she'd just head the hell away. But I had no such luck. She could sense vulnerability. And she preyed on it, like some long necked, cross-eyed vulture.

Huchmala sat down in the empty stool next to mine at the sculpture table. She glanced at my deer. "Deer often represent innocence."

My deer represented an offering to two stone lions so I wouldn't get eaten. But I nodded, acting like I drank her Kool aid.

"Do you feel like you've lost your innocence? Or you're about to in some way?" She blinked.

Behind her, a Hispanic dude grinned at me. "I'll take your innocence." He held up his fingers to create a hole, then used a finger from his other hand to fuck it.

"Here." I tossed him my half deer. "Take it. I'll start a new one."

He glared at me, but with Huchmala there, he couldn't do much. I used a wire to cut myself a fresh slab of clay and started smacking it like bread dough.

"Good, get your aggression out." Huchmala nodded. "Acknowledge those feelings of frustration and powerlessness. We all have so much less control than we think we do and so much less than we want."

We all have so much less earwax than we want, I thought. I knew some students actually wore earplugs in her class, but normally she didn't bug me. Normally, Huchmala fluttered over to the painters and bothered them. Part of me was tempted to make a ceiling light flicker on the other side of the room to see if I couldn't get her to go away.

I took a deep breath and stared at my clay. You can do this. Turn a lumpy block into a deer. I grabbed a carving tool, but Huchmala reached over and stopped me.

"Wait. I saw what you did last time, Hayley. You sketched and measured and then cut. Like a surgeon. But sometimes, in life, you just have to feel your way through. Sometimes, the discovery process is as important as the result. I want you to make a deer. But I want you to make it by hand. And I want you to take at least five classes to do it."

My eyes widened. I only had class three times a week with her. That would make the project take almost two weeks. What was I supposed to do that whole time? "But it's just a deer."

She smiled, her eyes almost reaching my forehead. "It's never just a deer. And this way, by the time you're done, it'll be more than just a deer to you."

She left me at the table, staring wide-eyed at the Hispanic dude who was turning my previous half deer into a head mounted on a trophy board.

I looked back down at the lump of clay in my hands. I gave myself a pep talk. And then, I just embraced the insanity. If I had to spend two weeks on a frickin' deer, I was gonna make the best life-sized replica of Rudolph anyone had ever seen.

I LICKED MY LIPS AS I STARED AT THE WALL IN HO'S CLASS ON SATURDAY —six days since I'd unraveled the twerking spell—worrying again. I'd had all my tutoring sessions with Malcolm, each one hotter than the last. Yesterday, I'd summoned up the courage to try footsie. I'd nearly internally combusted while we played Connect Four and I thought about all the other parts of our bodies I wanted to connect.

My hormones and my dirty dreams weren't helping anything. I still didn't feel quite right about telling Malcolm what I wanted. And each session he'd asked me why I'd picked him before I came here. I'd just shaken my head and refused to say anything, rather than lie to him. Any kind of half-truth seemed to rile him up.

And Grayson. That dick. I'd tried writing a few spells to get back at him, but nothing had stuck yet. I was gonna have to get more creative. His smirking face from lunch ate at me. I didn't know how I'd transition from this battle royale we had to a teammate scenario. And trying to connect the dots felt like jumping from A to Z and skipping all the letters in the middle. I didn't know what came next, only that something else needed to before I could approach Grayson.

Heat flashed over my panties and I started in my seat. I glanced at Malcolm, who used his eyes to point at Professor Ho.

Aw shit. Jackie Chan was staring right at me like he wanted to karate chop me in half.

I cleared my throat. "Sorry, sir."

"Sorry, for what, Ms. Dunemark? For disrespecting me by treating my class like it was naptime? Should I bring you a blanket and a stuffie next class?"

Soft laughs dotted the room.

I pressed my teeth together, hard, swallowing down any retorts. Ho gave out detentions the way dentists handed out free toothbrushes. Every single class at least one person got one. I lowered my eyes in submission, hoping maybe Ho's shifter animal would get the hint. I also tilted and exposed my neck.

"Dunemark, I asked you to tell me about magical shields. You can answer me and then come up to the front to get a detention slip."

I swallowed a groan. I shoved myself more upright in my chair and said, "Magical shields have been a part of weapon design for as long as history's been written. Humans and magicals have worked together to try to enhance shielding technology with magic. It started with repellent spells for swords and shields, progressed to castle walls, and so on, until lately they've been trying to create a purely magic anti-ballistic missile shield that doesn't require launching actual missiles, just air detonates the missile set to strike."

"Biggest issue with this kind of protection?"

"Shield spells can be one of two things, strong or long-lasting. The stronger you make a shield, the shorter its lifespan."

Ho's eyes narrowed at me until they were slits. "Correct." He whipped around and walked back toward his desk. He filled out the detention slip, and I sighed but went to retrieve it. As I walked up the aisle, I had to pass Laura. I scooted toward the far side of the aisle, avoiding her because I saw her scratching away on a strip of parchment underneath her desk with her wand. I didn't know if that spell was for me but—

My foot fell like a block of lead. I couldn't lift it. It felt like a brick was attached to my leg. I glanced down to see my leg was encased in a giant wooden club.

I tried to lift it. Almost threw my back out. But the best I could do was drag it across the ground with a horrid, low screech.

Professor Ho turned around, impatience in his eyes as he held out the slip. When he saw my leg, his eyes glanced sharply around the room. "Who did this?"

Not one mouth moved. Not one eye blinked. Not even mine. I wasn't going to let Ho have the satisfaction of punishing Laura. Not when I was going to do so myself.

Ho trudged down the aisle and stared up at me. "You did this to yourself, Dunemark?"

I just stonewalled, mentally preparing for a second or third detention.

Ho shook his head. "You're a fool." Then he turned and marched back to the front of the class. "Everyone gets detention Sunday, since you all like to cover for one another." His eyes flicked dismissively over my leg. "Get to the nurse so she can unravel that."

I tried to walk out. Tried but couldn't. I ended up hunched and dragging my heavy club foot like some Igor in a horror flick.

A chair scraped behind me and footsteps sounded. Suddenly, I was scooped off the floor like I weighed nothing and held bridal style. I glanced at Malcolm, surprise lighting me up. He had both our backpacks over his shoulder. He trudged past Ho without a word, and the professor didn't say boo, which made me slightly resentful even through my gratitude.

When we turned the corner in the hallway and I finally felt like I wasn't about to get yet another detention slip from Ho for talking, I said, "Thanks."

Malcolm just shook his head. "Why do you mess with these idiots?"

"Just one of them. I'm messing with Grayson. That fucktard Laura just can't help inserting herself in our feud."

"But why?" Malcolm's gaze traveled over me and I could feel his curiosity the way I could feel shadows, like soft feathers against my skin.

I swallowed hard as I looked him over, liking the way my arms looked linked behind his neck far too much. I fought against the urge to stroke the back of his neck, where his hair tapered off. I couldn't lie to him. I knew Malcolm wouldn't let me lie to him. That it would piss him off. But at the same time, the truth felt sudden. I didn't know if he trusted me yet. I needed him to trust me. And that meant I was caught in a never-ending loop of do I or don't I. I blew out a breath.

"Just tell me the truth," Malcolm said. "Why are you so obsessed with this war with Grayson?"

"The same reason I'm obsessed with having you as my tutor."

Malcolm's eyes narrowed and his head tilted as he tried to interpret what that might mean.

"I chose the two of you," I said, slowly, each word weighing as much as the stupid trunk on my leg.

"For what?"

But we'd reached the nurse's office for this building. (Building A and B each had their own nurse; at Metamorphose they needed two, maybe even four for all the fights that went down.)

The nurse saw us through the window in her door and popped her head out of the door and sighed when she saw the molting tree bark. "Well, come on then." She waved us inside.

Malcolm carried me in like a gentleman and set me on the exam table. He put my backpack on the floor next to me and then leaned in. "We will be discussing this more later." And then, in a move that left me frozen, his lips brushed over mine. His lips were as soft as flower petals, just barely grazing my mouth, a hint of his minty breath fogging up my thoughts. As soon as the kiss began, it was over, and he was out the door, leaving me spellbound, wondering what had just happened.

The next hour flew by as the nurse puttered around and clicked onto her computer and did research before writing an unraveling spell. I didn't even notice the weight of my leg or the fact that my foot fell asleep.

All I could think about was the fact that Malcolm Bier had just kissed me.

24

THE KISS COMPLICATION spurred me into a distracted frenzy, meaning I sought out any and every distraction I could think of in order to stop myself from thinking about *it*. Shit, romantic complications had been the last thing I wanted. And yet, here I was, dealing with them. I shook my head and focused on other things, like the fact that Grayson was letting his little bitch do his dirty work. I hadn't even retaliated for the twerking yet and she'd attacked me.

I let my ire fill me up and spur me on so that I was working into the wee hours of the night. But finally, I came up with a brilliant plan. One that punished both him and her. I wrote out a spell that was so long and complicated that I had to grab a brand-new roll of parchment out of my closet before I could even start.

And then I fell asleep, a naughty, nasty grin lighting up my face. Of course, when my alarm went off on Sunday morning, I deeply regretted the late night.

Running was gonna be such an awful pain as I struggled to keep my eyes open and not kiss a tree. Kissing trees made me think of Malcolm, which made my hands wander south during my shower. I leaned against the black and white tiles as my hand circled my clit. I thought of Malcolm's face whenever he'd called Bullshit on me. That intense, dark stare. I thought again of how soft he'd kissed me, and I felt sure, that if the nurse hadn't been watching, that his kiss would have been just as hot and intense as his stare. Malcolm's kisses would be brutal.

On the other hand, Zavier's kisses would be light and teasing—flipping between pecks all over my body and a very playful battle of the tongues.

Evan's face floated through my mind too. And I didn't even freak out about it. I thought about kissing him just as warmth surged up my spine. Evan's kisses would feel as light and magical as a rainbow. That's what I'd always believed. The thought of him pushing back my hair, caressing my cheek, his eyes full of adoration—my finger worked faster and faster, flipping between the images of each guy like magazine pages. I came hard on my hand, leaning my cheek against the wall and moaning as my nipples touched the cold tile and an orgasm lit me up.

After, I washed off my hand and turned off the shower, feeling slightly more awake. I stuck my hand outside the shower curtain and blindly reached for my towel. But there was no towel there on the rack. I pulled aside the curtain.

Grayson Mars stood in my bathroom, glaring at me. His fierce, six-foot-tall figure radiated anger. If his eyes could have glowed red like those stone dragons, they would have. He held my towel hostage in his hands, five feet away from me.

Guess he'd discovered my new spell.

I tried not to smirk as I used my hand to wipe the droplets from my face. It was clear that he had no intention of giving me my towel. Had he heard my orgasm? I glanced down at his sweatpants. A massive erection rose like a damned pole in a circus tent. I couldn't tell if it was from listening to me or the spell. I guessed the latter.

Still, the fact that he'd stopped to listen instead of stomping right in and yanking aside my shower curtain gave me a little courage. And more than a little attitude to go with it. I stepped out of the shower and grabbed my hair, twisting it, letting the water splatter across the floor. I ignored him, pretending his eyes didn't hungrily roam my body even as he stepped back out of the splash zone.

When I reached for a spare towel under my sink, giving him a nice view of my hard, newly toned ass, Grayson reached his limit. He stomped closer and growled, "You evil woman! What did you do to my dick?"

I grinned up at him as I wiped my skin down with a towel. I made my voice as innocent and conversational as I could, though derision snuck into my tone. "What? Don't like your dick tick?" I smiled up at him before I wrapped the towel around myself.

I wandered toward the counter and grabbed a brush, highly aware that Grayson's anger had me excited in more ways than one. I downplayed it. I sprayed some detangler in my hair and started combing through the wet strands.

Grayson appeared at a loss for a second. "That's what this is? That black thing? You put a goddamned *bug* on my cock?"

I looked at him in the foggy reflection caused by my mirror. I tried to ignore the fact that my nipples tightened while I watched his angry face. I hadn't added him to this morning's clit fest. But tomorrow, I was pretty certain his angry face would be the one I saw when I made myself come.

"Get rid of it," Grayson ordered, taking a step closer to me.

I slid sideways in my narrow bathroom. I put on my fake innocent face. The one designed to set professors off into a fit of fury. "How do you know I did it?"

Grayson slammed into me, shoving me away from the counter and across the room. He pressed my back into the wall as his body skimmed mine. I could feel a very prominent bulge at the front of his pants. If I didn't know better, I'd have thought he was enjoying this just as much as I was. But I did know better. Right now, a massive magical tick was sucking blood through his dick, keeping the thing engorged and stiff, and swelling until it was roughly the size of a water balloon. He'd have a permanent hard on until he could unravel my spell.

"Serves you right for sending your little girlfriend after me instead of manning up and doing it yourself," I snarled.

Grayson penned me in, one hand stopped me from ducking out the door. The other hand started for my neck. But then he thought the better of it. *That's right, fucker. You don't want to do that,* I thought.

I waited until both his hands were planted on the wall on either side of me. They curled into fists.

"I didn't send her," he grudgingly admitted.

"Tell her that. She thinks you need your honor defended like some little beta." I lifted my hand gently and brought it to his cheek in a mock pity move.

"Get rid of it," he seethed, jerking away from my hand, his hips twisting as the tick made a sucking sound not too far off from a dirty blow job.

I drank in his anger like it was potent whiskey—the kind of shit Claude brewed in his backroom. Only, Grayson's anger tasted so much better. This kind of high, this kind of power was so much better. I looked right into his dark, beautiful brown eyes as I said, "I can't get rid of it. Only you can."

He punched the wall, cracking the plaster next to me. But I didn't flinch. I kept my smile firmly in place. "All you have to do is apologize ..."

I ducked underneath his hand as a pathetic 'sorry' dropped from his lips.

I turned back in the doorway and looked at him over my shoulder. "Apologize. And mean it. Then the spell will unravel on its own."

I grabbed a spare towel from my dresser. Then I slid on my panties and sports bra, getting dressed for Cross Country while Grayson Mars' eyes traveled up and down over my body and he vibrated with fury.

I blew Grayson a kiss goodbye.

The billionaire's son didn't say a single word.

I RAN NEXT TO EVAN THROUGH THE TREES. LUNDY AND THE REST OF the class trotted ahead of us, the sound of panting and footfalls filling the forest.

Despite his height, Evan shortened his strides to match mine and we fell to the back of the pack quickly. The weak winter sun drifted down through the leaves and gave our faces a sickly cast.

When the torture had ended and we finally got to cool down, Evan touched my shoulder. Then he gestured down a path that broke off from the main gravel track and wove through the trees. "Walk with me?" he asked.

Curiosity filled me. I hadn't spoken to Evan since he'd seen me break down. If I was honest with myself, I'd been avoiding him. I just didn't know how to handle the new reality with him—this semi-truce. I didn't know what he wanted, but I nodded, still so out of breath that I couldn't speak. I shoved my hands on the back of my head, elbows jutting out, and followed the guy I considered my first love and my first enemy into the woods.

Once we were far enough from our classmates that our conversation wouldn't be overheard, Evan paused and glanced back at me. His blue eyes went from uncertain to sad. "I've been asking around about people with vamp family members or friends or whatnot."

I stilled. And though my heart was already beating fast, somehow it managed to go faster.

He cleared his throat and tried to make himself sound more detached, more clinical about what he'd found out about vampires. "You remember Alaina Aldridge?"

"Our old piano teacher?" I asked.

"Guess she tried to go Unnatural a couple years ago. It didn't work out. I played football with her son, Jeff."

I just nodded, stretching my sore calves as I waited for him to get to the point. I gritted my teeth. I'd forgotten how roundabout Evan could be. He was so obsessed with the little details. He couldn't force himself to get straight to the point. The little details had made him kick my ass at Risk every time we'd played. But it was damn annoying when I just wanted a two-sentence summary.

"Anyway, Jeff just graduated and he's working in Miami now, at some joint magical-norm tech start up. But he said that last time he went to try to visit his mom to donate they told him she'd been moved."

I stopped stretching. "What?" My tone was sharp and panicked.

Evan raised his eyes and nodded. "Right? Where's their authority to do that?"

"What happened?"

"Well, Jeff complained, got the runaround, they said they'd get the transfer paperwork over to him. That was six months ago. He tried to file a missing person's report, but the Pinnacle doesn't consider Vamps magicals and the norm government doesn't either."

I clenched my jaw, and despite how sore my body was, I started to pace between two trees in our tiny clearing. I threw up my hands. "So, a vamp can just disappear into a fucking logistical black hole?"

"Yup. Apparently."

My fist slammed into a tree. I was so angry that I didn't even register the pain for a second. "They don't have to feed them. And if they just disappear—it's no fucking big deal." I closed my eyes and shook my head. I tried to focus on my breathing because my heartrate was out of control.

Two hands landed softly on my shoulders and I opened my eyes to stare up at Evan. "The rest of the world just see monsters," he said.

"Only because the Pinnacle—" I cut myself off and ignored Evan's curious gaze. "So, Jeff's mom is just gone?"

Evan nodded. "I also called a couple of Institutes out here to see if it was just an east coast thing."

"And?"

"I pretended I had a brother who'd just turned, and I needed to find a space for him ASAP."

Anxiety kicked around my throat. "What was the wait time?"

"Two days. Every facility I called said that they had availability."

The wind whipped up and chilled the sweat that slicked my back. But my shiver had nothing to do with the cold. My hands reached up and covered Evan's where they rested on my shoulders. I squeezed, my fury and anger and heartbrokenness flowing out from my hands into him. "So, it's everywhere. Vamps are going missing everywhere."

I felt like I'd just looked down at my feet only to find I was balanced on a tightrope hanging over a canyon. About to fall. Someone was taking vamps. Helpless vampires who'd gone magically mindless.

Vamps who couldn't defend themselves. My eyes flew up to Evan's and pleaded. "How can we keep him safe?"

He sighed and pulled his hands away from mine so he could pace. I watched him think for a few minutes, trying to come up with a solution myself. Vampires were notoriously fast and hard to catch. That's why ceremonies to go Unnatural had to take place at designated facilities. The people who attempted the spell had to sign waivers and chain their ankles to the ground before they started. Guards with animal tranquilizers stood on platforms that overlooked the spell zone. Every middle school magical had to watch like twenty godawful, afterschool-special-style videos about it. Matthew was in a room, but could we really get in there and chain him up? Could we smuggle him out?

Evan paused his pacing to break a twig off a nearby tree. He stripped the leaves as he thought, frowning. "Getting him out of there is the obvious solution. I don't have rights to request that. And you're not quite legal."

"Psh. A few more weeks."

"Even so, pretty sure your mom has the authority. We could disguise him, I guess. Not sure how well that would work. And where the hell would we keep him?"

I licked my lips. There was one person I knew who could write a damn fine spell to change her appearance at will. One person who was somewhat sympathetic to my connection with vamps. One person who was going to be here later today. "If I can get him out of the facility, do you know of a place we can keep him safe?"

Evan's mouth quirked to the side. "I don't want you doing anything illegal—"

I started to laugh. Manically. Brokenly. Tears came to my eyes and I had wipe them away several times. I ended up sitting down on the forest floor because I gave myself hiccups. It took a long time for them to subside. Evan ended up sliding down to the ground with his back against a tree and waiting for me to regain my sanity.

When I'd finally calmed down, he asked, "What was that all about?"

I shook my head.

Evan scuffed a shoe over the dead leaves that coated the ground. "If I had to guess, it has something to do with 'Project Matthew.'"

My stare hardened. "How the hell did you remember that?"

Evan's smile was dark. It wasn't the happy expression I'd seen on him growing up. "You think I haven't been spelled to forget shit? You think my mom just sat around and let me mope and remember the worst night of my life as it replayed endlessly?"

My stomach dropped and my eyes widened.

"People have tried to magically fuck with my head ever since that night. I've always been a good Unraveler."

I stared at the ground for a moment as confused thoughts and emotions mingled to make me feel foggy, unsure of my next words or next steps. "You didn't want to forget?"

"No. What kind of person would I be if I just erased my best friend because it was hard? Because it hurt?" His tone cut like a sword.

I pulled my knees up to my chest and stared at a stinkbug that trundled along. Stupid thing. Didn't it know it was winter? "My mom takes Calm spells. Haven't seen her off Calm in over two years."

He nodded sympathetically, running an agitated hand through his hair. "That sucks. For her and for you."

I didn't answer him, just studied a dead bush. "When I think about before ... it feels like heaven. Like I literally *had heaven* and didn't know it. This," I gestured around us. "It's purgatory."

Evan just listened. Waiting. Somehow, he knew I wasn't finished.

I pulled myself to my feet and dusted the leaves off my clothes. Then I stared down at him, where he sat. "Where I'm going after this, you don't want to follow. Because I'm going to do anything it takes to bring Matthew back."

I turned.

"I want to help." Evan's voice felt like a hand grabbing mine.

I shook my head.

Evan stood and stomped over. He overtook me easily and stood towering over me. "You think you have the right to take saving him from me? I'm the one who—"

But the bitter truth spewed out of my mouth, erupted like lava. The truth that had turned my childhood crush into ash. "The one who dared him?"

"What?"

"My mom told me that you were both high on Bubble and decided to go into that facility and try the spell."

"That's not fucking true! How could I get it right if we were high? How'd I be able to fucking write if I was floating into the walls? Matthew wanted to do the spell. I told him we should wait. I wanted to practice more. Part of me didn't even want to fucking do it—"

"It wasn't his idea!" I protested, but a tiny worm of doubt wriggled inside.

Evan shook his head and held up his hands. "You know how obsessed he was with curing vampirism. He was convinced he had to do this to really understand the spell—"

That sounded exactly like Matthew. When he'd wanted to understand human anatomy, he'd built models everywhere. Robotic models. Hands. Feet. Arms. And then the fucker had enchanted them to chase me around the house. He'd always been a 'hands-on' learner. But why would mom lie? Why ... in the middle of her grief over Matthew and then Dad, would she take away the one other person I'd loved with all my heart?

I couldn't believe she'd do that to me. Now, maybe. Not out of heartlessness. But because Calm had fucked her up. It had taken away her fire.

I narrowed my eyes and studied Evan, unsure. Had mom been wrong? Had she been so twisted up by grief that she'd told me wrong? Had she been confused? I looked down and shoved my hands into the pockets of my sweatpants. But then it came to me. "I know how we can solve this."

Evan threw his hands up. "How?"

"Dad!" I yelled.

My father appeared just behind Evan. I leaned around Evan's giant, muscular form to see him. "Dad, how you doing?"

Evan said, "What the fuck?" just as my dad blew a raspberry at me.

"Hey kiddo." Dad winked.

I glanced back at Evan who was staring at me with a wrinkled brow. "My dad's a ghost."

Evan shook his head. "No." He started to laugh. He pushed his hands through his hair. "No. Really? Come on."

Evan's skepticism was normal. Since only Darklights could see them, and since we were so damn rare, ghosts were not something the masses actually believed in. They weren't something taught in school. They'd been 'debunked' by scholars. When Dad had first appeared, I'd had to scour the internet for a tiny diary by a dead Darklight in order to find anything documented in the last century about ghosts. It seemed like the rest of my kind didn't want to be deemed insane. But the fact that Evan fucking Weston, who'd known me since basically the day I was born, didn't believe me—that right there pissed me off.

It made me want to punch him in the nads. I pursed my lips and said, "Dad, possess him."

Evan's eyes immediately widened. "Hayley—"

But he didn't get another word out before Dad side-stepped into Evan's body. His own form disappeared, and only Evan was left, blinking at me.

"How about a bow? Can you handle that, Dad?" I asked.

Evan's eyes widened and he bent from the waist as he said, "What the fuck!" He wrenched back up. But clearly, he hadn't bent forward on his own. That was all Dad's doing.

"Can you make him stand on one foot?" I asked.

Evan's right foot lifted about a quarter inch off the ground before he slammed it back down.

"Still don't believe my dad's a ghost? Dad, make him smack himself on the face."

Evan's hand lifted, but the smack never came. His hand just vibrated in midair until I saw my dad hop to the side, exiting Evan's body like he was hopping off a bicycle.

Dad was breathing hard. "That possession stuff is hard work." He put a hand on his chest, like he'd just gone running.

"But you're improving," I told him. "Nice job."

Evan glanced at me, and then around the clearing, his eyes searching, his chest heaving. "What the hell was that?"

"Ghosts exist on a wavelength only Darklights—"

Evan shook his head and held up a hand. "I get that. I'll have questions later ... but I get that. But I didn't know your dad ... Mr. Dunemark?"

Dad reached out and tried to shake Evan's hand. That just made Evan yank his hand back as though he'd been frozen. Evan stared at his hand, then up at me, and back at his hand.

Apparently, ghosts reduced him to a speechless four-year-old. I didn't have time for that.

"Dad, were Matthew and Evan high that night they tried the Unnatural spell?"

"What?" My dad looked at me and his expression fell. I could literally see the memories fade as his brow lowered and his mouth drew up into a bow.

My heart crackled like tissue paper getting carelessly squashed and tossed aside. My eyes glossed. "Dad?"

Dad faded from sight, the confusion never leaving his features.

"Dad?" I tried to call him back, but he didn't return. My fist went over my chest and I just had to stand still for a second, my hand keeping my emotions crushed inside so that they wouldn't spill out and let Evan witness another breakdown.

A minute later, Evan came over and threaded his fingers through mine. He just stood like that, for a second, holding my hand, keeping me from floating away. And then he asked, "Did he leave?"

I nodded. "Sometimes he just … forgets things. One minute he's him. The next …"

Evan's hug swallowed me up in warmth and tenderness. I let my head rest against his torso, and I hugged him back for all I was worth until the loneliness receded. When I pulled away, I looked up at him. "Dad's lab had just discovered a cure for vampirism before he died. It's at the Pinnacle. I'm going to steal it. And cure him."

Evan didn't even blink. "I'm in."

25

I HAD to meet Potts at the front of the school. She was staring at the butterfly fountain when I walked out and found her.

"Little cheesy, don't you think?" she asked, jerking her head toward the butterfly fountain.

"Lotta cheesy."

She eyed me in my skinny jeans and one of Matthew's old sweatshirts. "You look a little rough."

I shrugged. "I have detention later today, and apparently detention here means free manual labor, so they don't have to hire extra staff."

Potts grinned. "Then they're doing it right." She clapped me on the shoulder and turned me around. "Gimme the grand tour."

I walked her through the admin building, pointing out all the boring things adults liked to know—like the low recidivism rate of graduates —stuff I'd accidentally memorized from the website after visiting it so much.

Potts's eyes scanned the place and then slid over me. "Not bad." She hefted her red and grey boho jacket up her hips and shoved her hands in the knitted pockets. "Tell me more about that guy you were mad about last week."

I smiled thinly at her. "We worked it out. Happy?"

Her eyebrows rose. "How?"

"We sang Kumbaya and ate marshmallows around a campfire. This place likes to do wholesome stuff like that."

Behind me, one of the other students snickered. I turned to look at the guy and Potts flicked my nose. "Don't do that," she warned, "or I'll have to bust out the cat videos. I took several this week, knowing I was going to come see you."

I led her through the quad, dodging around different huddles of students. I noticed Grayson's posse was missing their fearless leader. That brought a smile to my face. Guess he hadn't figured out how to unravel my dick tick. I really hoped he didn't. I wanted nothing more than to see his face all contrite and pleading… possibly on his knees as he apologized.

"Well, that's a conniving face you have there. You don't happen to be thinking about that Mars boy, do you?" Potts asked as she grabbed a stick of gum. She offered me one, but I refused, cocking my head and staring at her until she divulged, "Your mom said you have a big crush on that loser." Potts shook her head. "I don't believe it." She smacked her gum between her teeth.

Speak of the devil and he shall… Grayson Mars whipped around the corner of Building A. He was dressed all in baggy sweats. He yanked on my arm and pulled me toward him as Potts exclaimed, "Hey, you prick!"

Her choice of words was just too poetic. I couldn't help but laugh. I laughed so hard I almost didn't hear Grayson's apology.

"I'm sorry," he said, just as Potts came barreling into him. She wasn't strong enough to knock him over, but she shoved that shoulder into him like she believed she could. She had enough force to make him stumble sideways and clutch his aching, rock hard dick. "Owww!"

Potts froze when she realized I was laughing, not scared about being manhandled. Her eyes traveled from me to Grayson, taking in the giant swollen balloon inside his pants, and then traveling back to me, a million questions written all over her scarred face. "What—?"

I ignored her, focused solely on Mr. Mars. I held a hand to my chest in mock confusion. My bitch persona slid onto my face in full force. And I felt comfortable again. I hadn't gotten to play with bitchy face too much since I'd come to MAD. I missed her. "Wait, I'm sorry. I thought you were saying something. But I was laughing so hard I couldn't hear it."

His eyes narrowed and I could see his temper flare, but he took a deep breath and closed his eyes. "Hayley, I'm sorry. I'm sorry for what Laura did to you. And for what I did."

A weird slurping, popping sound occurred and Grayson's eyes widened. He reached into his pants.

Potts freaked, swinging her purse to hit his shoulder. "Do not take that thing—"

She stopped talking when Grayson's hand emerged from his sweatpants clutching a red round ball. It could have been confused with a water balloon, if not for the strange sheen and the wriggling legs. Grayson dropped the tick on the ground, and it exploded with a splat. Blood stained the sidewalk.

He and Potts both jumped back. I smacked a hand over my mouth, torn between laughter and complete disgust.

Grayson shook his head and walked off. But he called over his shoulder, "Don't think this is over!"

I gave him my signature wave.

Potts dug a tissue out of her purse and pressed it to her nose as she asked, "Hayley, what the hell is going on? And what was that? God … the smell."

I led her away toward the trees. "That's just how Grayson and I show affection. We're big on pranks."

"That didn't look like a prank. That looked like an alien bug—"

"It was a dick tick." I sat down on a bench and watched one of the stone lions patrolling in the distance.

After a minute, Potts joined me. "Explain."

By the time I'd gotten to the dick tick, tears of laughter were running down her face. "Oh, man. That's brilliant. I'll trade you. You wanted that lost eye spell? I'll give you that for the dick tick." She chuckled and dabbed her eyes with her tissue.

I shook my head and licked my lips. I glanced around, making sure that everyone else was enjoying their free Sunday afternoon out of earshot. "I actually wanted to ask you for something else."

I gave her the rundown on the missing vampires and my fears for Matthew.

Her face ran the gamut from shocked to angry to contemplative. "I can't pull him out and keep him anywhere, if that's what you're wanting," she said. "I don't have anywhere secure or safe enough to keep him. But … if you trust me … I can pull off some pretty great spell combinations so that they think he's missing—"

"I can hack the system to say he's been transferred," I offered.

Potts put a hand over her heart. "First off, don't ever tell *anyone* that again. You're lucky I'm bound by doctor-patient confidentiality."

I rolled my eyes. "Please, you probably tell your cats all my secrets."

"Shnookums likes to know about my day."

"Ever thought Shnookums might be a Pinnacle spy in disguise?"

She wagged a finger at me. "I'm not worth spying on, kid. I've got about thirty bucks left at the end of each month and no real agenda. This place, though, is a different story. The Pinnacle probably has eyes in here." She raised an eyebrow and jerked her head in what she thought was a subtle manner toward the navy-shirted Zoo members. They lazed on a blanket on the grass. One of them was creating fireballs that floated just above his hand. Another ate a sandwich. Without their navy shirts, I would have thought they were just a random collection of students.

I glanced at Potts, wondering how she could tell, but she held a finger to her lips and shook her head. I wondered if it was a doctor patient confidentiality thing. The curious part of me wanted to hack her files. But I had more important stuff to do. I changed the subject and asked, "Why do you think vamps are disappearing?"

Potts spit her gum into her tissue and then gave a raspy laugh. "What's the one thing vamps have that magicals don't?"

I stared into her mismatched eyes as I answered. "Immortality."

She gave me a tongue click and a finger gun. But there was no humor in her voice as she said, "Bingo."

"But ... Alchemiken's a joke. There's no such thing as the magical transference of genetics."

"Yet." She crossed her legs and stared across the courtyard. "What do you want to bet that some rich fuck is trying anyway?"

My very soul burned with anger. She was right. I just knew she was right.

26

I HAD to cut short my meeting with Potts in order to go to detention. She didn't seem to mind, because she had some historical tour lined up for her 'free vacation weekend.'

The tour sounded like torture, but it was probably still better than my detention, which was a miserable affair. Our entire class had to take turns digging holes far away from campus, and shoveling giant, rock-sized stone lion poop into said holes. Since stone lions pooped rocks, I first argued that this was a useless waste of time. Once I smelt the stone piles, however, I was really glad that none of them existed near the girls' dorms.

A couple of people puked, but nobody got to quit. Not until it was time for us to clean up and go watch another amazing showdown at the weekly tournament. I stumbled out of the girls' locker room, my hair still damp because I was too lazy to dry it all the way. I was determined to find Evan and tell him about my conversation with Potts.

It was strange, but comforting, to have him as an ally. To not be completely alone in this quest anymore. And even though I hadn't gotten the answers that I'd wanted when my dad had appeared, my gut told me to trust Evan. It told me he was in this, one hundred percent. My chest warmed, thinking that. I gave a little half smile.

Malcolm walked up to me just then. Even though he was freshly showered too, and I could smell the herbal scent of his shampoo, he'd done his hair completely. And he wore a dark, fitted black shirt with his jeans, the kind of shirt that made me think of fifties gangsters and pecs. His pecs looked amazing in that shirt. "Thinking about me?" He gave a wink that was breathtaking, even in the dull grey light of dusk.

"I am now," I told him, widening my smile. My heart picked up a little. It was the first time I'd seen him since the kiss and my fingers hummed with electric energy. I didn't know exactly what to do with my hands. I grabbed onto my backpack straps and tried to pull on my cool girl persona, but Malcolm wouldn't have any of that.

He leaned forward and brushed a strand of wet hair off my cheek. "No faking it. It's okay to be nervous." I laughed shallowly, until he leaned in and his lips grazed my ear. He whispered, "I am."

Holy shit.

His eyes were intense as he pulled back. He reached out and grabbed one of my hands from my backpack. He wove our fingers together and said, "I didn't really get to talk to you during detention."

Ho had split us into groups, making sure that neither Malcolm nor Laura was with me. "Probably a good thing. I only dry-heaved, but still not something I think you need to witness."

Malcolm gave a dark laugh and a chill raced down my spine, a chill not put there by the weather. It settled on my ass and gave it a cold, frosty bite, making me jump.

"Hey! What was that for?" I asked, self-conscious as people turned to stare at me.

"I've been thinking about our last conversation," Malcolm said, his fingers sliding up and down between mine.

My throat tightened. "Can we ... discuss it after the tournament?"

Malcolm raised a single brow.

I didn't pay any attention to the tournament, not even when the floating bubble spun like a tornado had caught it up and both the competitors were flung into the center. They were stuck, floating there, until the faculty retrieved them.

I only watched everything else out of the corner of my eye until, between bouts, Zavier and Evan marched over to us.

"Hey, flirty friend," Zavier scooped me up and set me onto his lap, ignoring the fact that I was holding Malcolm's hand. Then he glanced over at Evan. "I left a hand for you."

Evan shook his head but sat down on my left. Zavier ended up grabbing both our hands and smacking them together until we awkwardly held onto one another in order to avoid his annoying tactics.

"There. Now everybody's happy."

"You're the only one who's happy and I can feel that happiness poking me in the back," I retorted.

"Relax. Look around. Guys share here all the time." Zavier gestured to a girl three rows beneath us who was surrounded by five guys. "So long as everyone's in the know and cool with it."

I swallowed hard when one of the guys behind her started rubbing her back and another leaned over to peck her on the cheek. My chest felt like that pressure cooker Maria always used to make our pot roasts. I glanced over at Malcolm. His gaze back was calm, completely unconcerned, like this was normal. When I looked over at Evan, he was still wearing a frown, but his fingers stroked my palm. I swallowed hard. I felt like I needed to say something, to apologize or ... something. But before I could say anything, my boobs suddenly doubled in size. Then tripled. They looked like cantaloupes. "Dammit Grayson!"

Zavier laughed first. Then Malcolm. Then even Evan, that traitor. I glared at all of them as my hands went to protect my breasts and help hold them up. They were fucking heavy!

"Help, you jerkwads!" I leaned forward as my chest became weighed down by two watermelon-sized appendages.

Laughter rose around us as people started to notice what was happening. My eyes scanned the gym until I spotted him. Grayson Mars leaned against the double doors at the back of the gym. I narrowed my eyes at him, but at the same time, respect bubbled inside my stomach. I gave him a one finger salute. He returned it, laughing, before he pushed open the doors and left me to my misery.

Evan took up a spot in front of me, blocking the view of most of the other students as he stared down and studied me. Zavier kept a hold on my lap, mostly so he could say things like, "When we figure out how to reverse this, should we go all the way back to normal? Or can we keep her boobs like porn star size? Anybody wanna vote?"

If I could have reached backward and slapped him, I would have. I scolded all of them as my boobs began to hit my waist. They were hanging out from the bottom of my shirt and my bra was about to break—thank God it was one of those super elastic cotton ones. I hunched over and used the bleacher floor in front of us to help me hold them up and hide them from everyone. "Stop joking and just make this go away, now!"

Beside me, Malcolm said, "Looks like a directed growth spell, but unraveling isn't my strong suit."

"Evan!" I pleaded.

Evan already had out his wand and ink. He glanced over at Zavier, who said, "If you got this, I got you."

Then Evan nodded and knelt in front of me so he could write on the bench next to my massive, overflowing breasts, which were starting to look more like huge anacondas than breasts. One of my bra straps snapped.

From the gym floor, Professor Huchmala called out, "Hayley, what's happened? Do you need help?"

I turned fifty shades of red. All the professors stopped what they were doing, preparing for the next fight, and turned to look up at me.

"Just a prank! Reversing it now!" Zavier called down.

"Please, hurry," I whimpered.

Evan's hand flew across the parchment. Zavier's hand lifted and pointed right at Evan ... and the bear shifter's hand became a blur, until all I saw was the smoking trail of parchment and the orange sparkles lifting from the spell. Seconds later, my chest was back to normal, though my shirt and bra ... those were ruined.

But I didn't even notice that the collar of my shirt sagged forward or that a bra strap hung limp against my stomach. I turned around on Zavier's lap and punched him right in the chest. "Motherfucker!" I said. "You're a *Tock*?"

MALCOLM PULLED ME AWAY FROM THE GUYS AND HELPED ME OUT OF the gym, silently. Evan had tried to follow at first, but Malcolm had shaken his head and led me away.

"Are you okay?" Malcolm asked me.

I nodded. "More mad and embarrassed than anything."

"It was pretty mean, what he did." His eyes narrowed.

"Well ..." I thought about the dick tick. "Let's say ... he got his first. But don't worry, I'll get him back again."

Malcolm shook his head and stared up at the night sky for a minute. When he glanced down at me, his expression was serious. "So, I've been waiting patiently."

I swallowed hard. I knew what Malcolm wanted to know. I jerked my head toward the girls' dorms then started walking toward the building. I didn't check to see if he followed as my hands nervously yanked at my stretched-out shirt, my fingers as worried as my head. I felt like it was too soon. I hardly knew him. I didn't feel ready to ask him to help me.

Evan had been a different matter. Beneath the fury, I knew Evan. I knew that he'd sold his bike to the neighbor kid the time that Matthew had crashed his, so that they could be bikeless together. I knew he'd always snuck me exactly two cookies whenever the two of them stole a sleeve of Oreos from the kitchen because he knew Matthew would inhale the rest. I knew who Evan was and how he reacted and what made him tick.

I didn't know that much about Malcolm. Only that his palm over mine made mine sweaty. Only that his chin dimple made me drool. And that he liked games. And preferred anarchy to the Pinnacle. But was that enough?

I wracked my brain for anything I could do to delay what was about to come. I felt like we needed to know each other another month, maybe four, before I asked him to do something so monumental.

I avoided eye contact with Malcolm and when the chaos of the tournament ended and a crowd of people surrounded us and surged toward the dorms, I dragged my feet.

Malcolm's hand reached out and nudged the bottom of my chin until I looked up at him. He waited until the students were mostly gone, only the professor chatting and the maintenance staff cleaning up the grounds. "Hey."

"Hey."

He saw my nerves and let my chin drop. He grabbed my hand more firmly and pulled me toward the dorms. He marched me into the building and waited patiently while I let us in and brought him up to my room.

I closed the door behind me and turned to face him like a prisoner turned to face the executioner. *How are my nerves gonna hold up at the Pinnacle?* I wondered, feeling sick at how weak-kneed I was. But at the Pinnacle, I'd be in control. Here, I was about to hand control over to Malcolm. And I honestly wasn't sure what he'd do with it.

Malcolm stood in the middle of my room, his blonde hair darkened by shadows. He set down his bookbag. But he didn't go recline against my dresser or hop onto my bed like Zavier might have done. He stood with his legs spread and his hands behind his back. And somehow, his presence filled the entire room. My bookbag slid off my shoulder to the floor, forgotten.

Malcolm looked over at me and commanded, "Come here."

My arms crossed over my stomach and I swallowed as I made my way over to him.

Malcolm reached out when I was directly in front of him. He gently pressed on each of my arms until they were down by my sides. Then he waited, in agonizing silence, until I glanced up at him. "What are you afraid to tell me?"

"Everything."

"Why?"

I studied his eyes, my tummy tightening. "Because you can say no."

A tiny grin lit his face. "Try me."

I opened my mouth, ready to spill my secrets to one of the hottest guys I'd ever met. But what came out was, "Dost thou know mine secret... what infernal wind blows upon my tongue?" Fear turned to disbelief. To horror. My hands flew to my mouth. My eyes went wide.

Malcolm raised his eyebrows, blue eyes skeptical. "Is this another game?"

I shook my head frantically, my orange streaked hair whipping back and forth as I dropped my hands. What spilled out my lips was more gibberish. "In truth, there's no such game afoot, my lord." My hands clamped back over my mouth. What was wrong with me? My mind sped to the obvious answer. Grayson. He'd found a way to up the ante. "That black-hearted knave! That pustulant boil! Grayson Mars—the fool! I shall trample thy weapon, break thy sword in two…"

Malcolm leaned back against my dresser, relaxing the dominant pose he'd had before. Now, he snickered at me. "Is this Grayson's revenge? You two seem to go back and forth with prank spells quite a bit. Should I be jealous?"

"Jealous? Of that bull's pizzle? My wrath shall burn that three-inch fool to non." I yanked at my hair, furious and amused at the same moment. What the motherfuck was I saying?

Malcolm didn't help matters, adding, "I feel like you need to jump up on the bed and hold a skull in your hands or something, Shakespeare."

I shook my fist at him for making fun of my hardship. I went over to my bed and hopped up, like I was being a good sport. But I grabbed my pillow and launched it at him. "Thou mockst' my misery, most cruel sir." I tried to keep an angry face, but I couldn't. I sounded like a complete idiot! That fuckwad. That clever bastard. Ugh! I started to laugh and threw myself face first onto the bed.

Shit. I had a late night of unraveling ahead of me.

I glanced up at Malcolm. He shook with laughter. His face turned red and he clutched at the pillow until he was bent over gasping. "I take back anything I ever said about you messing with Grayson. Keep doing it."

Grayson's spell saved me that night, though I'd never have admitted it to him. I wasn't ready to confess everything to Malcolm. It was too soon. We needed to know each other better, trust each other more first.

Instead of spilling my guts, Malcolm sat next to me on my bed and helped me work through the spell. He actually taught me a neat little spell that you could write to reveal the original spell. The Latin letters and numbers from Grayson's work shimmered in midair. It made it twice as easy to come up with the unraveling spell I needed so that I could talk again. Still, even with all that help, unraveling took until after one in the morning, because every time I tried to contribute to the conversation, or even write out my ideas, what came out was stupid Shakespearean gibberish. Grayson didn't mess around. He'd gone full communication blitz on this spell.

Luckily, Malcolm wasn't a quitter. And that night, as we unraveled the spell together, I realized how well we worked as a team. And how good he smelled. And how warm his arm was against mine even when he wasn't sending out tiny jets of fire in my direction.

When Malcolm snuck out my window at one a.m., I closed the curtains and turned away with a dreamy smile on my face. But then a tapping at my window had me turning back. I opened the curtains and the window to see him perched on the sill.

Malcolm gave me a tiny, goofy grin in the moonlight. And then he whispered, "But soft, what light through yonder window breaks?"

I giggled and said, "You are such a nerd!"

"She speaks. O, speak again, bright angel!"

I leaned down, putting my elbows on my side of the sill. "Go to bed, Malcolm."

He didn't listen. He leaned forward and pressed his lips, chilled by the winter night air, to mine. Our lips caressed one another as he slid his hand behind my head and threaded his fingers through my hair. And then he deepened the kiss, the warmth of his tongue plying my mouth. He leaned in further and I felt his chest press against mine, felt his heartbeat racing and my chest strove to match its pace. My head spun and burned from the power of the kiss, and just when I thought I might faint, Malcolm pulled back.

We stared at one another in the stark moonlight, memorizing each other's features—raw, honest looks exchanged by two people who knew that they were connected in a way that defied description.

Malcolm stroked my cheek and winked.

Before I could invite him in, he leaned back and said, "And thus, with a kiss, I die!" He waved a dramatic fist in the air. Then he started to climb down the wall of the girls' dorm.

I leaned out of the window to watch him. "You're a dork!" I called down to him.

"Whatever, Shakespeare." He jumped the last six feet. He looked up at me one last time a soft smile on his face.

A loud stomp from one of the stone lions broke the magic of the moment, and Malcolm ran off to the guys' dorms.

I stayed in the window, staring up at the moon and wondering just how relevant *Romeo and Juliet* was for Malcolm and me. When he found out ... would everything be okay? Or would it all blow up in my face? If there was a tragedy in store, I wasn't ready for it.

27

I MADE my way down to the guys' dorm four days later. I was pissed that Grayson had gotten me twice in a row with a spell and I hadn't gotten him back yet. Pissed.

Somehow, miraculously, my tongue and lips and I had managed to hold Malcolm off from all the questions. I hadn't told him anything yet. Instead, our tutoring sessions had become heavy make out sessions—which was just fine by me. I wanted to keep them that way as long as possible.

I hadn't really had a chance to talk to Evan because he had standardized testing this week instead of class. So, I couldn't tell him what was going on. Zavier had been stuck in there too, so I'd had nothing to do with my time but plan for sweet, sweet revenge.

It was only the second time I'd been to the guys' dorms. It felt stupid, because I'd broken into different parts of campus at all my old academies—though none were quite as dangerous as this. But tonight, I was nervous. The back of my neck was sweaty even though the temp had to be a crisp, lash-your-face thirty degrees because March had decided to turn into a cold-hearted month. I needed to cool down. I needed to be cool like March.

But I was about to search Grayson's room. I'd violated his privacy and personal files to the max. But there was a disassociation with that. I had been attacking from a distance. I had been bombing his bunkers with drones like norms did when they tried to destroy their enemies. But going in with boots on the ground? I had to wipe my palms on my jeans. I'd broken into Malcolm's room and it had worked out. I knew I needed to do the same with Grayson. But the idea of him catching me ...

Grayson's anger was different from Malcolm's. Malcolm got quiet. Disappointed. Domineering. Grayson was more the punch-your-lights-out type. Though I kind of hoped our feud was changing that. Still, if he found me snooping, all bets were off.

Think of it as practice for the Pinnacle, I told myself as I drew shadows around me to avoid a faculty member who walked through campus, doing a last check for the night. I reached the grey stone facade of the guys' dorm and looked up. I swallowed. Grayson's room was on the sixth floor. Not that Metamorphose had thousands of students. It didn't. A few hundred at most. But the guys tended to get violent. So, I'd been told the boys were spaced out every other room. Magic supposedly blocked the empty rooms and green Peaceful Thought amulets housed in abstract sculptures hung from the hallways—one of Professor Huchmala's hokey creations.

I started to climb, my fingers aching only two moves into my rock-climbing attempt. Dammit. This was harder than it looked. Way harder than the gym's rock-climbing wall. It made me respect Grayson's crew's escape and Malcolm's descent from my window all the more. If I had to scale the Pinnacle, I was screwed.

I sucked in my complaints and forced myself to muscle through. Every bit of my concentration went into handholds and footholds until I wasn't a person, I was just a machine. *Extend arm, tighten foothold. Ratchet grip down until knuckles are white and shift body weight. Repeat.*

I took a break on the third floor, crouching on a windowsill to shake out my rapidly numbing hands. Why did I do this again? I should have broken in through the front door and gone up the stairs like I had when I'd gone to Malcolm's room. But that had been during school hours when no one was home. I wouldn't have made it anywhere close to Grayson's room at night when the rooms were occupied, even with my shadows around me. His little minions swarmed the place like bees. He was their little queen, ruling over the hive-minded dopes willing to lay down at his feet.

I had it on good authority that Grayson had tutoring tonight though.

I took a second to peer into the room beyond my window ledge. It was dark, so at first, I assumed it was one of the empty rooms, the buffer zones. But then I heard a moan. I drew my shadows closer-- and the nosy voyeur inside me stuck her face closer to the glass. I made out figures on the bed. At first, I was confused. There were too many legs.

I turned on my heat vision and realized that there weren't two people on the bed. There were three. Two guys and one girl— based on their size. My cheeks flushed and I immediately looked away. Awkward. My mind twiddled her thumbs and stared at her feet, scuffing her shoes, but my body grew warm. That was a sign. I definitely needed to move. I raised my hands and grabbed the top of the window frame. My eyes scanned the wall and looked for a new handhold. I latched onto a groove and started to pull myself up. My left foot slid over into the grouted crack between two stones. My right foot lifted off the ledge and snuck forward in space. But then my fingers slipped, and my foot smacked into the glass.

Fuck!

I scrabbled to get a better hold and swing my right foot away from the damned window. What could possibly be more humiliating than being caught? Nothing. I clutched at the stones like a bear clutches tree branches that are far too small for its massive paws. Beside me, the window slid open and a girl's head stuck out. I pushed a combination of shadows and light at her to blur her vision in case she looked my way. But she didn't look my way. She looked down, leaning out onto the ledge. Her wild mane of dark curls was immediately recognizable. Laura. Grayson's girl.

My eyes widened to the size of dinner plates. I hadn't expected Grayson to be the kind of guy who shared. He came across as such an alpha asshole. My nipples tightened at the thought of him in that light. I didn't bother to scold my body. It was gonna react how it wanted anyway. But my mind was moving a mile a minute. This was all the more reason to get into Grayson's room. I didn't know what was really inside his head. I needed to. I needed to solve the puzzle that was him and figure out what made him tick. And he was occupied right now. I had the perfect opportunity.

"I dunno," Laura's voice drifted up to me as she struggled to close the window. "Maybe a bird flew into it or something."

I waited until she was gone to move, my fingers and toes screaming their disapproval. By the time I made it to the sixth floor and Grayson's window, those same digits were past the point of pain. My fingertips bled as I pulled myself onto Grayson's ledge and propped myself up in the ancient window, thanking my lucky stars that the architect of Metamorphose hadn't made the ledges tiny. Grayson's room was dark, like I expected, though a light shone from under his bathroom door. He must have forgotten to turn it off. Or maybe he'd run in there to snag a box of condoms before his threesome.

The images that rolled through my mind at the thought of that made my stomach tighten. But I also felt a tiny prickle of something else. Something undefined. I wasn't quite sure what. I shook it off. I was wasting time.

It took several minutes before I could pull my travel-size self-inking wand and a bit of parchment out of my shirt.

I fiddled with the parchment, trying to unroll it against the glass and giving up, unfurling it across my knee. I took a deep breath and steadied my hand before I started to write an Unlocking Spell.

The window flew up as I was writing. Shocked, I leaned away on instinct. And that's when I fell. My heart slammed into my throat with so much force that I was choking on it. My head rushed toward the ground. Through my feet, I saw the open window. Grayson leaned out of it, his eyes black pits as he watched me fall. My feet scraped down against the brick wall and smacked against the protruding window ledge on the floor beneath Grayson's as I fell.

Pain. Rang. Through. Me.

My last thoughts should have been of Mom and Matthew—but Grayson's eyes held me captive and I couldn't think of anything else. They took my breath away. The cold determination in them. The black fire. They slammed into my spine and made me dizzy. I couldn't hold eye contact—though I wanted to—my eyelids fluttered, and my stomach flip-flopped like I was riding a roller coaster. My eyes closed and my inner ears must have been off-balance because I felt like I was rising, not falling. But everything about my body was off. I'd been flooded with heat when I first fell backward. Now I was covered in goosebumps. I struggled to open my eyes. But my eyelids wouldn't cooperate. Not even when I landed.

That was when I was certain I was dead. My heart must have stopped mid-fall. Because my landing felt as soft as a cloud. Like I'd just lain down in bed ready to drift off to sleep.

ANN DENTON

I WOKE UP TO THE FEELING OF SOMETHING WARM AND A LITTLE BIT rough pressing into my cheek. I sighed, leaning into it without opening my eyes, my body sore all over. I wanted that warmth, wanted to steal it and make it mine like that Greek story about the man who stole fire from the gods.

"You dead, nemesis?" A familiar, low, growly voice asked.

I forced my eyelids apart. My mouth dried out.

I stared up at Grayson's face, lit by some warm yellow incandescent bulb that made him glow like an angel. An angry angel, whose thick eyebrows were drawn together as his warm hand moved from my cheek to check my pulse.

The feel of his hand on my neck sent my heart racing. And not entirely from fear.

I licked my lips. My throat was dry, but I managed a jagged, "But you were having a threesome." Not the best thank you, but my mind was still just shifting out of first gear.

Grayson's face contorted. "What?"

"Laura and you and some guy on the third floor ..." I had to pause to swallow. My mouth felt like it'd been stuffed with cotton balls. Come hell or high water, I was not scaling the Pinnacle from the outside.

But I'd hardly completed my thought before my asshole savior had disappeared, leaving the door to his dorm room ajar. I blinked stupidly for a minute before I realized what was going on.

Shit.

I tried to sit up. My muscles weren't having it. My entire back felt like a giant bruise. Grayson must have lifted me back up here with his Force. My fingers stroked his comforter, imagining it. His hands extended, the gust of wind that had rushed underneath me and lifted me until he could wrap me in his arms.

A strange feeling drifted over me. It was a graceful sensation, like an Olympic ribbon dancer was spinning inside of me. It was a long, drawn-out emotion that twisted and turned and made the air around me look like it was full of beautiful hidden shapes and possibilities that I could see if I just looked hard enough.

I used my arms again, trying to sit up. But I still couldn't manage. So, I stared at Grayson's ceiling, looking at the popcorn texture that had been pierced by pencils thousands of times as bored students threw the writing utensils like darts instead of doing their work.

One pencil was still stuck in the ceiling above Grayson's desk. It looked just like mine. So did his walls. I wondered what else we had in common.

It took me several minutes before I realized my state of mind must have been affected by this whole fall thing. I'd been laying here filling my head with unimportant questions for Grayson like "What's your favorite color?" instead of trying to figure out what protection amulets he had hidden around the room to prevent me from antagonizing him.

My eyes turned to the corner behind his desk. I could see a pink amulet there, its light faint in the darkness. Pink light encased in a glass amulet sphere. That generally meant the spell was emotional. Interesting.

I waited on Grayson's deliciously soft mattress; he'd obviously replaced the standard school-issue stone slab with a giant marshmallow. Gradually, my arms started to respond to my demands. I'd just weakly pulled myself back up onto my elbows when Grayson came storming back into his room.

He slammed the door behind him. He grabbed his backpack near the door and threw it across the room. It smacked into his wall with a loud *crack*. Grayson started pacing like a madman. "Those assholes! They promised—"

"I take it you were never at the threesome?" My voice was wry, but I couldn't help sucking in air through my teeth and grimacing. *Fuck, I hurt.*

Grayson paused and stared down at me. "I forgot you were here."

"I'd leave if I could," I retorted. "This is as far as I've been able to move." My mind was still having little brown outs from shock.

He sighed, scrubbed a hand across his face, and walked over to me. Once again, his big warm hands touched my body, starting at my legs and feeling them.

"Hey!" I growled.

"I'm trying to see if anything's broken," he scolded.

"Well why don't you ask me instead of mauling me?" I groused. "Nothing's broken. But I feel like a giant bruise. I'm going to be as purple as that purple monster-thing from McDonalds."

"Grimace?"

I fell back onto Grayson's pillow, my arms giving out. "Is that its name? How appropriate."

Grayson rolled his eyes and went to his desk. He pulled out his wand and parchment and ink.

I panicked. Fear shot like a dart through me. "Hey! No fair. I'm incapacitated. You can't put a spell on me right now."

Grayson paused what he was doing. He turned sideways in his desk chair and planted his feet on the ground, elbows resting on his knees. "What were you doing tonight?"

"Coming to spy on you," I admitted with a grumpy exhale. "None of the new spells I've been trying on you have worked."

A twisted sort of smile crossed his face. "What spells?"

I narrowed my eyes at him.

"Oh, come on, they didn't work anyway. Tell me."

"I tried to make you randomly shout, 'I'm a dickhead!' in class."

The twist to his mouth grew painful looking.

"What else?"

"I tried to cast a spell to make the front of your pants permanently wet. Or make your wand turn limp every time you touched it."

"Why am I seeing a theme here?" Grayson asked, moving off his elbows and leaning onto the back of his chair, tilting it back onto two feet as he gave a smile.

"Cause you're a dick," I told him bluntly.

"Well, you're a cunt."

I made a sour face at him.

"You deny it?"

"No."

"A dick and a cunt." He laughed, lowering his chair to the ground and turning back to his desk.

"I told you not to spell me!"

"And what are you gonna do about it?"

I tried moving my legs, but they were still shaky. I had to watch, with bated breath, as Grayson wrote a spell. The parchment burnt up and curled into glittering blue sparkles as he did it. The sparkles wove through the air before they disappeared. And all I could do was shoot eye darts Grayson's way and hope they pierced his jugular.

My hand felt the spell first, like a gentle spring breeze. It was warm and hesitant. It entered my skin and flowed through my body. My sore muscles grew calm and stopped screaming. The ache that had filled me head to toe retreated like the tide. My eyes widened as I realized what Grayson had done. He'd healed me.

I sat up, feeling fresh and revitalized. Grayson watched from his chair, a solemn look on his face. I tested out my feet, which minutes ago had been as useless as an empty tissue box. I stood up and my eyes locked on Grayson.

I opened my mouth to say 'thanks', but he cut me off.

"Truce?" he asked, tilting his head to study me.

I stared into his eyes for a long minute before I responded. He'd just found out that his somewhat girlfriend was a cheater. Should I go easy on him? I weighed my options like a penny-pinching shopper weighs the fruit in the produce aisle. His eyes looked dull, duller than they had when he'd made me twerk.

Sometimes, people needed nice when they were hurting. Sometimes, they needed easy. But other times, as I knew far too well, they needed a goal. A distraction.

I walked toward Grayson until I was right next to his feet and he had to tilt his head to look up at me. I reached out and put my hand to his cheek, mirroring how he'd checked on me earlier. Then I gave his cheek a hard pat. I leaned in and whispered, "Truces are boring."

I walked out, knowing his eyes burnt a hole in my ass.

28

I PUT off telling the guys for one more week, mostly because I wasn't certain what to tell them or how to phrase it—I could hardly believe that the time had actually come—though I told myself that I was waiting to hear from Potts.

I'd given her cash to order us a couple burner phones. Mine came in on Wednesday and I carried it around in my pocket, checking it constantly— like a stereotypical girl the morning after a hookup. Anxiety built throughout the day. Was she gonna call or not? Dammit.

Finally, a video call buzzed the phone around five p.m. I'd been sitting outside enjoying a rare random evening of dry weather by studying at a bench instead of in my room. I snatched up the phone and jabbed at the green answer button.

Potts immediately started in without a greeting. "Well, I think that's about as good as I can get it. Nobody should see him." She flipped the camera view on the phone so that I could see the stark cement walls of the visitor's viewing room at the Institute. She walked closer to the window, the view shaking in her hand like it was some horror movie.

My heart started to beat quickly in anticipation.

ANN DENTON

She held the camera up to the mirror and I flinched, expecting Matthew's long claws to strike out at any second. But they didn't.

"See? In the corner?" Potts asked.

I squinted and tried to see the dark corner she was showing me.

"I don't see anything," I responded, frustrated by the awful signal.

Potts rapped on the glass. Movement flashed in the corner. Tiny wings and a small black creature … "Is that a bat?" I asked.

"Yup."

"But only Unnaturals can shift."

"Technically true."

"So…"

I could hear Potts sigh. She flipped the view from the vampire containment cell back to her face. She bit her lip, looking a little like a child expecting a scolding. "Sometimes you have to shake things up a little and try mashing two things together. I did the Unnatural Spell on him again, only, I wrote the spell to apply to him instead of myself. And while Unnaturals can't technically pick their animals … I combined it with a bat mating scent spell in the hope that—"

Fury. My vision flickered to thermal imaging unconsciously. Potts became a flat mass of red and orange on screen. I stood up from my bench and nearly dropped the phone because I was shaking so much. "You did *what*!?"

"Well, it's not like he could turn vamp again!" she protested.

My hand clenched on the phone. "You are so lucky you're across the country right now," I growled at her. If I was in that room right now, I'd have jumped her like the Fangs did here.

"The glass window is spelled against magic, so that vamps can't accidentally blast their way out, but I'm gonna write a level eight illusion spell and lay it in front of the glass so nobody can see or hear him flying in there," Potts added. "If they look, they'll just see an extra blanket. If they go in there, for some reason, they'll just feel an extra blanket. It'll all be an illusion ... and it's a strong one, so I'll have to come back every few days and redo it ... but I think it should work."

I closed my eyes and forced myself to take a couple deep breaths. Potts was right. I talked myself down. I might not love her methods, but the guards would never notice him now. And it was a lot of work on her part to do all of this, any of this, for me. She had no reason to help. Gratitude trickled into the cracks of my angry shell and broke it apart. I could hack into the system now and put in some fake transfer paperwork.

"Thank you," I told her, my tone stiff. I blew out a breath and tried again. "Thank you."

"You're welcome."

I spent the rest of that night hacking into the mainframe, erasing video footage of Potts, forging transfer paperwork, etc. While I was in the mainframe, I clicked onto some of the old transfer paperwork in order to forge it more accurately—attention to detail was key. At the bottom of the document, I noticed a familiar symbol next to the signature. The Pinnacle had authorized these transfers.

I tried to make out the chicken scratch signature. The best I could guess, it looked like Ginny Stone.

That was weird.

I opened a second transfer document, for another vamp. Same signature. A third. Same.

One hour later, I sat back against my bedframe, back aching, mind whirling as I stared out into the shadows of my room. I'd tried to hack the Pinnacle employment records, but they had a nasty, little dataworm spell darting around inside their servers. It had nearly latched onto my computer—if it had, it would have sucked my hard drive dry and helped them figure out who I was. I'd had to set my laptop aside and come up with an info dump onto one of the Pinnacle's servers, a nice delicious meal of Wikipedia goodness that it couldn't resist. I'd probably left some poor norm schmuck in the IT department frazzled when the server blew.

I blew a frustrated raspberry in the dark. Ginny Stone's identity was going to have to remain a mystery ... for now.

My skin grew cold and the acid in my stomach churned like lava. The Pinnacle was transferring these vampires, making them disappear. But why? Was Potts right? Were they using these vamps for genetic research? When she'd said that, I'd initially thought some mad scientist or maybe even some company ... but the government was taking vamps and not even really covering it up.

Of course, most people only saw what Professor Wolfe saw—monsters. They didn't care what happened to them.

My eyes scanned over the transfer page for the latest vamp—a woman named Kahli. She'd only been twenty-two when she'd tried the spell, forty years ago. I closed my eyes and tried to envision being stuck inside those awful stone walls for forty years, with a diet just above starvation level. We didn't know what kind of mental processes vamps had, just that their rabid behavior was dangerous, their natural born powers could shoot off at random, and that they drank blood.

But I'd thought I'd heard Matthew calling my name. My heart pinged. I believed, deep down, that my brother's mind was still in there somewhere.

I didn't have time to dig any deeper before the sun rose and blinded my bleary eyes. I rubbed my forehead and sighed. I wished for a second that I had an Energetic amulet to get me through the day. But I didn't. I rolled out of bed and had to rely on good old caffeine and Gatorade before my run with Lundy.

We ran underneath the threat of rain for the third time this week. I hated the Pacific Northwest and its gloomy weather. During the run, Evan and I deliberately fell behind and I updated him. His eyes flashed when I told him about the connection to the Pinnacle. "Did they all go to the same facility?"

I shook my head. "Different places. But all major cities. New York. Los Angeles. D.C. Except for Cape Canaveral in Florida. A couple just got transferred there."

"They're moving them to big cities? Closer to more norms? That doesn't make sense. Why hold them there? That puts more people at risk."

I grew quiet as a couple members of Fang got too close. They glared at Evan, baring their teeth, one of them flipping him off. He didn't respond, just grabbed my arm and had me slow down further until they got far away.

"Wolf shifters." He shook his head. "As if we get to choose what animal we become."

"Well, I don't know everything that goes on with the Pinnacle. But Claude's always got a million weapons projects going on with them. The Pinnacle could be using them as ... I dunno—back up, in case we're ever invaded? Imagine some army having to face off against them."

Evan shook his head. "But they can't be controlled. It would be chaos. I guess maybe they could air drop them into other countries. But, if they're basically gonna force them to be soldiers, they should get family releases and stuff. Compensate the families."

I laughed. "Why? When they can get away with it and no one cares?"

Evan shook his head and rubbed at his chest. "I just ... I feel like something worse is going on."

I bit my lip and stared ahead toward the trees, trying not to let Evan's fear infect me. *Matthew's safe,* I recited in my head. *Potts made sure he's safe.* "Potts was sure that some twisted mad scientist was using them for experiments. Like, Alchemiken-crazy, weird, gene-level stuff."

"You think someone's continuing the work from your dad's lab?"

I shook my head. "If they were, he would have told me about it. I think."

Evan reached out and his hand brushed down my arm until his palm reached mine. Then he picked up my hand and held it. We stopped the pretense of running at all and just walked hand in hand. My eyes drifted to where his fingers wrapped around mine. His hand had gotten so big since the spell. "I wonder why you became a grizzly," I said softly.

"They're loners." He shrugged as we reached the edge of the tree line, and the buildings of the academy appeared again. In the distance, other students stretched after their run. Evan stared up, watching the grey clouds roll in.

"You're not a loner." I protested.

"Since the spell, yeah, I am."

Those simple words mangled my insides. Evan's handsome face, his stiff jaw, his haunted eyes as they lowered to mine, made me twisted with guilt. He was only alone because I'd let him be. Because I'd believed my mom when she said it was his fault. I'd never even questioned it, wracked by sorrow. It had been easier to blame someone. Easier to deal with the flames of hatred than the depths of despair.

I pulled my hand out of Evan's and wrapped both arms around his waist. I buried my face in his chest and started to cry. I'd left him alone. The boy I'd said I'd loved for three years, the boy I'd written about in my diary, whose last name I'd doodled in all my notebooks. I'd abandoned him. And he'd followed me anyway.

Evan's arms slowly slid over my shoulders, gently rubbing circles along my upper back. Eventually, his arms wrapped around me and he crushed me into him in a giant hug.

It was a hug to end all hugs, something I knew that I'd replay in my mind over and over again for years to come. It was a whole body hug, the kind where his fingers dug into my flesh and he lifted me off the ground so that my feet dangled in the air, the kind where he pulled me so hard against him that I felt breathless. It was a hug that was years in the making, that was the physical embodiment of apology and acceptance in one. It was a hug on the outside, but on the inside, it was two souls touching, acknowledging for the first time just how desperately they needed one another. Because out of anyone in the world, only Evan shared my love for Matthew, my grief. Only he knew who I was before and who I'd had to become. He was the only one who could ever fully appreciate that fall from grace.

A shrill whistle broke our moment, and we turned to see Coach Lundy striding toward us, his short man legs carrying him faster than most short men could run. "Break it up, people. No PDAs." He waved his arm, gesturing for me to move backward.

I gave Evan one last, long squeeze and then I let go, because I had to. But as I backed away and pretended to stretch, my eyes held onto him, latched onto his stare so that I could stay connected to at least one part of him. Gratitude and a long-latent desire thrummed inside me. My pulse bounced wildly. I licked my lips and Evan's lashes lowered so his eyes could trace the movement. The air between us thickened, and as a storm promised to rain down on the academy, another type of storm brewed between us. The kind of storm that was full of drops of sweat and the wild lightning that seared your eyelids as an orgasm raged through you.

My body tightened in anticipation. It was coming. Evan's eyes promised it was.

Of course, Lundy ruined the moment. "Love birds, you need to separate before your doe eyes make me lose my breakfast. Stretch out!"

I turned away from Evan then, but didn't leave. Instead, I sighed and started stretching my calves. I'd need to be nice and limber later ... I hoped.

Evan stretched his arms and then bent in half until Lundy strode off to break up a fight that the Fangs had picked with another student. That's when Evan walked over in front of me and said, "Hailstorm, I think it's time. I think we need to bring the guys in."

I rubbed a hand down my face in exhaustion but also in fear. I chewed on my lip. "I don't even think ... I think there's like a sixty percent chance Malcolm will say yes. Grayson's up in the air. Zavier ... I still haven't background checked that jerkwad, but he's got a tracking device. It's his last shot here, I dunno ..."

Evan stared down at me, his blue eyes studying me, taking in my nervous lip bite even though I tried to stop it before it started. He'd taken my hand and said softly, "They'll be in, Hailstorm. Don't worry."

I shook my head. "How do you know? I mean ... taking on the Pinnacle? Grayson's dad is running for office. Do you really think he's gonna be up for robbing it?"

Evan's lips quirked up. "Yes, I do."

"Why?"

His hand rose and tentatively touched my cheek. His expression filled with so many different things. Sadness. Longing. Heartache. "Because who could say no to you?" Then he turned, and before I could say another word, he walked off.

29

APRIL SECOND. Yesterday was the day that everyone celebrated fools––but today I couldn't help but wonder if I was one.

I gulped as I walked through the quiet library, toward the study room, feeling more inexperienced and intimidated than I'd felt in years.

It was my eighteenth birthday, though I didn't tell anyone. The day itself had lost its meaning a long time ago. The only birthday wish I had was that I wouldn't fuck this up.

I stared into the study room through the glass, feeling unsteady on my feet. Evan, Malcolm, and Zavier already sat inside.

That made me bristle. I'd wanted to be first to this meeting, but I pushed the emotions down. Defensiveness wasn't gonna get me anywhere.

I swallowed hard before pushing open the door. I'd spent all day psyching myself up after inviting all the guys to the library. Only Evan knew why.

The other two had curious looks on their faces when I walked in with a laptop bag.

I gave a tight smile to each as I set my bag on the table of the study room, where Malcolm and I normally had tutoring. I didn't say anything at first as I took out my laptop and flash drive, fingers twirling the little grey stick nervously as I waited for Grayson.

Malcolm watched me with the cold, evaluating look he got when he was trying to decide if I was being honest. He didn't say anything, but that look itself piqued my nerves as I booted up the laptop.

When Grayson pulled open the door, he had one of his cronies with him. He hadn't come alone, like I'd asked. A spike of panic stabbed my stomach. But I tried to keep a cool face as I said, "Sorry, no room for extras."

"You've got your harem here, why the hell don't I get back up?" Grayson raised a thick brow.

I blew out a breath. "Because I wanted to see if you wanted to join them."

Grayson stared at me, eyeing me up and down. His eyes got caught on the flash drive that I fiddled with—I scolded myself for the tell. But I was more nervous than I'd ever been. This was do or die. All or nothing. My cool-girl persona was shot to hell.

Grayson waved off his goon. "I'll call you if I need you."

"You sure, man?" The tattooed, nose-ringed guy that Grayson had brought along eyed us all suspiciously.

Grayson waved a hand, and immediately, the rest of us were suspended three feet from the floor. "I've got this," the rich boy smirked.

I tried to ignore the fact that he'd just made me as powerless as a puppet and how giddy I was that he could lift all of us at once so easily. I smoothed my features.

His bodyguard harrumphed but stomped off.

Thank fuck.

Grayson let us down and came into the room, closing the door behind him.

"Take a seat," I offered him the last open chair. I had to nail this pitch. He had to say yes.

"I'll stand, thanks." He leaned against the wall. His eyes roamed over all of us and I could see by his rigid stance that he wasn't quite as casual as he pretended to be. "So … what's this really about? I doubt you need a PowerPoint to explain how to fuck you … except maybe for that dumbass." He nodded toward Zavier.

"Nah, I already got that PowerPoint lesson … from your mom," Zavier replied with a grin.

Grayson shot a jet of wind at Zavier, who merely held up a hand. Z turned into nothing more than a blur as he streaked around the table and back to his seat faster than I could blink. Zavier sat back down, smiling. The blast of wind Grayson had shot hit Zavier's face just as Grayson looked down and found his pants and boxers around his ankles. I tried not to look as he hiked his pants back up, but damn, he was hung.

Grayson's eyes flashed with anger and he lifted his hand again.

I pressed my lips together and sighed, flicking my hand so that Grayson and Zavier's vision immediately went dark. They couldn't attack each other if they were blind. "This is my fault for thinking a crew of all guys would be less drama than girls."

"Crew?" Malcolm asked, leaning forward and putting his elbows on the table.

I tossed Malcolm the flash drive, my darkness wavering. I turned my attention back to the other two, focused on keeping the darkness steady as I said, "Evan, want to explain while I keep thing one and thing two in time out?"

Malcolm pulled my laptop toward himself and stuck the flash drive in.

My stomach clenched as the files opened and Malcolm's eyes widened just a bit.

"Hey, I wanna see. And he attacked me first!" Zavier whined. "Come on, Hayley. I'll be a good boy."

I rolled my eyes but released both of them. Grayson just turned to stare at me for a moment.

Malcolm looked over at me in disbelief, shock clear as daybreak on his face.

I tried to force some swagger, but it didn't work. The entire speech that I'd prepared flew out of my head. But I had to say something. What came out was, "Hi, I'm Hayley. I'm a Darklight. And I want you to break into the Pinnacle with me."

Grayson threw back his head and laughed. But when nobody joined him, he stopped. "No. Wait. You're serious?"

Malcolm turned my laptop around so that Grayson could see some of the schematics he was looking at. "Yeah, she's serious." My tutor's eyes went to mine, his expression stern.

I swallowed hard, lowering my gaze to the floor. *Fuck.* I hadn't meant to throw it out there like that. But there was no backtracking now. No way to softly introduce the topic anymore. I just had to keep moving, though I mentally cringed, kicked myself, dipped myself in tar and feathers. I felt like a damn fool.

I wanted to hurl. But I couldn't. I had to shove that all down. *You can't make it to the fourth quarter and just give up,* Matthew's stupid sports metaphors rang in my ears, his voice just as taunting in my mind as it had been when he'd said it.

I blew out a breath and looked back up at them. No time for cowardice or second-guessing. I was doing this. And I needed them on board.

A chair scraped backward, and Zavier stood up. His expression was confused. "What are you planning to steal?"

"The cure for vampirism," I told him. "The Pinnacle has a serum in their vault boxes."

Something flickered in his eyes. "I've never heard of a serum."

"My father's lab completed it just before he died. The Pinnacle bought his company out from under my grieving mother and her asshole new husband less than six months later."

"Proven serum?" Grayson asked.

"So I've been told. The data was erased—and I mean completely corrupted and wiped from drives, someone didn't want it found—before I learned about it. The Pinnacle doesn't want the serum to exist." My voice trembled with rage.

"Why not?" Z wondered.

Evan jumped in. "We aren't sure. We've been investigating. But vamps are disappearing left and right. The Pinnacle's transferring them out of institutes where they've lived for decades. And they aren't reappearing at the institutes where they've been reassigned." His statement was followed by a long moment of silence, where everyone in the room processed what had been said.

"Sending them where?" Grayson's voice was uncharacteristically soft as he leaned forward and clicked on one of the schematics, pulling up a large shaft that descended from the seventh floor of the Pinnacle to deep underneath the ground.

At least he's listening, I thought as I fought the urge to wring my fingers. "Still working that out," I replied. "But, that's off topic. We get this serum; we can stop that. There won't be any more Vampiric Institutes. No need. It supposedly allows them to think normally." So I'd been told. By a ghost. I didn't add that shit yet. Baby steps. Okay, well I'd screwed up the baby steps part of it. But still …

"Why would the Pinnacle hide something like that?" Z scratched his head, leaning back in his seat.

"Because whatever they're using vampires for, they want them *as is*," Malcolm theorized. "They want them mindless and controllable. They want them rejected and forgotten by society. So they can use them."

His words made the air grow cold. Or maybe he did it with his power. Either way, goosebumps rose on my arm. "It's evil, whatever it is," I whispered. I kept the tremble from my voice only because I pinched myself on the arm, hard. I wouldn't get weepy. I would only let myself stay angry about this. Anger was better motivation.

"It's what every regime does. Abuse the weak." Malcolm's face twisted with anger in a way I'd never seen before.

Malcolm turned to me, standing up in front of Zavier and eyeing me speculatively. "But why this cause? Why would you risk a life in prison for a cure for some freaky arrogant assholes who were overconfident in their own abilities and are now 'suffering the consequences of their choices?'" He used air quotes around the last part, which was good, because otherwise I'd have wanted to punch him.

Grayson chimed in. "He has a good point."

Fuck. This was not how I needed this to go. I knew it was too much to expect them just to jump right on board, but still, I'd hoped they would. I glanced over at Malcolm, who didn't say anything, his expression stony as he stared at me. Had I judged them wrong? Did these guys really think so little of vampires?

Evan nodded encouragingly.

My eyes went around the room again. I didn't know what to say to make Grayson say yes. I wasn't sure about Z. But Malcolm ... honesty seemed to be the key for Malcolm. He wanted power, just like anyone else in the world did. But not the same kind of power. He didn't want it in stacks of cash. He wanted it in knowledge. Vulnerability.

I swallowed hard before I pulled up my phone. I swiped to an old picture of Matthew and then walked over and showed it to him. "I want the cure for my brother."

Malcolm took the phone and glanced back and forth between the picture and me for a minute. Then he stood up in front of me.

Shit. He was going to walk out. He was going to leave. I held my breath, waiting for his rejection, trying to school my features and be ready to take one on the chin. *Grow up, Hales. You knew this could happen.* I had a Memory Spell prepped in my notebook in case I needed to use it, to wipe all their memories so they forgot this conversation.

I started going over the first lines of the spell in my head as Malcolm approached me, his face as unreadable as stone. He handed my phone back and his fingers brushed mine. His skin was blazing hot. The air around us warmed. His burning fingers touched the edge of my arm. I felt the heat seep through my sleeve as he traced a path up to my neck.

Oh, God, just end it. Just say no and be done.

But was he furious? Did he think I'd used him? Shit, I didn't want him to think that. No matter what, I didn't want him to think that. Honesty tumbled from my lips. "Look, I want the cure for my brother. And that's selfish. And I came here to school so I could recruit you and Grayson. But ... you hate the Pinnacle—their bullshit laws. The very fact that they're keeping a cure from people? Evil." I shook my head and glanced from Malcolm's stern face to Grayson's. Crap. I couldn't tell if they thought I was crazy or if they were taking me seriously.

I couldn't tell if they were interested or not. I couldn't *tell*. And that made me nervous, wired, buzzing with anxious energy. It pushed me to try harder—even if I came across as desperate. I had to try harder.

I raised a hand and gestured at the playboy. My hand shook and I quickly retracted it. They didn't need to see that. "Grayson here is a fucking genius who's living in a shadow." I made eye contact with Grayson. "Some of those spells you've pulled on me are brilliant. You're a lot smarter than you like to pretend. You are *good* at spell writing. Your dad might have gotten magicals to Mars, but you'd eclipse him if we set you up a lab and a year or so from now you came out as the person who 'invented' a serum to cure vampirism."

Grayson raised his eyebrows.

I swallowed hard. That wasn't enough? My stomach churned. I'd profiled him for months. I'd been sure that Grayson's issues with his dad were …

Zavier interjected, "Wait. Wait. That's still doesn't—"

I kept my eyes on Grayson, trying not to plead. My words came out stiff and stilted. "There are labs in China right now investigating Alchemiken. Wasting their time. I have six mil stashed in offshore accounts we can use to fund the production. Use your dad's lab contacts and flip one of them to work for us. I have a contract all drawn up here." I pulled a contract that had cost me a small fortune out of my laptop bag. "It makes the four of you partners in the lab, with Grayson's name on it." I slid the thick document across the table. "In less than a year, you'll all be billionaires."

I glanced down at Zavier in his seat. He was easier to deal with, easier to read than the other guys. Or just more relaxed. I wasn't sure. I didn't feel sure of anything anymore. But I kept on with my pitch. I had to get through it. Even if they said no.

I had to let them know just exactly how big an opportunity they were turning down. "How much do you think a magical would pay in order to avoid the risk of becoming a blood-crazed vamp? A thousand bucks a pop? Ten thousand? Fifty? I want something selfish. But I don't expect you all to risk everything for altruistic reasons. I've thought this through."

Z licked his lips, an admiring smile spreading across his face.

I glanced over at Evan, who was leaning back in his seat, beaming.

My chest started to blaze with excitement. Z was smiling. Evan was smiling. Had I done alright? Was it going better than I thought? I glanced around at each of the men in the room, feeding on the rising energy. Grayson's eyes were brimming with the vision of exceeding his father.

Zavier gave me a wolf-whistle. "You are so hot right now, I can't even."

But Malcolm brought us all back to reality. "You say this like you think this will be easy."

I looked back at him, his hair flip crisp and perfect, and just as stiff as his posture. Dammit. I'd lost Malcolm. He was gonna say no. *Shit. Fucking shit.* I wanted to stomp my foot. I felt like screaming. Instead, all I could do was grit out, "I don't think it'll be easy. But with you all, it'll be doable. I've been planning this job for two and a half years."

Malcolm returned to his seat and linked his fingers. "Well then, show us."

I walked over to the computer and flicked my hand up at the projector on the ceiling. My light power activated the electrons swirling through the electronics. The projector turned on, displaying the Pinnacle's layout on the library wall. I pointed my other hand toward the study room window and tossed a shadow over it, so that no one else could see in. "Grayson, can you lock that door, please?"

Once the door was locked, I flicked on the 3-D tour of the Pinnacle I'd created. I spoke as the image roamed over the outside rotunda, complete with its golden friezes. "So, bad news first. The Pinnacle is the most magically locked down building on the planet, more secure than any of the presidential bunkers … Outside, there's unique and effective ground security. A group of prairie dog shifters roam the grounds. They bark out alerts during off hours."

Zavier chuckled. "Prairie dogs? Really?"

"They're really good watch animals," Evan stated. "I've been looking them up. They have specialized calls for different predators, including humans. The Pinnacle always has a guard on watch who's a prairie dog shifter so that someone can interpret the calls. Asking around in the shifter community, they've stopped eighteen break ins in the past year."

Zavier gulped. "Eighteen? That's all?" He sunk a little into his chair and put his head on his hand. "Eighteen. Shit." He looked a little pale, and tried to laugh that off with a chuckle.

I continued, "The first three floors of the building have lasers, pressure sensitive floors, an extensive pat down and security process, wolf and fox shifters to sniff out amulets…"

"So, easy stuff then?" Zavier scoffed.

I grinned at Zavier, who looked like he might be about to hyperventilate. "No, not easy stuff. The first three floors are a no-go. We'll be flying in," I nodded toward Grayson, who just grinned back at me.

"Once we do get inside, we're going to need to go down to the vault, a hundred and fifty feet below ground. There's only one entrance."

I waited for a second, so that my visual aid could catch up with me. When it displayed a little kitchenette fashioned like an employee breakroom, I continued, "The entrance to the vault is in the fridge. It's on the northeast wall and it's spelled to look normal, but there are no actual shelves inside, per my contact. It's an illusion. You have to have a Good Intentions Amulet on you to get the fridge to open, then we'll have to climb into it and descend a ladder down a tube that looks a lot like a large sewer pipe."

Zavier rubbed his chin as he studied the picture. "That's a long tube. And that's it? Climb down?"

I shook my head. "The tube is lined periodically with fire spells. We'll need an Icefire to cool them down." I looked toward Malcolm.

Malcolm tilted his head and asked, "Why me and not the bear shifter?" He gestured toward Evan, not aggressively, but curious.

"We need a subtle touch. We need the flames to decrease but not die completely so the sensors don't activate. And Evan's got a different job. He's going to be our Unraveler." I sped up the video to get through the tube and display the vast underground bunker with its many doors. It looked like something right out of a horror movie. Maybe I shouldn't have colored the video that way, but it was better to imagine it awful now and be relieved later, than for the opposite to happen.

My breath quickened as I imagined us getting closer to our goal. "When we get underground, the entire floor is dark. There's only one Darklight on staff at the Pinnacle right now, and she absolutely has to be with whomever goes in, because any other ounce of light—anything that's not magical, will trigger an alarm and cause the entire floor to be deprived of oxygen."

"Well, that all sounds completely doable—" Zavier grinned. "I mean, piece of cake, why hasn't anyone done this before?"

"Not quite finished." I wink at him and pull up the vault door. "This is the vault. Our serum is inside. In order to open the vault, we'll have to have an Honesty Amulet on us and use a Pinnacle-authorized wand to unravel the ever-changing vault door spell ... in under three minutes."

Zavier started to laugh. Then he smacked the table with a laugh. He laughed until he made himself cough. All eyes turned to him as he pounded on his chest. When he finally regained control of himself, he said, "You do know that the longest any Tock has ever—in recorded history—been able to slow time, is two minutes, right?"

I grinned at Zavier. "That's because they haven't been dirty friends with me."

Watching his jaw drop and his eyes grow hooded was one of the highlights of my life.

Evan added, "Hayley's power level rating is a hundred. Only five other magicals have ever been rated that high." He was grudging when he added, "That kind of power up …"

"So, you in?" I asked.

"In you?" Zavier grinned. "Fuck yeah. Been waiting for this for months."

I rolled my eyes. "You better be sure. We're talking about permanently risking your dick. Besides the teenage horn dog, anyone else?"

Malcolm looked at me. "You're telling the truth. But I need to see for myself. How'd you get all this intel? Maps? Inside info?"

I turned to look at Grayson who just gestured at Malcolm. "What he said."

I swallowed and straightened. Then I called out, "Dad, can you come here please?"

30

My dad appeared in the study room, though no one could see him but me. He waved and said, "Hayley, there's been a bit of a development—"

I cut him off, because I couldn't stand around talking to someone invisible. "Just a sec. Can you possess Malcolm real quick, please?"

Malcolm's eyes widened and he stood. "What?"

"Malcolm, meet my dad." My dad pointed a finger at Malcolm, confirming he was the intended target. I nodded. "My dad died a week after my brother was turned, right as his lab discovered everything about vamps—"

"Suspicious," Grayson said.

I turned to look at him, my chest hollowing out. "Yeah." My throat dried up. "It is." I hadn't ever thought so before, because Dad had never had time to announce the serum. Nobody really knew about it. Of course, I hadn't known then that the Pinnacle was using vamps for nefarious purposes.

Dad's head popped out of Malcolm's torso, completely unaware that I was having a miniature meltdown. "Hayley, what did you want me to do?"

"Oh, sorry. Can you make him touch his head?" I asked.

Dad gave a nod and slid back inside Malcolm, who shivered and whispered, "What the hell is this?" When his left hand jerked up and started to muss his perfectly styled hair, he shouted, "Hayley! What the hell are you doing?"

Grayson stared at me. "Is this some kind of prank spell?"

I shook my head. "Dad, can you leave Malcolm and go visit Grayson for a sec?"

Dad walked out of Malcolm's body and tried to give him a handshake. "Nice to meet you."

"Dad, he can't feel you shaking his hand."

Malcolm's face was stuck somewhere between awe and horror. "Actually, I kind of can. The air particles get a lot colder." He reached forward and swiped his hand through the air. He swiped through Dad's arm at first, but then gradually backed off, until he was kind of petting my father's outline.

Dad glanced back at me. "He's powerful."

"I know."

"What'd he say?" Evan asked.

"He said he liked Malcolm better than you and that I have his blessing to date Hales," Zavier needled.

I laughed. So did Dad, who couldn't resist punching Zavier in the gut for that. "No blessings!" Dad chided.

Zavier immediately grabbed his stomach. "Damn, Evan, that's cold."

"I didn't do it."

MAGICAL ACADEMY FOR DELINQUENTS

Z's eyes widened when I scolded my dad. "Not fair when he can't retaliate, Dad."

Dad just shrugged and adjusted the collar on his shirt.

"Sir, um, sorry. Just joking," Z apologized.

I pointed over to Grayson and Dad sighed, walking over with his hands in his pockets. "It would be a lot easier, if I could just shine onto the wall, like your darn computer."

His words triggered a revelation. Potts popped into my head for a second, her snarky voice saying, "Mash things together." Maybe … maybe something like that could work. I turned toward Zavier. "You've bragged about your thieving skills. How easy do you think you could break into a room here on campus?"

Z shrugged, nonchalant. "Easier than any of the mansions I've hit before. Why? What do you need?"

"Can you go grab a Recollection Amulet? We made them in Barron's class, but she locked them away until graduation."

"Sure."

"Right now?" I bit my lip.

"Now, now?" Z asked.

I nodded.

He sighed. But then he strolled out the door with a jaunty, "Don't do anything dirty without me." He sped away so quickly that all that was left was a rush of wind.

When Zavier got back, I had everything ready for the projection spell. My computer was packed away and my flash drive was tucked into my pocket.

Zavier held up a glowing navy amulet with a little smirk on his face. "Definitely owe me a blow—is your dad still here?" he looked around the room.

My dad grabbed onto Grayson's hand and lifted it to smack Z across the face.

"Hey!" Z protested.

At the same time, Grayson also yelled. "What the fuck?" He jerked his arm down.

"Yeah, Z, my dad's still here. So cut the naughty jokes. Sorry he stole your arm, Grayson. He's been working on possessions in case we run into trouble at the Pinnacle and he needs to help out."

Grayson shook out his arm. "Feels weird. But don't worry about it, nemesis. I've had worse."

Malcolm grinned from his seat. "Possessions. That's a new one. Never worked with a ghost before. This could be interesting."

I tried not to crow over the fact that Malcolm had just sounded like he might opt in. I tried to keep my face nonchalant as I glanced over at him. But that was hard as fuck when he sent a zing of heat across my panties. I sucked in a breath.

Dad asked, "What's wrong?"

I shook my head, face growing red as Malcolm hid a smile behind his hands. "Just thinking through my spell." I blew out a breath. "Okay then. This is what I'd like to try. Amulets only work on living things—"

"Thank goodness because I'm not a huge fan of talking corpses." Zavier stuck out his tongue and shivered, making a disgusted noise.

I glanced over at Evan, who had leaned over to whisper something to Malcolm. I cleared my throat. "Evan ... is it okay if Dad possesses you again?"

He straightened. Then my handsome stalker nodded.

I tossed the amulet to him. "Great. Can you go sit by the wall where we had the projector showing?"

As Evan dragged his chair over with a screech, I grabbed my parchment and wand. I tapped my wand against my chin, splattering myself with ink. But I didn't bother to wipe it off. Magic ink tasted a little like strawberry jam. There were weirdos on campus who were even addicted to it. I stared at the knots on the table and made sure I had the spell that Professor Wolfe had used to show his memories clear in my head. Then I wrote.

A floating mirror appeared above Evan's head.

"Evan, can you think about that time you beat Matthew at Fortnite?" They had been vicious rivals over the video game.

Evan grinned and the memory of my freckled brother pouting appeared on the surface of the mirror. "Okay, keep thinking about that. I want to try something. Dad, can you possess Evan and then start thinking about the Pinnacle?"

All these years, I'd been basing my schematics off what dad said, having him look over my shoulder and double check everything. My stomach fizzed with excitement at the possibility that I might actually get to see things for myself.

Dad walked over to Evan and sat down on top of him, like he was trying to sit in Evan's lap. But he sank through my stalker's giant thighs and leaned back until he faded completely into Evan's body.

The image on the floating mirror flickered. Matthew's face faded, replaced by a security guard at the Pinnacle. The man had huge bags under his eyes that gave him the appearance of a hound dog. He scratched at the chess rook and diamond logo on his shirt as he glanced over at a monitor. "Please proceed to the shifter sniffing station."

We floated through the halls of the Pinnacle, to places the public couldn't go. My dad's memory of floating into the breakroom crossed the screen. He approached a stout man wearing a tan suit and a woman with purple hair whose face was turned away. I watched as a thin hand held out an orange amulet toward the fridge door—it must have been her hand. Immediately, my mind started doing calculations.

Malcolm must have read my mind because he said, "Honesty amulet. Crap. We're gonna have to figure out how to get around that." He raised his fingers to his lower lip and started plucking at it in thought.

We watched the worker's thick hands reach right through the very realistic fridge shelves and grab onto something invisible just beyond them. Only once the man stepped forward and started descending could we see the rungs of the ladder. We heard a rushing sound, like water, and the view on the wall turned, looked down, and saw that two rungs down, the tube was engulfed in flame.

His pudgy hand reached out—

But the vision changed. The image on the wall swirled and suddenly there were two hands on a steering wheel. An older man's hands with a wedding ring. His voice filled the room, excited. "Yeah, they found it! I can't believe it. We've been working on this for six years. And just when I thought I'd lost all hope ..." It was my dad's voice. But ... that would mean this memory was from before my dad died.

My throat caught. I leaned against the table; not sure I could handle seeing something from before Dad passed. Even if it was just his drive home from the grocery store.

There was an awkward pause in the memory—a long span of silence where the car stood still at a stop sign much longer than necessary—and Grayson looked toward me, confused. "Phone call?" he mouthed.

I shrugged. But an eerie feeling swept over me as I watched and listened and the car started to move again. Grayson must have noticed, because he walked over and stood next to me. "You okay, nemesis?"

"I dunno," I whispered back.

On the wall, the view turned to look out at the sunset that sent orange streaks across the passenger seat. I recognized that tan leather. It was from the car my dad bought once he thought the Porsche would be a good gift for Matthew. He'd only had that car for six months … this memory had to be close to his death.

My hand slipped into Grayson's. I started squeezing his fingers as I watched the screen. My heart wasn't quite to full panic mode yet, but the steady thud-thud sped up when Dad's voice spoke again. "Yeah … yeah, I guess I can wait for you. Let me just pull over here. Yeah. Um, I'm by Sixth and Marron. By the train tracks."

My heart sprinted to the edge of the Grand Canyon and leapt off.

Dad kept talking. "Yeah. I'm gonna call Trudy, she'll be so excited … oh. Yeah. You're right. Better wait to tell her after."

I realized I'd tucked myself into Grayson's side. "Sorry." I shook my head and tried to back away. But the tears started when Dad parked on the side of an empty street and put his favorite song on the car stereo. "Desperado" played through the speakers. Dad started to sing off-key. Grayson pulled me into his side and Zavier somehow squished in between me and the table, taking up my other hand.

"Hey, hey, what's wrong?" Z whispered, tucking a strand of my hair back.

My eyes didn't leave the screen. They were glued there, terrified and mesmerized at once as the sunset burned a brilliant red before it started to dip.

"I think … this might be the night my dad died," I whispered. My hands started shaking.

"We can stop, Hales," Z whispered in my ear. "Just ask your dad to leave Evan."

I shook my head. "No. We can't."

"Yeah we can." Grayson tried to pull away from me and step toward Evan, but I yanked him back.

"No. We can't," I growled. "My dad got hit by a train. There was basically nothing left … But you just heard him. Someone went to meet him that night. There could have been someone else in the car with him. Some family out there somewhere could think their loved one went missing. Got kidnapped. Somebody might have been suffering three whole years, not knowing."

Bile rolled through my stomach as the sun set within the floating mirror and the view turned toward the clock dial. 7:52 p.m. My father had died at 8:03. I started to sway where I stood, but when each of the guys tried to convince me to at least sit, I refused.

"Shut up," Malcolm growled at them. "This is her truth. She wants the truth."

The sky in the floating mirror grew dark and my imagination ran wild. Until there was a rap at the glass. Grayson immediately turned toward the glass window on the side of the study room. But the tapping wasn't from there. It was from my father's memory.

Dad's hand pressed the unlock button and the passenger door opened. A man's legs were visible. Then he bent and climbed into the sports car.

Claude King sat down.

My insides snapped like whips. I was stripped raw. "Claude," I whispered.

Claude turned to face my dad, an eerie look in his eyes. "You have it?"

Dad's hands reached into his coat pocket.

My heart started thumping-pumping-jumping. My head started spinning, spinning, spinning, pinnings, inningsp, nningspi, ningspin …
—…— …

Dad took out a glowing red vial. It looked like neon.

The world slowed down.

My existence narrowed.

I became nothing but eyes as Claude's fingers lifted ... and blasted my father with ice.

Paralyzed.

Dad was paralyzed.

I was paralyzed.

Motion was impossible. Movement was a dream. A distant, uncontrollable thing. A wish.

Claude took the vial, pocketed it, and climbed out of the car. My dad was stuck staring at the passenger door as it closed. *Click. Whoosh.* The rush of wind and distant traffic floated through the room as another car door opened. Hands fumbled around my father's frozen waist, releasing the emergency bake and shifting the car into neutral.

Dad's car lurched forward. *Smack.* The car door slammed shut and through the passenger window, the shadows changed as Dad and his car rolled down the hill, gaining speed. In the distance, a bright light, the kind people describe when they talk about heaven, shone.

It grew bigger and bigger.

Hoowooot. Hooowoot. A train whistle sounded.

My knees gave out and I collapsed. Grayson's grip was the only thing that stopped me from falling.

"Enough!" Zavier leapt up and shouted. "Enough!" He leaned forward and grabbed the Recollection Amulet off of Evan's lap.

The horrific scene cut off. I stumbled away from the guys just as my dad stumbled out of Evan's body. He shook his head, like he was clearing it. Then he glanced over at me.

"Where am I? What's going on? Who are you?"

I leaned forward and puked. Right on the floor.

I would have pitched face first into the puddle of sick if two huge arms hadn't engulfed me.

Evan scooped me up as Grayson released my fingers.

"We could go to the police, report this," Zavier offered softly. "Show this memory to them."

I shook my head. I scrubbed a hand over my face. My throat ached. "Without Darklights on the squad … even with them, my dad's memory isn't as reliable as it used to be. Being a ghost … it's hard. I don't think a ghost's testimony …" Plus, with Claude's connections … Anger and hopelessness felt like a wire being pulled taut inside me and dragged over my insides, scraping them raw.

Grayson added, "Not to mention the fact that if your mom is anything like my father, anything you say will be suspect."

I glanced dully over at him and nodded. I had no idea what lay at the foundation of his relationship with his father. But he was right.

Evan turned to the others. "I'm taking her back to her room." He moved me around in his arms so that he cradled me, his arm now tucked under my legs.

I shook my head, trying to clear it, though I didn't try to leave his arms. I wasn't ready to stand.

I struggled to push back the images from Dad's memories, or the fact that he was at the door of the study room, trying and failing repeatedly to turn the handle. He'd forgotten he was dead—he did that sometimes. I turned my eyes away, trying to blink back the sheen that made the room get glossy.

I shut my eyes, took a deep breath, and said, "I can't leave until I know if everyone's in." I opened them to find Malcolm and Grayson staring at me.

Malcolm asked, "Who was that man?"

To my surprise, Grayson answered before I had a chance. "That's Claude King. He's the asshole who told my dad to run for office."

Grimly, I added, "He's also the asshole who married my mother." Claude had known about the serum. "He took the serum. He killed my father. Married my mom. Sold our lab to the Pinnacle."

Evan added, "So, he's the one experimenting on vampires. Making them disappear."

I tossed up a shoulder. "Looks like it." Hatred vibrated through me. The years and years of feeling my skin prickle with distaste any time the Clod entered a room suddenly felt justified. I hadn't just loathed him because he'd married my mom. Or because he was a sadistic asshole. My hand rose to touch one of the scars along my neck as vindication soared through my veins. I'd sensed the evil in him lurking under the surface.

I shoved all that away. Emotion had no place in this heist if I was going to pull it off. Claude was simply another enemy. A bigger one. At least now, he was a known entity. I knew what his endgame was. I knew his goals. I knew why he always had chosen ice to punish me— the sadistic fuck.

Deep breath. Clear your head, I scolded. I turned to look at the two potential members of my team. I needed to focus on them right now.

Malcolm's eyes probed me as he thought. Then a gentle flicker of warmth ran up my spine. Behind me, Evan made a noise of surprise. But my lips curved into a smile. I knew Malcolm's decision seconds before he uttered the words, "I'm in."

I turned to look at Grayson. He gave a slow nod. "No truce, though."

I grinned weakly at him. "Never."

31

ZAVIER WALKED INTO THE GIRLS' dorm like he owned the place. He sweet-talked and joked to distract some girls hanging out in the first-floor lounge, while using his hand to speed up time behind him as the guys and I walked through so that nobody else saw all of us. The girls might make an exception for him, but someone would be bound to call Professor Huchmala, our dorm monitor, if a whole gaggle of guys just strutted in.

Evan carried me up all three stories over my protests. He handled me like I was a china doll and only put me down once we reached my bed.

Malcolm and Grayson set my things down, and then there was an awkward moment where the guys sized each other up.

Evan broke it by saying, "I'm gonna stay with her tonight. I think it's best if she's not alone."

Luckily, Zavier walked in just then, and broke up any brewing tension. "I call dibs on tomorrow night. And Hayley," he leaned over and winked at me, "it's not gonna be all backrubs and pillow fights."

"So, what you're saying is you want me to paint your nails instead?" I joked weakly. My throat felt raw and I needed to brush my teeth. But I wasn't quite ready to leave the bed. I wasn't quite ready to leave the distraction.

"Night after that," Malcolm called out. He didn't say anything else.

Grayson didn't speak for a minute and I wondered if it was too awkward for him.

"I'm a big girl—"

"Saving the best for last, I guess," Grayson grinned. Then he clapped a hand onto Malcolm's back and the two of them walked toward the window. "Come on, Zavier."

The other three left and Evan went and locked my door, before heading to my bathroom. He came back with a prepped toothbrush and a glass of water.

I sat up, drinking the water gratefully before I brushed my teeth.

"I can run you a shower or something if you want," he offered, a pink blush creeping over his cheeks.

I shook my head.

"Do you want me to help you to the bathroom so you can change?" he asked.

I held out my hand, toothbrush still jutting out from my teeth. He helped me grab some clothes from my dresser.

I went into the bathroom and changed, feeling self-conscious and a little bit nervous. I didn't really know why. Evan had spent the night at my house a million times before. When we were younger, I'd even lain on the living room floor next to him. I had probably been seven the first time I stayed up longer than the boys. I'd stared at Evan's eyelashes and the way the moon hit his cheek for nearly an hour that night.

After I'd changed, I found Evan sitting at my desk, rolling his wand back and forth across the surface. Clearly, something was bothering him.

I slid underneath the covers and patted the bed beside me. "You don't have to stay over—"

"Happy birthday," he interrupted me. "Um. I know that was a sucky end to your birthday. I'm sorry."

I shrugged. "I got what I wanted." I scrubbed my hand over my face. "I kind of can't believe they said yes."

"I can. Having that contract ready-made was genius, by the way," Evan complimented me.

"Thanks." We stared at each other awkwardly for a bit. "You know, beds are a lot more comfortable than chairs. You can sleep over here."

Evan self-consciously made his way over and laid down on top of the sheets.

"It's not the seventeenth century, you know," I teased him. "Sleeping under the covers with me isn't going to ruin me."

He rolled his eyes with an adorable blush, climbed out of bed and took off his shoes, then climbed back in again. His hulking form was like a mountain next to mine. The heat that rolled off him was like a volcano. He offset the night chill perfectly. Part of me wanted to snuggle up against him. But the other part of me didn't know if he was okay with that. Or ready for that. Particularly with a line of guys behind him.

We stared at each other in the dark for a moment, before I used my palm to create some tiny droplets of light between us. They glimmered like fairy lights. I let them swirl through the air and settle around Evan's head like a crown.

"Do I look like a princess?" He raised his brows.

I giggled, like I was fucking seven, and waved the lights away. "Sorry. Too much time around Zavier. Thank you for staying. I really don't want to go to sleep right now," I admitted. "After that—"

"Want me to distract you?" he asked in a gruff whisper.

I smiled, my body immediately getting hot and bothered. My nipples perked and my breathing grew shallow. My eyes traced Evan's biceps and I waited for his kiss, anticipation coiling in my stomach.

Instead of leaning forward to kiss me, Evan pulled a complete one-eighty. He rolled onto his back and propped his head up on his arm. He stared up at my ceiling as I stared down at him, confused and a little embarrassed. Had I read the situation wrong? Had Zavier been wrong when he said Evan was in love with me? *OMG. Does Evan just think of me as a kid sister?* Was it guilt that had been driving him to follow me all these years?

"You know that birthday prank? Where we decorated the school?" Evan's words interrupted the ten-car pileup that was my mind at that moment. Thoughts and fears and insecurities were streaking in from every direction to smash into each other and build a hulking mess.

It took me a minute to process his change of direction, his words, and answer him. "Um. Yeah. Why?"

Evan glanced over at me and then back up at the ceiling. "It wasn't Matthew's idea."

"What?" That revelation had me sitting up in bed. I'd given Matthew shit for months about that and he'd just laughed, punching me in the shoulder and saying he bet I'd be even more embarrassed next year. My hands clutched at the sheets and I turned to look at Evan.

"Why would you want to embarrass me that bad?"

"Embarrass you?" Now Evan leaned up. "Shit, I didn't mean to embarrass you, Hailstorm." He swallowed and I could see his Adam's apple bob slightly. He closed his eyes and sighed. "I thought Matthew was just giving me shit when he said you were pissed."

"Yeah. Um. No. I pretty much wanted to die. I hated people looking at me back then."

"Well, fuck."

Based on Evan's reaction, his downcast face, the birthday thing hadn't been meant as a prank. My voice was thin as I asked, "Why would you do something like that?" Hope started to melt away the fear around my heart.

I watched Evan, waving my hand so the glimmering drops of light hovered just around his face so that I could see each micro-expression. Fear. Resolve. Resignation. More fear.

Evan's hand reached down under the sheets and he pulled up his wallet.

At first, I thought he'd just decided not to answer me. But then he pulled a little pink square of paper out of the slot for bills. He held it between his thumb and pointer finger, staring at it, before he sighed and handed it to me, saying, "Here."

I took the little square and unfolded it. As I did, recognition washed over me. The pink paper had little purple lines on it and one of the edges was ripped. It was a page from my diary. I unfolded it to see the words 'Hayley Weston' surrounded by a heart.

I glanced back at Evan.

His eyes avoided mine. "Um. I'm sorry about the birthday thing. And about this one time I stole your diary—"

I grabbed onto Evan's massive shoulders and turned him toward me. And then I attacked his face with kisses. I pummeled him with my lips, pressing them to his cheeks, his jaw, even his nose. I punctuated each peck with scolding. "You. Are. The. Biggest. Jerk. Ever. Don't. You. Know. Diaries. Are. Sacred?"

Inside though, my heart was a dove on fire, dazzling and impossible and miraculous. My hands traveled over Evan's massive chest, caressing his pecs, lingering on his shoulders, sparks of electricity lit up a metal button on his shirt. Evan had liked me. He'd stolen my diary page and then done this massive, foolish, typical-teenage love-struck boy thing for me. And it was amazing. The sepia taint of that memory fell away and it became technicolor.

My lips continued to dance over Evan's skin. And gradually, his lips joined mine. Like a shy girl being led to her first dance, hesitant and excited, and full of nervous energy, his lips stepped on mine, tripped. I just laughed and he tried again. The second time, he got it right.

A tear of joy streaked from my eye when his arms wrapped around me and he pulled me in tight and began to kiss me for real. Not hesitant anymore. Evan claimed me. His tongue demanded mine and his hands covered my hips and back, encasing me in warm, bright love. And for a second, I forgot how broken I was. I forgot how mangled my heart had become.

When Evan held me, I felt like the old me again. I felt whole.

He laid me down on the bed gently, like I was made of porcelain. His tenderness made me laugh and pull him closer.

"You aren't going to break me," I whispered.

"I'm going to try." He smiled back.

And then Evan ripped off his shirt. He was built like a superhero crossed with a mac truck. His muscles had muscles. My greedy hands reached up to touch them all. But he wasn't having that. He reached down and carefully unbuttoned my pajama top, then leaned me up so he could slide it down my shoulders.

The way his breath caught when he saw my bared breasts made me feel beautiful. It made me feel powerful. It made me wet.

His head dipped and he captured a nipple in his mouth right away—like he couldn't resist, he just had to taste me. He sucked on my nipple, flicked his tongue over it and then around, teasing me. His hand rose to play with my other breast, caressing first, then pinching and tweaking.

My arms raked down his back and when his tongue hit me just right, I arched up into him. My vision started to get blurry at the edges, just as it always did when I was getting close to an orgasm.

"Evan," I whimpered.

He stopped and pulled back, leaning over me. I was panting, soaked, ready and frustrated. "Why'd you stop? I was close," I whined.

He reached up a massive hand and caressed my cheek. "I've waited to hear you say my name like that for a long time."

Oh, be still my fucking heart. Another tear threatened me, but before it could fall, I leaned up and captured Evan's lips again. I showed him with my kiss how much he meant to me. My hands roamed down the washboard planes of his stomach and I started to undo his belt.

He pulled back long enough to say, "Hold on, protection."

"Top drawer of my nightstand. Anti-Conception Amulet."

Evan got off the bed, shedding his pants as he bent over my nightstand. I lifted my pelvis and shed my panties and pajama pants, eager to feel every inch of his skin against mine. Evan set the amulet near us and pressed a button to activate the spell. Then he crawled onto the bed between my legs and caressed them. His rough palms felt amazing against my sensitized skin.

"How do you like it? What's your favorite way to come, Hayley?" Dirty words spilled from his mouth and made me twist my hips in desperation.

I looked up at him, surrounded by my fairy lights, but still full of shadows, like some dark sex god. "I'm not very creative," I whispered. "I usually just use my fingers."

"Well, we'll have to change that." Evan grinned down at me. "But we'll do it your way first. Touch yourself."

I kept my eyes on him as I slid my fingers down my stomach. I dipped them between my soaked lips, gathering the wetness there, before I brought them up to circle my clit. I was fully waxed, so the skin was smooth everywhere and it wasn't long before my clit was aching for more.

I teased myself as I watched Evan, letting myself get wound up, but not quite ready to come.

When Evan reached down and started to stroke himself, I realized just how thick he was. Most dicks looked like carrots … but his was a full-on cucumber. It was thick all the way from head to base. And it grew even thicker as Evan watched me raise my hips and play with my pussy so he could get a better view.

I loved that watching me made him get harder. I loved the unashamed way he pulled my thighs a little further apart so he could see more.

My mouth watered and I wanted to taste him. But when I pulled my fingers away, Evan grabbed my hand and put it back.

"Get to the edge and tell me when you're there."

His fingers mingled with mine and we circled my clit together. My fingers were smooth, his rough, and my clit loved the change in textures. Evan kept stroking himself slowly as we played, and my breath grew shallow. My thighs started to tremble.

"I'm—" I didn't get to finish talking before Evan shoved our hands away and replaced them with his hot dick. He rubbed himself over me, using the thickness of his shaft to spread my lips wide, using my lubrication and spreading it up and down across my clit.

Fingers ... fingers were okay. But the feel of a smooth, hot, hard dick sliding over my sweet spot was a million times better. Choirs sang in my head and I came so hard I nearly bucked Evan off the bed. He stroked through my orgasm, pinning my hips with his hands and thighs and continuing to draw out the pleasure until I cried out, "Stop. Stop!"

When he stopped, that's when I actually noticed his weight. "You're gonna crush me," I wheezed.

Evan laughed and pressed himself up onto his elbows. "Was that a good one?" he asked.

I nodded, hardly able to open my eyes, I was still so dazed.

Evan leaned down and pressed a soft kiss to my lips. "Good." And then he lined himself up with me and began to press inside. He was so big that my pussy lips stretched too far, and I started to whimper.

Evan pulled back a little. "We'll take it slow, Hales." And then he kissed me, and his fingers went to either side of my clit as he slowly pressed back in. He played with me, and put his mouth back on my nipple, letting pleasurable sensation battle the pain of being stretched by him. Until ... Evan's thick dick rubbed right over my g-spot. And I nearly came right then.

"Yessss," I wailed, caught somewhere wild between pain and pleasure that I'd never been before.

Evan realized what had happened, because he pulled back and carefully stroked in again, stopping when I gasped. He did it a third time, slowly, until he knew exactly how deep he needed to go to drive me wild. Then his tongue went to work on my nipple as his thrusts grew faster. I smoked. I simmered. I boiled over. The feelings inside became too much. Words didn't work. Images stopped. I just felt. I was nothing more than sensation and ******* stars.

"Evan!" I cried out as I came, clutching his forearms.

When I went limp, Evan released my breast and pushed up onto his hands. He hovered over me, thrusting shallow, eyes piercing me. "Say my name again, Hayley," he asked roughly, as sweat dripped down his brow.

"Evan," I repeated, watching him as he arched up and faced the ceiling, coming apart in silence.

Afterward, we cleaned up and laid back down, forgoing clothes because we had something better. We snuggled together, sharing body heat. The magical buzz underneath our skin flared out randomly. Evan put a flurry of snowflakes into the air above us but melted them before they could touch us. Fairy lights shot from my hands and filled the room. I could only hope no professors were out on patrol, or they'd wonder what the hell I was doing. But I couldn't hold all that power in.

My clock radio flickered and static fuzzed and then it turned on, my power flickering through it, sparking the electronics inside.

"What's going on?" Evan asked.

I giggled. "It's me. Well, technically, you caused it." I waved my hand. The stations flipped, one to the next, until some station playing Norah Jones' "Come Away With Me" was playing. I left it there, music flowing through me.

"I thought you had light powers," Evan murmured, kissing the top of my head.

"Radio waves are on the light spectrum," I responded, loving the little tingle that ran through my body at his kiss. "I've just never had access to them before."

That made him grin. "Oh."

"Yeah. Oh."

Evan and I turned and laid on our sides, facing each other. We exchanged glances that teetered between shy and ecstatic, playful and awed, as jazz singers crooned love songs in the background.

"I've always loved your blue eyes," I confessed.

"I've always loved your smile," he returned.

His hand came around me and curled me in closer. I fell asleep thinking all was right with the world for the first time in years. I fell asleep dreaming about this heist, visualizing us pulling it off.

Of course, dreams were easy. Reality was not.

32

We met up in the woods on Sunday for our first official practice for the heist. We met near an old shack that had originally been built for the stone lions to sleep. But apparently, they preferred dozing on some rocks on the far side of campus. Thank goodness.

The shack was apparently a well-known spot for the gangs. But Grayson had his goons clear it out so we could use it.

When we walked up, I wasn't that impressed. It was little more than a massive rundown barn at this point. The paint was peeling, and the bird shit stains had piled up over the years to make it a very uninviting spot. I wasn't surprised that the gangs claimed it though. It was the most privacy you could get at MAD. I looked over a spray paint monstrosity that Professor Huchmala probably hated (if she knew about it) of a wolf. The paint dripped from the eyes, nose and edges. Whoever had done it had clearly been a novice tagger. *Lame.*

I turned to face my crew. That word still rung oddly inside my head. I had a crew. I'd done it. They'd said yes. The very thought brought a smile to my lips.

We formed a circle, facing each other for an awkward second, in the green shadows under the trees. Every eye landed on me and I felt the weight of expectation. It was a different kind of expectation than I was used to, however. I was used to people watching, expecting me to fuck up. These guys were watching, expecting a leader. That was a different pill to swallow.

I kicked a pinecone before I said, "Okay then. Assignments. Recon is mostly done, though we probably need to suffer through a couple more rounds of possession like yesterday to verify more of my dad's intel. I also have an interview, I hope anyway, coming up at the Pinnacle, to verify last minute items."

The guys nodded and I turned to my fifties-era bad boy. His blonde hair was a little less than perfect today, which made me smile. I wasn't the only one nervous. "Malcolm. I need you to come up with a couple things. A femme fatale or a wham bam, maybe a who blew. You decide. We'll probably need a couple levels of distraction strikes so we can slip inside."

Malcolm nodded. "I've got a few ideas."

I added, "The big thing is to get the ground security focused on something else so we can get in. Because if we get taken down by goddamned prairie dogs, I'm never letting you live it down."

Malcolm laughed and grabbed his laptop. "Got it." He went and sat with his back against the outside wall of the shack, just below the crappy, drooling wolf painted on the side. He propped his laptop up on his knees.

I grabbed a bag full of crappy sculptures I'd made in Huchmala's Art Therapy. I tossed them Grayson's way. He caught them and held one up.

"Been playing play dough with a five-year-old?"

I ignored his jab. "Use that spell you used on my boobs. Make them bigger. Then see if you can safely lift them and yourself seventy feet into the air. That's how high we need to be to hit the seventh story."

Grayson smooshed the head of one of my clay guys and gave a nod. Then he trotted off a little bit to a clearing, so he had space to work. He easily lifted the figures the first twenty feet. But after that, they started to wobble.

I heard him curse when one of them flipped sideways.

I turned to Evan. "I need you to practice unraveling spells." I pulled a sheet of paper out of my back pocket. "I paid a couple guys to come up with the hardest, most complex spells they could. Time yourself. I've got solutions here too, so we can check it. But we need to see how long Z needs to buy you."

Evan took the paper, letting his fingers linger over mine. He gave me a small, private smile before he nodded and headed into the shack.

I turned to Z who had leaned against a tree and was smacking some gum obnoxiously. "So, boss, whatcha' want me to do?"

"If we need a wand, you're our sticky fingers. You and I need to look through a list of Pinnacle possibilities and see who the easiest target is." I gave him a half grin. "I mean, technically, we could take Claude's wand—" I was tempted to take it and just leave it behind in the vault after we finished the job. Let the Pinnacle decide what to make of that —either he'd be ruled incompetent or guilty.

But Z saw right through me. "Nope. No way. I'm sure you know better than to have a personal attachment to a mark. You need to keep a clean head."

I shrugged. "Worth a shot. Let's go sit and find a target."

"Do we have a timeline for all this?"

I took a deep breath and said, "We could try summer break--"

But Malcolm interrupted me, standing up from where he'd sat. "Two weeks," he stated firmly. Then he flipped his laptop around and showed me a magical news site. The headline featured the Unnatural Ball. "Ball's three blocks away from the Pinnacle," Malcolm explained. "Perfect spot for a little Boom Chicka Boom."

My heart clenched. Was he insane? That was impossible! We'd just gotten together. They'd just agreed. "Two weeks?" I shook my head. "No—"

Malcolm reached out and grabbed my arm. "It needs to be two weeks, Hayley. If I'm gonna pull off my part of this, it's gotta be then. The Unnatural Ball will have a huge group of people. If I can rile them up, that will be the best distraction for those guards and prairie dogs."

My feet felt heavy. My brain convinced my eyes that I was hallucinating. I blinked. But Malcolm was still there. The article about the ball was still on his computer screen.

Behind us, three clay dummies smashed into the ground and broke as Grayson lost control. A clay hand came flying in our direction and landed near our feet. I stared at it. Only the middle finger remained. It literally looked like fate was flipping me off.

Zavier looped his arm around my shoulders. "Hey. Bright side. That's spring break. So, at least we don't have to sneak out of here, too."

I looked over at Z, who started to play casually with my hair like this was no big deal.

I only had one word. "Fuck."

33

I HIT UP TIA—BECAUSE if anyone knew how to get me things I needed in a rush—it was her.

-Hey, long time no chat. Wanna date for the Unnatural Ball?-

I was totally willing to pimp out Evan for the night if it earned me a couple favors. Tia's response was exactly what I'd hoped for.

-OMG. Are you serious right now? I'm gonna die. Gonna die. Calling.-

My phone rang a second later. I answered, grinning at Evan who pouted as he sat on my bed across from me.

"Hey!" I said.

"Who?" Tia cut through the bullshit, didn't bother to greet me, and got right to business.

"You know my stalker?"

"Evan Weston? You want me to go with Evan fucking Weston? Are you on Bubble right now?"

"Nope."

"Thought we hated him."

"Things changed."

"For real?" I could hear the excitement in Tia's voice. She wanted this—bad. All the kids at Medeis did.

"For real. He and I made friends. And I've got a date—"

Her squeal was louder than a pig's. I had to hold the ear away from my phone. "It's Grayson isn't it?!" Her voice was loud enough to carry through the room.

Grayson looked up from where he leaned against his windowsill, a quizzical smile on his face.

I licked my lips and winked at him. "You know it."

"Giiiiirl!" I could hear the springs on Tia's bed as she jumped up and down on it. "This is gonna be the best. You're the best—"

Her dad yelled from somewhere, "Tia, what's going on?"

And just like that, Tia's salty attitude was back. "Nothing! Okay. Just celebrating the return of shark week!"

"What?"

"You know, because there's blood in the water?" she screeched.

I tried to hold my hand over my phone, but it was too late. All the guys in my room wore disgusted faces.

"Um, Tia?" I said.

There was a long, potent pause. "Evan's right next to you, isn't he?"

"Yup."

"Fuck my life."

I laughed. "Well, good news. The ball isn't until next week, so shark week should be over."

"If I haven't killed myself by then."

"Don't you dare! I need you to help me go dress shopping. Plus, I need to see if you know anyone."

"Yeah, for what?"

"I need a couple amulets. And um ... some fire-resistant outfits."

"Say what?"

I cleared my throat. "There's a stupid hazing thing out here ..." I trailed off, crossing my fingers in the air as I stared around at the guys.

Tia blew out a breath. "I told you that you didn't belong at that place. That's fucking dangerous."

"I know. So ..."

Tia sighed and said, "Yeah, I got a cousin."

NOT EVERYTHING WENT AS EASY AS CALLING TIA. BUT SHE HELPED ME check a couple things off my list, so then I focused on others. Like where I could get an authorized wand. Doing the spell to get into the vault with any wand that didn't have a Pinnacle-approved core, would set off a Sloppy Spell. Some guy in the eighties had found that out the hard way when the Break Spell he'd been writing to try and crack the vault door apart literally cracked every bone in his body.

I was not interested in having the same experience. So, we had to lift a wand. Zavier had been demonstrating his competence all week, bringing me Professor's ties and people's phones he'd stolen. He'd even brought me a bra, which I'd nearly slapped him for until I realized it was mine. He'd stolen it off me and I hadn't even noticed.

That had earned him a kiss in the middle of the quad and me a detention.

I gritted my teeth as I studied the faces on screen. I'd already spent nearly a year getting to know the Pinnacle's security staff. But they didn't have wand access to the lower levels in the bunker. I needed someone at Claude's level or just a step below. Not a lot of choices.

I looked up from the computer and stretched my feet out on my bed. My back was sore, and I stretched, before looking across the room. Grayson sat at my desk working on a project for his Math and Literature class. I glanced over at Grayson as he wrote, a book of Emily Dickenson poems open on the desk next to him.

Something about that was hot. About the fact that a huge, burly masculine guy like him hunched over the wounded words that poured out of a dead woman's heart. I stared at him for a while, my face outlining his figure. He would glance at his book every so often and then hold up his phone to take notes.

A quiet, productive evening was actually the last thing I'd expected. The last couple nights, Malcolm and Zavier had kept me busy. In more playful ways. Malcolm had brought over a chess set and made me play strip chess with him. Every time I lost a piece—I was horrible at chess—I lost an article of clothing. We'd ended up making out and his fingers had done amazing things inside my panties while we'd rolled around on the floor.

Zavier hadn't even come over with the pretense of doing any kind of work. When I'd opened my window for him, he'd crawled in, stood up, grabbed me by the hips and thrown me on the bed like a caveman. We'd gotten hot and heavy but hadn't gone all the way. He'd kept saying he didn't want to ruin me for all others yet.

I'd laughed and gone down on him, expecting him to change his mind. But he'd come in my mouth instead. And then reciprocated. Three times. My eyelids fluttered thinking about it.

After those encounters, I was a little disappointed to actually be making headway on the heist. But maybe Grayson was the most serious of all of us. I'd heard he'd made an excuse to get out of Study Hall yesterday and go practice in the woods with the clay dummies. He'd managed to keep three of them in the sky.

Grayson chuckled as he glanced between his phone and his book.

"What are you reading?" I asked. I didn't think Emily Dickenson wrote anything funny.

Grayson looked over at me. And for some strange reason, his chuckles turned to laughter. Not just laughter. Howling. He slapped his knees and held his ribs.

"What the hell is wrong with you?" I asked, setting aside my laptop and going over to check his forehead. But I passed the mirror on my dresser as I walked his way. I stopped dead, staring at my reflection in horror.

My face was neon green. Bright fucking green. Like poisonous frog green. My hands flew to my cheeks. Then I turned to Grayson and tackled that jerk. I pummeled him, but my fists did nothing to stop his laughter. And with how hard his damn abs were, I doubted he even felt my punches. I shoved at him, trying to get a better grip, and his shirt slipped up, revealing those delicious abs.

Grayson looked up at me, "You're turning green all over again!" He snorted. "It faded for a second when you were pissed. But ... I'm just that irresistible, I guess."

I sat up next to him, staring. "You sound exactly like Zavier right now. I think you two need to stop hanging out."

"Well, this prank was his idea."

"WHAT?"

"They've been watching you on video chat all night." He held up his phone, where the other assholes in the crew were all gathered, faces crowded the screen. Every single one of them was contorted in laughter. Grayson pulled the phone back from me and hung up on them. "Any time you think dirty thoughts about any of us, your face turns a specific color. Pink for Z. Blue for Malcolm, white for Evan..."

Horror. Serial killer chasing me through a dark alley horror filled me. I leaned back down and punched Grayson's chest as hard as I could. "You're evil!"

"Evil genius," he snorted again, lifting his shirt.

My eyes couldn't help it. Those abs were unreal.

"Green again," Grayson taunted.

I couldn't retaliate magically. I didn't have time to write a spell. So, I reverted to the age-old torture. Tickles. I tickled Grayson Mars until he gasped, until he begged. I didn't stop until there were tears in his eyes.

"You're distracting me when I'm supposed to be picking a mark," I said.

"You should already know your mark," Grayson said from his spot on my floor. "There's only one person out there who has to go down into that bunker all the time. Only one other person who could randomly wander into the Pinnacle and see your dad and screw everything up for us."

"Who?"

"The Darklight. Ginny Stone."

34

Ginny Stone proved to be a ghost—but not the kind I could see. The woman was a freaking mystery. Other than her signature to transfer the vampires, and that one vague memory my dad had of her, I couldn't find documentation on her anywhere. No birth certificate. Nothing.

The Pinnacle had erased her. So had the American government. That could only mean one thing. They were working together.

Norm government files were so much easier to hack. While they purchased spell protection, too many of them didn't know how they worked. They didn't understand that a spell's power faded with time. And the red tape to get new purchases approved meant that there were all kinds of pretty little gaps where I could hop around.

I was searching during Study Hall when I got nature's call. I closed my laptop and grabbed the hall pass from Professor Torrez's desk. He was snoring, a pile of half-graded Magical History papers in front of him.

When I went into the girls' restroom, it was empty, mercifully. It didn't stay that way, however. Shoes clicked across the tiles and sneakers squeaked and soon I heard the dulcet tones of Laura Whitehall. I gently lifted my feet from the floor and set them on either side of the stall door. I didn't have time for petty girls today. And I'd already had one of her lackeys try and knife me on our run. Evan had scared the kid off. But if she found me alone—I could hold my own. But I didn't have time to recover from a knife wound. Not when the clock was counting down.

Laura's feet stopped in front of the mirror. A zipper sounded and then a little *pop* as she opened her lipstick. "He hates that bitch. What the hell was he doing in her room?"

"Heard he pranked her, I wouldn't worry about it," another girl said. "You know they have that war going on."

Laura snorted. "I don't think it's just that. He's not taking me to the ball anymore."

"WHAT?" The indignant shriek echoed around the room. "No way he's taking that whore."

"I'd already bought my dress and everything."

"He shouldn't even get to go, he's not an Unnatural."

"Please. His dad can buy his way into anything."

"Fucking bitch. We should get one of those Fang dudes to shift and let him loose in her room. You know they mark the shit out of everything."

Laura's laugh was brittle. "I know where Callum is. Let's go find him. He'd probably do it just for fun."

I stayed still and silent as they finished up their makeup and left. Then I stood and let my power flash under my nails, lighting them up. If Laura wanted to do this, I wasn't gonna stop her. I was just gonna make sure she got caught.

THAT NIGHT WAS MALCOLM'S NIGHT SINCE HE AND EVAN HAD TRADED. Evan had tricked Trusk, the Spell writing professor into testing him with the most complicated spells possible, feeding into the professor's hopes that Evan wanted to make it out of here and get a job with the Pinnacle. Every professor seemed to aspire to teach a Pinnacle-bound student.

When I got to Malcolm's room, backpack in hand, video feed of my room playing on my phone, I expected another board game. Instead, Malcolm grabbed my phone and backpack, tossing them down.

He backed me up against the door, pinning me with his hips.

Immediately, my nipples tightened. Malcolm gave me a dark, knowing look. Then he slid his mouth over mine, teasing me with those lips. I grabbed onto his honey hair and yanked his mouth down to mine so I could take what I wanted. But, ever the patient torturer, he simply gently stroked my arms until I lowered my hands. Then he bound both my wrists in one of his large palms and returned to teasing kisses.

I pulled back and whined. "I thought the point was for you to fuck me for a power up. Why haven't you taken me yet?"

Malcolm chuckled. "You think I give a shit about the power up, Shakespeare?" Something in my heart skipped at that. My breath caught and I leaned up onto my tiptoes, so I could kiss him better and show him what that admission meant to me.

But he just backed away again. When I tried to kiss him harder, or press my pelvis forward, he simply leaned away until I was utterly frustrated and completely wet.

"You're mean," I pouted, jutting out my lower lip.

"You're impatient. I'm winning, by the way." His lips gently brushed over my jaw.

"Winning what?" I sighed, tilting my head to give him better access.

"A new game. The rules are—the person who comes first, loses."

"But I want to come first."

"Then you're going to lose."

"Maybe I don't care about winning," I said, trying to sound impertinent. But Malcolm knew better. He'd trained me better than that. Any little game he wanted to play, I always wanted to beat him. He stoked that competitive streak in me. "Dammit!" I tried to pull away from him, but he wouldn't have that. Instead he spun us around so that my back was to the middle of the room.

He chuckled as he moved my hands behind my back, where he secured my wrists together once more. He pressed lightly against me. "See what a fun game this is?"

I laughed into our kiss. "It's not at all fun, you jerk."

"Come on, Shakespeare, you like my games. Admit it." His tongue darted out and traced down my neck to my collarbone. I arched into him.

"God, yes."

"Are you gonna try and win this one?"

"Hmm..." His tongue was so distracting. But then I cleared my head. Focus, Hales. Focus. The damn man had my hands trapped behind my back like a big fat cheater. I'd have to use something else to persuade him. I pulled apart my legs and straddled one of his thick, muscular thighs. And then I started to slowly grind onto him as we kissed. Not hard enough or fast enough to make myself come, but just enough to soak my panties underneath my skirt, just enough for him to feel the heat and friction.

I started to moan, pouring it on a little bit, hoping he was one of those guys who liked little mewling sounds.

Malcolm's kisses got harder. He nipped my bottom lip. Yes, it was working. I held in a smile. I could beat him--even with both hands tied behind my back.

That's when one of Malcolm's hands abandoned my wrists and snaked up to trace around my nipple.

My head fell back, and I forgot to grind for a moment as the sensation filled me. I closed my eyes and just waited for that moment when he'd tweak my nipple and send lightning bolts down my spine.

But Malcolm didn't tweak. I opened my eyes to glare at him and he simply smiled. I wriggled, trying to free my hands from his hold. But I couldn't.

He grinned. I gritted my teeth and tried to shove my breast further into his hand, but he lowered it completely, setting it on my hip instead.

"You bastard," I cursed him.

Without hands, I decided to use the next best weapon in my arsenal. I stole my mouth away from Malcolm's and instead spent a moment sucking on his pulse. It was racing, which made me smug. He wasn't nearly as in control as he liked to pretend.

I licked down to the edge of his shirt and then leaned forward even farther, forcing Malcolm to drop my hands as I bent at the waist. I quickly reached around to grab at his pants and undo the button. But that was as far as I got before he locked my wrists to my sides. But at least they weren't behind me. I could work with that. I straightened and went back to kissing Malcolm, to letting our tongues dance.

Slowly, I rotated my wrists in his grasp until I could point my palms at his legs. and then, taking a page right out of his book, I trailed warm, summer-like sunshine over Malcolm's crotch.

When he moaned, I felt like a fucking queen. A fucking queen. I'm the *fucking* queen. I laughed inside.

Until ice formed on the tip of my nipples. *Oh shit!* It melted quickly, Malcolm transformed it into water, and it soaked the front of my shirt as he took me from cold to hot. My nerve endings sang and cried at the same time. It was pain and butterflies, and it left me panting.

I bit his lip hard in retaliation and yanked my hands out of his grip, latching back onto his hair. I jumped up and wrapped my legs around his waist, games forgotten, burning need replacing every other thought in my head. I pressed hard against Malcolm, rubbing my panties over his hard bulge until he walked me backward and dumped me onto the bed.

Malcolm's eyes were rabid, uncontrolled; he looked like I'd never seen him before. He yanked on my shirt and I had to help him pull it over my head. He didn't even bother taking off my bra, he just shoved the cups down under my breasts and let them prop up my mounds. His mouth sank down and devoured me, swirling and flicking until my hips rose and I rubbed against his body like a cat in heat.

"Enough," I growled, shoving him off. I grabbed the base of his shirt and tugged upward. He didn't help, just laid there while I struggled to unwrap my prize. His perfect torso, chiseled abs and pecs with just the tiniest bit of blond hair. And freckles. Malcolm had freckles on his chest. I had to kiss every single one. I bent forward to do just that, kissing each precious spot as my hands reached down and traced Malcolm's bulge through his pants.

Malcolm gave me a minute to worship him before flipping me back over onto my back. He knelt in front of me and flipped up my skirt. He slowly dragged off my pink lace panties. And then he propped each of my legs on his shoulders. "Remember, the game is whoever comes first loses." He grinned. And then his mouth latched onto my clit.

"Fucking cheater!" I moaned, but I didn't mean it. Because he sucked gently on my sensitive folds before running his tongue down and up and down again, priming me. His tongue was warm and wet, and he kept it flat and soft against my sensitive skin. I had to fight not to writhe against him. I wanted to shove his head further into me when he lightened the touch of his tongue. But that's when he brought his finger up to play with me.

Malcolm heated the tip of his finger with his fire power, in the way only he could. He dragged that warm fingertip over and across me. He dipped it inside, and I howled. It felt like my pussy was steaming--so fucking hot I started to clench even though he wasn't even pumping his digit into me.

I screamed my disappointment as I shoved him off me and took control again. I straddled Malcolm and undid his pants with shaking fingers because I was so close to orgasm, because I was so furious that I'd been denied—that I'd denied myself so that I wouldn't fucking lose this game. I roughly yanked his pants off, saying, "You'd better have a damned Anti-Conception Amulet in your pocket."

"Of course, I do," Malcolm smoothly reached around my struggle to get his pants worked off and pulled the glowing green amulet out of his pocket. He set it above his head on the bed.

"Thank fuck," I growled, because I didn't want to have anything between us. I got Malcolm's pants down, only to realize his stupid shoes were in the way. I decided he didn't need his pants all the way off. I'd just ride him.

I crawled back up the bed and mounted Malcolm like a good little cowgirl. I didn't sink onto him right away, instead I teased the head of his dick, running it slowly up and down my sopping length until we were both breathless. Then I lifted my hips and sank slowly onto him. I had to pause halfway down because he was longer than I expected.

His hand came up to my cheek. "Don't do anything that hurts, Shakespeare. Okay?"

I pressed my cheek into his hands. "You're sweet."

His eyes were dark and serious. He whispered, "Hayley, I need you to ride me now. And I need you to come."

I leaned forward, my breasts dangling above his face. "Yeah?"

Malcolm reached up and fondled my right breast as I sank even lower on him. "Yeah. If we come together, nobody loses." His other hand sank to my hip and started to shoot heat across my thigh, pulsing tiny threads of heat.

He made me lose it. I lost all sense of caution, all sense of self-preservation, as I sank down on him the rest of the way and swiveled my hips. His heat magic stroked my clit and he leaned up to take my nipple into his hot mouth.

I rode him harder and faster, letting my eyes sink closed and just feel. My core felt like tinder catching flame and burning hotter and hotter, the embers blowing up and swirling through my stomach and my mind. I was fire. Malcolm's magic warmed a little further. I rode faster, panting, sweating, scraping my nails down his shoulders as he sucked my breast harder, distending my nipple. And then I hit that peak—that haze where everything in my eyesight became lacy because my eyes couldn't focus. "Malcolm!" I cried, not wanting to go there without him, but unable to stop myself.

Malcolm's hand dug into my hip and his other wrapped around my back. He gave three, hard, pelvis-breaking thrusts into me and then ... we exploded in bliss together.

After we came down, I lay on Malcolm's chest, breathing hard, light flaring randomly from my palms. The buzz of magic in my chest just prolonged the heady sense of satisfaction I felt.

Malcolm stroked my back. "I'm impressed."

I leaned up onto my elbow so that I could look down at him. His eyes glowed like orange flames with the extra power he had in his system. The orange eyes were beautiful with his honey hair in a way that was completely unexpected. And intimate. A sense of possessiveness overwhelmed me. Those post-sex orange eyes were mine. Should be mine. I tried to shake off that foolish, presumptive thought and instead reached down to trace his lips. I loved how swollen they were from my kisses. "Why are you impressed?" I asked, leaning down to taste his mouth one more time.

When I pulled back up, Malcolm's eyes burned red hot. "I'm impressed because I was sure you'd lose."

I laughed—until Malcolm's arm swooped behind me and rolled us over so that he ended up on top. He leaned down and ran his nose along my neck. "I want a rematch," he whispered.

He got one.

35

I CAUGHT Laura bright handed later that night. When I went back to my room around midnight, the smell was awful. It didn't just smell like wolf urine. It smelled like that Fang bastard had marked his territory by expressing his anal glands. I used my sleeve to cover my mouth and went out into the hall to dial Professor Huchmala, our dorm monitor.

"Someone broke into my room."

Huchmala arrived wearing a floral flannel nightgown that looked like it might have been from the 1800s. Her odd eyes stared up at the corner of my door frame. But as soon as I cracked my door, she backed away, practically choking from the scent.

"What the hell?" She gagged and called some maintenance men on her phone. "Make sure you bring a Force to blow some air through this place." Then she knelt in the hallway and pulled out her wand. She wrote us each a quick nose-deadening smell so that we could walk inside.

"How did this happen?" she asked, her voice high-pitched from the spell. It essentially acted like a nose pinch, only it was much more effective.

I gave a shrug and pulled on my innocent persona. "I dunno. I was just studying in the common room—" (My eyes blinked vapidly, trying to convince her I was there and totally not fucking Malcolm in the guys' dorm). I shook my head and puffed out my lips. "I overheard some girls talking about hazing me the other day, they don't like me much, so I did kind of try to set up my room a little ... to at least be able to figure out who was after me."

I pulled a jar of paint out of my backpack and held it out for Huchmala to examine while I made my way to the window ledge. Sure enough, the UV reactive white paint I'd used to coat the ledge was smeared. I lit my hand with UV light so that the ledge glowed bright orange. "See? They've probably washed their hands, but with a UV light, maybe their sink will still have traces of the paint."

Huchmala's mouth drew into a thin line, her normal hazy hippie artist demeanor falling away. She marched right out of my room to the door next to mine. She banged on it.

It was a long night, sitting in the hall, watching as every girl in the place had to present her hands and her sink for my UV inspection. It was a good thing I didn't care about friends. It was a good thing it was nearly spring break. Because that night I became the most hated girl at the academy.

I didn't give a fuck. The satisfaction of shining a light on Laura's sink, watching her face—as what she'd thought were invisible droplets of watered-down white paint glow bright orange—was worth it. The way Huchmala grabbed Laura by the scruff and dragged her off made me giddy. The feeling was better than any temporary friendships I might have made anyhow. I was on a countdown again. In another week, I'd either be back here, playing it cool and biding my time, or I'd be locked up. I didn't need high school girls and their drama. There was no time in my life for friends. My thoughts flicked to the guys. But we were more than friends. They were my crew. I didn't have time for other friends, I reminded myself as I gathered up one or two items that didn't smell horrific and followed the maintenance crew up to the attic. That thought reminded me of Emelia. I wondered for a second how she was doing. But that wonder was interrupted by the maintenance crew unlocking an attic room on the fourth floor so that I could sleep up there for the night.

The room was dusty, but the Force janitor was nice enough to clean it for me. I fell asleep fully clothed, on a bed that didn't have sheets, and dreamed about Matthew chasing me through the hallway with a toy snake he'd enchanted to hiss. I woke up smiling, though tear tracks stained my cheeks. I was gonna get my brother back. I could feel it.

THE NEXT DAY I HAD A LEVEL FIVE SPELL WRITING TEST IN PROFESSOR Trusk's class. Unlike my prior academies, which taught students all the way up to level eight spells (the type of spells required by the Pinnacle), MAD was more interested in getting students to graduate and hold base-level magical jobs at energy plants—wind and water power were the typical career paths for most magicals.

Even with only a level five spell, I had to help walk a guy to the nurse's office.

One dude ripped his arm open when he mixed up the order of some instructions. Since I'd finished my spell first, as I always did in that boring-ass class, Trusk called me over.

"Hayley, come here please." The professor with the walrus-sized mustache summoned me to his desk as he wrapped the guy's arm in gauze. The blood immediately soaked through the bandage and the smell of seared flesh reached my nose.

I had to swallow hard to avoid nausea.

Trusk pushed the guy toward me. "Take Ben here to the nurse's office. But go the long way around. Do not go past the faculty lounge." Trusk's beady brown eyes stared steadily at me. "Got it?"

My stomach churned when I realized the implications of what he said. It was lunch time. Half the faculty shifted at lunch time. I'd had to feed them during detention before. I pressed my teeth tightly together to keep my face expressionless in front of Ben, who looked like he might pass out. I nodded.

I dragged him through the halls and out around to the front of the admin building. He got so heavy at that point I had to set him down on the front steps and run inside to the nurse's office. As I ran, my burner phone buzzed inside my cross-body purse—the buzz from it was different than my normal phone. Potts was the only person with that number.

If she was calling, either something had happened to Matthew or she had information.

I didn't get a chance to call her back until I'd gotten Ben settled with the nurse and washed off my hands. I took the long way back to class, in case any of Ben's blood had gotten on me. I ducked behind the corner of Building B and dialed.

"Hey," I said in a low voice. "I'm in class and I'll have to get back. But I wanted to see if something had happened."

"You know that friend-with-benefits I've got?" Potts responded.

Annoyance and suspicion crept over me. She better not have called me to terrorize me with awful stories again. Was she referring to the guy who'd actually made it to Unnatural? I thought for a second. That was the only guy she'd ever mentioned, so I assumed she meant him. "Yeah."

"He just had a job interview with a lab."

"Okay?" I glanced at my watch. I had maybe a minute before Trusk started wondering what was taking me so long.

"The lab creates polyurethane coatings, enamels, that sort of thing. They're filing for a patent for a new kind of paint."

"I'm about to leave—can you get to the point?"

"This new kind of paint is magically reinforced. They're calling it Eternal Paint."

I spotted a stone lion heading toward me through the trees. Shit. I didn't want to be caught by it. I slid around the corner of the building. But then I was facing the quad. I squatted down, trying to make myself less prominent in case someone was looking out the window.

"The point, Potts?" I growled.

"He smelled something odd in one of the vats when he went through their plant. Shifter nose, you know? He stole a sample while he was there. Tested it. Guess what they're using in that paint?"

"I don't have time for Twenty Questions," I growled, deciding to stand up and just walk back to Trusk's class. This conversation was going nowhere.

"He found blood. And not just any blood. Vampire blood. They had vats and vats of this paint."

Dread.

Horror.

Disgust.

I stopped walking.

I froze right in the middle of the quad, phone held to my ear. "Why?"

"All those studies they're doing on finding ways to make norms magical ... you and I thought they'd be doing something to find a way to make magicals immortal. But nobody's gotten there yet.

Meanwhile, vamps are just sitting there. Like cattle in a pen *for eternity.*"

I got where she was going. Claude's favorite phrase morphed in my head and spilled out my lips. "What a waste of eternity, that could be put to better use," I whispered, heart cracking. "God, that makes me sick."

"Doesn't it though? There's a lovely little article in this morning's paper about an entire set of new rockets preparing to go to Mars and then to its moon. The magical heat shields for space travel—yeah, those are intense. Burn up rather quickly from the bit of research I've done. But the interesting thing is they're now claiming the rockets will be reusable due to new, unspecified 'advances.' And if you follow the more elite papers, there are a couple journalists hinting about expensive new shield spells written with a special ink. They're saying the U.S. is better protected than ever before ..."

My own vision went dark for a second. I was so stunned that my power overwhelmed me. Goosebumps rose on my skin. "Are you sure?" I whispered. *This is so widespread already? So many people have bought onto this? Agreed to this? Do they even know?*

Potts sent me links to the articles.

I scrolled through them, feeling dizzy and off-balance as I did so. The world beneath me had shifted. I didn't even stop when I saw one of the stone lions head toward me. The stone monster shocked me when he scooped me up into his mouth.

At first, fear lit through me like lightning. *So, this is how I die,* I thought. *And I was so close.*

But the beast cradled me with surprising gentleness between his massive teeth as he tromped toward the administration building. He made no attempt to eat me, even when I tried and failed to wriggle out from between his teeth. The lion's warm breath blew across me as he set me down on the just-greening grass by the butterfly fountain and pinned me to the ground with his paw. He let out a roar (to alert the faculty I guessed). Sure enough, an assistant marched outside, retrieved me, and led me to the headmaster's office.

This office was dull compared to the one at Medeis. Spartan, just like most of MAD. I stared dully at Headmaster Griffin's bald head while he droned on and on about responsibility and crap like that.

I didn't really listen.

My mind was a million miles away, still reading through the articles, still replaying Potts' last words over and over.

"The Pinnacle isn't experimenting on vamps. It's killing them."

36

Zavier showed up on our last day before break with a picnic basket hanging over one arm and a blanket on the other. I looked up at him from the bench I'd been sitting at for the past hour, fruitlessly searching for this ghost of a woman—Ginny Stone—through U.S. government files. The best that I could find was that she was fifty years old, based on a scrap of a doc that I unscrambled which included a birthdate. The Pinnacle was doing a good job of keeping their top-level Darklight a secret.

I sighed and shut my laptop when Z sat down next to me on the stone bench. He plucked the computer off my lap and put it into my backpack. "I can help you forget about that. Come on."

I grabbed my bag and followed him toward the woods. Once we were on the path, a little away from the buildings, Zavier slid his hand into mine. For once, he didn't make a naughty comment like, "Oh, your hand is silky smooth, bet that would feel good against my cock."

"Are you doing alright?" I asked him, glancing up from his tattooed forearm to study his dark eyes.

"Peachy keen, jellybean," he grinned. But the smile slid away quickly, and I could tell it wasn't real. Zavier had something serious on his mind today.

Was he nervous about the job? Was it too much? He and Evan had practiced together several times, Z slowing time as Evan scribbled furiously across a page, trying to unravel spells. It wasn't perfect yet, but they still had most of Spring Break. The ball wasn't until next Saturday. They were just over a minute and a half short on time, as expected.

Z still hadn't slept with me. Neither had Grayson, but Grayson insisted his power could handle things without a boost. Based on the Mars family, I was betting Grayson was telling the truth. But, now that I'd researched Z, I knew he needed the boost. His power ranking was a seventy-four out of a hundred. It was good. And he was smart. But that extra bump would push him to the top and give us what we needed. Z hadn't mentioned sleeping together, hadn't even really kissed me since this whole thing started. It made me worry he was having second thoughts—either about the job, or me.

The second option felt even worse than the first. I'd gone and majorly fucked up this job. No wonder pros wouldn't work with me. Because I was very attached to all these guys. And Zavier ... I'd thought he'd be the most enthusiastic about this power up stuff. But for all his naughty talk, was he shy?

I glanced up at Z again. He chewed his lip as he dragged me around Grayson and through the pine trees up a small ridge.

Gray nodded toward us for half a second before returning his concentration to four clay figures he was levitating in midair. I looked back to watch him and then up to see his clay dummies. They floated just at the tops of the trees, around forty feet. Gray—who absolutely hated to be called that, we'd discovered, so we'd all immediately started referring to him that way—he lifted the figures slowly, trying to hit fifty feet. His forehead was covered in sweat.

"Nice work," I called as we walked off.

Z led me farther into the woods, on a path and then off a path to a little clearing I hadn't seen before. It wasn't all that different from any other clearing, except for the rotting tree trunk that fell across the middle. I guess that made this place special somehow because Zavier stopped and declared, "Here we are."

"Dead tree trunks are so romantic."

"Yeah, well I tried to find a rotting pumpkin patch but—wrong season," Zavier retorted.

I glanced over, lost. "Why?"

"Because it'd be gourd-geous."

I laughed. "You're ridiculous."

"You're right about the dick part of that statement." He pumped his hips in a lewd dance for a second. And my familiar silly Zavier was back.

"I wouldn't know. I haven't gotten to see that dick," I teased as I helped Z spread the blanket. But then I worried I'd overstepped. "Hey, I'm sorry."

He laughed. "That's a first."

I punched his shoulder. "Stop. I'm sorry. I shouldn't have joked about that." I bit my lip. And then a thought occurred to me. *No. Z isn't a virgin, is he? Impossible. Shit.* What was I gonna do if he was a virgin? How did I ask about that without being a total jerk?

He leaned back on the blanket, eyes twinkling. "I like this little nervous you. Almost as much as spitfire you. Why are you nervous?"

I huffed and tried to ignore him. No way I was gonna ask that. I also had no intention of answering his question. Both options made me highly uncomfortable. Instead I moved to open the basket. "What are we gonna eat?"

He laid out the blanket and said, "I got the cafeteria people to make us something special. Mac and cheese since it's your favorite."

I glanced up sharply. "How do you know that's my favorite?"

"First off, not everyone's oblivious. Second off, you've stolen at least three packages of the premade stuff from Malcolm's room. If I feed you, will you tell me what you were thinking?" Z asked as he dished some mac and cheese into a bowl for me and then brought out a bowl of strawberries.

He wouldn't let it drop. Of course. I was gonna have to tell him something. Otherwise, Z would call Malcolm over so that I'd spill my guts.

The guys had realized that Malcolm had this uncanny ability to make me tell the truth. I wouldn't put it past them to use that against me. I stared down at the blanket and said, "I don't get why you haven't ... you know ... made your move."

"Maybe I want you to make it." Z raised a brow.

"What?" I sat back, stunned.

"Yeah," Zavier bit into a strawberry. "That's definitely it. I want you to seduce me."

"We don't have time for that!" I exclaimed, a little alarmed. "Plus, I thought you said you were a wham bam, thank you, ma'am--"

"Nope. Recently changed that policy. See, can't be that guy anymore. Cause this chick I like has three other dudes hanging around."

"But dirty friends--"

Zavier cut my reply off by shoving a strawberry into my mouth. "Don't worry. I'll go easy on you. If you mess up in your attempt to make a grand romantic gesture, I'll forgive you. Once. But if you mess up twice ..." He shook his head. "It'll be awfully hard for me to focus on our job if I haven't been properly wooed."

"Wooed? Wooed?!" I threw the back half of my strawberry at him. Of course, the jerk used his Tock power and avoided it, moving fast as a flash. "Z, I'm about to have a heart attack right now. Malcolm says we can only pull this off next week!"

He shook his head. "Yelling isn't very seductive."

I took my spoon and flicked a noodle at him. He ducked that too. "Seductive, I'll show you seductive!" I growled. I climbed to my feet and Zavier scrambled away from me, running through the trees and laughing. I chased him, which was an impossible quest, because any time I got close he'd extend a hand, blast me with power and slow me down until I felt like one of those ridiculous movies where people ran through a field toward one another.

Eventually, Z relented—once we were both panting, and I had a stitch in my side. He dragged me over to a dried-out creek bed and we sat on a flat boulder next to it, feet hanging down the tiny ledge.

I didn't speak while I caught my breath. But when I had, I flipped our silly mood and turned it serious. I didn't know how to seduce Z. But I needed him to know how much it meant to me that he'd said yes. That he'd done so quickly, and with so much less hesitation than Malcolm or Gray, that he was willing to risk his entire future for me … it made my heart swell and skip along like a sailboat full of dancing wind. At the same time, that knowledge loomed over me, made me feel like I was underwater, trapped in a submarine that was just one wrong move away from nothingness. It was so much pressure.

I grabbed a twig and started to strip the bark from it, feeling as naked as that little limb. "You know, I need you more than you need me."

Z looked over at me but didn't say anything.

I stared down at the twig as I dug my nails into it, trying to make sure I didn't leave a single piece of bark. "It makes me nervous to ask so much of you. If anything goes wrong and happens to you or the guys

..." My voice cracked and I broke my damn stick. "If I could do it alone, I would." I tossed the stick into the creek bed.

Next to me, Z sighed and put his arm around me. I hugged him hard and tight. "Zavier."

He hugged me back for a long time. He stroked my back. When he spoke, his voice was light and conversational. But I glanced up and saw his jaw was tight. "The last job I was on ... there was a guy. We'd worked with him a couple times. Good guy. Guy I trusted. But when push came to shove, he left me and my cousin out to dry."

My fingers tightened around Z's waist. "What happened?"

"Alarm we didn't expect got triggered. He got away, but we'd been down in the vault, feeding money up to him. We both got snatched." Z sighed and ran a hand through his hair. "I'd never been caught before. I get into a lotta shit here because of my vibrant ... personality. But out there, I used to be what people in the biz call a whiz man."

My heart and throat grew tight. Not that I was worried about Z disappointing me. Any one of us could fuck up any part of this job at any moment. But because Z was worried about disappointing me. He cared. My entire being gave a sigh of relief.

I had to reciprocate. He'd just admitted fallibility. He'd just admitted his weakness. I had one too. I leaned back and undid the top button of my shirt. Then I pulled my collar to the side.

Z tilted his head, his brown eyes curious.

"I'm gonna tell you something I haven't told the others yet. Because ... because it's hard for me. But also, because it might be a weakness. Or a distraction. And someone needs to know. Claude ..."

"The guy from the memory?" Z asked.

I nodded and grabbed Zavier's hand. "My mother's new husband," I reminded him. I stared down at his pale skin for a second before I flipped his hand over so he could reach out and touch me. Then I raised his fingers and placed them on my neck. Slowly, I dragged them around. I let the pads of his fingers travel over my scars.

Z's eyebrows shot up when he realized what he was feeling. His fingers tightened slightly on my neck before he relaxed his grip. Still, he swallowed hard before he spoke. "He did that?"

I nodded, pulling his hand down and setting it in my lap before I reached up to button my shirt. "Yeah. And I need you to make sure I stay focused. Because after everything ... I really want to hurt him. Especially knowing what he did to Dad. But revenge won't save Matthew. And the reality is I probably only get one shot at the Pinnacle before they're onto me ..."

Z grabbed my hand and laced our fingers together. I stared up into his deep brown eyes. I felt vulnerable, which was foreign and awful and joyous all at once, because it felt like I was about to jump off a cliff. But at the same time, I trusted Z would catch me.

I cleared my throat before I said softly, "I need you. I need your help. I need you to keep me focused. And I need you because you keep the dark away." My eyes misted and I blinked back the tears. I refused to cry. "Some of those needs might just be for the job. But that last one? Z, that one's always gonna be around." I leaned forward and brushed my lips hesitantly against his.

Z didn't share my hesitation. He crushed me to him and pulled me onto his lap. His tongue wrestled playfully with mine and his hands stroked down my back. But he ended the kiss far sooner than I wanted, pulling back with a smile.

"Hales?" he said, softly, tucking a bit of my hair behind my ear.

"Yeah?"

"Next time a guy wants you to seduce him, you just need to take off your shirt."

My jaw dropped. *"What?"*

"Maybe the bra too. But, you know, slowly. To make it classy."

I threw back my head and laughed. Then I hit him. "That's all you wanted? And I just spilled my guts?"

He shrugged. "I'm a simple man."

I tackled him shoving him back on the rock until his back was flat against it. We both shook with laughter.

Z wrapped his arms around me and pulled me down to him for a kiss. At first, it was just as fun and playful as Zavier always was, but after a while, it grew deeper, more intense. He pressed me against him, and I could feel how much he wanted me. I wanted him just as bad. I let my fingers get tangled in his just-fucked hair. I started to rub against him, pulling back and saying, "I'm gonna seduce you so good," then reaching for the next button on my shirt.

Z was the one who stopped us again, sitting up with me still on his lap. He put his hand over mine as he caught his breath. He gave me a peck on the lips, "As much as I want to do this, and I really do, we need to talk."

"Okay."

"First off, I don't think we should trust the power boost. That's just chance. That time gap is huge. No living Tock has hit that time. We need a second Tock. And I know a guy—"

"Z—"

He cut me off. "Second off, I don't think Malcolm's bombs are gonna be quite enough. We need to hedge our bets. I think we need to pull another stunt. Bonus is, this one we can aim at that shit stain your mom married."

I leaned forward, intrigued. "Yeah. What is it?"

"It's a little something that we in the business call a Leery."

37

BECOMING the nemesis of a billionaire's son had its perks. Gray had his private jet come pick us up. The guys had all told their families they were going to stay with him—and what magical parent would say no to that?

I got to ride on the jet, but mommy was too conservative to let me actually sleep over at a guy's house. Plus, she was all a-titter about my Pinnacle interview. I'd pretty much forgotten about it.

-Did you order a suit?- She texted me as we boarded the plane.

-Forgot. Midterms-

-Good! We can go shopping!-

I groaned as I stared at the text. Shopping was an all-day event with my mother. Evan glanced over at me. "Well, you have to get a dress for the ball anyway," he said. "Invite Tia."

I set everything up and then relaxed against the seat as the guys all settled in around Malcolm to learn how to play that board game I'd seen in his closet—Azul.

I bowed out, grabbing a soda and moving toward a plush leather seat in the front. I set down the soda can on the table in front of me and pulled out a folder. (Malcolm refused to put anything into digital form. We had an extensive argument over the spells and programming I could do to keep his plan safe. I lost said discussion when he took off his shirt.)

I flipped through the first few pages of the plan he'd dubbed "Mice in a Maze." He didn't want to build a fire bomb—his signature style. Partially because we wanted to remain anonymous. And partially because he had far more interesting ideas about how to drive a pack of shifters wild. I pulled up one particularly juvenile-looking sketch of a stink bomb. "How exactly are we getting these set up?"

Malcolm just winked at me as he laid down some blue patterned tiles on the board and made Gray groan. "Same way I got all my other stuff set up, Shakespeare. I've got a system."

"But security—"

Malcolm paused the game and pulled out a hat. He shoved it onto his forehead, ignoring the fact that it decimated his fifties hair flip. The hat was old and battered with a Pepsi logo on it. "Security doesn't ever pay attention to the delivery guys."

"You sure? I thought that was just some—"

"He's right," Gray said. "We get water, groceries, and shopping deliveries at home. My dad always has probably thirty randoms a day go to his office. As long as they look like they're just doing their job, nobody even makes eye contact."

I looked back at Malcolm's drawing, which included eggs, milk, and vinegar poured into a soda can and left to sit for a week. "But you're gonna have to reseal these. And what about anyone that tries to drink from the cans before the party?"

Malcolm glanced at Gray. "Has she forced you into bed yet?"

Gray grinned and shook his head.

Malcolm turned to Z. "She making a big deal about the fact that you're gonna have to magically remove that monitor around your ankle?"

Z shook his head, "She knows I stole the key day one." But then he stage-whispered to me, "You're in trouble."

They all turned to stare at me. Malcolm's magic turned my skin to ice. He was ticked. "I'm the expert, Hayley."

I tried to backtrack. "I'm sorry. I'm just double-checking…"

"Let me be the expert."

"She's just worried," Evan tried to defend me.

Malcolm's eyes narrowed. He looked up at me and pulled the cold away. "The answers to your question are magic and math." Malcolm looked down and placed a row of tiles on his board, filling his card and beating the guys.

I sighed and turned back to his file, stomach churning. I didn't like annoying him. I was annoying myself with all this worry. But it felt like it was too soon.

Malcolm left the other guys and came over to sit beside me. He cracked my soda and took a sip. Then he set it in front of me and pointed his hand at it. The metal around the tab heated and melted until it thinned and smoothed across the top. Then Malcolm flipped his power. Ice crystals formed on the soda can. It swelled. And then it burst, sending soda everywhere.

"Hey, man! There's a cleaning fee!" Gray complained.

"You can afford it," Malcolm shot back. Then he grabbed my hand. He leaned forward and stroked my palm. "Trust me, Hales. I've got this."

I swallowed hard and nodded. "You're right. I'm sorry. I do trust you."

He stared at me long and hard for a second. "You'd better. Because your life is in our hands."

A small airplane pillow went flying through the air and smacked him in the head. We both looked over to see Z crossing his arms and shaking his head from his seat. "Way to freak her out more, dick."

"It's the truth," Malcolm stood and threw the pillow back at Z, who caught it.

"You can tell the truth without being harsh."

"Okay, you tell her."

Z leaned over in his seat to peer around Malcolm. "We've got you, Hales. You can trust us. And Malcolm's too scared to say he has feelings for you and he'd go to the ends of the earth—HOLY FUCKING SHIT! My balls!" Z collapsed, sliding out of his seat onto the floor of the plane. One second, Z was on the floor holding his crotch in agony. The next he was gone and there was an airplane blanket around Malcolm's shoulders. An airplane blanket, tied off at the neck, and nothing else. Z had slowed Malcolm down and sped himself up enough that he'd stripped Malcolm completely naked. And I hadn't even seen it.

Malcolm's face was scary as he stared down at himself and then back at Z.

Oh shit. My heart raced as I glanced between the two of them. It looked like World War III was about to go down. Midair. Right in the aisle in front of me.

"Little cold in here for you, Captain Smeckle?" Z grinned.

"Whoa! Whoa—let's not forget we're all working together—" Evan said.

Both Malcolm and Z turned to stare at him. Malcolm didn't bother to cover up at all. Instead, his hands went to his waist, elbows out, superhero style.

A tiara made of ice appeared on Evan's head. "Sure thing, Princess," Malcolm retorted. "We'll keep it sweet."

Gray snorted. So did Z. The two of them started laughing so hard it felt like the plane was going to vibrate. Evan reached up and touched his crown. He pulled it off and laughed. Then he set it right back onto his head.

Z tossed Malcolm his boxers. Malcolm dragged them on and sat back down. The two of them started playing a new round of the game like nothing had happened. Other than the occasional snicker, the guys seemed fine.

I shook my head. If some girl had pulled shit like that with me, she'd be on my 'hate forever'—bitch talk her and try to curse her children—blacklist. But dudes razzing each other was like a bonding ritual. Guys were fucked in the head. Except … maybe so was I. Because there was one guy I liked to taunt.

I glanced back to see them all playing, bursting into occasional laughter. All but one. He sat and played. But he wasn't quite as loud as the others. Not quite as boisterous.

I reached into my bag and grabbed my wand. I knew how to fix that. And it only took one little level six spell.

Two minutes later, Malcolm trounced everyone. Just as he was sitting back to enjoy his victory, Gray said, "Just wait—BOOBIES!"

Everyone stared at him a second, and then cracked up. Including me. I didn't even try to be subtle as Gray turned in his seat, rising onto his knees to peer at me over the back of the chair. He shook his head at me. "You unoriginal—FAT BUTT NUT!—What the hell? You—BROCCOLI BREATH!—gave me—DUMP TRUCK!—Tourette's?"

My ribs hurt from laughing so hard. "Not just any kind. Toddler Tourette's."

"Eat sh—I HOPE GUMMY BEARS PEE IN YOUR HAIR!" Gray started laughing. He thumped the seat back with his fist.

I just smirked, wagging a finger at him. "Now you know a little about what that Shakespeare spell felt like."

Evan wheezed after laughing so hard. "Gummy bear pee! That doesn't even make sense."

"Neither does your—YOU LOOK LIKE YOU CAME FROM THE DONATION PILE!"

That one even brought tears to Malcolm's eyes.

Gray pushed off of his seat and grabbed his bag from the floor. He jabbed a threatening finger in my direction but didn't dare open his mouth. I just gave him my signature finger wave, one that had become almost affectionate when I gave it to him.

He stared at me in mock disappointment as he grabbed a notebook and pencil so he could figure out how to unravel it. But then he looked over at Evan. "Hey, this is your job. Come help me—YOU FATTY WATTY SHOE FACE!"

After another round of laughter, Evan walked over and plopped down next to Gray. Z even stood by and helped them speed through the spell when Evan finally pulled out his wand to write.

"Alright, Preschool, let's get you fixed," Evan grinned.

I sat back in my chair, feeling a little self-satisfied. This crew was coming together.

THE SHOPPING CREW THAT MOTHER SURROUNDED ME WITH HAD IT together, the way demons had it together in hell. We'd gone to a norm store, because even though magicals could make clothes, magic always seemed to fit exactly to your form, which was not the most flattering. Mother was a believer that a good seamstress could hide nearly anything, make nearly anyone appear beautiful. So, we went to her favorite shop. The women fitting me for a rush custom suit and gown pinned me and poked me with evil efficiency that I had no doubt was designed for maximum torture.

Mom *ooh*ed and *ahh*ed like this was a wedding dress fitting. She disappeared twice during it, no doubt to go swallow some more Calm in the bathroom. The fuckers that sold to her liked to mix it in with sparkling water, so that no one could tell that the can she carried glowed with green magic inside. Her elegant hair and outfit couldn't cover up the fact that she was too thin—that she cared more about the spell than eating.

Tia just shook her head as she watched all the chaos. One of her aunts made dresses, so she was off the hook. She didn't have to stand there like a pin cushion. She just ran a tongue over her black lipstick and said, "I'm not even jealous of how hot you're gonna look in that dress after seeing this."

Mom looked at fabric swatches from her seat. "Are you sure you don't want another color, honey?" She held up a red silk. "We could re-dye your hair and this would look—"

"I want black, Mom." I cut her off but tried to soften the rejection with a smile. I wanted black in case I needed to pull on my shadows—in case part one of the plan went to shit.

"But, with your hair streaks, won't that look … Halloweeny?"

I sighed. But Tia nodded. I'd come to like the orange hair streaks a little. But, if we were busting ass to run away from the Pinnacle after this job, I didn't need to be memorable. I sighed and nodded. "Fine. Let's go get my hair dyed."

Tia yipped like a puppy and I stared at her for a second—she'd gotten so caught up in the girlish excitement of this dance that she was actually smiling. She'd lost her 'death to the world' attitude.

At the salon, while Mom got her nails done, Tia and I sat and talked as our lowlights sank in.

"Okay, so … Evan. He's like super-hot," Tia cleared her throat. "Do you know … is he seeing someone?"

Panic. Awkward panic. I felt like I was doing that awkward side-step in the grocery store aisle, where the person in front of me and I keep stepping the same way and blocking each other. Crap. What did I tell her? "I'm not sure. I think he might be. But, it's not something he talks to me about."

She pressed her lips together. "Okay. So, maybe just a friend thing. But … maybe not." The little jump in her tone at that had me feeling all kinds of anxiety.

I had to put on my fake ditzy, happy persona to keep up with her. Because I really just wanted to march Evan over to the nearest tattoo parlor and make him get 'taken' written across his torso. Maybe on his neck too. His forehead. But that would be ridiculous. And Evan was only going to the ball so he could help Malcolm out. I shoved away my claws and gave Tia a big smile. "Yeah, this whole thing is gonna be so cool."

"I've heard that at midnight, the shifters all go into different rooms to shift based on their animal."

"Oh, I hadn't heard that!" I lied.

"You didn't look it up?"

I had. Extensively. I knew the building had fourteen entrances and exits. And that Malcolm was planning to make all but two impassable. But I touched a foil wrap in my hair and said, "When Grayson asked me, that was kind of all I could think about."

"God. I know! It's like a fairy tale. Or like a stalker romance," Tia gushed. "I can't believe you went all the way out there for him and actually got together."

I laughed. She was right about the stalker part. The romance? I wasn't sure where Gray and I stood on that yet. His face flitted through my mind. I did love the little war we had. I would have even called it mental foreplay—if I was sure he was interested. But Gray … well, he'd just been through that breakup. And we had a job to focus on. I should have been more focused on the job with the others too. Sometimes, though,

Mom walked up just then, showing off the new bejeweled nails she'd gotten. "What are you two girls giggling about?" she asked, stealing an empty stylist's chair and rolling it over to sit next to us.

"Our dates."

"I'm so excited for the both of you." Mom reached out and rubbed my hand and I realized it was the first time she'd touched me since I'd gotten home yesterday. She'd been passed out from Calm when I'd walked in the door. I tried not to let the sting of that realization enter my face and just enjoy the fact that she was here now.

Tia's stylist led her off to finish up her hair. It was just me and Mom. I stared down at where she held my hand. Then I brought my hand to cover hers. "Love you, crazy lady," I said, using an old term that Matthew and I used to tease her with.

She smiled softly at me. "Love you, too." Her eyes teared up. "I know it's been hard, Hales. But I just … Dad would be proud of you. I want you to know that. An interview at the Pinnacle. I knew you could do it."

I squeezed her hand and said, "Not without you. I know you pulled those strings."

She laughed. "I just want the best for you, honey. You're so bright. And not just your hands," she used an old joke my parents had beat to death over the years. Mom reached up and patted my cheek. "You're so strong, you know. Stronger than I've ever been."

"You're strong."

She shook her head, glancing down. "I'm not. Your dad always called me his flower. It's true. I need to be tended. It's just who I am." When she glanced up her face was full of regret and pride and a million other things.

Her expression tugged at me. Because it was the first time that she'd been fully vulnerable around me in years. I squeezed her hand. "It doesn't have to be who you are," I told her.

She bit her lip. "It is though. But you. You aren't like that. And you have no idea how happy that makes me." She rubbed my hand, almost like she was rubbing it to soothe herself.

My heart hurt at hearing how little she thought of herself. "Mom, you think you're weak. But you've helped me through the dark times. You're stronger than you think."

Mom leaned over and kissed my cheek. "You're a sweet girl. This is the perfect moment to ask me for anything you want, now that I'm all teary and buttered up."

I laughed. "What makes you think I want something?"

"You're a teenage girl. Give it five seconds and you'll think of something you want."

"How about I just get to postpone my Sunday appointment with the counselor?" I asked. "I'm gonna be tired after the ball." I actually hoped that I'd be at the Institute then, giving Matthew his cure…

"You got it." Mom laughed. "I kinda was expecting you'd want jewelry for the ball."

I shrugged. "Nah. Everybody there will be trying to out-sparkle each other."

"True enough."

I smiled up at Mom, my heart warmed by her presence for the first time in a long time. My enjoyment was short-lived because her phone buzzed. Mom pulled it out and answered. "Mmm-hmm." She spent a minute 'mmm-hmming' before she said, "Perfect!" and hung up.

"Who was that?" I asked.

Mom tilted her head. "Oh! Ginny, she's so sweet. She's Claude's secretary, you know. She's out getting her own dress for the ball. Great minds."

I stopped stock still.

"Ginny? I thought his secretary was named Tina."

Mom laughed. "Oh no. Tina's been gone for months." She made a ridiculous face. She swiped through her phone. "That girl's brain wasn't bigger than her nipple."

I just smiled and shook my head at her. My parents used to make a game of trying to embarrass Matthew and me by saying scandalous things. It felt like our talk had brought back the old version of her, if just for a moment.

Mom just continued, "When Claude found Ginny, it was a godsend. Oh, look, here she is at dinner with us, we took her out for her birthday." Mom turned the phone around to show a picture of her and Claude huddled together in a booth. On Claude's other side, huddled way too close to him, was a girl with unnatural cherry red hair. His arm disappeared underneath the tabletop in a way that was suspect to anyone except my oblivious mother. But it wasn't the hand that drew my eyes. It was Ginny's face. Her very young (very unpierced in that picture) face.

Emelia's face.

Thunderbolts lanced my chest. *That bitch. Claude sent her to spy on me.*

It was a good thing I'd spent three years practicing my arrogant, disinterested face. Because otherwise, I would have blown everything. "Hmm." I took the phone and looked at the date.

It was a match for Ginny Stone's birthday. I glanced up at the photo again. Ginny must have had an excellent plastic surgeon. Or else her spell writing was beyond formidable. I was betting it was the latter.

Dad had said Claude was having an affair with his secretary. He'd forgotten to mention that the bitch was way more than just a secretary. She was the Pinnacle's top Darklight.

38

THE GUYS WORKED and lived out of Grayson's pool house. The pool worked well for when we staged full re-enactments in case Gray ended up dropping us. He was good enough to slow us down and flip us over so we could belly flop 'gently' into the pool. Z's smart mouth got him in trouble more than once.

"Come on, Preschool, it's not like this is hard." Z's taunt made Gray's eyebrows draw together and the rich boy dropped my Tock from twenty feet, flipping him face down so that his belly smacked hard against the water. When Z surfaced, sputtering, his belly was as red as a Classic Crayon.

A few of Grayson's "friends" from Crush flew out from Cali and showed us the best ways to outfox animals in case we had any trouble during the "Stampede" part of our plan—aptly named by Z. My power to blind shifters only worked half as well as I wanted, because their noses were so good. Burning their paw pads was our quickest solution, because I could blast them with light, and it didn't require spell writing or amulets. We were already going to need to carry two amulets as it was.

Malcolm tried repeatedly to write some spells that simulated the pheromones of a female shifter in heat. He wanted to drive the shifters mad at the Unnatural Ball. When he thought he'd found the right combination, he grabbed a cooler full of pheromones and brought us all out to the woods to test it. "So, we get everyone outside with part one: Stinky Stampede. Then we use the sprinkler system and add this." He held up a test tube full of pale pink sparkling magic.

"Why are pheromones pink?" I asked, offended. That seemed like a bunch of bullshit.

"They just are," Malcolm responded.

"I don't like this idea. Think about the chaos," Evan protested.

"Exactly," Malcolm replied, pushing aside a branch as we walked deeper into the shade of the trees. "If we get lucky, a couple guards will abandon their posts over at the Pinnacle to help deal with a group of rut-crazed shifters. If I can get enough different animal scents mixed in there, it will be a shit show of different shifters running around trying to mate. The prairie dogs will be so distracted, the outdoor videos will be full of chaos, it will make our flight to the seventh floor and the first part of the night way easier."

"Except that will mean a hundred sets of eyes outdoors that could see us," Evan protested.

Malcolm shook his head. "Let's say you scent a female in heat. You really gonna look up to the sky to find her? Nope. You're gonna be scanning all around you. You think the woman next to you is gonna look up if you shift and go full grizzly? Nope. She's gonna scream and book it. I've made sure not to get any avian pheromones, so we don't worry about flying shifters. Now, come here please," Malcolm gestured toward a large oak tree in Gray's yard. Wrapped around the massive trunk was a thick chain.

"What is that?"

"Well, I have to test out my pheromones."

"But Gray has friends—" Evan looked to me for support.

"We don't need outsiders knowing every part of our plan," Gray replied. "Even though they're my guys ... we should only trust anyone outside this circle with limited info. They know their role. I pay them. That's it. No questions asked."

I gave Evan an apologetic shrug. "At least, if it makes you horny, once you're human again, I can—"

Evan clipped the metal restraint around his waist immediately. He turned to Malcolm. "Okay. Go."

Malcolm stepped forward with his spelled vial full of 'female shifter in heat' pheromones. Z reached into the cooler at Malcolm's feet and grabbed another, a grin on his face as he swirled the liquid back and forth inside it.

"Hey, Z, that's overkill, don't you think just one—" Evan didn't even get to finish his sentence before Malcolm tossed the sparkling pink liquid into the air in front of my stalker.

When Evan shifted with a roar, it was a frightening sight. His skin crackled with lightning and he roared as his clothing ripped and shredded. Hair sprouted all over as his bones morphed and he grew three feet taller.

I scooted closer to Malcolm as Evan wildly strained against the chains that held him. "Um, so, it worked," I said in a low voice, as Evan swiped at us, his claws looking as long and terrible as daggers.

"Yup," Malcolm smiled.

"So, do you have any way to reverse it?"

"I could write a spell, but that would take a while," Malcolm said. "We're probably better off just waiting for him to calm down and shift back."

"Okay," I agreed, uneasily. "How long should that take?" Evan's massive bear boner was red ... and just plain scary. It was huge and stuck straight up as he dry humped the air in front of him. He gave a moan, and I couldn't tell if it was in anger ... or something else.

Evan roared again and lunged, driven mad by the hormones.

"Are you sure you gave him the right dosage?" I asked.

Malcolm wavered his hand in front of him. "Maybe it's a little strong."

"We don't actually want people to get hurt," I added as we watched Evan struggle against the chains.

The tree trunk behind him made a cracking sound that made every hair on my arms stand up.

Malcolm bolted toward Gray and Z, who each had a vials in their hands. "Bet you could use this for all kinds of fun things," Z said. "Imagine tossing this on some of the Fangs at school."

"You fucktards!" Malcolm yelled, snatching away the vials. "those aren't toys! They're biological weapons!" He yanked the test tubes out of their hands, but Z had uncapped his. Female shifter hormones splashed down the front of Malcolm's shirt.

"Ugh, that stinks!" Gray took a step back.

Evan's roar was three times as loud as any of his prior roars. He strained again and I heard a *swhink* before the chains holding him fell to the ground.

My mouth went dry. *Oh, holy fuck.* I bolted for the nearest tree.

"Oh shit!" Gray said as he flew upward, out of Evan's path.

Malcolm's eyes widened in terror as Evan ran—straight for him.

Z raised his hand and shot power at Evan, turning the bear's run into a slow-motion dance. Zavier waved his other hand frantically at Malcolm, shouting, "Go! Go! Run! And cover your ass!"

MAGICAL ACADEMY FOR DELINQUENTS

Malcolm darted through the woods, both hands firmly on his butt as Evan struggled in slow motion to reach him. Z's manipulation of time made him seem to almost float in the air with each bound he took.

I couldn't help but swallow a giggle.

Z pulled out his phone and swiped over to video. I ran to him and smacked it out of his hand. "No, Asshole! Help me speed write a spell to stop this!"

"But, but—"

Gray interjected. "Don't worry. You help Hayley. I gotcha covered." And then he held up his phone and chased after the pair, laughing wildly as Malcolm shot power at Evan's back paws and turned them into ice blocks, so that the horny bear slipped and slid across the ground. Z's power seemed to diminish because suddenly Evan slipped and slid faster and then made it to Malcolm. He pinned the blond underneath him and started dry humping.

I had never written a spell so fast.

And Gray might have laughed until he'd collapsed; Z might have pitched face first into a poolside chair—worn out because he'd expended so much natural power trying to slow time; Malcolm might have buried his face in the grass, red-faced from embarrassment, but me?

Buck-naked Evan threw me over his shoulder and hauled me into his bedroom, marching without a word past Gray and Malcolm's friends. He slammed his door shut and then pressed me up against the wall, yanking up my skirt and shoving my panties down around my thighs. Then he lowered his face and stuck his tongue onto my slit without warning.

At first, I was too sensitive, and yanked back on his hair. But Evan growled and pushed his face back into me, using his breath and fingers to warm me up. At the same time, he pumped himself quickly.

When he came on my skirt seconds later, I groaned in disappointment.

But then Evan said, "Oh, we're just getting started. I had to take the edge off." And then he scooped up a drop of his cum that had landed on my thigh and fed it to me.

The heat blazing in his eyes made me lean in and press against him. "Well, then, if we're not done, get back to work."

He grinned as he dipped down below my waist again. His tongue teased my thighs this time, then slowly worked toward my center.

This time, the soft, gentle licks he gave me made the muscles in my legs start to hum. My mind went limp as sparks started to shoot through my nerves. Evan brought up his fingers and slid them slowly into me. First just one finger pumped leisurely in and out, getting me ready.

When I was close, but needed more, I whispered, "Evan."

Like he could read my mind, he added a second finger. He curled them as he pumped into me. When I was teetering, on the brink of bliss, he added a third and started to pump his fingers so hard that my ass repeatedly smacked into the wall.

"Yes!" I whispered.

Evan flicked his tongue faster over my clit as his fingers pummeled me.

I rose, higher and higher, until I felt like I was floating. Then I fell over the edge into pleasure. I shuddered and pulled Evan's hair as I rode his hand to completion, completely wanton and shameless.

When I came down, Evan picked me up and threw me onto his bed. He stalked toward me, only remembering to grab the Anti-Conception Amulet at the last minute.

But when he climbed over me and rubbed his hard staff against my slit, he said, "I'm not gonna go easy on you today."

"Good," I reached down and guided him inside of me, and he quickly rammed in all the way to the hilt, making me arch with pleasurable pain.

He'd already stretched me with his fingers though; the pleasure overtook the pain after a few more strokes. That's when I lifted my hips further, reached up and traced his biceps, and told him, "Harder."

Evan grinned and held onto my shoulders. He rode me so hard the bed slammed into the wall again and again.

When he got close, he reached down and used his fingers to make sure I got there too. His thick fingers circled my clit and then rubbed it, then spanked it, driving me insane to the point that I was shouting for more, not caring who heard me.

When I came, my vision went black. That's how intense my orgasm was. It sang and echoed through my body, like I was a bell that Evan had rung. I could feel it down to my fingertips, which prickled even afterward.

As I came down, and Evan fell face first onto the mattress beside me, exhausted, I said, "I'm definitely gonna bribe Malcolm into making more of that pheromone for me after this job." Out of control Evan was too hot to resist.

39

To practice another aspect of the heist, Gray had also purchased a tube slide for us. He'd had that set up in the massive lawn in the backyard. I had no doubt that the staff thought we were crazy, all climbing into the tube slide and making our way down again and again like elementary school kids. They didn't see the char marks inside the tube as Evan set fires and Malcolm put them out.

They also didn't see how insanely tight our fit was on the ladder rings we'd drilled into the tube. We'd determined piggyback was the only way we could descend, because Dad's latest memory projection showed that the fire rings were spaced every three feet. Even doubled up, Malcolm and Evan would have to chill down twenty feet of flaming circus rings at a time, for the entire three-hundred-foot descent. In our twenty-five-foot practice slide, we had to go up and down twelve times to simulate the same effect. We ended up tired, coughing like smokers, and horribly grumpy.

During one of our trips down the tube, the guys started chipping at each other.

"Don't fucking rush me!" Evan growled at Gray.

"Oh, okay, yeah, this is just some leisurely stroll through the Pinnacle. Not like guards are gonna be on our tails or Hayley's gonna have to hold off a dozen different cameras simultaneously—take your time. Flame whenever you feel like it."

"Calm down, Pony, I'm sure Evan's just distracted because he gets to have Hayley rubbing up against him," Z said grumpily from Gray's back. He absolutely hated that his size meant he was always forced to ride either Gray or Evan, the two most massive members of the group. His normally chipper nature turned nasty in the tube.

"Call me Pony again," Gray threatened.

"Hold on, Horsie," Z pressed his buttons.

"Guys, shut up," I scolded both of them.

But it was too late. Gray blasted us all with air and we shot out of the tube like a cannon, high into the air.

"We'd better not fucking die, moron!" Malcolm yelled.

My heart spun like a pinwheel. My arms and legs spread out like an 'x' in a useless attempt to slow my fall. *Holy hell!* The earth rushed at me like a linebacker.

Five feet later, Grayson caught all of us, one by one. He left Z for last. Then he slowly had us all descend to the grass. We collapsed on it, coughing and shaking from the adrenaline. My stomach felt like it was stuck in a whirlpool. I put a hand over my forehead and closed my eyes, trying to shake off the awful feeling. "I don't think we're gonna survive practice long enough to pull this shit off," I muttered.

"Nah," Z said. "We just gotta keep a cool head and not get our little pony tails in a twist."

Every single one of the guys blasted him. Z ended up spinning like a top, three feet off the ground, wearing two ice mittens, with pants that were singed across the ass so his boxers showed.

He just grinned. "That's the opposite of what I'm talking about, fuckers." Then he turned to me. "Hayley, they're picking on me." He jutted out his lower lip. "I'm just trying to help them practice their focus. I'm gonna need you to kiss my boo boos."

I laughed where I lay. But I forced myself to my feet and yanked Z down by the arm. Grayson released Z reluctantly. I raised a brow until Malcolm melted the ice mittens. Then I stared down at the three of them. "Z's right, you know. You gotta be able to ignore distraction. Unless you all want to wait another year—" My stomach tightened at that thought. How many vamps would die in that year? How many would be treated like some damned natural resource instead of a person, drained and used and tossed away?

Grayson leaned up on his elbow from where he'd been laying in the grass. "No. We do this now. I dunno about you all, but I've been planning to go Unnatural all my life. I don't wanna screw up that spell and … nobody should have to end up like that."

I nodded.

After that, we inched forward, from total disasters to not sucking completely. I still had nightmares about failure—getting caught in the tube, a guard spotting us, the shifters guarding the vault attacking … there always seemed to be something else to worry about.

The nightmares got so bad that I gave up on sleep. I decided to sneak out in the middle of the night and float around in Grayson's pool on a flamingo raft as I magically screwed with Gray's security system. My goal was to ensure I could 'adjust' the light on camera lenses at the Pinnacle, using my power to create a false scene. A scene where nothing moved, and nothing happened to ensure the guards wouldn't notice us. Grayson's security system was top of the line. There were at least three cameras aimed at the pool from the house. I played with all of them as I used my feet to push off the edge of his pool and float around under the stars.

The redundancies in Grayson's video system were a pain until I learned how to not only cover the screen but to shove my power at the electrical impulses along the wires, too.

It took fifteen attempts. Gray's home security company called him so many times that he stomped outside with his cellphone to his ear, trying to see what was going wrong. When he'd seen me, he told the security company, "Apparently, my dad's testing things. So, call me and let me know, but don't send out the police if he sets off the system."

Then Gray shut his phone and waded down onto the steps. He sat down with the water lapping at his ankles, wearing nothing but a tight blue pair of boxer briefs that highlighted *everything* in the most delicious way. He asked, "You okay?"

I nodded. "Just practicing. Thanks for not calling the cops on me." I winked.

He laughed. Then he sat there in the darkness, in companionable silence, giving me my space as I practiced and failed again and again. Gray waited until I got it right. Then he stood up. "Okay. Well, I'm gonna sleep a few hours. But if you need me—"

It was the first time he'd made such an open offer. Of all the guys, he was the most closed off. I smiled, the fears tugging at me receding a bit.

"Thanks Gray."

I'd watched him walk back into the house, wondering if I should take him up on his offer, hop up the steps and go confide in him. But I hadn't decided by the time he disappeared into the shadows of the house, so I missed my chance.

OVER A PIZZA ONE NIGHT AFTER WE'D ALL SPENT THE AFTERNOON focused on individual practice, Z said, "You know, a couple days ago, I would have said we were goners. But now, I totally give us a three percent chance of surviving."

Gray blasted Z's ass backward all the way into the kidney-shaped pool.

I glanced over at Evan. He just shook his head and took another gigantic bite of pizza. He swallowed it after hardly chewing and said, "You better get going so you can pick up all our stuff from Tia's."

"Will you keep them from killing each other?"

"No guarantees."

I grabbed our amulets and suits from Tia's, paying for them with cash and a full hour of pure torture under her barrage of questions about Evan and Grayson and Evan again. I answered the best that I could, but mostly I stared at her. She wasn't wearing black lipstick. For the first time in years, she had on a nude color. Crap. Evan was in trouble. Or I was in trouble.

But she was helping us out in a huge way. I owed her more than she knew. I shoved aside the jealousy monster that appeared, fangs snapping, at the thought of her hands touching Evan. I thought instead of the page in my diary that he'd saved for all those years and a blush rose on my cheeks.

"OMG. You're so into Grayson, it's so cute. You just stop and get all dreamy over nothing," Tia sighed.

I pressed my lips together so I wouldn't tell her the truth. But I was constantly having to shove aside responses like that to all of them. This 'hit it and quit it' plan of mine for me and my crew had gone all to hell.

I didn't answer her, I just wrapped my arms around her waist in one of her most hated forms of affection. I gave her a big squeeze. "You're the best, T, but I kinda promised I'd meet Gray after this," I told her, pretending I was so lovesick I couldn't wait to see Gray. The thing I berated myself for was that it was halfway true. Ugh. Part of me just wanted to tell Tia everything. But that would make her an accessory. It's why I didn't tell her or Potts any more than absolutely necessary. If things went sideways, Tia would stay innocent.

I hugged her harder, guilt eating at me. Tia didn't even chide me for the hug. She giggled. "This ball is gonna be so awesome!" she exclaimed as she walked me to her front door and handed me a bundle of fire-resistant black bodysuits.

I skipped the last few feet to my car. I really couldn't wait to see my crew; my feet were jangling a million times a second in anticipation. Being around the four of them had become a little like an addiction.

I parked my red Porsche in the circle drive at Grayson's. It was crowded with cars, which was unusual. One of the cars was a delivery truck screen printed with sodas all over the side. I shook my head at Malcolm's resourcefulness. I'd told him he was in charge of all the chaos pre-heist to keep eyes off us, and he'd taken to the assignment with gusto.

I walked around the side of the house, carrying our shiny, glowing new amulets in a box. Gray's staff knew me by now, so I just waved at the gardener as I passed.

I reached the pool house, this modern white building that was decorated in the pale white and pale blue that only the uber-wealthy who never actually use all their living spaces can pull off.

I yanked open the door to find the living room crowded. At least fifteen different dudes I didn't recognize stood around chatting with my guys. "Whoa! I didn't know we were having a party today." I gave a fake smile. My interview and the ball were tomorrow. The heist was tomorrow. We were less than twenty-four hours from execution. What the fuck were the guys thinking? I glanced around at them, trying to decide who I needed to throttle.

Z wove his way through the full room. As he passed by the giant tower of stink bomb of soda cans the guys had assembled for Malcolm, Gray called out, "Watch it! Don't knock those over!"

"I've got it, Preschool," Z chided, holding up a hand to stop Gray from harassing him further.

"Who are all these people?" I asked, handing the box of amulets over to Z, who tucked them under one arm and then grabbed my hand.

Z smiled and bobbed his head side to side. "Couple new guys are from Crush. Drivers. Two are Malcolm's friends—chemists. Don't worry, they've been vetted. And Gray bribed each of them with a wad of cash as thick as my—"

"Clearly, they're gonna want more cash," I retorted.

Z chuckled. "You know that's a lie." He steered me through a crowd of men covered in tattoos and muscles, magical iridescent scars gleaming on their arms and faces, motorcycle vests declaring that most of them were part of Gray's gang. At least that made me feel a little better. None of them would have much incentive to go spill their guts to the Pinnacle. They'd probably get wrapped up with charges first.

Z stopped walking in front of a mountain-sized man who stood alone, leaning against a wall. "And here ... drumroll please ... is my cousin."

I stopped midstep, staring up. Z's cousin was tall, cut, and intimidatingly hot in an "I'll fuck you but then I'll have to kill you," kind of way. His pictures didn't do him any justice. My face probably only reached his ribcage. His pecs were massive, the size of my head. His hair was gelled and pushed back off his forehead. His face was one of those All-American masterpieces, the kind of face that was attractive from infancy until death. The guy had probably never known an awkward day in his life. Tattoos wrapped his huge muscular arms, like Zavier's. But where Z was dark and his eyes were playful, this guy was dirty blond and his blue eyes were hard as stones.

I swallowed hard and then extended my hand to be polite.

"Hi, Andros. It's nice to meet you. Z didn't tell me you were his cousin." My hand hung awkwardly in midair as Andros didn't move from his spot against the wall, just eyed me.

I retracted my hand and glared over at Zavier, who'd seen every last one of my files. He knew that Andros had been on my list. I'd crossed the guy off because he'd been in jail. All these months ... dammit all.

Z just grinned and waggled his tongue at me. "Gray knew a guy who knew a guy who got some cash to bail him out. I figured it would be a good surprise since we need a second Tock."

"You say we do." I raised my brows at him.

"We do," Z said with a sharp authority I'd never heard from him before.

Andros leaned forward and glared down at me. "You gonna fuck my cousin?"

Whoa. Awkwardly personal. But Andros looked like he could split my skull in two with just his fist. "Umm.... I think that's up to him?" I looked at Zavier in askance.

"He means, are you gonna fuck me over," Z clarified, his stiff posture melting, eyes dancing with mirth.

Humiliation took off its clothes and streaked across my face. "Oh. Nope. Not that kind of fucking. Definitely not into that," I shook my head.

One of Gray's bikers shouted, "Did I hear someone just say fucking?"

Gray interjected. "No. You didn't." Then he ushered his guys outside, leaving me stuck between Z, who was bouncing on his toes in excitement like a little kid, and Andros, who stood like a giant reaper. I expected him to pull out a scythe and gut me at any moment. Damn. That level of scary would make most the Pinnacle guards shit themselves. Just thinking about that made me giddy. How had I not realized how huge he was?

"Zavier told me this job is personal for you," Andros said.

"Yes."

"Personal is bad. You make mistakes."

"Yeah. True. Sometimes you don't have a choice though."

"We get stuck in there, what's the plan?"

I had a plan for that, actually. A plan inspired by Potts. A plan that probably wasn't the best or the safest thing ever but was still better than nothing.

"We get stuck, you guys can slow the guards and speed me up. I'll write a level eight illusion spell to make you all look like inanimate objects. Pens, screwdrivers, crowbars. It lasts seventy-two hours." I pulled the strip of paper that Potts had mailed me (which had the spell she'd done on Matthew) out of my pocket. "You all will be picked up as evidence as part of my break in. When you guys come to, you'll be in an evidence containment facility in the back of a police station. Lots of contraband spells, wands, weapons in there. A lot easier to break out of than the Pinnacle."

Andros' eyes scanned the page, double-checking my spell writing. "How do you know they won't look for this kind of thing?"

Before Malcolm I might have lied. I might have pretended to be sure of myself when I wasn't. But he was convinced whole truths were better than half-truths. And some of that conviction had rubbed off on me. "I don't."

Z took a step toward me. "Hey! We hadn't talked about this spell!"

I shrugged. "I'm not letting you guys take the fall when this is my job."

"So, would you like something to drink?" I asked Andros, trying for awkward politeness.

"No."

"Eat?"

"No."

"You want to sit down?" I looked over at Z, trying to hide my 'what-the-hell' face. How was I supposed to work with the one-word answer freak? He hadn't even said if he was up for the job. If he wasn't, that illusion spell was getting put on him whether he liked it or not. I couldn't have him interfering. I'd stuff him into my pocket as a pen for three days and then hope I could spend the rest of my life running fast enough to get away from him.

"Andros, she's good people," Z said, trying to smooth things out. "I mean, when she's not torturing us."

"Wow, that was totally a glowing recommendation," I growled.

"Well, considering you're a Darklight, I know how important glowing is to you." Z grinned like a little shit.

He knew just how to make me want to strangle him. "I'm gonna make your dick into a glowworm if you don't—"

"I prefer the term glow stick. Or maybe glow branch. Maybe glow trunk."

"I'm gonna shove you in my trunk and seal up all the air gaps if you don't—"

"Okay," Andros interrupted us, handing back the spell. "I'm in."

I raised a brow. "Really?" I guess he found the illusion spell good enough insurance.

"Yes. You just have to follow through on the glow stick thing after this job. I want Z's dick to glow through his pants like a little, tiny firefly."

"Deal," I grinned. Immediately, my mind retracted the death-reaper image. Andros was just an oversized cuddly teddy bear who understood why Z needed death threats on the regular.

Z immediately punched Andros. "Hey, excuse me. My dick is way bigger than a firefly."

"Nah."

"It is."

"I guess we'll see if it is after the job," Andros replied before he turned back to me. "I also want five million dollars."

I swallowed hard. That would wipe out most of the research money I'd set aside.

But Gray's voice came from somewhere behind me. "Done," his voice wrapped around my ears as his hand wrapped around my waist. "Is your dress hot?"

I shrugged, more concerned with the fact that he'd just offered to cover five-million freaking dollars to help me out. "Like it matters."

"It matters."

I smiled up at him, trying to stay cheeky, not to show how much I was reeling inside from his gesture. "I can sneak a mini-wand inside it. I made sure of that much."

"But is it hot? Is it gonna make it hard for me to concentrate?" He put his chin on my shoulder in a gesture that was incredibly intimate for him. It was almost possessive. Heat traveled through me and my heart gave a giddy little clap. I liked it.

But I tried not to show it. I shrugged casually. "I guess we'll find out."

"Dammit, Hales, I need to be able to focus."

That made me grin in a way I couldn't hide. Of all the guys, Gray was the most reticent. I'd been intimate (or almost intimate in Z's case) with the others, but he was still on the fence. Or he had been. Was he coming around?

Andros looked between me and Gray. Then he turned to Z. "I thought the girl was with you."

"We kinda have a timeshare thing going," Z replied casually, not at all upset.

Grayson and I both grabbed whatever was nearest (chips in my case) and tossed them at Z.

"I'm not a fucking timeshare, dipshit!"

Grayson's weapon of choice was far better. His water bottle smacked Zavier across the chest. "Whoa! We don't throw things, Preschool!"

"Call me that again, Firefly. See what happens."

From across the room, Malcolm called out from his spot crouched over a series of super-science-y looking vials lined up next to a pile of amulets. "If you guys are gonna fight, take it outside. I've got the sodas over there and if anyone knocks over my pheromones here, I'm gonna be pissed."

Zavier sighed. "Fine. I'll be the bigger man. Wouldn't want to injure you anyway, Preschool."

And that did it. Gray went off like a bomb. He dove at Z, who moved out of the way, too fast for Gray to catch, of course. But, avoiding Gray meant Z didn't look where he was going, which meant he knocked into the stack of painfully constructed stink bombs.

I watched in horror as the first one fell to the ground and burst.

Putrid, disgusting, vomit-inducing smells immediately wafted through the room. But that wasn't the worst of it. I watched, and it felt like the entire world slowed down, as more soda cans toppled over.

Shit!

"No!!!" Malcolm's cry of dismay stretched and slowed and got deeper, like a movie using slow motion. The cans tumbled over one another slowly. Slowly.

I realized that Z was slowing time. I raced forward to help. But as I got close, as my hands closed around the first can, I realized that I was stuck in the slow-motion magic too. I could only save two cans, because once I held them, I could only move as slowly as they did.

"HELP!" I screamed, my voice deep and twisted like a man's.

Everyone in the room helped. But, ultimately, that didn't matter. Sixteen people holding thirty-two cans didn't compare to the hundred that fell and cracked open, releasing noxious fumes.

My stomach twisted. *Dammit all to hell.* I held my breath and my eyes watered as I ran for the door.

So did everyone else. We barreled outside.

I glared at Z and Gray. "You idiots! You stupid, careless little boys!"

Z set down his can on a table and held up a hand. "Hayley, it was an accident!"

"We can't afford accidents! You just gonna fuck around inside the Pinnacle?"

"No, of course not—"

"This isn't some game, Z. This isn't just some random job. You fuck up that serum, and my brother's chance at life is gone. Gone!"

"Hales—"

I spun around and refused to listen to him. I stomped off passed Gray's house to the front yard so that I could be alone. I was so angry that the power in my hands flickered and I kept throwing random shadows onto trees. It looked like I was surrounded my monsters.

The guys cleaned up without me. Packed up without me as I stood alone in my rage.

An hour later, Malcolm came alone to find me. He stood off to one side and studied my face. "We're gonna have to move headquarters. The smell's too bad. No one can sleep back there."

I nodded stiffly.

"Gray's guys have a place."

I just nodded again, letting the shadows in my hands creep across the ground, slink through the grass like black snakes.

"I'll find a way to fix it, Shakespeare," Malcolm said.

I turned to look at him. "How? We're out of time—"

Malcolm stepped into my personal space, glaring down at me. Heat wrapped around my legs, stroked up my spine, flicked my nipples. "Are you questioning me?" he growled.

I shook my head.

He stepped back. "That's right. I'm the expert. And I'll make it work." Then he walked over to my car. "Come on. Let's head over to the new headquarters. I have directions."

ONE OF GRAY'S DRIVERS HAD AN APARTMENT ON THE FAR SIDE OF TOWN, on the wrong side of the tracks. The complex was brick and nearly every window had the kind of dusty blinds that would make Potts proud.

Malcolm and I got there first, before the rest of the crew. We rinsed the awful stink-bomb stench off in the pint-sized showers at the tiny three-bedroom apartment. When everyone else arrived, the place felt too crowded—and the smell was unbearable even though we opened every window and door.

Malcolm sat down with his two cronies and immediately started to brainstorm new solutions.

After Gray showered, he sat down on the plaid couch with two of his dudes and went over driving routes for before and after.

Z and Andros sat down next to Evan, who had been outside during the entire debacle, practicing unraveling in his notebook. He was practicing yet again, with a new spell that one of my dark web resources had given us. I swear, he was nearly as fixated on this plan as I was. My chest grew tight as I watched him. I hoped, for his sake as well as Matthew's, that we could pull this off.

Feeling claustrophobic, still a little angry, and also just a bit scared, I left. I walked outside, dragging my feet along the sidewalk, toeing the cracks for a minute, before checking in with Dad. "Hey, Dad?" I called out.

Dad appeared in front of me. He looked a little less solid than usual. A little bit hazy. He wore the damned hated Fedora again tonight. I smiled at that. "Hey kiddo," he said. "You've been busy."

I glanced at him in surprise. "How do you know that?"

"I've popped by once or twice—"

Immediately, I cringed, hoping Dad hadn't seen anything less than PG rated. Evan and Malcolm had both been eager to repeat our private sessions. And what girl could say no to either of them? "Um..."

"It's really brave, sweetheart. But you don't have to be the one to do this, you know."

I shook my head. "Don't, Dad."

"Honey, just tell someone."

I laughed. "You think I didn't try that? Two years ago, I started talking to that reporter. He called me a tin-foil hat loon. All those pros I've tried to recruit just laughed …"

Dad shook his head and put his hat in his hands. He played with it. "I don't like it, Hales."

I squinted at him. "What's changed?"

"Something feels off. I go into the Pinnacle and things look the same. But they don't feel the same. I don't think you should do this."

His worry cut me open and wrapped me up like a warm blanket at the same time. It had been a long time since I'd felt any kind of parental authority or affection. I reached my hand out and let it hover in the air. Dad reached out and touched me, sending prickles that felt like paresthesia over my fingers. I had to pull back and shake my hand awake.

I gave Dad a sad smile. "Dad, I promise, it'll be okay—"

His face went blank. I saw the spark of intelligence in his eyes fade. Dad floated up for a second and hovered in midair. He glanced around for a second, confused. But I saw him clench his eyes shut and give a pained grimace.

"Dad?" I stepped forward.

But he disappeared.

It hurt, like always, seeing him fade into the night. But I'd never asked before if he could still feel things. He never talked about how losing his memory felt or if it felt like anything at all. But did it? Was some part of him aware he was fading away? Could some part of him still feel the heartache I gave him even if he didn't know where it came from?

I closed my eyes and breathed in the scent of fresh spring air and wondered what exactly I was putting my father through. I blinked and stared up at the solitary streetlight with its dim yellow glow and wondered if death was just as full of frustration and agony as life.

40

I STARED up at the Pinnacle as I stood before it, ready for my "interview" aka my last little chance at recon. It was an intimidating building even in the daylight. The round marble structure had arch upon arch that led into what appeared to be a shadowy abyss. The gold friezes above each arch gleamed with ancient carved gods who looked real enough to jump off the building and eviscerate you with their lightning bolts.

Maybe it was the Pinnacle's resemblance to the Colosseum and the bloody tortures that the original structure had held up as spectacle that made me so disgusted as I stared at it. Or maybe it was my knowledge that the Pinnacle was responsible for hundreds of missing vampires—my search on the dark web turned up new missing vampires each day—and was withholding a serum that could cure thousands of its citizens, instead charging their families a monthly fee for caging poor vampires like zoo animals. Yeah, I didn't get any reverent vibes from the building.

I stood staring for a second as long lines of people in suits trotted in and out like ants. My eyes scanned the grass lawn that nobody walked on. I could see the prairie dog mounds every so often breaking up the turf. There was even one fuzzy brown bump in the distance that might have been a little head peeking out.

It made me laugh to think that the tiny rodents were the big bad protectors of the Pinnacle—its first line of defense. I watched the guards at the doors. Second line. Adrenaline buzzed through my body. I felt drunk and energized at the same time. I had to suppress my light and clench my fists as I looked up the thirty stories. Twelve more hours. Twelve more hours and I'd either fly or fall to my death. I'd either get Matthew's serum or be torn apart by cursed amulets in an underground bunker. *There are worse ways to go.* The memory of the faculty ripping apart entire slabs of meat—gnawing on the bones—came to mind and I shuddered. *Maybe.*

"Ready?" Claude asked beside me, lazily. He was smirking, thinking I was intimidated about this interview, probably.

He tried to put a hand on my shoulder, but I moved quickly to avoid his touch. I'd tried to spend as little time at the house as possible, avoiding him until the inevitable. I'd managed not to even see him until today, when he'd shown up at the front door with Mom smiling next to him and offered to take me to the 'office.'

Even though I was the one who'd subtly hinted to Mom that Claude walking me in might improve my chances in my interview, seeing the fuckwad was almost too much. Just thinking about him made my insides blister. It was like rubbing a raw wound with salt.

I took a deep breath and focused on what I needed to accomplish today. It was time to implement Zavier's Leery. And, if I had time, I wanted to ensure we had the path to the breakroom correct. I wanted to count cameras. The list in my head doubled in length. I wanted—

Claude slid his hand onto my shoulder. I jumped like I'd been bitten by a snake. Some of his coworkers had turned to smile and wave at us, ignorant of the demon that inhabited Claude's body.

Time to sow the seeds of discord. I happily let angry words slide out, while keeping my chipper mask. "Thank you so much for bringing me today. You know, without your help, I probably wouldn't be able to find anything. I mean, I can hardly walk and breathe at the same time as it is. Who knows what would happen if I had to press that number eight button on the elevator?"

"Hayley—stop," Claude growled. His glower, the one he reserved for me, descended for a second and I skittered backward, drawing a look or two.

But Claude quickly restored his fake smile and gestured toward the door, like he was some kind of gentleman. I knew better. And I was gonna make sure the people here did too.

But ... Zavier's voice rang out in my head. "Make sure you get in his head. Just like you did with Grayson. He shouldn't see anyone else; he should be so pissed at you. You want to push him to show who he really is ... once people see ... the rumors will fly. But not too big, Hales. Not huge. That's the key to a leery. Get the suspicion simmering. It'll bubble up on its own after that."

I ignored Claude's outstretched hand and strode up to the building. *Murderer,* I mentally spat on him. *Not too big. Not too big,* I reminded myself. *Get the rumor mill started. But if you push him in a big way, you'll look like a jerk, too.*

Claude's anger prickled; I could feel it on my skin as the hairs stood on edge. But he didn't say anything as we reached the massive front doors. They were open for business hours, flanked by four massive men in uniform, breast pockets embroidered with the Pinnacle's chess rook topped by a shining diamond.

I swallowed the lump in my throat that formed when I thought about tonight. *Shake it off. Next five minutes. What can you do? Prick the boil. Boil the prick.*

I joined the line for security, pulling out my wand and my ink. The ink pot was run through an explosives scanner and my wand was inspected to ensure it was solid and not a weapon spelled to look like a wand. The wand itself was checked against the wand registry to make sure it was mine.

A bored security guard with two wide iridescent scars running in parallel lines down his left cheek (magical mistakes, no doubt), handed back my wand and said, "Please head over to the shifter sniffing station."

I grabbed my wand and ink and walked to another line. I should have bit my tongue and bided my time a little. But he was right there, smiling, making small talk, calling me his 'daughter' to people. The fucker.

He deserved any discomfort and embarrassment I could give him. He deserved more. My fingers itched to give him more. I smiled and gave a little wave when he introduced me to someone. Then I leaned up and asked through my wide grin—teeth clenched, "Other than abusing children like myself, what have you been doing for fun lately? Or who? Anyone else new I should know about, stepfather?"

Claude's face grew stiff. His hands slowly went into his pockets. He was clenching his fists in there, I could tell. But he made no move to retaliate.

I smiled up at him and giggled—a high-pitched annoying giggle that even hurt my own ears.

It must be nice to have self-control. To be so superior and sure of your murdering self that insults mean nothing.

I leaned up and whispered with mock sympathy, "Oh dear, Claudia, don't tell me you've been rejected by someone? With all that money you stole from my dad's estate, I'm sure you can buy yourself another companion." Inside I was both giddy and on edge. He had to be close.

The scent of singed cotton reached my nose. He was burning the inside of his pants.

A pathetic sense of satisfaction stole over me. It wasn't enough. Nothing would ever be enough to punish him. But it was something.

Another security guard called out, "Next!" and grabbed my arm, maneuvering me over to a little carpet with two footprints on it.

"Stand here." The security guard stepped back and waved the fox shifter on duty over.

I was slightly distracted for a second. But they put the fox in a sweater with a Pinnacle symbol embroidered on the back. I realized their strategy—who would want to steal from a sweet little fox? I kind of wanted to pick him up and take him home.

My attitude changed seconds later as that shifter put his nose to my ass for what seemed an unreasonable amount of time. *Pervert.*

Once we'd passed through security, I turned to Claude and started up again. "Maybe you can get a spell for a new personality. I've never tried that. But it can't be that dangerous, right? I think that one movie star bought one. What's her name?" I pretended to think as we got onto an elevator crowded with people.

I thought I'd lost my momentum with the fox shifter, thought that Claude had had too much time to cool down. But maybe the personality thing got to him. Or maybe all of it. I didn't really care.

Because the asshole had come out to play.

Claude grabbed my arm and pushed me toward the sidewall near the back. I made myself trip and look alarmed as I huddled against the wall. Two women in pencil skirts glanced my way and I gave them a small smile, then looked at the floor and cringed when Claude stepped up to me.

One of them glanced between us.

Seed planted.

Time to let it sprout.

Just a little.

I had to pull this off carefully. He'd never hurt me in public before. Never even in front of my mother. A sick, twisted part of me wondered if I could get him to do it. Ruin his perfect little facade of 'good guy' in front of everyone. Or would that be too much? *Balance*, I told myself. *Just push a little. No full-on brawls like at home.*

I couldn't help cringing at Claude's touch as he pushed me toward the elevator wall. Bile rose in my throat. He disgusted me on a level no one else ever had. His touch was like raw fish and razors mashed together—disgusting and sharp.

I had to clench my teeth when the fucker smiled and introduced me to the person next to him as his stepdaughter. A string of curses as long and colorful as a rainbow filled my head. By the look on his face, the guy could sense my hatred. Quickly, I tried to change my look from fury to fear, glancing up at Claude and cringing.

The man on the elevator glanced between us, curious.

Claude noticed. His hand moved up my arm on the side closest to the elevator and clenched down. But he didn't hurt me.

I was gonna have to sell it without that. I bowed my head and let tears form in my eyes, then acted like I was trying to hold them back. The man and the two women in the elevator glanced at me again.

Was it enough?

When the bell dinged and the door opened, other people got on and off in the midst of morning chatter. The man and one of the women left.

Claude leaned forward and said, "You think you're so smart, don't you?" His hand slid to my neck.

My body instantly recoiled, knowing what was coming. He only touched my neck for one reason. I closed my eyes and tried to talk myself through the panic that was bouncing through my veins. *Fuck. Buck up, girl. He's just a murderer. Just the fucker who's disappearing vamps.* I had to take a second to realign my thoughts. Tonight, there'd be this kind of pressure. Tonight. Was I jeopardizing it, toying with Claude? Had I done enough?

My fingers started to shake. I grabbed onto my purse, clutched it to me, to hide the shaking.

Shit.

I decided to stop. To just stop. To get through this interview and get away from him. I had to suppress this volcanic hatred inside. As much as I wanted to destroy him, I needed Claude there at the ball tonight. And even though I wanted the rumor mill swirling, I didn't want to make it a whirlpool. I didn't want him disgraced today. Tomorrow… that was a different story. But tonight, we needed him at the Unnatural Ball because he was the only connection to Ginny Stone that I'd been able to find.

Claude's hand grew tighter on my neck.

I'd already pushed too far.

His fingers found the scars he'd given me and started to trace them. My stomach jumped, on autopilot. I lurched forward, knocking into the person in front of me.

"Sorry," I apologized, trying to scoot away from Claude. But in such a small space, it was impossible. Even though people got off at every floor, more got on. We were just as crowded as we'd been on the first floor.

I held onto my thoughts like I was clinging to a life raft as Claude slowly inched his hand closer again. Alarm nipped at my heels, but I tried to kick it back.

Claude's hand pressed into a new spot of skin, an unscarred portion. The cold burn started instantly. My entire body clenched. I couldn't think for a second. Thoughts of escape lit up my mind like a flashing neon sign.

I tried to think of my mom. Dad. Pull up Matthew's face. I tried to float away and get my mind into a different space. But the pain chewed at me. My hands itched to blind or burn him. But blinding him wouldn't stop him with his hand already on my neck. And burning him would be too obvious, it would light up the whole elevator.

"I'm gonna be sick!" I yelled, yanking out of Claude's grip and stumbling to the front of the elevator.

Everyone quickly moved out of my way and let me take up the middle front.

When the elevator dinged, I shoved my way out, not caring what floor I was on. I ran haphazardly to the nearest women's bathroom. I stumbled into a stall, heart racing. I locked the door and just leaned my forehead against it.

I'd pushed too hard. Claude had always been careful. He'd never hurt me in public before. Why would he do that right before my interview? Was it a warning that I take it seriously? A lecture would have sufficed. No, my hand reached up to touch my neck and I realized it was wet. He'd made me bleed. He'd never made me bleed before.

Either I'd gotten to him, or he'd taken his little punishments to another level. The thought of the first gave me a wretched sort of thrill but the thought of the second possibility made me sick. Claude wanted to control me. Break me.

I undid my shirt and checked the back. Only a tiny spot of blood marred my collar. I could hide that. I rebuttoned my shirt as one of the women from the elevator walked into the bathroom. She beelined right for me.

I swallowed hard and blinked. Shit. She'd seen. How to play it?

"Are you okay?" she asked, reaching gently for my left shoulder.

I tried to nod but ended up gasping as that strained my wound. I tried to play it off. "Yeah. Yeah. It's just a lot of pressure—"

"Claude's your stepfather?" she asked.

I blinked and nodded, not allowing the disgust to roll over my face. "Yeah. He just ... Mom and he ... just really want me to do well." I reached up and touched my neck, like I was self-conscious. I was sure to run my fingers over the wound and bring them down bloody.

Her eyes went wide.

I pretended to hide my fingers, to close my hand. "I ... um ... I've gotta go to my interview." I bolted from the bathroom, leaving her behind. In the hall, I reached into my bag and grabbed antibacterial foam and a tissue and cleaned my fingers.

Claude was waiting for me, leaning against the wall, just down the hall. I ducked my head and stared at the floor tiles, just like I did at home when Mom yelled at me after any encounters between Claude and me. I glanced up hesitantly. His smile stretched wide, as fake as artificial sweetener. But his eyes smoked like coals. He grabbed my arm as soon as I was in the hall. He leaned down and whispered, "I know what you're doing. Don't think you'll get away with it."

The warning chilled me to the bone. *He's only referring to my attitude ... isn't he?* I wondered, as we climbed back into the elevator. He had to be. And he thought he'd won. He hadn't seen the look on Betty Sue's (or whatever-her-name-was) face.

I bet that by sundown most of the women in the office would know about how Claude terrorized his poor little stepdaughter.

My thoughts rambled and wondered and wandered. I nearly forgot to pay attention when the elevator opened on the seventh floor to let people out, I almost didn't notice the construction. My eyes flickered toward the plastic sheeting and didn't register it for a second.

Then my mind screamed, "No!"

I shoved my hand between the doors as they almost closed. "Wait! That's my floor!" I shoved out of the elevator. My eyes widened in horror and my stomach dropped out from under me. The seventh floor was under renovation. And they were moving walls right next to the employee breakroom.

My eyes flickered from spot to spot. Cameras. Two less than expected. But I saw a laser beam streaming behind the construction plastic.

Fuck. Fuck. Fuck.

Claude yanked me back. "Nope, silly goose. You're on eight." He chuckled fakely as his hand went to my neck and his nails dug into my brand-new wound.

I didn't even notice.

I had bigger problems.

41

I HAD to fake my way through the interview.

"And what do you see yourself doing in five years?" Amara asked. She was a magical woman near fifty, wearing a purple suit. She sat in the middle of the three magicals interviewing me, so I assumed she was heading the internship program.

I gave her a tight, no tooth smile and rocked back and forth on my seat. This stupid interview was eating up time. I needed to get out of here. I needed to take the extra minutes before that murdering asshole of a stepfather came to collect me and I needed to go see what was happening on the seventh floor.

I let my voice shake a little. "Well, um, I'm not sure exactly. I do like research a lot. But I—" I shoved a hand over my stomach and pressed my lips together hard. I widened my eyes and stood abruptly. "I'm so sorry." I grabbed my purse and covered my mouth. I bolted for the door, letting out a little retching noise once my back was turned.

Amara said, "Poor thing!" as I shoved the door open.

One of the male panelists just said, "Ew."

I hurried out into the hall and around the corner. Once I'd made it that far, I checked to ensure Claude wasn't there. Then I straightened my shirt and walked quickly to the nearest stairwell.

Most magicals were too lazy to take the stairs, thank fuck.

I hurried down as quickly as my black pumps would allow. I took a deep breath before I opened the door on floor seven. I reached into my purse and grabbed the little, handheld jar of UV paint. I unscrewed the lid and dipped a pen from my bag into the paint. Then I closed the jar, pulled the door open and walked out, calm and wide-eyed as a stupid doe.

Immediately, I spotted two cameras in the corners that would be an issue. My heels clicked in time with my heart as I walked by a meeting room that could serve as our entry point. The room had all glass walls, even those that faced the hall. It had sleek leather chairs. But more importantly, it had a huge glass window we could cut out and the table was big enough for us to lay the cut piece of glass on it. I tapped my pen against the white wall next to me, marking it with an X just like a treasure map.

I walked further down the hall, toward the elevators. Three more cameras. A security guard walked past me and sniffed. Then he turned around and looked at the sheets of plastic taped to keep construction dust from spreading. "They painting already?" he muttered.

I stiffened. *Crap.* I kept walking, forcing myself to go slow even though my instincts wanted me to run. I took a deep breath, trying to stay cool and collected, pulling out the letter with my interview information from my purse to cover up my paint-dipped pen.

The guard stared a moment longer. "I didn't even think all the walls were up over there. Hacks." He shook his head but then turned and walked on.

I let out a giant sigh of relief, leaning against the wall for just a moment.

But then I checked my watch. I only had five minutes before Claude came to get me. I had to hurry. I picked up the pace, striding quickly down the hall, shoving aside the construction plastic. Three rooms had been torn apart. They were stripped down to studs, electrical wires and plumbing pipes exposed like veins and bones in an anatomy class.

Just past the construction, through one of the open walls, I could see the remains of the breakroom. The countertop, employee table, and fridge were still intact, though they were covered in dust. I could count three cameras left in that break room alone.

I smelled the sizzle of melting plastic, but ignored that, because it came from one of the exposed rooms. Not my target. Not my problem.

I took a step forward, leaning to the side to check for a fourth camera in the corner. And that's when I realized, the floor ended about three feet in front of me. After that, the hallway was nothing but steel beams spaced every four feet.

Shit.

A laser beam hit me, and an alarm sounded. A construction worker appeared, and I backed up in a hurry.

The guy darted over, pushing me back through the plastic and yanking off his yellow hardhat and goggles. "What the hell are you doing?" he demanded.

I blinked rapidly. "I'm sorry. I'm sorry. I'm just here for an interview. I got turned around. I thought I was supposed—"

"An interview? You an idiot? We got live power tools and magicals heat sealing shit all over the place in there."

I let my lower lip tremble. "I'm sorry." I shuffled back again and ran for the elevator. I pressed the button.

It dinged and I stepped on, pressing the button for Claude's floor. Forget him picking me up. His secretary was our Darklight target. Possibly, probably a spy, given the lack of a digital trail I could find on her.

I needed to know what I was up against.

The elevator doors opened on the twelfth floor and I got out, striding down the hallway lined with much nicer doors than the ones below. These doors were thick wood painted shiny black, with embellishments along the edges. There were no glass walls here, no windows into the offices of the Pinnacle's council members. They got privacy.

I read the brass plaque next to Claude's door and then turned the knob, letting myself into the front room of his office.

There, sitting at the desk, reapplying lipstick, was Ginny. I planted my feet and dropped my jaw in what I hoped was a good expression of shock. "Emelia?" I asked. Shit. I sounded a little over-the-top. A little too much like a soap opera. *Pull it back,* I scolded myself.

Ginny dropped her lipstick.

She stood, showing off more of a figure than I'd ever seen at Metamorphose. She hurried toward me in her tight, black dress, wringing her hands—a super fake look of contrition on her face.

At least I wasn't the only one with B-list acting skills.

"Oh, my goodness! Hayley?! You're here!" She swept me into a tight hug.

That's when I had everything I needed. But I couldn't just walk away. Cue teenage theatrics. I pulled out of the hug and shook my head as if I was dazed. "Mom and Claude sent you to … what? Spy on me!"

Ginny held up her hands and waved them in protest. "No! No! They were nervous about you going to that school! Actual criminals go there, you know! They didn't want you to get hurt." She blinked at me with the most pathetic look of concern I'd ever seen.

I wanted to burst out laughing. The pair of us were as fake as Terra Lysour's tits. But that would give me away. And Claude had already made me uneasy. Better to stick with the teenage drama llama act. "I can't believe them!" I pushed Ginny and she took a step back, her mask falling for just a millisecond to anger. "I can't believe you! I thought you were my friend!" I turned around and rushed for the door, yanking it open and hurrying down the hall. I took the stairs, instead of waiting for an elevator.

As I walked down the twelve floors, I took notes in my phone about every camera placement, and a couple of landings that looked like they had magically pressurized floors intended to blast unwelcome individuals with air. If we had to make our escape in an unexpected manner, the stairs were doable, not ideal.

When I reached the first floor, I called Gray to see if one of his guys could pick me up. "Sure," he said. "Everything go okay?"

"Perfect," I told him. "Tell Z and Andros that their target keeps her wand strapped to her left shoulder."

Gray's driver, Jim, picked me up. But he didn't get to take me back to the guys, because my mom called.

"You got sick? And then just left Claude?" She was in a tizzy.

"Mom—"

"Maybe you shouldn't go to the ball if you're sick—"

"Mom, it was nerves."

"Then why did you leave Claude? Why didn't you let him take care of you?"

She was so clueless it was infuriating. But ignorance was her shield. I wasn't gonna be the one who cracked it. So far as I knew, Claude only attacked me. He'd never hurt Mom. Whether it was because he actually cared or the fact that they didn't have any kind of prenup to protect his money, I wasn't sure. "He's working. I'm fine. I got a ride."

Mom was silent on the phone for a minute as she fumed and debated whether it was worth arguing with me any further. She must have decided it wasn't because she said, "Fine. I'm sorry about your interview, honey. Next time. I'm sure you're not the only kiddo who had an issue with nerves."

"Thanks."

She sighed. "I have us booked for a hair appointment at three. Are you still up for that?"

"Sure," I responded. If tonight went south, the hair appointment might well be the last quality time I'd ever get with her.

At first, I made an effort to chat and giggle with Mom, but when one of the workers took her to the back for a youthful face-lifting spell, I shut down.

I sat like a zombie, face stone as I ran through spell possibilities in my head, mentally walking through our new route again and again. At one point, the hairdresser even leaned down and whispered, "Honey, whoever your date is, he can't be that bad. Take some Bubble in your pocket and float away after a few dances." She patted my shoulder. "Chin up."

When she noticed the new cut on my neck, she looked at me with pity, taking a new perspective on what she thought my 'date' had done. "Maybe we should leave your hair down. Beautiful mermaid locks, yeah?"

I'd just nodded and white knuckled through the session, knee jangling, hoping Malcolm had come up with some kind of resolution to the stink bombs he'd lost, hoping Z and Andros were as good as they said they were, hoping Gray's arrogance about a power up didn't lead to our downfall, hoping Claude and Ginny didn't have a nice long chat this afternoon about me and realize anything was off.

There were so many what ifs. So many places this heist could go wrong. The hairdresser finished my curls and spun me around to look at the mirror. *I might end up in jail tonight,* the thought ran through my head as I fingered the curls, which looked like something out of a magazine. *But I'll have the finest damn booking photo if I do.*

I LEFT THE SALON AND DECLINED MOM'S INVITE TO GO TO AN EARLY dinner before we finished getting dressed for the big event. I drove over to the cruddy apartment that was our new headquarters.

Malcolm and his delivery truck were gone by the time I pulled in. I pouted over the fact that I didn't get to kiss him goodbye. Technically, I'd given him all kinds of good luck kisses last night. I still wanted another though. I'd become greedy like that, obsessed with what kind of new naughty game he'd have in store for me when he shut his bedroom door.

But Malcolm needed all afternoon to set up. He'd left with a new collection of soda cans and over a hundred pounds of specially prepared, magically spelled stink-ice.

I sighed as I walked past a norm and knocked on the apartment door. I glanced at the sky, hoping the weatherman was correct and the weather would stay chilly. We didn't need the ice melting early.

One of Malcolm's nerdy lackeys, Ben, let me in and I immediately gave him the new timeline. He rushed off to change our timetable and swore he'd let everyone know.

Then I walked into the living room. Catcalls and whistles from Gray's biker friends immediately rose up. The bulky foursome, our driving team, had bowed down the couch under their weight as they studied maps so they could help us make a quick getaway. Each one of them was in charge of a separate car—one outside on every street surrounding the Pinnacle. All the cars would serve as a diversion if we were made, otherwise, they'd be available so that we could bust out and fly toward whatever road happened to be nearest.

"Hey there, cutie! How about a little kiss for luck?" Jim, the guy who'd picked me up earlier, asked.

His friend, an older guy with a grizzled beard, smacked him on the side of the head. "Don't talk to Gray's old lady like that."

"Thanks, Bear," I nodded toward the bear shifter who went by his animal name. He gave me a wink as I walked toward one of the back bedrooms. Hearing him call me Gray's lady made me teeter on the brink of elated and a little intimidated. I shoved that feeling aside. I needed to check in with everyone still here and stay focused. Sorting out what Gray and I were or weren't could come later.

I checked in with Z, who was stuffed into one of the tiny spare bedrooms—sharing with Evan, who wasn't there. Z was dressed in jeans and a t-shirt but was just sitting to put on shoes.

"Hello, Sleeping Beauty," I teased. "Why aren't you dressed? I know I didn't wear you out last night. So, what gives?"

Z turned, abandoning his sneakers. When he saw me, his face lit up. But not in his normal dirty, teasing style. He gave me a smile full of warmth that slid down inside my chest like melted butter. He walked over, planting his bare feet in front of me. "I'm jealous that Gray gets to see you in a dress," he said before pressing his lips softly against mine.

"You could see me in less than that if you'd give in," I needled him. Evan and Malcolm had been more than eager last night, when I'd spent alone time with each of them.

He pulled back and tilted his head. "I know. But I've been thinking. And I've decided I want the girly 'wooed' thing. I want you to wine and dine me and take me on dates and send me flowers…"

"Are you serious?" I couldn't tell. Z was so full of jokes and pranks and absolute playfulness. But his tone didn't sound playful.

He shrugged shyly as he stared at the ground. "Yeah. When you yelled at me … you know after the stink bomb thing…"

"Yeah?"

"I didn't like it. People always yell at me. I'm always halfway in trouble. But when you were mad at me, I didn't like it."

I shook my head. "What?"

Z licked his lips. "It's 'cause I care what you think of me. I don't like you thinking bad things about me. I've decided no dirty friends with you. I wanna try the relationship thing."

The apocalypse happened. And I missed it. There was no way Z, dirty-flirty friend was actually saying this for real. Except, he was. "I already fell for this once."

"I'm serious." His face was stark. Pale.

"Even when you know there are other guys …?"

He met my eyes. "Yeah."

My cheeks heated at the look in his eyes. But my mind was overwhelmed. I punched his chest. "This is not the day to drop this on me, Z!"

"Sorry." He stepped back.

But I couldn't leave things like that. I couldn't leave Z feeling vulnerable, couldn't stand the hurt look in his eyes. I scooped my arms around his waist and tugged him back into me. "Oh, no you don't,

Zavier Kieltyka. After this job, I'm gonna woo you so good your head's gonna spin!"

He laughed. "Which head? Because let me tell you, the lower one is much more flexible."

I squeezed him as I chuckled. "There's that foul mouth I've come to love." I leaned up on my tiptoes and kissed him.

"Why today, Z?"

He shrugged. "Well, you've been fixated on this job for so long. It's been your life's purpose. After you achieve it … you're gonna need a new one."

I tossed my head back and laughed. "Oh, my fucking God!"

"What better purpose than pursuing me?" Z couldn't help himself.

I poked him in the stomach repeatedly, jabbing him for all I was worth. "You are so arrogant!" But I didn't mean it.

Z captured my fingers and brought them to his mouth. He kissed my fingertips. "You love it."

I did. My smile proved it.

Reluctantly, after the moment passed, reality came back. I pulled my hand back. "I'm not gonna see you until we're in the trees. You be careful tonight."

He bopped me on the nose. "You better worry about yourself, short stack. And I know it will be tempting, but please resist spending all evening googling presents for me."

I shook my head and rolled my eyes. "I'll try. Where's Evan?"

"Went to help Malcolm with deliveries. Still don't know how they got on the list of suppliers for the ball."

I grinned and dusted my shoulder off. "When you know a hacker, it's not too hard."

Z shook his head. "Get outta here. Go get hot for Gray."

"You gonna practice with your cousin?" I asked Z, heading toward the door.

He held up my panties, one side of the thong ripped where he'd apparently torn it off my body. "Already done practicing."

I shook my head as I yanked down on my skirt. "Bastard!"

But I left with a smile on my face.

42

Grayson picked me up in a stretch limo. I'd ridden in limos before. But I'd never had a guy step out of one, holding a dozen roses for me.

There are some things in life that every girl wants even if she doesn't know she wants them. The sight of him in a tux, staring up at me slack-jawed was one of those things.

A nightingale warbled in my chest and then flew around, tickling my rib cage with the brush of its happy, soft little feathers.

I took a step down the stairs and that broke Gray out of his trance. He hurried up to grab my hand.

"You look amazing, nemesis," Gray breathed. His dark eyes became hooded as he glanced over my black silk dress.

The dress was a floor length gown with an asymmetrical top. Part of the collar jutted upward and came to a point near my shoulder. The gown then hugged my figure until it reached my hips. It flared out and fell to the ground. A liberal slit on the left side showcased my legs and the tall, rhinestone encrusted stilettos I wore. The back of the dress had an asymmetrical slash through the middle, so that most of my back was exposed. I held a silver and rhinestone encrusted clutch in my hands.

Gray handed me the blooms, which were an array of colors. "Your power is kind of multi-colored, so I thought maybe a variety—"

I smiled and smelled them. "They're beautiful. Thank you!"

I turned back to see my mother peeking out the door, spying on us, a tearful grin on her face. I rolled my eyes. "Mom, would you like an excuse to come out here and meet Grayson instead of spying on us? I have these flowers you could put away."

Immediately, Mom straightened and pulled the door open. "Why, Grayson, so good to meet a guy who can tolerate Hayley's serrated tongue."

He laughed. "I can see where she gets her wit. And her beauty. Nice to meet you."

My mother shook Gray's hand. For once, I didn't see her shaking. She must have recently had her hit. I smacked that sarcastic thought away and tried to just enjoy the moment. I took a mental snapshot of the two of them together, halfway wishing that this was just a normal night and just a normal ball. But it wasn't.

Mom took the flowers from me and winked. "You kids run along and have fun. Don't do anything I wouldn't do."

"One Mars heir coming up!" I joked.

Grayson's face paled. I grabbed his hand. "Calm down dude. You know we don't have time for that." "How could you—"

"Mom got pregnant with Matthew when she was hardly older than me. It's been a running joke for years."

Grayson helped me into the car, shaking his head even after he sat. "You're crazy."

I shrugged. "You're the one who agreed to help me. Wanna back out?"

He leaned his head back against the headrest saying, "I'm crazy for not wanting to."

I giggled and tossed his arm around my shoulder, hugging his side. "Too bad we can't do some Bubble before we pull this job off."

He snorted. "That might actually help me lift your fat asses off the ground."

"Yeah but think of that fire tube. Not so good once we're in there." I glanced at my phone. "Almost time to do a check in with Malcolm. Did his delivery truck get off okay earlier?" I ran through the mental checklist of the hundreds of things we had to get right to pull this job off.

"Yeah, he's good." Gray leaned forward and opened the minibar in the limo. "We can't do Bubble tonight. But we can have a quick drink." He pulled out two mini shot bottles of scotch and untwisted the lids. He handed me one. "To pulling off the craziest shit the Pinnacle has ever seen."

We clinked our bottles.

Then we downed our shots. It felt like fire racing down my throat. Awful! I started to cough. "Damn."

Gray laughed and grabbed me a water bottle so I could rinse away the pain. Then he set me on his lap.

I stared down at him. He'd looked up at me in awe earlier. But I hadn't been sure if that was part of the act for Mom and Claude. My legs grew warm from where his skin touched mine. My stomach tightened. Anticipation, that weird amalgamation of lipstick and matches, preparation and kindling flame, built inside me.

"Two minutes," he said. "Let's pretend for two minutes that this is a real date and not a job."

That match inside me fell onto my lady bits. They ignited with a *whoosh* as Gray's hands went to my waist and started to trace over my hipbones.

"Okay," my voice came out soft and breathy.

Gray's eyes grew hooded. "I'm glad you chose me, nemesis."

I smiled and stared at him, soaking up his lusty expression. Who needed scotch when a guy looked at them like that? I wrapped my arms around his neck. "You've made a pretty wonderful villain yourself."

Gray opened his mouth to argue the villain bit, but I leaned forward then, letting my lips hover just above his. His eyes studied mine for a moment before he closed the distance. His lips were big, fuller than mine, and soft. The way he pressed them to me was tender, gentle. He kissed my lips, and then the corner of my mouth, before returning to my lips and slowly building our kiss touch by touch. His lips widened and his tongue darted out, teasing me for a second before he swooped down and took my lower lip between his teeth. My toes started to tingle, and I pushed my hands through his shorn hair, loving the rough texture against my fingertips.

Gray's lips left mine and traveled down my neck to my pulse. His hands pressed down the length of my spine, reeling me in, smashing my dress against his tux. Then he slid his hands up my sides and over the sides of my breasts.

"Dammit. I want you to rip this dress off," I panted as his tongue danced along my neck.

He pulled back and chuckled. "Maybe next time. I just wanted a taste." He flexed his fingers. "I can feel the power surge just from that." He spread his fingers and sent a little ribbon of wind across my skirt, making it dance while he checked his Rolex. "We'd better check in with Malcolm though."

I pouted, jutting out my lower lip. But then I climbed off Gray's lap and grabbed a burner phone. I dialed the only number that I'd saved to contacts, Malcolm's burner. "You ready?"

"Yup. Everyone's in place. Stage one will start after you and Gray have your big moment."

I flipped the phone shut and nodded to Gray. "He's good. Your getaway drivers ready?"

Gray winked.

I sighed and grabbed my compact. "I'd better fix my lipstick."

But Gray reached out and grabbed my hand. "Don't," he said.

"But then everyone will know we were--"

"Exactly," Gray replied as the car pulled to a stop. A valet pulled the car door open. Gray reached over and snapped my purse shut. Then he handed me out. After he'd climbed out himself, he took my arm.

"Let's go be scandalous," he grinned down at me.

"Bet I can make a bigger scene than you," I told him.

"Nemesis. You're on."

Then Grayson led me up the stairs to the Atrium, the giant glass building built purely through magical construction. Diamond panes of glass were stacked upon each other with no mortar or metal to hold them together. Magic kept them suspended and locked in place like delicate puzzle pieces. Overhead, the panes on the roof were not just diamond-shaped, they were prisms so that the entire place was filled with dancing rainbows. Tonight, those rainbows were cast by spotlights that a hired team of Force magicals had hovering outside the building.

Gray and I looked out over the crowded ballroom from the entryway. We had to descend several steps to get to the main floor, which held a ballroom that then had archways leading to other meeting rooms, a huge banquet hall, and several verandas so that people go outdoors and get some fresh air.

I shook my head. All this elegance and these magicals would be shedding their expensive clothes and champagne glasses so they could mill about in fur and sniff one another's asses. Because that made them superior.

I shook my head at the ridiculous way the world worked.

Evan's voice sounded in our ears. The earpiece was part of a norm spy kit he and the guys had bought, because it made them feel more James Bond. "New schedule just given for the night. Apparently, to avoid any sort of animal in-fighting, each species has been assigned a specific time to shift. Bears aren't 'til 12:15 a.m. so that's good. But wolves are up soon."

Malcolm responded over the earpiece. "What time?"

"Forty minutes."

"Set your clocks, then. That's gonna be our go time," Malcolm said. "It's about five minutes later than I'd intended, but it will be worth it if the wolves are already shifted."

Gray responded for us, smiling and giving a fake wave to an elderly lady. The woman was loaded down with diamonds. "Looking good," he told her, and the rest of us.

I held onto Gray's hand and stopped him from descending the steps, not caring that a couple behind us bumped into him and pushed past us muttering complaints. I needed to get a lay of the land. We had to find our target. Ginny Stone was supposed to be here. I wanted her wand. I wanted her to be worried about it and not us. And I wanted her wand implicated in the break in—if anyone ever discovered it.

My eyes traveled over the floor of the ballroom. I didn't spot Zavier, but his cousin Andros stood out like a sore thumb. He was too tall. He'd be too obvious. I shook my head.

"I'm not sure about Andros," I whispered to Gray.

"You gotta trust us," Gray replied. "If Z says he's cool, then he's cool." Gray dropped my hand and instead offered me the crook of his elbow so we could descend. "I see your mom beat us here. She and Claude are over there. Should we go say hi?"

I didn't want to be anywhere near Claude. I didn't need him anymore, except as a lure for Ginny. And I could use him as that lure from far away.

I glanced around and realized that Mom and Claude were in a cluster of men, but that off to one side of the room, a group of women in black dresses that were a little less gaudy than the rest, stood talking, occasionally looking over at them. I hoped that was the rumor mill at work. But it might have been wishful thinking.

I was about to refuse Gray's suggestion, when I saw a bright red shock of hair weaving through the crowd, heading toward them.

"I think I see her," I said. I lifted my hand and tried to subtly point as I pretended to fix my hair.

"Found the dunce and the Ace," Gray reported. In addition to the spy earpieces, the guys had also come up with code names for us and our marks, against my express wishes. The dunce was their name for Claude. Originally, they'd wanted to name him Boomer, but I'd nixed that norm insult because it gave his age away. Ace was obviously Ginny.

Teenage boys.

Andros' gruff reply was, "On it." Then he moved like a panther, deftly following the bright red hair through the crowd.

I rolled my eyes as Evan's voice sounded in my ear. "Roger that, Preschool. Barbie's heading your way. Get ready for playtime."

Gray led me down the steps into the crowd. My ear buzzed with Malcolm's voice. "You have forty minutes."

"Wanna dance?" Gray asked me. He didn't wait for my answer as his arms wrapped around my waist and he whirled me to the left. He leaned in and whispered in my ear. "You really do look hot. And I love your panties—"

"Way to rub it in," Z's voice interjected. "Can you focus now, please?"

Gray smiled and took my hand and started to lead me in a waltz. He was good at it, which wasn't surprising.

"Daddy made you take dance lessons, huh?" I asked.

"Yup," he replied before sending me out for a spin. I wasn't the best dancer, but his thighs and hands pressed firmly against me and directed me exactly where I needed to go.

I spotted Laura, dancing nearby, her dress a short, sparkly pink sheathe. Her curls were piled high on her head. And while she clung to her date, her eyes were fixed firmly on Grayson. We spun, and he saw her for the first time.

His footsteps faltered. He swallowed hard. He spun me around so that his back was to her. But as we continued to dance, he kept spinning so that he could see her. At first, he was subtle about it, but after a while, Grayson gave up on formal dancing. We started to sway in place. And his eyes didn't meet mine a single time.

"I think I need a drink," I glanced over at Laura, who was staring steadily back at Gray. I tossed my fake smile on and tugged on his hand.

I pulled Gray over to a side room, where drinks were artfully stacked in buckets of ice. For all that the Unnatural Ball had an upper-class, ballroom feel in the front room, there was a barbecue hoe-down feel in the room that housed the food. That was because all the predatory shifters insisted on meat and lots of it. Apparently, there was another room with a salad bar, but we didn't go to it. I didn't have time to eat, anyway. With my stomach full of buzzing nerves, eating was probably a bad idea.

Gray grabbed me a soda with a grin. "Here, Hottie."

"Ha ha." I refused him and went to grab a water bottle. Then I touched my ear and asked Malcolm. "Water bottles are safe, right?"

"Better use the water fountain if they have one," he replied.

I sighed and set the drink back. "Well, never mind." I turned when I heard a howl behind me. I leaned out of the room we were in to see a line of Unnaturals waiting to go into a side room three doors down. "Wolves are starting."

"Better hurry," Malcolm replied.

I spotted Laura, sans her date, making her way down the hall toward us. I looked up at Gray. "Excuse me, I better run to the ladies' room." I ducked down the hall, scooting around the line of people waiting to proudly turn into wolves. And shit! Potts was there, in line next to some old dude.

I ducked behind a pillar. It must have been her 'friend with benefits.' I scooted around the pillar, careful to keep my back to her. Crap. I didn't want her seeing me. Not right before this. The damn woman would pester me and somehow get me to spout the truth.

I walked back toward Gray, heels clicking. I'd meant to give him more time. But, hopefully, he was smoother than I anticipated.

I glanced to the side, spotted my mom, alone and wandering through the crowd, the dull look of a fresh Calm spell on her face. She looked gorgeous, in a wine-colored satin gown with long sleeves.

I hurried over to her, giving Gray another minute. "Mom! Why are you by yourself?" I glanced around. "Where's the husband?" I did my best to keep my tone civil. I didn't want Mom alone and unprotected when things went down.

"Just wandering, you know, chatting with people." She grinned. "Claude's got a big meeting with Grayson's father coming up. Some big project—oh, shrimp!" She grabbed a shrimp appetizer off a waiter's tray and ate it.

I turned and let my eyes scan the room. Claude and Ginny were headed this way. Fucking good. The ruthless pair of them wouldn't let themselves be trampled. Mom just had to stay in between them. After I saw the targets, my gaze immediately found Andros, a head above everyone else. He slowly started making his way closer at my nod.

Mom gave a little shriek. I turned, looking her up and down to see where she was hurt. But she wasn't hurt. She was pointing.

I turned to see Grayson and Laura wrapped up together. Laura's hand stroked the side of his face. He leaned into her touch with a heartbroken expression.

Rage that I didn't expect lit me up. I nearly laughed in surprise at it. Because—really—what kind of claim did I expect to have on Grayson?

I grabbed Mom's hand, making her appetizer plate crash to the floor as I dragged her toward them. "He promised—" I forced my voice out in a strangled squeak.

And then, then … the bitch leaned up and kissed him. Laura planted her lips on Grayson and the fury I'd felt before was nothing. My hands itched to burn the girl. My hand crushed my mother's, so that I'd resist.

"WHAT?" Mom's outrage made heads turn.

Laura backed away from kissing Grayson. Her smirk turned wary when I stepped toward her. She thought she was so much better than me; she thought she had a shot. She still didn't get it.

My eyes glowed. I dropped Mom's hand and pointed my palms at Laura. The power boost I'd gotten last night from Evan and Malcolm made my hands light up like nuclear reactors. I started to shake.

"Hayley, calm down. He's a jerk, love. Nothing more," Mom tried to soothe me, but I shook her off. I let Claude pull her back beside him.

I took another step toward Laura and smiled when fear lit her face. The light and darkness in my palms started alternating fritzing sign at one of those motels that people rented by the hour. It made me look broken. I turned from Laura to face Grayson. "You said you were done with her!" I screamed at the top of my lungs.

The ballroom went silent. Every Unnatural head turned to stare at me as I pulsed like a strobe light. "You fucking liar!" I screeched.

Then there was a hand on my shoulder. Claude pulled me back, spun me around. The waterworks started at his touch, like Pavlov's fucking dog. I couldn't stand his touch. That demon.

Next to him, dressed in a red cocktail that matched her cherry hair, Ginny Stone tried to melt back into the crowd. But the darkness escaped me and wrapped around everyone nearby in pitch black shadows as my sobs reached volcanic eruption levels. "Grayson Mars, I'm fucking done! Do you hear me! Done!"

Just like Cinderella, I fled the ball.

43

I RAN AS FAST as I could in heels to the parking lot, which was a hell of a lot slower than all those damn movie actresses. I wondered briefly if there was such a thing as a stunt double for running in heels. It seemed like there should be. My eyes scanned the plethora of limos and town cars littering the parking lot, until I spotted a tall, dark figure wearing a leather jacket. I beelined for Jim.

Jim opened the door for me, and I asked, "You crushing it tonight?'

He winked at our passcode. "Yes, ma'am. Tips are gonna be good." Then he pulled open the door.

"How's the time looking?" I asked as I wiped away the mascara that streaked my cheeks.

The beefy biker checked his watch. "Four minutes," he said.

I nodded as I pulled off my chandelier earrings and handed them to him. He took them with a nod. "You be careful," I warned him, before climbing into the limo.

He leaned down and gave me a sincere smile, one that stretched the iridescent scars on his right cheek. "You too, little princess."

I flipped him off. "Get outta here. I gotta change."

He laughed as he shut the door.

I scrambled into the limo's interior and hurried out of my dress, sliding on the fire-resistant suit that Tia's second-cousin twice removed or whatever had gotten for me. The black suit fit like a glove, molding to my body with the help of spelled stitches. I slid on some boots just as the limo door opened and Grayson slid inside.

"Damn. Got a breath mint?" he grumbled. "Laura tasted like dog."

"You probably tasted secondhand dick from the blowie she gave your friend on the drive over."

Gray immediately stuck his tongue out and made a gagging sound. Then he quirked a brow at me as he pulled his tux jacket off. "Did I sell it okay? Not really a drama student here."

"Yeah. You did. I kinda want to throw this heel at you." I showed him the pointy side of my shoe.

He laughed as he wrangled his bow tie off his neck. Then he glanced around the limo. "Isn't Evan supposed to be back here already? I thought we'd timed it so he and I should get here at the same time."

"True." I touched my earpiece and asked, "Evan? You there?"

He didn't respond. Malcolm's voice came through. "And stampede in three, two, one..."

It sounded like a football stadium when Malcolm's stink bombs went off. Part of me really wanted to open the sunroof and look out, but I was supposed to be wearing my little teenage mask of self-pity and broken-hearted woe. So, I wouldn't get to witness his triumph firsthand. But I could hear it, as people shrieked at the godawful smell. Retching sounds intermittently pierced the cacophony.

I peered through the tinted window, watching as people hurtled out onto the lawn that this building shared with the Pinnacle. They trampled over the prairie dog holes in their desperation to escape the foul stench. Once, but only once, I spotted Z's cousin darting in and out among the wealthy, his hands blurred as he stripped them of pocketbooks, jewelry, wands.

Malcolm's voice came online again. "Part two: Mindless frenzy in three, two, one."

I watched as Malcolm's delivery truck rolled by.

My hand flew to my ear. "Wait! Princess is still out there!" My heart jumped as I scanned the parking lot. Worry prickled me. Evan was supposed to be back at the limo already.

His first assignment for the night had been to show Tia a fun time to pay her back for the suits and then fake a stomach illness and get her out of there. Where was he? Had he driven her home? Or was he still on the grounds.

"Anyone hear from him?" I asked.

A chorus of 'no's sounded in my ears.

"Princess?" I tried the coms, touching my earpiece to activate it. Princess was Evan's code name for the night. The guys had tried to push for horny bear, but he wouldn't have it. Why he'd preferred Princess ... guys made no sense.

"Princess?" I tried again.

Evan didn't answer.

My stomach started to whirl. Had something gone wrong already? If I'd expected anything to go wrong, I'd expected it to be with Claude or maybe Laura. I hadn't expected Evan to have any trouble.

Crap.

Malcolm's voice sounded. "4-H, we're losing our window. People are scattering."

"Do it," I replied.

The sprinklers on the lawn went on with a whoosh. Screams from women in thousand-dollar gowns turned to shrieks of terror as their dates roared and transformed into wolves, bears, lions, even snakes as thick as my torso, that slithered along the ground.

Gray finished changing and I turned to look at him. "What are we gonna do if Evan ..."

"We'll have to push through," Gray responded, taking my hand.

I swallowed hard and shoved aside emotion. I nodded. "Guess it's time to go to the meetup spot."

Gray motioned to his driver, who pulled out and drove us to the opposite side of the Pinnacle building--the side with all the construction on it

"Z's meeting us at the trees, right?"

Gray nodded and rubbed my palm. "Yup. He and his cousin should be finishing up 'Masquerade.' Soon as they drop all those jewels, they'll be here."

I shook my head, heat flooding my neck as I rubbed it. I blew out a breath. "Covering a heist with another heist—"

"We've got to explain away all the chaos we've caused. People are gonna be looking for a reason."

I nodded.

"It's a solid plan."

I nodded.

My entire body felt like it was balanced on the head of a pin. I felt like some cirque act, suspended high in the air, nothing to catch me.

Gray let go of my hand and flicked my boob.

I recoiled. "Ow!"

"Stop it, nemesis. Don't freak yourself out. Ride the adrenaline. Don't let it ride you."

I turned to look at his dark brown eyes drawing my strength from him.

"This is just another prank. Just another fuck you."

The driver stopped and Gray pulled me out of the car into the frosty night air. The cold seemed to wake me up, to drive away some of the hot worry that was stewing in my stomach. Seeing Evan standing under the trees, a mask covering his nose, lifted it further.

I marched over to him. "I tried to radio you like three times."

His cheeks reddened. "Sorry. Tia was ... harder to get rid of than I expected."

Jealousy flared inside me like a blow torch. "What? Why?"

"I ended up telling her that I'd had a crush on you for years in order to get her to back off."

The flames ebbed and I gave him a small smile. I turned to see Zavier and Andros walking toward us. Malcolm followed just behind them.

"You get it?" My gaze went straight to Andros.

Z grinned. "A better question is what didn't he get? Damn! Those women were swimming in diamonds."

"You dropped those right?" I glared; my expectant expression immediately turned to a frown. "Half those gems will have seeker spells on them."

"Relax. I dropped them with a couple of Gray's guys. They're on it." Andros' reply was casual. Too casual for me. Like he wasn't taking this seriously.

"Did you get Stone's wand?" I repeated.

Andros held up a silver wand. Then he tucked it into his shirt.

I smacked my hands together and then held up my hands. The darkness unfurled from them like calligraphy, like beautiful swirls of ink. I let my power caress each of my crew's faces. Then it swirled down and swallowed them up.

"Okay," Gray said. "I'm up."

"Not yet," I replied." I took my left hand and flicked my fingers, letting tiny pinpricks of light float out and settle over each of them. Now, we'd be indistinguishable from the starry sky. Once we were done, we lined up and stared at the Pinnacle.

The building rose, tall and imposing, the white stone arches glinting in the light from the parking lot and a tiny sliver of crescent moon. We'd lucked out with the moon's phase. It wasn't bright.

The shadows created by all the sculptures carved into the walls made my eyes play tricks on me. Even though I controlled darkness and light, my eyes still thought they saw movement. My pulse pounded so hard that I thought I might fall down dead where I stood. I closed my eyes and took a deep breath, focusing on the shit meditation techniques that Potts was always pushing on me. Calm wind. Waves. I counted my inhales and exhales until my heart was at a manageable 65 mph and not the fucking Indy 500 pace it had been at before. It didn't help things that sex with some of the guys had made my power sizzle beneath my skin all damn day.

Shit. Control it, I scolded myself.

Like the asshole he was, Grayson strode over to stand beside me, his bulk making me feel small. "Ready?" he asked.

I nodded. He lifted us up slowly until we were past the treetops. I could see the chaos around the edges of the Pinnacle building. Norm police, magical police, and several Pinnacle guards were trying to herd aggressive, rutting shifters into cages--comforting sobbing women--taking the statements of bystanders. Not an eye looked our way as

Gray floated us through the sky. He pulled us around the corner of the building, and I pointed a hand at one of the far lights in the parking lot, making it flicker and burn out.

A couple eyes turned in that direction, but still, no one looked up, even as we edged around all the boards and planks and construction, toward them.

When we reached the window, Malcolm and Evan glanced over at me. I spread a blanket of darkness beneath our feet as we hovered, then lightened it a bit to fit with the surrounding light. "Do it," I ordered.

Both of them shot narrow beams of fire at the window, melting lines into the glass. They cut out a giant square from the pane, large enough that we could step through it. Their cutout fell forward, toward us.

That wasn't supposed to happen—my thoughts went into slow motion as I watched the rectangle of glass pitch forward and start to plummet.

Holy fuck.

No.

My mind saw the glass hitting the sidewalk below us, transforming into a spray of sharp little droplets--ending us. Every head would turn. Every eye would look up. We were done. Baked. Cooked.

"Preschool," Z growled, diving down. He reached for the glass and caught it. Barely. His fingers clung to the edges like clamps.

I turned to look at Gray, who'd been supposed to catch the glass. His face was covered in sweat. It rolled down his forehead, dripped over his eyes.

Shit. He was nearly maxed out.

I swam through the air toward the window. "Inside. Now! He can't keep holding us," I whispered shouted. I don't know if they heard my words. I could hardly hear myself over my pounding heart, but they saw me. Malcolm and Evan followed quickly. We climbed inside and I turned to Gray.

"Come on, Preschool. What's wrong? Can't handle a couple guys?" I taunted.

Gray turned to face me, and his expression grew angry.

"Thought your magic was stronger, didn't you? Bet you're wishing you'd gotten that power up right about now."

Gray's brows drew down and Z started to rise with the glass. Slowly, but he started to rise.

"You lazy bum. Daddy can get entire rockets to Mars."

A growl erupted from Gray's lips and Andros shot through the sky and into the room. He tumbled to the floor.

"And then there was one," I said. "Come on, Preschool. Any little old Force could do what you're doing now."

Z rose farther, enough to hand the glass through the hole to Evan and Malcolm, who carefully took it and walked it to the side of the room. They set it on some table or something, but I didn't look over at them. I kept my eyes locked on Gray's as Andros yanked on Zavier's hand and dragged him up the side of the building and into the room.

"Alright. You're done, hottie. Come here." I put my hand out.

Gray took one shaky breath before he shot forward and barreled into me. I slammed to the ground. The wind was knocked out of me and my ribcage ached. But I smiled and reached up to wipe the sweat from Gray's brow. "You okay?" I asked.

He rolled off me and laid on the floor. "Yeah. Just a couple hundred pounds more than we practiced with. Jolly is heavy as fuck."

"I'm pure muscle," Andros glared down at him.

"And happy about it," Z said. "That's why your codename is Jolly."

Andros glared at him.

I took a minute and gave Gray a minute to recover before I climbed to my feet. Then I glanced at Malcolm. "How far off our time are we?" We had to make it from our current spot on the sixth floor and through the laser and construction debacle on the seventh floor in less than twenty minutes because that's how often the guards were scheduled to make their rounds.

"Five minutes," Malcolm replied.

Fuck.

44

"Dad," I called.

Dad appeared, wearing a Hawaiian shirt and flip-flops. "Hayley!" He glanced around. "Wow, this is some crew. You did it, kiddo." He smiled at me, but then I saw his expression start to fall.

Shit. My heart stuttered as I ran up to him. "Dad, remember that clay wolf Matthew painted for you? The red one with the blue spots?"

Dad's eyes lit up at the memory. "Yeah. He gave it to me. But then he carried it around himself for three days cause he was so proud of it."

I grinned. "Dad, can you go check this floor and find out where the guard on patrol is for me?"

"Sure, sweet pea." Dad sauntered off.

Andros stared down at me, brows raised. "What the hell?" He turned to Zavier. "You brought me in on a job with a crazy?"

Z waved his hand casually. "No. Hottie's dad's a ghost, that's all."

Andros' nostrils flared. "This isn't what I signed up for."

I turned to him and snarled. "Well, you're welcome to walk down the stairs and let yourself out then."

He reached for me, but Evan stepped between us. Then Malcolm. And Z. Even Gray. My crew lined up in front of me, arms crossed, staring at him.

The testosterone built to intolerable levels.

I cut through it with a terse, "Look, how do you think I got all my intel?"

Andros opened his mouth to argue but Dad popped up next to me a second later. "Round the corner. He's talking on his walkie."

I nodded and smiled. "Incoming with a handheld radio? I can work with that." I cracked my fingers.

"How? You're a Darklight," Andros protested.

Malcolm leaned against his desk with a smile. "Yeah, but radios are part of the electromagnetic spectrum."

I looked at Dad. "What direction is he in?"

Dad pointed right. "Badge says Melvin."

I turned that direction and extended my hand toward where I imagined Melvin was striding through the hall. My light waves couldn't go through walls. But radio waves were larger. I shoved hard--radio control was something I'd only developed since my first time with Evan. But I closed my eyes to focus, trying to feel if my beams were going in the right direction. It felt like a tiny tingle when my power connected. I shuffled the station, just like I had with Evan.

Behind me, the guys tensed.

"I hear footsteps," Andros whispered.

I heard them too. The *tap* of a boot coming closer. Shit. I didn't want any confrontations. Not this soon. Not until we were down below.

Preferably none at all. I moved my fingers, fluctuating the radio signal.

"Hello, hello?" the guard's husky voice traveled around the corner.

He was close.

Too close.

Fuck.

I had to do more.

I touched my finger to my earpiece and kept my other hand extended, flicking the station for both my system and the guards until our radios were synced. "Melvin," I let out a pained whisper.

"Hello? Hello? Trina? You okay down there?" Melvin's voice echoed in my ear. But more importantly, his footsteps paused.

"Help," I whispered. Then I waved my hands and cut both our devices, turning them into a storm of static. My pulse thundered as I waited to see what the guard would do. Would he fall for it? Or would he realize someone was magically fucking with him?

Melvin's footsteps sped up ... but in the opposite direction. He'd taken the bait. It bought us time. But only a limited amount. If he got down there and realized he'd been tricked...

"He's gone," I said.

Z clapped me on the back, but I waved him off and focused on Dad.

I stared at Dad's Hawaiian shirt and pulsed energy toward him accidentally, making him glow slightly with ultraviolet light. "Dad, I need you to follow him. Let me know if he takes the elevator, because I can stop that--"

Gray protested, "You'll have your hands full with cameras."

I held up a hand to shut him up, my concentration focused on my father, as if I could *will* Dad's memory to stay. "If Melvin takes the stairs, I need you to make him fall."

Dad's eyes widened and he swallowed.

"Nothing permanent. But a broken leg or something that would immobilize him would be best."

Dad nodded and faded away. I closed my eyes and blew out a shaky breath.

I turned to the crew.

Andros shook his head. "I don't like it. We should have just killed the guard."

"You don't have to like it," I snapped. "Not your job. Not your call."

"Foolish."

I stomped off, waving my hands toward all the video cameras and freezing them in place.

But a little niggling part of my mind couldn't help but worry that Andros was right.

45

We reached the construction zone without incident, everyone walking behind me as I froze the camera transmissions so we could walk past and unfroze them seconds later so that the guards wouldn't notice a time lapse.

I held up a hand to stop the guys. "Okay, so this is where it's gonna get tricky. Gray, I hope you're feeling better because you're gonna have to bat clean up if someone missteps."

Gray looked wiped out, but he nodded. I pulled aside the plastic. "Okay guys. So, clearly Dad missed a little something during his trips here. I'll keep the lasers in check, I'll leave them active but arc the lines above us like I'm a prism, but we're all gonna have to move together, because I can only do so many at a time and they're at a couple points across this mess. So …"

"Shit!" Andros leaned over and stared down at the drop to the next floor. Then he stared across the gap, which was at least thirty feet wide.

His leaning made me nervous, it wouldn't take much for any of us to lose our balance on the steel beams we needed to cross. Bile rose in my throat, but I tried to overpower the foul taste with sarcasm. "Jolly, at least make an effort not to fall. It'll be really hard for me to keep the lasers appearing active and knock out cameras I can't even see on the floor below."

Andros straightened back up and glared at me. "I do not like that codename."

I shrugged. "Sorry. Mid-job, can't change it." Zavier had picked the Jolly Green Giant for Andros' codename. The huge man was so scary that I loved the irony of the name, even though I didn't like when he glared at me about it.

"Conga line!" Z grinned and came forward to grab my hips.

I shook my head. "Take this seriously."

Malcolm lined up behind Z and the other guys followed suit.

Malcolm said, "Hottie, if you're ready, I'll count us off."

I pointed a hand up toward each of the video screens, letting light eke out of my palms, patterning it in a replica of the room—bright silver beams and dark bundles of cords and unmoving shadows. Then I sent that image floating toward the camera lenses and let my image cover them like a film. They flickered. I closed my eyes and tried to imagine the audio components. I tried to feel them out like I did the guard's handheld radio just minutes before. These wires were duller, smaller, harder to locate. I pinched my fingers together and shoved darkness toward them, interrupting the current.

"Cameras down," I whispered.

Then I turned to face my next foe—lasers. I hadn't even practiced with lasers. I'd only learned about them today. *Thanks, Dad.* The sarcastic thought rolled through my head before I could suppress it. I knew Dad struggled with his memory. *Focus, Hayley. Focus.*

I had extra power thrumming through me from spending time last night with Evan and Malcolm. But still ... I'd already disguised our entire group as we'd flown through the sky. I'd already taxed myself taking out a radio and then the hall cameras.

I took a deep breath, squared my shoulders, and glanced at the little norm laser boxes as if I was a cowboy and this was a showdown. Me versus them.

As I stared at the thin red beams that crisscrossed in front of the hole in the floor—to keep magicals from unknowingly plunging to their deaths—My chest vibrated like a guitar string. If I'd had time, I might have sat down and figured out a spell I could write to trick them. But I didn't have time. I just had to use my natural powers and hope they were enough. But seeing Gray struggle to bring us up here, after he'd practiced and practiced, knowing how strong he was and how good his control was, that shook me.

I raised my hands toward the boxes, letting red beams shoot from my fingertips. Laser lights were more concentrated, amplified. They took a lot more power to create than a broad-spectrum light. At first, my beam pulsed. It wasn't a continuous wave. I stared up at it, punching despair so that it couldn't grab me and tug me down. *Shit, try harder, Hales. Don't suck so much,* I pulled up a phrase Matthew had often used on me, one that pissed me off and made me work harder. I stared at the beam and cracked my neck. I had to make it steady. I had to make it stronger. I tried to close my ears to the noise of the guys shuffling behind me. I craned my neck up and pushed my beams harder.

A bright, unconcentrated beam of light shot from my hands, bright white and rainbow around the edges.

Shit.

"Is that supposed—" Andros started to say but someone shushed him.

I clenched my fingers and reined the light in again until I had a narrow beam of red. It wavered for a second, like icing lines on a cake. But then it grew steady. Part one. I separated my hands and shot a laser beam at each of the transmitters on either side of me. My beams connected with theirs and I painstakingly lined my hands up so that the light met and reflected back at exactly the right angle.

"Okay, I'm gonna try to arc the light. Then we move." I took a deep breath and started to lift my hands.

But Dad popped up in front of me, startling me, forcing me to step back. I almost lost the light.

I could see, as if it were happening in slow-motion, the light beam start to break. I moved as fast as I could—but it still felt like I was running underwater. I shoved my hands back up and reconnected the red laser by shooting two beams from my right hand, one beam toward either sensor. I shoved out my left and felt for the connections inside the sensors, those mechanisms that would go off if they sensed a lack of electricity. I shoved light into them, letting the electrons fill them so they didn't notice any gap in coverage.

I did all that in milliseconds, though it felt like years to me. When I finished, I was breathing hard. I looked up at Dad and snapped, "What?"

Dad shook his head. "You have to hurry. I made my guard trip. But the guard another level down heard him in the stairwell. He's on his way up."

Fuck me with a damned sequoia redwood.

I froze. "New plan. I'm gonna get low. You all are gonna walk over me."

"What?" Z asked behind me. "Why's there a new plan?"

"My dad says a guard is headed this way right now." I said as I took a knee on the edge of the floor, just before it dropped off. "Get over there. See the fridge? Head toward it. Once everyone's past me, I'll walk around," I glanced over—I'd have to take the beam without any crossbeam supports. I'd have to walk across it like a balance beam. "I'll take the other beam, get ahead and disable the other laser."

Nobody protested. They stepped over my right shoulder in single file and shuffled out onto the large steel beam just as I felt sweat start to bead on my forehead. Lasers were harder than I'd thought.

Once Andros had edged across to the first crossbeam, and could hold onto something with his hands, I carefully started reducing the laser beam from my hands, backing up and slowly letting the original beam get closer to reconnecting. It felt like I was handling my grandmother's Fabergé egg. Or some tiny glass figurine. Delicate. Finally, my beam was only inches wide. I slid back on the floor further, retracing my beam millimeter by millimeter.

I heard footsteps.

Shit.

I retracted all at once. The light beams reconnected, and I reached out with my hand shoving more light at the sensors as I ran to the right, toward the beam without any guys on it. My guys were already at the far end of the construction zone, waiting for me to come repeat the process and let them past.

But I stared at the narrow beam in front of me. It was a good twelve-foot drop to the floor beneath. And I'd never been good at gymnastics. I sat down on the beam and started to scoot.

"Are you kidding me?" Andros said.

"Shut up," I muttered as I scooted along, quick as I could. It was not quick. Not quick at all, considering I could hear the guard whistling as he opened and closed doors, checking out rooms behind us.

"Stay there," Andros growled at me. Then, in a move that would have impressed any jungle cat or ballerina, he jumped from his beam onto mine. He hardly even had to waver his hands up and down once to regain his balance. I stared up at him in slack-jawed disbelief.

That only lasted a second before he scooped me up, threw me over his shoulder and crossed the beam in three steps before shaking me loose and setting me down. "Here. Go."

I shot my hands out and interrupted the laser beam on the other side of the hole. Andros climbed over me. Then I let the beam reconnect as I hurried over to do the same for the other guys.

But I was too late. The plastic curtain that cordoned off the construction zone wavered and crinkled. I saw a shadow moving behind it.

My heart felt like the drum solo at a rock concert. It was a rolling, raging pounding mess that nearly made me deaf. *Fuck. Fuck.*

A man stepped out from behind the plastic, flashlight in hand.

46

I PULLED the shadows tight around us, sucking all the light between the lasers out of the room. I couldn't even see my hand in front of me as I extended it and killed the guard's flashlight.

I heard the man smack his flashlight and mutter, "Stupid thing. Just replaced the batteries."

I waited, holding my breath, for him to pull out his wand and parchment and write an illumination spell.

But the guard didn't seem to think that was necessary. He turned, pushed back through the plastic, and shuffled away.

I think every one of my crew members and I sighed at the exact same moment.

I slowly let the shadows retreat, once I was sure the guard was gone. I looked over at each of the guys, checking their faces. "We all good?" I asked.

Z nodded. Malcolm nodded. But Gray looked a little shaken. The other guys had all pulled jobs before, but I think facing a second guard had taken its toll on him.

"I almost made that guy fall forward," Gray breathed.

"Hey, you didn't. And he left. Don't dwell, nemesis. Or I'll have to make your dick glow whenever I write that spell for Z's."

Zavier scolded me. "Codenames. I'm the magnificent Firefly. Which is a lie, but a funny one, so whatever."

Malcolm just raised a brow. "You gonna lift those lasers any time soon?"

I leaned forward and let lasers shoot from my hands again. The beam was higher on this side, so Gray had to levitate each guy a bit before they could hop over. When all was done, and the beam was back to normal I turned to face the breakroom only to see the issue that had made my guys pause.

Everything in the breakroom was coated in dust. If we touched anything, we'd leave tracks.

I turned to Gray as I pulled the Good Intentions amulet out of my pocket. It glowed a pale lilac. "I hate to say it, but, you're up again."

Gray closed his eyes and tilted his head back toward the ceiling. "I should have gone with a power up."

"I don't mind waiting and watching," Z said.

I ignored him and walked over, sliding my hand into Gray's. "After this, you get a break. Evan and Malcolm are on next."

Gray nodded. He gave my hand a single squeeze before letting go, opening his eyes, and pointing his hands at me. "I'm gonna lift you first."

I nodded. "Remember, we're handing the amulet person to person. You can't get into the tunnel without good intentions." I held up the little orb that fit into my palm. "Clear your minds. We're going down there to help people—make sure you're focused on that."

Z tossed out. "If you can't focus on that, throw in random thoughts like pizza toppings. Mushrooms, olives, pineapple—"

"Firefly, be serious," I gritted out.

Andros held up a hand. "He is being serious. Our grandmother used Good Intentions amulets on us when we were younger. They can be outsmarted by random thoughts, neutral thoughts."

I nodded. "Good to know." I checked in with Evan, who stood silently in the back. "You good?"

He gave me a slow nod. I didn't know how to take that, but we didn't have time for more. We had to move. The goal was to get down, unravel the vault and get out in twenty minutes, before the next guard.

I tapped Gray's arm and he lifted me and Malcolm. I floated sideways through the kitchen. I reached inside the door handle of the fridge and used my forearm to open it so I wouldn't leave fingerprints. I was also careful not to touch the outside of the handle and disturb the dust. I climbed just inside the fridge, using my legs to prop me up on either side of the tube. Three feet below me, fire blazed. I felt like I was poised over the mouth of a dragon.

Malcolm grabbed the amulet and squeezed in next to me. He took up the tiny bit of floorspace in the fridge. He handed the amulet back and turned to stare down at the tube, analyzing the flames—we'd only ever practiced with theoretical knowledge of the fire source—while I held the amulet out for the next person. The fit with Malcolm and I was tighter than we'd thought it would be, our torsos pressed against each other. Every tiny movement he made jostled me, which made me press my legs even harder into the sides of the tubes.

I counted down the seconds, waiting for him to begin.

The heat on my calves went from tickling, to biting, to melting. "Smeckle, I need a little relief."

"One sec," Malcolm said.

But a second later, Evan was floating in front of me and I was handing him the amulet. There was no way his ass would fit in the fridge with us. "You need to just blast it with ice, what's the problem?" I growled.

Malcolm retorted, "I can't just ice it, that's the problem. There are thermometers in here. I've used them before. Practicing. If the temp changes too quickly, then it's just like the lasers. Alarm."

"Shit." I tried to wriggle so there was some room for Evan. He shoved himself into the fridge, which pushed Malcolm into me. I felt like my ribs might crack. Evan was too big, half his torso hung out of the fridge. "Can you go any faster?" I wheezed.

"Trying."

I couldn't reach my earpiece to tell Gray to stop sending people. I just had to shout with my eyes as he floated Z toward us.

"I can't see," Evan spoke, "but point my hands and tell me what I need to do."

Malcolm elbowed me in the face, making my nose smart, as he rearranged Evan's hands. The heat in the fridge, from all three of our bodies and the fire a few feet below felt unbearable. I felt like a melting wax figure.

"We aren't blasting with ice; we're just lowering the amount of flame."

"Don't forget our body heat compensates," Evan said.

"On three," Malcolm said. "One, two, three…" They both shot luke-warm water toward the fire, which turned the kitchen from an oven into a sauna as the water hissed and steamed.

Condensation settled on my face.

"Again."

They blasted again, and suddenly, Malcolm started to wriggle past me. "Got it."

Thank goodness, because Z was right in front of us.

Malcolm climbed down, using his hands to maintain the flames around us at barely there levels with one hand, while keeping a sauna-like heat in the air going with the other. I followed, taking up a position on his back as he fed his hands through the rungs of the ladder and blasted the next ring of fire below us.

Dazed, I touched the ladder rungs with my forearms, using my fire-retardant suit to test them. They were surprisingly cold. *Thank magic!* Then I held onto the rungs so Malcolm could focus on the fire. Evan crawled down above us, until his feet were right in front of my face.

The way down the tube was crowded, and three times as hot as when we'd practiced. By the time we reached the pitch-black subterranean level, we were all sweating, miserable, angry.

I lit a small space around us, and we all sat for a second. Evan conjured up ice cubes for us to suck on and Malcolm cooled the air around us slowly. Both of them looked ready to keel over when all was said and done. But we weren't even to the vault yet.

I closed my eyes, shoving back my sweat-plastered bangs and felt around the room for any devices Dad might have missed. Five cameras pointed at the vault door.

"Fucking ghosts," I muttered around my ice cube as I extended my hands and slowly covered their feeds with black shadows.

"What's up?"

I shook my head and gestured for another ice cube from Evan. "Just had to take out some cameras, that's all."

We marched together to the vault door, which was steel, and round, and as impressive as any bank vault I'd ever seen.

I knelt in front of the door, on the rough concrete floor and pulled a tiny roll of parchment from my pants pocket, then a tiny vial of ink. "Wand?" I held my hand out to Andros. He gave me Stone's silver wand.

I wrote out the spell I'd learned from Malcolm, when he helped me unravel Gray's Shakespeare prank. The spell for the vault glittered in the air and Evan used a pen and paper to write it down as quickly as he could while Zavier stood, pulsing magic into the air so that the Latin words wouldn't dissolve too quickly.

"Got it," Evan said.

Just then, Andros, who was watching his watch, standing out of the range of Z's spell, called out, "1.5 minutes. Z's got about thirty seconds left in him."

Evan nodded.

I looked over, stomach churning, as I watched him write on the notebook. I couldn't be sure if the sweat rolling down his brow was left from before, or if he was as nervous as I was.

I glanced back up at the door, and as my hand moved, so did the door's gleam. Like it was winking at me.

My heart felt like it was leaking into my body. Like I was a tea bag steeping and somehow my essence was leaving me. Soon there'd be nothing left. Because this serum was all I'd wanted for so long. I'd obsessed over it. Behind that door was the promise of a future for Matthew.

It felt like I was staring at heaven's pearly gate—waiting to see if it would open for me. So close. Would it be? Would it be true? I'd seen the serum in Dad's memories. But he had no memory of it actually working in front of him.

As I stared at that vault door, adrenaline making me feel light-headed, I wondered if it was all just a dream. This cure. Was it just some pretty picture my dad made up, some windmill giant, some fake Don Quixote-like quest? Something—anything to give me purpose? To get me through those hard times?

My stomach churned at the thought that the serum might not be real. Had I built my entire life around a lie? People did it every day. Convinced themselves things were real. Gave themselves false hope. Was it worth it? Most of them would never know. Their lies were less concrete. Goodness, kindness, joy. They were devoted to ethereal things. Emotions and beliefs.

Me?

I'd built everything around this. Done everything for this moment. Was it worth the slings and arrows I'd shot?

Or would death have been easier?

When they opened that door, would I realize that forgetful bliss was the better option?

I realized I'd stopped breathing. I forced air into my lungs. I might want to die after this job. But I'd be damned if I died before I knew.

Z stepped back and Andros stepped up. And Evan took out his wand. Out of the corner of my eye, I saw him start to write.

I shoved aside my thoughts and pulled out the Honesty Amulet. *Thoughts are the enemy of action,* I repeated one of Matthew's old lines, the one he'd used on me when he'd built the zip line off our roof. "Don't think, Hayley," he'd told me, "Just do."

I looked down at the amulet. It glowed, a dull orange glass triangle in my hand. I walked over to Malcolm with it and said, "Remember, I'm going in there. Opening drawer 94. But I don't want to take the cure out of here. I just want to study it."

Malcolm studied my face. Then he shook his head. "Not good enough. You're lying. You want it to0 much."

I tried again.

Again, Malcolm shook his head. I wanted to yank my hair out in frustration. But I blew out a breath and tried again. "I just want to see the serum so I can help people."

Malcolm started to shake his head again when Z snatched the Honesty Amulet from me. "I just want to look at this serum. I mean, I've heard so much about it, I kinda just want to see if it's real."

Malcolm nodded.

Z looked at me.

My heart cracked a little, knowing that I wasn't going in there, that I wasn't going to get to pick up the amulet. But outcomes were more important than glory—more important than living out the stupid fantasies in my head. "Get it done."

The vault door swung open with a creak and Z strode inside the vault room full of metal drawers with me lighting his path.

He didn't hesitate when a deep, magical voice inside the vault boomed, "State your purpose."

"Drawer 94. I want to check on the serum, see if it's real."

The amulet glowed brighter in Z's hand and then faded. He pocketed it.

"Access granted," the magical male voice said.

Z scanned the rows of deposit boxes. He walked through slowly, each step echoing in the metallic vault room. He crouched and checked a number, then turned to me and nodded.

He'd found it.

My body felt like a helicopter. Spinning and whirling and mechanical and completely beyond my control. All I could do was hover as Z slowly pulled open drawer 94, careful to use the side of his hands to pull the curved handle and avoid leaving fingerprints.

Evan came over and grabbed my hand, squeezing tight. I glanced up, momentarily pulled from my out-of-body experience. Evan had almost as much riding on this moment as I did. His jaw was tense, black hair plastered to his forehead.

I squeezed his hand back as my eyes returned to Z.

Even if the serum wasn't there. Even if the serum didn't work … I'd tried.

And the journey had brought me back to Evan, had brought me to my crew.

In a way, this quest had given me all the ethereal things people search for all their lives.

A purpose.

People to share it with.

Zavier reached into the drawer and pulled out a vial that was slightly longer than his hand. It glowed with yellow-green light. Zavier stared at it, then into the drawer, then back at the vial. He used his elbow to push the drawer shut.

His every movement felt like pinpricks. Every step made my heart jump forward. I wanted nothing more than to run forward and put my palms underneath his to make sure he couldn't drop that vial.

Z walked back toward us, staring at the vial in his hand. "Mushroom, olive, pineapple, orange juice, soda crackers, lemon-lime," he chanted as he walked through the vault door. The door swung shut behind him, closing with an ominous clank. The dial spun on its own and golden magic fell from the ceiling, renewing the protective spell on the door.

I ran toward Zavier and grabbed the vial, which felt so inconsequential in my hands. Too small. Too delicate.

I stared at it, chest heaving. It felt like I'd just run a marathon and swallowed fourteen doves. My heart felt heavy and light—I was falling and flying—and there was a cooing noise coming from somewhere. As I cradled the vial, I realized it was coming from me. I was cooing at the vial, like it was my baby.

It was.

It was my baby, my prize, my Golden Fleece, my everything.

I turned to the guys with shining eyes. I made blurry eye contact with each and every member of my crew.

Gray leaned against a wall, still exhausted and recovering. Andros stood straight and so fucking tall, his arms crossed, looking as gruff and intimidating as the first time I met him. Malcolm wore a small smile, which was actually huge for him. Evan was openly crying. And Zavier was bouncing around the room, giving out high-fives and backslaps.

"Thank you," I said, shakily, as I swiped at my eyes. I didn't have words. They weren't enough. That was all I could say.

But each one of them nodded, as if they understood.

We'd done it.

We had the serum.

Disbelief left my head in a fog as I carefully retrieved a padded pouch from inside my fire-retardant suit. I placed the vial inside. "Time to blow this popsicle stand," I said, with a teary grin.

But cold prickled along my back.

Ice formed along my neck like a collar.

"Don't thank them just yet."

Claude's voice set me reeling. I turned to face my father's killer, who appeared out of thin air, as though he'd been down here, hidden by a disguise spell, waiting for us. Claude's smile practically dripped with blood. "Hayley, don't just stand there. Aren't you going to greet your daddy?"

BOOK 2 AVAILABLE NOW!

AFTERWORD

Thank you so much for reading about Hayley and her crew! I hope you love their magical adventures as much as I do.

Thank you from the bottom of my heart for supporting my dream of constructing beautiful worlds with words. If you liked this book, please leave an Amazon review. It's how indie authors like myself make it into the algorithms at Amazon so other readers can find us. Plus, your reviews keep me motivated so that I can write more books for you!

XOXO!

There's info about more books, my newsletter, and my facebook group on the following pages, in case you want to be like Evan and stalk me!

ACKNOWLEDGMENTS

A huge thanks to Rob, RK, Ives, Thais, Harley, Sue, and Elle. I appreciate all the butt-kicking. Thanks to my cover designer, Logan Keys at Cover of Darkness, whose artwork inspired this story, and my amazing ARC readers.

MORE BOOKS

Tangled Crowns Series

My first reverse harem series is the Tangled Crowns series. It's a medieval fantasy with an enemies to lovers story, princesses, knights, castles and dragons in the first book. It's medium burn.

Knightfall - Book 1

MidKnight - Book 2

Knight's End - Book 3

Lotto Love Series

My second reverse harem series is the Lotto Love series. Its a contemporary, romantic comedy reverse harem about a woman who wins the lotto and decides she doesn't want a boyfriend, she wants a

MORE BOOKS

harem. She drags her best friend along for a Bachelorette style competition and crazy antics ensue.

Lotto Men - Book 1

Lotto Trouble - Book 2

Ruby - Jewels Cafe Series

I have a stand-alone, paranormal reverse harem romance set in the awesome shared world of Silver Springs, New York. It's about an angel trying to complete her Christmas miracle. This is a fated mates medium burn romance.

Ruby

The Lyon Fox Mysteries

If you liked the sense of humor in this story, you might want to check out my Urban Fantasy mysteries. They are silly and snarky and full of laughs with a slow burn romance.

Magical Murder

Enchanted Execution

Supernatural Sleep

Hexed Hit

Timebend Series

If you're in the mood for more intrigue, check out my Post-Apocalyptic Thriller series.

Melt

Burn

CONNECT AND GET SNEAK PEEKS

If you would like to read exclusive snippets from different characters, make predictions with other readers, see my inspiration for books, or just come hang and be yourself, I have a Facebook reader group full of amazing people.

Feel free to join Ann Denton's Reader Group.

ABOUT ME

I have two of the world's cutest children, a crazy dog, and an amazing husband that I drive somewhat insane as I stop in the middle of the hallway, halfway through putting laundry away, picturing a scene. I have a degree in Playwriting that I'm finally putting to good use! Ha.

Printed in Great Britain
by Amazon

362ff54f-52f5-4dec-9805-bef7d1c2bbdeR01